LAST OF THE GIFTED

Spirit Sight
Book One

Water Sight
Book Two

Marie Powell

A WOOD DRAGON BOOK

Last of the Gifted

Last of The Gifted contains the two books: *Spirit Sight* and *Water Sight*

Published by:
Wood Dragon Books
P.O. Box 429
Mossbank, Saskatchewan Canada SOH 3G0
www.WoodDragonBooks.com

Library and Archives Canada Cataloguing in Publication
Powell, Marie 1958—
ISBN : 978-1-989078-74-7

Author Contact:
Marie Powell
http://mariepowell.ca

Participation was made possible by funding from the Creative Saskatchewan Book Publishing Production Grant Program.

Character Guide

Hyw and Cat's family

Hywel (HUH-wel) or Hyw (huh-oo) ~ Welsh warrior
Catrin (KAHT-rrin) or Cat ~ Hyw's younger sister
Bran (brrahn) ~ Hyw and Cat's father, Llywelyn's steward
Adara (uhd-EHRR-uh) ~ Hyw and Cat's mother
Gawain (GAH-wayn) ~ Hyw and Cat's uncle
Rhys ap Cadwgan (hrrees ap kad-OO-gan) ~ Lord of Meirionnydd, Cat's betrothed

The House of Aberffraw

Llywelyn (thluh-WEH-lihn) ap Gruffydd ~ Prince of Wales
Elinor de Montfort ~ Llywelyn's wife (deceased)
Gwenllian (gwen-THLEE-an) ~ Llywelyn's infant daughter
Dafydd (DAHV-ith) ap Gruffydd ~ Prince of Wales
Elizabeth ~ Dafydd's wife
Gwladys (GLAH-duhs) ~ Dafydd & Elizabeth's daughter
Llyw (THLUH-oo) ~ Dafydd & Elizabeth's eldest son
Owain (OH-wayn) ~ Dafydd & Elizabeth's youngest son
Margred (MEHRR-grred) ~ one of Dafydd's illegitimate daughters
Rhiannon (hrree-AN-on) ~ one of Dafydd's illegitimate daughters

Other Welsh characters

Aeneus (eh-NEE-aas) ~ former head of Llywelyn's teulu (personal guard)
Bronwen (BRRAHN-win) ~ Cat and Hyw's friend
Cynfrig ap Madog (KUN-vrig) ~ Rhys' former steward
Dai ap Rhys (die ap hrrees) ~ warrior
Drem (drrehm) ~ butcher's son from Criccieth
Enid (EH-nid) ~ wet nurse
Emrys (EM-rris) ~ warrior, Hyw's childhood friend
Gwilym ap Einion (GWIHL-ihm ap eye-NEE-on) ~ master bard
Hywel ap Rhys Gryg (HUH-wel ap hrrees-grreeg) ~ Welsh lord

Other Welsh characters (continued)

Ifan (ee-van) ~ warrior in Llywelyn's teulu
Odgar (AWD-gahrr) ~ Welsh warrior
Maelgwyn (MYLE-gwin) ~ Welsh priest

The English

Edward I (Longshanks) ~ King of England
Edmund Mortimer ~ heir to Baron Roger Mortimer (deceased)
Gilbert le Clare ~ Marcher Lord (from the Welsh-English border)
James ~ Shrewsbury's son, Hyw's friend, half-Welsh
Lord Shrewsbury ~ Marcher lord, Hyw's foster father
Robert ~ son of Shrewsbury's cousin
Roger Lestrange ~ commander in King Edward's army
Sir Bellamy ~ English knight
Stephen de Francton ~ English knight
William de Valence ~ Marcher lord
Alan Acton, Gerald ~ soldiers who befriend Hyw

Don't forget to look in the back of the book for:
Historical Note
Glossary
Further Reading

1282

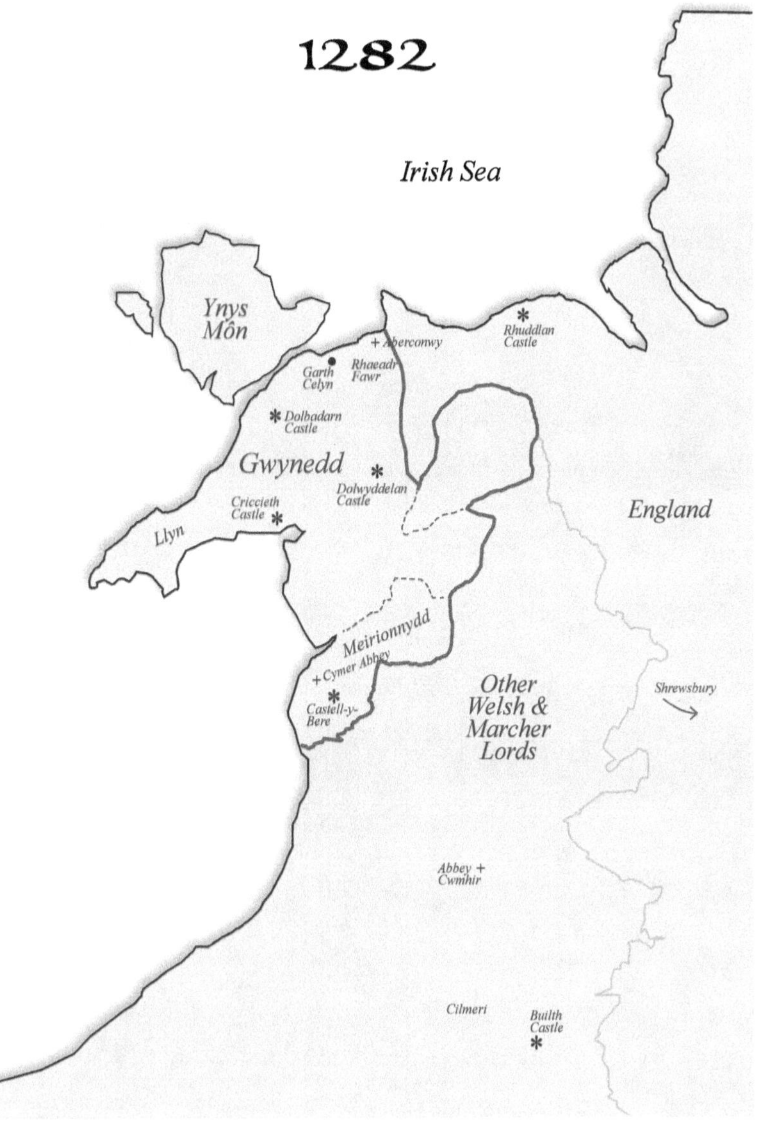

Irish Sea
Ynys Môn
Rhuddlan Castle
Aberconwy
Garth Celyn
Rhaeadr Fawr
Dolbadarn Castle
Gwynedd
Dolwyddelan Castle
Criccieth Castle
Llyn
England
Meirionnydd
Cymer Abbey
Castell-y-Bere
Other Welsh & Marcher Lords
Shrewsbury
Abbey Cwmhir
Cilmeri
Builth Castle

LAST OF THE GIFTED

SPIRIT SIGHT

MARIE POWELL

BOOK ONE

1

December 1282, Gwynedd, Cymru (North Wales)

He raised his arms, feeling bone and feather flatten against the wind, and knew himself tethered to air currents that smelled of salt and fish, somewhere off the horizon.

He ran below the bird, yet his mind and the hawk's mind moved as one. He could feel the dry December grasses beneath his bare feet, but he saw as the hawk saw: a flash of grey fur in the stubble, the swaying pattern of a tree branch.

He tried to turn the hawk's mind—his mind—to his will, and for a moment he succeeded. In the distance he could see the stone watchtower of his home at Garth Celyn, seat of the royal court of Wales. But the hawk's need was powerful, turning him back to scan the ground they circled. If he squinted—just so—at the yellow and russet clumps, he could make out the leaves of each tree. A shadow flitted from branch to branch.

Prey!

His talons ached for the soft flesh and his beak thrust forward—

No, not his. It was the hawk's beak that longed to rip the flesh from bone and feather. Hyw grasped the bird's thoughts again and turned its head toward Prince Llywelyn's tower. There! A streak of movement across the grass. Was it some grotesque beast from the past? He urged the hawk to circle until he could see it more clearly. A single horse and rider galloped toward Garth Celyn.

A messenger! Fast horses in wartime never bring good news. Had the English broken the peace again? Hyw gasped, and his connection to the bird faltered.

The hawk gave a piercing shriek. Hyw felt himself falling, as if he'd dropped from its talons rather than its mind. His feet—the same feet that had seemed to barely skim the ground a moment ago—thudded against the earth. He stumbled and the momentum of his running threw him, over and down until he braced his hands against the mountainside. He almost flipped again and bit back a cry as his fingers buckled, but his shifting weight came to a stop. *Tears have no place in a warrior's world,* his father had told him when Hyw had sprained his ankle five years ago. He flexed his fingers. Each one moved, painfully. Nothing was broken.

When he shared the mind of an animal or bird, he often lost the sense of his own physical body. He was becoming familiar with the consequences of coming back to himself. This time, though, he'd taken it a step further. He'd done it! He had made the hawk turn, so he could see what he wanted through its eyes, if only for a moment. It was easier with horses, because they loved him and he them—but they couldn't see any farther than the men riding them. Hawks and other birds would be more useful in a battle. Now he had proven it. He scarcely felt the dry spears of grass as he pushed himself up.

Hyw's first thought was to tell his father. But would his da listen? His da was Bran ap Maredudd, a trusted warrior of the prince's bodyguard. When Da bid him learn the ways and customs of their English enemy by going to foster at the court of Lord Shrewsbury, Hyw had gone. He spent four long years in the borderlands. But he had returned over a week ago. Every Welsh boy in training at Garth Celyn received a red sash on his fourteenth birthday, to mark his warrior status. Hyw had turned sixteen before he left Shrewsbury's court. All last week he'd waited, but his father had not brought him a sash. Hadn't even mentioned it.

On Hyw's first evening home, his mother Adara had seemed glad that his ability had manifested while he was away. It was his inheritance from her family, similar to her brother's, she'd said.

She'd even called it a "gift" that could help them. Bran had nodded but shushed her, glancing around at the priests and other wagging tongues in the Welsh royal court. He had not called on Hyw to serve the prince at Garth Celyn. But now Hyw had something to offer. Surely, now that he could control the minds of the creatures he bonded with, he could change his father's mind.

And what word did this messenger bring? If this meant war, Hyw would be needed. Wouldn't he? At the same time, Hyw felt a nagging doubt. What of James? They were best friends, but James was Shrewsbury's son and one of the *Saeson*—English. The enemy.

Fie on it! If his father rode with the prince, Hyw must be by his side. He would work harder to master his gift and to prove its value. He could prove himself—he would—if he could make his father listen. He would win his red sash. His cheeks burned as he sprinted for Garth Celyn.

As Hyw passed through the gates, he heard an anxious neighing. He sprinted across the courtyard toward the barns in time to see a young groom, holding the reins of a lathered horse. The sunlight caught a gleam of metal and Hyw saw a heavy English saddle, rather than the darker leather gear of the Welsh. The messenger's horse! The man who'd been riding it must already be inside the longhouse.

The groom crooned softly to the horse, but it blustered, jerking its head down. "*Hogyn da,*" he repeated, but the horse reacted as if he was cursing it instead of saying "Good boy." Hyw caught sight of its wild eyes as its head reared up again, and its hooves skittered on the packed courtyard. Could it be reacting to the language itself? Hyw felt the wrath beneath the horse's bay coat like a fist in his own gut. Warhorses were bred to be fighters too. How often had he dealt with their tempers in Shrewsbury's barns? He took a deep breath and held out his hand.

"Would you like me to try?" he asked in Welsh, and the groom passed over the reins.

"Why not? He's one of the *Saeson* too, after all."

Hyw took the reins and ignored the slur. It was mild compared to some he'd overheard since his return. After so many years away, he was like a stranger to his own people. He'd had to prove himself to the English in Shrewsbury's court, but it stung to have to prove himself again here at home.

He turned his attention to the horse, reaching out with his mind to make contact with the animal. He relaxed, probing the horse's mind to find the link that would bond them. He gasped as he felt his head lengthen. His back stretched. His nostrils filled with the smell of sweat and dust. Sunlight filtered across his blinkered eyes. He was all but overcome with a wild urge to kick out and pull away. He bared his teeth and snarled.

At the sound, he opened his eyes. It always felt real, but he knew it had occurred inside his mind and not in his body. He was able to join with the animal's mind, to see and think as it did. Yet from the look on the groom's face, he had seen nothing more than another boy calming a horse. Hyw stared into the dark intelligence reflected in the horse's eyes. Its skin shivered, but it stared back at Hyw with pride and defiance. As if he were an enemy, Hyw realized. Because he was Welsh? Hyw reached out once more, crooning in English as he had to the horses in Shrewsbury's barns. Gradually it calmed.

"I'll take care of him," Hyw said quietly in Welsh, and the horse tossed its head again. The groom held his hands up in a gesture that clearly said he was leaving Hyw to his fate and backed away to attend other duties.

As Hyw turned, he spied his father's lean frame by the doors of the longhouse at the other side of the courtyard. Bran was standing with Prince Llywelyn, easy to recognize in his black mourning clothes. The prince had no doubt been training with his men when the messenger arrived. Bran must have carried the news to the prince. Even now, they would be on their way to hear the messenger's words.

The two men appeared to be watching him. For a moment Hyw felt a faint hope that his father had seen him use his gift. Then he realized the groom standing right beside him had not known what Hyw was doing, so how could his father from that distance? Perhaps he could do it again, and use this horse to convince his father that his gift would be useful to the prince. But before Hyw could wave, they turned and made their way inside the longhouse.

2

"Deep breath," Cat's mam whispered, standing with her back to the heavy embroidered draperies that kept the cookhouse separate from the rest of the longhouse. She held a thin bread platter with an assortment of meats and a mug of the prince's best ale. Cat stood facing her mam, balancing her platter of cheeses and honeyed sweetbreads. Then her mam backed through the heavy curtain, holding it open for Cat to go ahead of her into the large open room.

Their guest sat cross-legged on the floor. He was one of the *Saeson*—English—but Cat wasn't prepared for how awkward he looked, knees akimbo, waiting for his refreshments. She managed to turn her smile into a welcome. After all, Cat and her mam had been hosts of Garth Celyn since Princess Elinor's passing last summer, and good hosts were expected to serve their guests. True, a messenger would most likely have been sent to the kitchen, but Mam had said this one was a special case. Messengers came and went often at Garth Celyn these days, and most were friendly and courteous. Hadn't the English Archbishop even stayed with them a fortnight ago? The English priests had looked much the same as the Welsh, and messengers were used to travel and adapted quickly. This tall, silent man in his riding coat and boots looked more like a knight than a messenger.

Cat placed the platter on the matt of rushes in front of the messenger and sat to his left. Her mam set her platter to the right, as she handed him the mug of strong Welsh ale. Then Mam knelt and took up the thicker piece of bread with the hollowed out middle that she'd had Cook save for their English guests—a "trencher" just as Cook used to make for Princess Elinor and her ladies—and Mam chose the best pieces of meat and cheese and set them into it. Mam was proud of the way she could adapt their Welsh fare to suit English tastes, but when she handed it to him, the man only grunted.

Cat wrinkled her nose and almost *tsked* before Mam caught her eye. Mam had asked Cat to make the traditional threesome for his meal, but he hadn't even greeted her yet. She knew Mam would expect her to make an effort, but before she could think of a question to ask, the messenger downed the ale and gestured with his head towards the door.

"Where is the prince?"

"He will attend you shortly," Mam responded, smiling. "My husband has gone to let him know of your coming."

At that moment the longhouse door opened for Prince Llywelyn, with Cat's da close behind him. The messenger stood, heedless of the platters, and Cat and Mam followed suit. Cat took a few steps toward Da, but something made her hesitate. The prince cast a deep shadow as the door slowly shut behind them. His black mourning clothes made him stand out against the colourful tapestries that adorned the walls.

Cat stared up at the prince's face, noticing for the first time the lines on his forehead and around his mouth and eyes. He had always seemed ageless, but Mam said he had been the country's leader for thirty years.

The prince smiled briefly at her as he passed, and Da laid a hand on her head in blessing. Cat touched the black band around her sleeve, a sign that she and her family shared in mourning for the Princess Elinor, who had died giving birth to the prince's first child, Baby Gwen. Cat still missed the princess and her ladies, who had brought so much colour and laughter to the longhouse. Cat ducked her head and said a silent prayer for the princess' soul, as Da began Llywelyn's formal introduction, tracing the prince's lineage back to Troy itself.

Her prayer and Da's voice were cut short when the bowing messenger began to speak, in English. "My Lord Llewellyn—"

"Prince Llywelyn," Da corrected, pronouncing the prince's name in the Welsh way.

"Erhm—My apologies, but time presses. I bring greetings from Baron Edmund Mortimer, lord of the March, the newly returned heir of Wigmore Castle."

"Yes, I knew his father and respected him," said the prince, his deep baritone echoing in the hall. "I trust the new Baron is well?"

The messenger faltered for a moment, his mouth gaping like a fish pulled out of the lake. Cat realized he must have forgotten his memorized message. What manner of messenger was he? Frowning slightly, the prince gestured for the man to continue.

As he began again, Mam leaned down and whispered in Cat's ear. "Go and see to Gwenllian for me, if you please."

Cat started to remind her mam that she'd already checked on Baby Gwen when the messenger first arrived. What could change in an hour? Besides, she wanted to stay and hear what the Englishman had to say.

"Please, Catrin," Mam repeated firmly. Cat knew better than to argue when her mam used her full name. She moved toward the kitchen, but as she passed the draperies separating it from the main room, she lost herself in their heavy folds and stood very still. She often hid there to listen to the kitchen gossip, but today she was more interested in the strange Englishman.

"Attack!" she heard the Englishman say. She knew that word well enough. Those *Saeson*! They should have learned their lesson by now. Hadn't Da and the prince turned them back, time and again? But now they were coming once more. Why couldn't they just go back to their *Saeson* hovels and leave Cymru alone? Maybe Hyw would know. He'd spent years and years with them.

Then she heard the word "alliance." Did that mean friendship? She remembered the old Baron Roger. They'd had a feast when he visited last year, and she'd tasted her first pigeon pie that night. Cat frowned. She remembered another messenger a few weeks ago, bringing news of the old baron's death. That made the prince very quiet. Had they been friends? Maybe his son Edmund, the new baron, would visit and they could have another feast. She put a hand over her stomach and willed it not to growl at the thought.

"…this letter," the Englishman was saying. Cat peeked from between the curtains in time to see him step forward to hand a parchment to the prince. Llywelyn took the parchment, examined the seal, and opened it. He scanned it, then handed it to Bran. The messenger fidgeted as they read.

"Tell Baron Edmund that Wales accepts his offer of friendship," the prince finally said, in a commanding tone. "We greet him warmly as the heir to Wigmore Castle. He will be welcome here at Garth Celyn."

"My lord—" the messenger began.

"Your Royal Highness," Da corrected again, his voice threatening. "As befits the Prince of Aberffraw, Lord of Snowden, and still the Prince of Wales." Cat noticed her Da's hand move to his sword, but Llywelyn shook his head slightly.

"Yes, er, your highness, my master beseeches you to attend him at Builth," the man said, bowing formally.

Llywelyn stood with his arms folded. Da turned to him, and they exchanged a few words too low for Cat to hear. She was listening so hard, she didn't notice her mam returning to the kitchen with the platters and ale jug in her hand. Mam opened the curtains and Cat almost fell through them into the other room. Mam shifted the platters, took Cat by one arm, and pulled her through the kitchens to the outside door. The frown on Mam's face warned Cat not to argue.

"Gwenllian," Mam whispered loudly, and pushed Cat towards the hut next door, where Enid nursed the baby.

As Cat stepped into the hut, she found Enid twisting wool threads into yarn on her spindle as she crooned a wordless lullaby. "Lullay, lully…" The wet nurse had lost her own baby a few days before Gwenllian was born, and she'd moved down from her farm near *Rhaeadr Fawr* to nurse Baby Gwen instead.

Cat sidled up to the baby's cradle and stared down at her pinched little face. Baby Gwen's eyes were tight shut, and she held one fist up to her closed mouth. Cat felt a sharp pang of sympathy for Gwenllian, who had no mam to show her the way, and for Enid, who had no daughter of her own.

On her deathbed, Princess Elinor had made her mam promise

she would keep Baby Gwenllian safe. Hadn't Cat even heard it, when she'd carried more water and blankets to Mam and the other ladies? They had shushed her from the room, but she had waited in the hall. She could hear the princess groan and plead and finally scream until Cat ran outside of the longhouse and wept in the gardens. The next time she saw Elinor, she was laid out for burial, her body shrunken and her face pale and still.

Baby Gwen was all that was left of her princess now. Cat's thoughts took another turn. If Enid's baby could die, what about Baby Gwen? *No!* There had been too much death lately, and it would not touch this baby. Didn't she have Cat and her mam to protect her? And Enid, too. Between them, surely they could protect one tiny baby. Cat moved the baby's coverlet gently around her and sat nearby to listen to Enid's sad contralto.

3

Hyw was brushing the bay's hide to a mahogany shine when the kitchen boy found him.

"Lord Bran says to fetch ye," the boy panted in Welsh. Hyw wondered if his father had news of his placement at last. He told the boy he would come as soon as he stabled the big horse, and the boy ran back to the kitchens without another word.

At Shrewsbury, Hyw would have been expected to call another groom to look after the horse and immediately attend his lord's summons. But at Garth Celyn their lives were so dependent on the livestock—especially the horses—that he would be expected to finish with the horse before he reported to the longhouse. Besides, this horse would not respond to the Welsh groom. Hyw let the big stallion loose in an empty pen near the geldings to avoid friction between this aggressive visitor and the Garth Celyn stallions.

Then he quickened his pace to the longhouse, where he found Bran sorting his gear.

"There you are, Hyw," his father greeted him. "We must ride hard, and we need a squire who can manage the mounts. Are you up for another journey?"

"Yes," he said, and then shifted uncomfortably. He had still been a page when he left Shrewsbury. Saints knew he would have become a squire soon enough had he stayed, but he'd rather be a warrior and serve the prince and his father. This trip might be the way to show them what he was capable of, and so finally win his sash!

Bran turned to him. "Your prompt response makes me proud, Hyw," he said. "But you have my leave to reconsider. I know you've just returned, and you might want time with your mother and sister before—"

"No—that is, I will say farewell to them if I may, Tad." His father flinched at the formal term, but Hyw pressed on. He was the best choice for this job, whatever the circumstances, but he wasn't sure how to say it. "I know there is risk in any journey, with the English on the march, but I would go with you. Besides, none other has my gift—with horses."

His father scanned the room, even as the corners of his mouth turned up briefly in a smile. "Yes," he replied, "if your mam speaks truly, yours is a gift we will find most useful on this journey." Before Hyw could ask more questions, Bran returned to his sorting and dismissed him with a parting comment. "Best sort your gear and say your goodbyes tonight. We leave at first light."

Hyw's first thought was to find his mother. Adara was spinning near the window to catch the sunshine. When she saw him, she stood and moved to him for a hug. As she released him, her smile was genuine.

"How have you settled in, Hyw?" she asked as she drew him to the window seat, holding his hands in hers.

"Well enough, Mother," he said, loathe to tell her that he felt like a stranger again. During the years of his fosterage, thinking of her round, smiling face had brightened his heart. Shrewsbury's older lady had taken little interest in him, save the one time she referred to him as "yon Welsh cur." She spat those few words like a bad taste in her mouth, and the others of her court had taken her cue. He wondered what his mam knew of what had befallen him in Shrewsbury.

He blushed and tried to turn his head away. Adara dropped his hands quickly. "I forget how near a man you are already. Forgive me, Hyw."

"Do not fear it, Mam," he said, wishing he could reach for her hands again. She reached up then and brushed the hair from his eyes.

"That's what I was hoping for," she said. He looked at her in surprise, and she laughed. "For you to call me Mam again, instead of mo-ther." She emphasized the English pronunciation and he smiled, realizing he had been using the English words. Maybe he'd been acting like a stranger.

"Ah, what brings that flush to your cheeks, then?" she continued. "An English maid, left behind?"

"Nay, Mam," he answered quickly. "No English girl would have me." He spoke in Welsh, using "geneth" for girl with a smile, but at her look of concern he wished he had kept silent. The English girls had found little to their liking in his wiry frame. His copper hair earned its share of jeering from them, but it came, like his own gift, from his mother.

"Well," she brightened, "there will be time for a' that, now that you are home again. And glad I am of it." She laughed again, patting his folded hands.

He made a pained face. "Now is not the time," he told her. "I must take my leave shortly, to go with my father and the prince."

"So soon? But I had thought—" Adara broke off, realization dawning in her eyes. "Well, that is good news, is it not? Your da asked for you at last?"

Hyw nodded, on the verge of telling his mother that he was neither a squire nor a warrior yet, but she continued with a look of delight.

"I prayed he would call you to the prince's service, and now I will not need to prompt him," she said. "I am not pleased to see you ride to war, Hyw, but I believe this mission may help prevent one. If your da and the prince can bring the new Baron of Wigmore to their side, it may give the English king a reason to hold his advance at Rhuddlan. And I am well pleased to see you serve the prince."

"It is only one mission, Mam. I am not yet *teulu*," he said, referring to the prince's special bodyguard.

"And why should you not join your da there too?" she asked. He dared not admit he hoped to prove himself worthy, but she gave him a look as if she had read his mind. "Ach, we have tomorrow for goodbyes. Today we will make you ready. I have a fresh tunic for you."

"Not red, Mam," he admonished her, referring to the red tunics worn by Prince Llywelyn's *teulu*.

"Not yet," she answered, meaningfully. "And how does your surcoat?"

"Well enough, Mam," he mumbled as she looked his clothes over for tears to mend. As a page, he had learned to mend his own clothing in emergencies. But Adara's attentions also showed how much she cared for him, and for a moment he longed to throw his arms around her again. She often said she could call her gift when she needed it, and he wondered if he should ask her advice on using his to help him win his warrior's sash.

Before he could find the words, Enid entered, carrying Baby Gwen. Adara held out her arms for the child and began to hum softly. His sister Cat came in behind Enid and sidled closer to him. He reached out and pulled a strand of hair that had come loose before she could push him away. He had been surprised at how much she'd grown in his three-year absence. She would soon be fifteen. He wondered if arrangements had been made for her wedding, or if the war would delay that as well.

"Cat, your brother has news," Adara said. "And he needs his new tunic. Would you take him to fetch it?"

4

Cat drew her brother toward their mam's basket of sewing projects, while Enid and Adara took the baby to be admired by the other women. The tunic was neatly folded on top, waiting for the servants to come and put it with his things. As Cat shook it out for him, he told her he would be going to serve the prince as squire.

"You will be a warrior now, surely," she said, half listening. "Your gift can only help you get there." Hyw was lucky to have gained such control over his gift already. What would it be like to connect with animals like Hyw, or charm bees like their mam? Her own gift had not appeared. Some of Mam's family had no gift at all, but surely she would not be one of them.

Cat put that thought aside as she handed the tunic to him. "Don't fret. It will be red soon enough."

"It's fine," he said, taking it from her and unconsciously wringing the fabric with his hands.

"Then why aren't you smiling?"

He grimaced then, as if he was trying to smile. She made a face at him, and finally coaxed him into a grin. Then he shook his head.

"Your words reminded me of something," he said.

As his voice trailed off, Cat realized what he must be thinking. "James!" she said.

Hyw nodded, looking miserable. It was not the first time since his return. He often seemed stuck between the *Saeson* world and his own. She touched his shoulder.

"I cannot imagine it, Hyw. What it must be like to know you might meet a friend in battle."

"It's more than that," Hyw said, staring at the tunic in his hands. "James helped me forge my gift."

"He knows?"

"He guessed, one day when I worked with a nervous filly in Shrewsbury's barn. And instead of turning away or raising the alarm, he urged me to try with other animals. He helped me build something like a wall in my mind, to protect me from connecting with animals by accident. He kept my secret. It was—like a bond between us."

Cat wasn't sure what to say. Their mam had long warned them never to tell anyone outside the family about their special abilities. Did Hyw think of this *Saeson* boy as a brother, then? She almost felt jealous of him. Hyw went on to explain that James was the son of one of their father's cousins, so he was half-Welsh. Then she brightened and put her hands over Hyw's.

"I heard the messenger when he told the prince. You do not ride to war, Hyw. You ride to make an al- ally-" She paused to think of the right word in English. "Alliance."

"What else did you hear?"

Cat told him everything, even her thoughts about the strangeness of the man's dress and bearing, and his poor skills at delivering the message. "I could have done it better," she declared.

"Where is he?" Hyw craned his neck to look around the room.

"He is gone already," she told him. "Fret not, brother. The man was so anxious to leave he saddled his own horse for the journey." They both grinned at that.

"It seems strange that he would not break bread with us before he left."

"*Saeson*," Cat said with a dismissive shrug. She reached for his hand again. "Here, I made this for you," she said, taking a colourful finger bracelet from the basket and knotting it onto his wrist. "I made it for your birthday, thinking you would be here with us. Look, I braided in a few strands of my hair. The princess said everyone does it in France. For remembrance." She looked up to see him watching her, a look of concern in his eyes.

"Do you miss her very much?" he asked.

She raised her hand to her black armband again. Adara had called Cat into service when the princess first came to court. Princess Elinor and her ladies spoke only French and English and Cat's job was to sing children's songs and poems to help them learn Welsh. The princess had welcomed her. Later, Cat learned the complex meters of the bards so she could sing Welsh poetry to them. At the princess's insistence, Cat travelled with their itinerant court to visit the prince's holdings and castles. During one of these trips, Princess Elinor introduced Cat to Rhys, the boy she was promised to marry. If she had married Rhys, Cat would have become the Lady of Meirionnydd, but when the princess became pregnant, she asked Cat to put the wedding off and stay with her. Yet in the end, there was no help. Cat could not find the words to say how much she missed her princess, so she said nothing.

"I wish I had something for you in return," Hyw said. His face looked so serious.

"What of a deed instead?" she suggested. "Come and see *Rhaeadr Fawr* once more, before you go." Would he recall their old childhood races to the waterfalls? Before he could reply, she tagged him and ran off toward the path.

"No, you don't!" he cried from behind her as he followed, laughing.

The night's grey clouds had parted, allowing the wakening sun to slant off Tŷ Hir, the longhouse at the heart of Garth Celyn. This was her favourite time of the day. A wave of love for the peaceful and industrious *llys* washed over her. She shielded her eyes as she looked up, hoping to savour the moment, but she caught sight of the armed warriors pacing on the tower and shivered.

Sturdy wood and stone buildings fanned out from Tŷ Hir, creating a small town that made up the royal *llys*. Already people filtered into the courtyard to bid farewell to Llywelyn's *teulu*, the trusted warriors who made up the royal bodyguard. Cat stood with her mam, counting the warriors. At first, she was surprised not to see more of them: only about twenty men, counting her da, wearing his gold torque around his neck and red sash across his coat of mail. Her brother held the reins of the prince's horses. Of course, it took fewer warriors to make friends than to fight off enemies. She felt a small swell of pride that her brother and father were included in this select company, twenty out of one-hundred sixty warriors.

Then she was struck by an overshadowing greyness, almost a feeling of dread. No! She almost said it aloud. But her da was already embracing her mam before he bent down to her. She snuggled into the warmth of his heavy fur cloak and put her arms around his waist.

"Tada," she whispered, using the phrase she had not used since she was a small child. He hugged her closer for a moment before releasing her and ruffling her hair.

"Worry not, little Cat," he told her. "We will be back before you know we're gone."

Hyw moved to hold Aeron, their da's brown warhorse, as Bran mounted, and then held the prince's huge black stallion steady for him. As she watched, Cat wished the messenger had remained to guide them. She suddenly thought of Father Maelgwyn. What had he said at Mass? Something about being rewarded by the "fruit of his mouth" while a transgressor would only "eat violence." She shivered.

"Are you cold, sister?" Hyw asked, draping his soft cloak around her shoulders.

"No, Hyw," she said, trying to give it back to him. "You will need this."

"I have another." He held it on her shoulders a moment before pinning it in front with the gold clasp from her woolen surcoat. "This cloak was a gift to me. It is much too fine for where we are going."

She felt the soft fabric, dyed a rich blue and lined with blue-grey squirrel fur. It was a mark of wealth. "Was it from James?"

Hyw nodded and began to turn away from her. Her earlier feeling of greyness returned and threatened to overwhelm her. To escape her thoughts, she flung her arms around him in a final hug.

"Fare ye well, Hyw. May God protect you and Da," she whispered, "and may you keep the prince from harm."

"We will," he told her, kissing her cheek. His mouth twisted into a lopsided grin. "You look after our infant princess." The grin lapsed into seriousness again. "And our mam."

"I will." She hugged him fiercely another moment before he turned to mount his horse.

5

Through the morning they rode hard when the land allowed, dismounting to lead their horses through denser brush. As he rode his father's gelding, Cadarn, Hyw clicked his tongue and the horse's ears flicked forward in response. He had taken special care to groom Cadarn the previous evening, and the horse remembered and trusted him. In his free hand, Hyw held the reins of Llywelyn's fresh mount, ready in case of ambush. Vox was a stallion, powerful and used to action. Hyw connected with him often to keep him calm and quiet. He found himself glad that, since this was to be a short trip with no hunting, Llywelyn had left the dogs behind—which meant fewer animals for him to marshal.

At first, it was a matter of keeping the horses abreast and not letting the stallion take the lead. The ground in several places was already covered with snow, making the narrow trail increasingly dangerous for the horses. As the path twisted, Hyw had to make Vox fall in behind Cadarn.

Vox pushed against the lead, snorting. Hyw didn't need his gift to know the stallion was not pleased to follow the gelding, but both horses were well trained. Hyw created an image in his mind of the bushes and thickets around them, projecting his sense of urgency to Vox in a strong command: *Enemies. Be watchful.* Vox's head veered from side to side once, as if he was scanning the terrain. After that, he followed, ears forward.

The men spoke little, and the prince even less. No one sang, as they would have on most journeys. Often the prince had surprised his enemies with the swiftness of his response to battle. His warrior *teulu*—the men he often called his true family—had it down to a discipline.

Hyw scanned for birds in the trees, especially the hawks with which he felt special connection. His gift would help the men avoid danger if it came. But with Bran riding behind Llywelyn, and Hyw at the other end of the line of warriors, how could he give the alarm without explaining his gift? How receptive would his father be, with the prince and his warriors so near?

They stopped to water the horses, which most of the men accomplished without dismounting. He'd forgotten what the *teulu* were like, but he soon learned what it meant to ride hard through the mountains. At one of these stops, he made his way to his father.

"Da, I am able to see farther than most," Hyw began, holding Vox's reins as the horses drank their fill. At his father's raised eyebrow, Hyw pointed upward at a hawk circling nearby. "I can see what he sees. But how can I let you know if I spot the *Saeson*?"

Bran looked around at the wooded stream, patting Aeron's broad neck. "Once, when you were young, you and I disturbed a nest of hawks, red kites, near Aber Falls. Do you recall the sound they made?"

Hyw nodded. The chicks had made a shrill near-whistling sound with a slight warble in its centre. He felt sure he could reproduce it. "If you hear that sound today, Da, it will mean trouble," he promised.

Bran nodded as he turned Aeron's head back to the path.

The day waned into the next morning as they pressed on. Years of early training under Aeneas served Hyw well. He set his mind not to feel the cold or the hunger that gnawed at him. They needed speed and stealth. There would be no stopping to hunt or make a fire. His mam had slipped him extra bread with dried meat strips from her pocket. He ate these from the pack he'd tied to Cadarn's saddle as he saw the other men do, and he would need to make them last as long as he could.

Several times he had to jump down to wade beside the horses as they crossed treacherous fords with fast currents. Hyw had to shake himself more than once, as he began to slide from the saddle in sheer weariness. Then in panic he connected with the hawks again, making certain no enemy was near.

They were forced to a halt at the River Wye, black and swollen to the level of its banks. Impassable.

The remnants of a bridge clung to the near bank.

"*Saeson*," one of the warriors grunted, and spat on the ground.

Llywelyn motioned for Bran and a younger warrior named Goronwy to walk aside with him. They stood contemplating the river. Hyw could see the younger man gesturing down the bank and across the river. Hyw dropped from the saddle and led the horses to the water to drink.

"What can you see?" Bran asked.

"There are two armies." Hyw stood staring at the sky, seeing through the eyes of a hawk as it spied on groups of men milling about a field. Some cleaned weapons, while others put armour on each other and their horses.

"Can you see the sigils?"

Hyw drove the bird closer and described what he saw on the banners of the enemy. Bran quizzed him carefully and then nodded.

"Giffard the Saxon," Bran said. "And Roger LeStrange. We must tell the prince."

Hyw watched anxiously as his da spoke with Llywelyn, just out of earshot. He had learned about the allies and enemies of his prince's house almost from the cradle. Giffard was Llywelyn's cousin by marriage. How must the prince feel to have his cousin turn against him yet again? Llywelyn questioned Bran and then abruptly turned toward the others. Bran nodded and smiled at Hyw as the prince rallied his men.

Llywelyn's response was decisive. "The English king is upon us. We must send word to our allies."

A wave of relief flooded Hyw. The prince had believed them, although Bran would never have named Hyw or his gift as the source of the information. Llywelyn was known as a modern Welshman, with tolerance but no fondness for the old ways. The prince acted quickly, sending a man back to Garth Celyn for his army, and others to muster his allies in Gwynedd and Powys Fadog.

"We will meet at Garth Celyn in no less than three days. All haste is necessary."

As the men rode out, Llywelyn turned with a gesture to Bran and the few men remaining. Hyw's heart was pounding as he brought Vox forward. He must go with them. He could use his gift to watch the enemy, to help protect his prince—and his da. But how could he convince them?

Then he heard his da's low voice. "We must bring my son."

Prince Llywelyn stopped for a moment and looked back at Hyw. The expression in his eyes was unreadable. Finally, he nodded.

The next morning, they arrived at Abbey Cwmhir. The imposing building sprawled across the field in front of them. At Llywelyn's gesture, Goronwy remained near the gatehouse with the horses in readiness for their departure. Hyw followed Llywelyn and Bran through the gate to the church and down the long stone nave, the main aisle of the church. The vaulted ceiling rose high above them, and Hyw counted fourteen bays.

"Impressive," Bran said softly, crossing himself and bending one knee as they came in sight of the altar.

"Yes," Llywelyn responded, kneeling also. He bowed his head for a moment and rose to continue down the aisle. "After this skirmish, by my troth, I will finish it." As Hyw knelt, he realized this abbey reminded him of the abbey at Aber, near Garth Celyn. The familiar look and style of this nave meant these were the White Monks, Cistercians, who believed in the simplicity of prayer and work.

The abbot saw them and came forward with two other monks in their characteristic white robes. Llywelyn turned the abbot aside, and they spoke in a low voice for a few moments. As Hyw politely turned to look again at the church, one of the monks clasped Bran by the arm, warrior style. The two embraced briefly, and then the monk turned to Hyw.

"He has certainly grown," the monk said, using his hand to mark a space by his waist, and then by the top of Hyw's head.

"Uncle Gawain!" Hyw threw his arms around his uncle in a bear hug that was heartily returned.

"We are grateful to have this chance to see you again," Bran added.

"And lucky, for I am traveling to Aberconwy this week," Gawain said. "Now I shall have an excuse to stop in on my lady sister."

"That would please her, I am sure," Bran said.

"Enough of this family reunion," Llywelyn said, clapping Bran on the shoulder. "The abbot has given me a blessing for our actions and a brother to ensure our success."

"You have missed the morning service, I am afraid," said the old abbot with a kind look. "I must remain, but I will give Brother Gawain a special release to attend you, to aid your mission if he can."

Llywelyn offered Vox to Gawain, since the horse was already saddled and their need to get back on the road was pressing. Hyw helped him check the cinches on Vox's gear before they mounted.

"Shrewsbury treated you well?" Gawain asked quietly, using the horse to mask them from the other men.

"He did, uncle, but—" Hyw broke off, unsure how to tell his uncle. "It seems I am like you."

"Oh? In what manner?"

"Mam says you and I have a similar—gift."

Understanding dawned in Gawain's eyes. "Then I may be able to advise you, Hyw." He asked a few quick questions, and Hyw answered as well as he could. Gawain paused to look at him. "I have such a gift, but only with horses. And I have never felt what you describe, as if you are becoming one with the creature."

Hyw was unsure what to say. His dismay must have shone on his face.

"I recall our grandfather speaking so of his early years," Gawain went on quickly, placing his spare robe into the soft leather bag attached to the horse's saddle. "Perhaps I will journey to Garth Celyn for Twelfth Night, so we can spend some time together. I do not promise to have all of the answers to your questions, but what I know I will share." He tousled Hyw's hair. "Together we may sort out your strengths. Meanwhile, we must get the prince into Builth Castle to meet his allies."

Hyw expelled a breath in relief, although he had not realized he was holding it. His uncle would make good his promise as soon as their mission was complete. Other questions crowded into his mind, and he blurted out the first one almost without thinking. "Is that why you packed a second robe, uncle?"

"You have sharp eyes, I see." Gawain looked into the distance, his expression almost sad. "I forget you children were born in war and weaned on watchfulness." Then he smiled a little as he continued checking Vox's saddle and gear. "And Llywelyn himself may be your model for it, forced to be watchful for so many years. This second robe may prove its worth. With a castle shut as tight as Builth, a simple monk may travel with less notice than a rival prince."

Hyw nodded, beginning to understand his uncle's role in helping Llywelyn. The prince would dress as a monk and the two would pay a call on the castle. Gawain turned his attention to Vox. It was strange to watch his uncle use their shared gift to make contact with the skittish stallion. Hyw wondered if he looked as intense when he used his gift, and if that's how James always knew. He wondered if others could tell, or if he could school his expression to hide it.

When Vox quieted, Gawain mounted. Bran motioned for Gawain to join him farther ahead in the line of men, and there was no more time for talk.

Later that day they neared Builth and stopped to make camp. Llywelyn and Gawain moved aside to speak together. Bran and the other men began to tend their horses, and Hyw took Vox and Cadarn to the stream. He dunked his own head in the cool water as the horses drank. As the waning sun glinted off the surface, he stared down at his reflection. With one hand he fingered the threads of the bracelet his sister had woven around his wrist.

Then he stood and moved onto the bank with the horses to remove their saddles. He took his brushes from Cadarn's saddlebag to groom them. He finished Vox first, and then turned to Cadarn. His father's gelding nickered softly as Hyw came closer and nuzzled at his side to take the small apple he kept hidden there. Hyw smiled, stepping easily to Cadarn's side as he had so many times before. He had been grooming Cadarn since he was a boy, before he went away to England. Sometimes it seemed the horse remembered him better than his old friends or his family.

As he finished brushing Cadarn's shaggy winter coat to a shine, he heard the clashing of armour in the distance. Could the men be practicing, with the English army so near? Cadarn nickered uneasily, swinging his head around and twitching his ears. Hyw put away the brushes and looked up, choosing a rook from a flock hovering overhead to be his eyes. The bird could hear the faint sounds of clanging armour as well, and he willed it to look closer. Its vision caused his stomach to fist: men fighting and bleeding in a clearing.

He released the bird, left the horses grazing on the bank, and sprinted toward the clearing.

6

At first, all she saw was water.

Cat was in the chapel with her mam and some of the other women, listening to Father Maelgwyn's baritone as he sang the prayers. She had worn the cloak Hyw gave her, and she stroked the rich material with one hand. The ever-present rain drummed steadily on the stone chapel walls.

"Let us pray," Father Maelgwyn sang. Cat focused on the raindrops dripping into the chapel through the arch of the window, as she drew in a breath—

—and suddenly she could see the wide, dark expanse of a river.

Was she dreaming?

She tried to open her eyes, but the picture became clearer. Black water rumbled, swollen and churning against the banks. This wasn't her familiar Aber. What river was it? Where was it?

She turned as if to ask someone, and saw her brother standing on the bank, staring into the water.

"Hyw!" She called his name, but he didn't look up. Couldn't he hear her? He snapped his head up but looked past her. And then he ran.

Things began to move around her. It was as if the scene broke apart and came together again. She was standing in a meadow. The stench of blood and death filled her nostrils. She heard a high-pitched whistle—no, a scream! Someone screaming. She raised her hands to cover her ears—

—and she found herself back in the church, kneeling. She

could feel the wooden balustrade in front of her, and hear the chant rising and falling around her.

"*Dominus vobiscum*," the priest sang in Latin.

The Lord be with you, Cat thought automatically, the familiar words anchoring her in the ritual.

"*Et cum spiritu tuo…*" she sang back. *And with thy spirit.*

Cat looked up and found her mam's eyes, which slipped from smiling to alarm. Without dropping a word of the prayer, Adara touched Cat's forehead and then drew her into her side for support.

"*Sanctus, Sanctus, Sanctus,*" Adara's clear soprano rang out. Holy, holy, holy. This was always the part of the *Te Deum* that Cat liked best, and she joined in, harmonizing automatically.

"*…Pleni sunt caeli et terra gloria tua.*"

Heaven and Earth are full of thy glory. Had she just seen some of it? Or was it a dream? She felt a chill like the spray from the waterfall on a wintery day. Father Maelgwyn warned of darker forces. Was that what caused her vision? Was her gift evil? But how then could it come to her in church? She turned to her mam, but Adara shook her head slightly and touched one finger to her lips.

When the service was finally over, Adara drew Cat aside to walk with her toward the waterfall. They had often walked together after church when Cat was younger, but they had been too busy of late. When they had gone far enough to be out of earshot, she told her mam what had happened in the church and what she'd seen.

"What—what is it?" Cat asked. "Do you think I really saw Hyw?"

Mam thought for a moment and then nodded. "It seems clear to me that you saw him. And possibly more."

Cat shivered, thinking of the churning water and the smell of blood. "What can it mean?"

"I know not, Cat. The meadow in your vision marks a change. If this vision is of something yet to come, if it is the future, then you must have seen it for a reason."

"What reason? What can we do?"

"Often a vision is a warning. If your gift is the Second Sight, we must not ignore it."

"Second sight?"

"It's an old gift, Cat," said Mam slowly. "One I haven't seen for a long time. My grandfather used the term 'seeing beyond the veil.' There are different ways that comes to us. We each bring our own nature to it. Like the connection your brother has to animals. My own brother—your uncle Gawain—has such a gift as well."

"And you, Mam." Cat thought about the way her mam could take honey from beehives without ever being bitten, and the way no gnats or insects ever bothered their banquets and campfires. "You're a bee charmer."

"Bee charmer." A smile played around Mam's mouth. "Yes, I suppose I am. I like that, Cat. And our grandfather had a strong gift. His started with matching his mind to the creature, as Hyw does. Later he learned to fully transform into the creature. My great-aunt—rest her soul—could see the future. Our grandfather called that the Second Sight."

Cat hesitated, unsure she wanted such a gift. "But I have no gift. Or at least, I thought I didn't. Why did this happen now?"

"Maybe because we need it now," Mam said. "I've watched for your gift too, but there has been no sign. It comes to men and women in our family, but it does not come to all. I thought you might be like my youngest sister, your Aunt Cadi. One or two of each generation have been passed over, and sometimes the gift will skip generations and pass to the children or grandchildren. My mam used to say it was to balance the scales. But perhaps that can change, if the need is great. As it is now."

"Then we must do something."

"We will send someone to give the warning to your da, that he may pay special heed to your brother." Mam put her arm around Cat and turned them both back toward Garth Celyn.

7

Hyw arrived panting, more with alarm than exertion. The reek of blood and sweat surrounded him. He crouched, looking around him for soldiers, but nothing stirred. Spotting one familiar figure lying on the ground, he ran to it. He turned the body without thinking. It was not his da's face. Relief so strong it made him giddy washed over him, before he recognized the man was one of the prince's *teulu* from Garth Celyn. The warrior's eyes were open and unseeing, and his skull above shorn off. Hyw crossed himself and reached forward to close the man's eyes with a blessing. Then he turned and retched into the grass.

"Help," someone cried behind him. Hyw turned to spy another warrior lying a short distance away. "Help the prince."

The man pointed over the hillock and Hyw ran, leaving the fallen warrior to bleed into the hillside. His neck prickled with panic. He raced heedlessly over the hill and almost into the arms of an armoured man. The man grabbed Hyw instinctively and swung him around with the momentum of his charge.

"Here now," an English voice said. "What's this?" Hyw found himself dangling in the air. He stared at a group of armed soldiers, who seemed to be merely standing on the hillside together.

Then he paled: Llywelyn was there, kneeling on the ground. A spear pierced his body from front to back. Yet the prince supported one end of the stake aloft, or perhaps it held him upright. Hyw realized the prince must have been surprised by the English soldiers.

Where was his da? And his uncle Gawain?

"He's just a lad, Mortimer," said another voice to his right, this one strained and thick. "Leave him be. Has there not been enough killing this day?"

Hyw dropped roughly to the ground as the soldier laughed. "This from the man who struck down the Prince of Wales? Have you a woman's will, de Francton? Bah. Take him then. Enough of this. It ends here, prince or no."

Before the men could stop him, Hyw leapt up and ran to the prince. His knees hit the ground in front of the dying man.

"Get me a priest," rasped Llywelyn, in English. Then his black eyes focused on Hyw, and he seemed to recognize him. In Welsh, Llywelyn said, "Protect my daughter. She is all my future now."

Hyw met the prince's gaze. Llywelyn's dark eyes never wavered. As Hyw stared into them, blood roared like a dark river in his ears and his mind seemed to expand. His consciousness opened to the prince. He saw himself kneeling in the field. He must be seeing through the prince's eyes, as if he and the prince were one.

The prince cried out, "God have mercy on our souls!" And the dark eyes broke contact even as the prince's head was cleft from his body.

Hyw saw as if through a veil as the English knight held the prince's head high in the air, roaring with triumph. Blood gushed from the prince's headless body, still kneeling in the field, impaled by the spear. And blood dripped from the knight's sword onto the grass.

Something like mist spread over Hyw's mind. Clouds appeared from nowhere to dim the sun. The world turned ashen, and then as red as blood. Stars fell toward him and birds plummeted from the sky like rain as the ground thundered and rose up in its place.

As if from far away, he heard someone screaming and did not know it was himself until he felt a blow on the side of his head. Then he heard and saw—nothing.

He floated in a sea of cool water and soft cloth. He thought of Elinor, her scent and the softness of her skin. But when he opened his eyes, he saw her not. Instead, he saw a blue-eyed man in a monk's cowl.

"Hyw, glad I am to see you waken," said the monk.

"Who is Hyw?" he asked. His voice croaked, and the monk sponged his lips with a wet cloth, dripping some of the water into his mouth. He swallowed.

He recognized the monk's voice. Or did the boy recognize the voice? He shook his head and almost swooned from pain. How could it be that he, Llywelyn, could see at all? Was he not dead at the hands of the traitorous Mortimer?

Was he in hell then? He almost laughed. Had he not already been there? Any place was hell, without his wife. Again, the anguish of her loss threatened to drown him, but the monk laid a cool cloth upon his brow. "Rest, Hyw."

"Nay," he rasped. "I am not Hyw."

"He is bemused," the monk turned to an armoured soldier at his side. "But he is strong. He will rally."

Llywelyn recognized the mounted soldier who had struck him down. Somewhere inside his mind he heard the echo of a name: de Francton.

"Murderer." He tried to rise, but his head felt thick. "I am not Hyw."

The monk looked at him deeply then, into his eyes. Llywelyn read a mix of shock and horror in his face.

"Can this be?" the monk half-whispered. Then his expression became thoughtful. He moved closer and spoke the next words into Llywelyn's ear. "Fear not, my liege. All will be well."

Llywelyn's eyes began to close. He heard a voice singing and thought of Elinor. He whispered her name as he sank beneath consciousness again. It was like floating underwater.

As he sank, he saw a lad swim past him, pulling hard for the surface. Why, it is Bran's son, he thought, and slept again.

8

Cat knew before the kitchen boy came to get her.

She was kneeling in front of Baby Gwen's cradleboard, shaking a clay rattle Llywelyn had made for his daughter. It was cleverly fashioned in the shape of a smiling pig, and whatever tiny stones he had placed inside clinked cheerfully. Baby Gwen reached out her chubby fists to the rattle—which Cat held just out of reach—and giggled. Cat sang a short rhyme about patience as she gave the pig to the excited baby. Enid smiled at them.

Cat took a drink to clear her throat and leaned forward to set the cup down, adjusting her new cloak to a more comfortable position. Her eyes caught the glint of the swishing liquid as her fingers brushed the fabric—

—and she found herself in a meadow, kneeling in front of Prince Llywelyn instead. The prince's face was contorted in pain. Then she saw her brother's face. The two faces merged so she could not tell one from the other as they fell into the raging waves of a dark river. Then she saw a head raised high in the air by a mailed gauntlet. She could not see the face. Was it her brother?

She heard an echoing laughter, a man's deep spiteful laugh, and it sent a shiver down her back—

—and she was kneeling in front of Baby Gwen again.

"Hyw!" she cried out. "Where are you, brother?"

But the vision was gone.

Startled, Enid set down her mending and stood. "What is wrong, child?"

Before Cat could answer, the boy appeared at the door.

"Your mam sent me," he said. "Ye must come—right now!"

A familiar young man looked decidedly uncomfortable in the hall, a small figure turning his cap over and over in his hands as he answered her mam's barrage of questions. Aeneus was there as well, his arms crossed over his chest and his face a grim mask. Mam paced in front of them. Cat had never seen her so anxious.

"We must go at once," Mam began as soon as she saw Cat.

"Hyw is hurt," Cat said.

"As you have guessed," Mam said, casting her a warning glance. Cat, flustered, turned to Berwyn. The son of another warrior, he had left recently to join the Cistercian order, but the abbot must have sent him back to tell the family the news. Cat's knees buckled as she recalled the mailed fist and the raging river of her vision.

"What of Hyw?" Cat broke in. "Is he alive?"

"Hyw lies in a sickbed in the abbey."

"Sickbed?" What good was the Sight, if it came too late to save those she cared about? She could not make sense of what she had seen. "What happened to him?

"The abbot did not say, and I could not tarry."

"And Bran?" Mam asked. "What of my husband?"

"I am sorry, my lady," the stable boy stammered, shaking his head. "There was no word."

"No word," Mam repeated, a worried frown creasing her brow. Cat flew to her.

"Lady, the *Saeson* will come to claim Garth Celyn," said Aeneus. "We will fight them." He turned to Berwyn. "Did your abbot tell you how many troops Edward brings with him?"

"Th-th-thousands," stammered Berwyn.

"How's that?" Aeneus stepped back and swung his arms expressively. "Tell me truly, boy. How many?"

"Th-the monk said, begging your pardon, sir," Berwyn stammered. "He said to tell ye they mean to—to—"

"Monk?" Mam broke in. "Was it my brother?"

"It was, Lady," Berwyn stammered. "He was with the prince in the field, he said. They let him go because he was in his robes, and because he demanded to look after Hyw."

"My brother lives," Cat whispered.

"God be praised." Mam kept her arm around Cat, who leaned into her familiar warmth.

"He said Mortimer comes in force, and to tell my lord Aeneus that your only hope is to flee Garth Celyn."

"We must secure Llywelyn's daughter. Tell Enid to get Baby Gwen ready for travel." Mam released Cat and turned to Berwyn and Aeneus. "Aeneus, you know my brother. He would never interfere if he was not certain. See to the men."

"I will see you to safety first, Lady," the warrior answered. "Whither thou goest."

Mam frowned and then nodded. "I know you will." She put one hand to her brow. "We will take Gwenllian to Criccieth Castle. Word came yesterday that Dafydd has sent Elizabeth there, with their children. The babe should be with her family."

Dafydd was the prince's brother and heir, and Cat realized he would now be the Prince of Wales.

"Aye." Aeneus nodded. "Criccieth is more fortified than our *llys*, and the garrison is loyal. With its twin towers between us and the English, the babe will be safe."

"Dafydd will protect her as he does his own children. Send to Anglesey for more defenders to make a stand here, lest the *Saeson* get through to burn our winter stores as they tried to do five years ago."

Aeneus nodded. "I will see to it."

"Once Gwen is safe, I must go to Builth." Mam turned to Cat, her unspoken concern for Da and Hyw bright in her eyes. She seemed about to ask something, but Aeneus took a step toward them.

"Nay, you must stay with the babe," he said. He raised his hands before she could protest. "I will see you both to Criccieth, and after I will go to Builth and fetch your son. And I will find his da or bring his body home to you. On that, I give you my word."

9

Hyw rose to consciousness only to sink again into a place he could not remember on waking. He sensed himself rising and falling, like the tides surrounding Garth Celyn. Yet he was not near his home at all; he was in a monk's cell, stark and cold. Whenever he woke, his uncle Gawain was there, sponging his brow or holding his hand.

"My da? I did not see him. Was he—?"

"Shh. There's no news, Hyw. I will tell you as soon as I hear. Try to sleep."

"Where am I?"

"You are in my room, Hyw. In the abbey."

Hyw glimpsed a soldier standing behind Gawain. "Who—?"

"Hello, boy," the soldier said, smiling at him. "Glad I am to see you waken."

"This is Stephen de Francton, Hyw. He brought you to us."

The man's name was lost inside him for a moment, as he struggled to remember. Yes, this was the man who had spoken for him on the hill near Builth. Instantly, rage flooded Hyw, bursting from inside and outside of him at the same time. He remembered someone hitting him on the head. And something else—a spear, blood.

Gawain saw his agitation and shooed de Francton from the room. Hyw closed his eyes and slept.

He could not tell whether hours or days flashed by this way. Finally, he surfaced in a cavern pool. He was able to float gently on its surface and was surprised when the water did not splash with his movements. It was blue, and thick, and as warm as a goose-feather quilt. He looked about to see reflections of light on the stone walls. Was he somewhere deep under the mountains of his home?

At the edge of the pool, he saw his uncle Gawain standing with his head bowed. His lips were moving, but Hyw couldn't hear what he was saying.

You, lad, he heard a deep voice rumble to his left. At the same time, he felt his own breath vibrate with the words. *You are Hyw.*

He turned to find the prince sitting on a rock at the pool's edge, staring at him. Hyw frowned. It couldn't be the prince. For a moment he couldn't remember why he knew that. Then his mind flooded with the sights and sounds of the hillside again. He saw the knight, sword raised, with his other hand grasping the prince's head.

Hyw flailed in the water. Sputtering. Drowning. As he disappeared underneath the blue surface of his consciousness, he heard Gawain's voice, and clung to the sound.

Hyw heard singing. The voice was low, as if from far away. It must be his uncle. Gawain sang of the mountain and its sleeping spirits. His words were not the Latin of Cistercian monks, nor the language of English lords, but the soft words of old Cymraeg:

"*Cysgu mae ysbrydion o dan y mynydd...*"

"*Spirits sleep beneath the mountain...*" Gawain sang of the world that had been, and the world to come. He sang of the pool at the edge of the world, and he sang of Hyw and of the gift they shared.

When Hyw broke the surface of the thick blue water again, he saw Gawain standing at the edge. His uncle raised his head, and

Hyw watched as Gawain's eyelids fluttered and opened. For a long moment they stared at each other.

"Where are we?" Hyw wondered.

"A safe place," Gawain told him, as if he could hear his thoughts. Or perhaps Hyw spoke aloud; he could not tell. Goose down seemed to fill his mouth. He concentrated and tried again.

"How came we hither?"

"The old songs," Gawain said, smiling. Hyw couldn't understand what he meant and thought he must be dreaming. Then he remembered the other dream, of English soldiers standing over the prince. He began to shudder. Gawain reached out to him with one hand.

"The prince yet lives, Hyw. He lives in you, if you will it."

"How can it be, Uncle?"

Gawain shook his head. "'Tis true."

Hyw reached out, and felt himself pulled from the pool, although he did not touch Gawain's hand. Then he realized he was not wet. What appeared to be a pool was not one at all. Hyw stood on the rocks at the cave edge as Gawain continued.

"It would seem that in the moment of his death, your minds joined. Whether you are kindred spirits, or whether it was mere accident, the true-born Prince of Wales is here with us. With you. When his spirit left his body, it entered yours."

What magic is this? The prince's low rumble came again, and Hyw turned quickly. He opened his eyes—eyes he thought were already open—and found himself in a bed in the bare monk's cell.

His uncle stood motionless, with his cowl hiding his face. Gawain had his head bowed and he was reaching forward, one index finger touching the middle of Hyw's forehead. Inside his mind, Hyw heard his uncle's voice, calling to him as if from far away: "Close your eyes, Hyw."

Hyw did and saw Llywelyn seated on a rock in front of him. Gawain appeared to be standing with them again, at the edge of the same pool-that-was-not.

"If I close my eyes, I can see you here."

Gawain nodded. "This is where the prince lives. Inside your mind."

Will you sell me to the Tylwyth Teg next? Llywelyn spat the old words for what the English would call "fairies" with contempt rather than fear. His voice echoed as if it were drawn from deep within the earth. *Is this some demented OtherWorld?*

"Nay, my lord," Gawain replied, his voice low and even. "It is but the gift with which our family has served yours all these years. As we serve you still."

The prince stood. *I told your great-grandfather I had no wish for your gift. I freed you—all of you—from those old bonds of fealty. I want freedom for all of our people. An end to these superstitions that cripple us.*

Gawain waited in silence. The prince moved restlessly and spoke again.

Was I wrong then? Am I being punished? Must all of Wales suffer, because of my mistakes? Because I chose to follow God, and not the old ways? Is that why—why my Lady Princess had to die?

"Nay my lord, I cannot think it. I also choose to follow God in this life, and to put my gift to His service. Our gifts are strong, but they are natural. Part of nature."

Then why did you not prevent her death? Llywelyn's voice thundered on the cave rocks, but Gawain did not shift his position.

"You know our family, my lord. You know our hearts are true. We believe human beings can be evil, but the gift has no power over the one who wields it. We bear no ill towards your Lady or any other. She was a pure and good woman, and as a woman our Maker called her home."

Gawain fell silent as Llywelyn's shoulders shook. The prince wiped his hand across his face. Hyw drew in a deep breath. He was not sure it was his place to speak, but he must.

"My mam says—" He faltered.

Go on, lad. The Lady Adara was Elinor's truest friend in life. What says she of my lady wife's demise?

"Mam would have acted to prevent it, if she had known. She told me childbirth is the most natural of events, and just as natural for a woman to give her life to save her child's."

For a moment Llywelyn did not speak. He turned from them, and they heard him groan. When he turned back again, his face was drawn, and his dark eyes glittered. *You, lad, you have the power to keep me here. Is that true?*

Gawain nodded. "If he agrees, you may share this time with Hyw. At least, until Nos Galan Gaeaf this autumn, when we must lay all restless spirits, for their sake and our own."

Then I will have ten months. The prince shook his head. *Mortimer did not act alone. It bears the mark of my old enemy, Gruffydd ap Gwenwynwyn—*

"My lord," Gawain said. "I must caution you. If you stay for vengeance you will corrupt your immortal soul, and this boy along with it."

Llywelyn stared at Hyw for a moment and slammed his fist into his hand. *To know, and not wreak vengeance! How can you ask me that? How can I not act?*

"You must not, my lord."

And who will stop me? This boy?

Gawain stepped closer. "In peril of your soul, and Hyw's, you must act only in justice while you remain among us."

The prince's face was red, and he snarled like his namesake, the lion. *Cannot vengeance for a wrong be a kind of justice?* His will was as powerful in death as his body had been in life. It was the first time Hyw had seen the prince's fiercer nature, but he had the sense to fear it. Would saving the prince's soul damn them both?

"You are no longer part of this world, to decide this world's justice," Gawain was saying. "How can you be sure what is God's will, and what is your own?"

Llywelyn struggled to bring himself under control. *Release me from this torment. I demand it.*

"I—I cannot, my lord," Gawain replied, faltering.

"Can I do it?" Hyw asked. "Can I release him?"

Gawain shook his head. "I cannot tell. In truth, much of this lore has died with those who knew it, in these past years of war. I have not seen it done since I was a child, myself, and then only on Nos Galan Gaeaf. All I can do is guide you to abide together until then, as best I know how, if you will accept my guidance."

"What will happen to us, if we do not?" Hyw asked.

Gawain shrugged. "Madness, perhaps. Or worse. It is a thing of legends. All I know is to follow the way as I was told it. There may be those who know better, but I know them not."

Then, from the centre of his fear, Hyw felt his gift begin to stir inside him like the pure bell tone of the harp. He began to see what had happened in the final moments of his prince's life in a new light.

From the beginning, Hyw had followed his gift. He let his instinct guide him. It stood to reason that what had happened on the hillside had been his gift again. But it was also his choice, and he had chosen to act. Wales needed her prince now more than ever. And Hyw had chosen to save the prince in the only way he knew. His family had always served Llywelyn's. And without thinking, he had chosen fealty. He, Hyw ap Bran ap Maredudd ap Rhys ap Eineon, chose to stand with his prince. And he would pit his gift, his fealty, his will, all that he was, against his prince's rage. He concentrated again and managed to make his thoughts known to the prince.

"You must let me act for you, my liege. As I saved your spirit that day, so will I act to save your soul."

Llywelyn contemplated Hyw for a moment before he spoke. *Some would call the Prince of Wales the soul of the country. Verily, may you save all Wales, master Hyw.*

Hyw nodded, crossing himself. He had taken the Church for granted. He understood the Latin, but he had never really stopped to think deeply about what the priests said. He hesitated now, unsure if he could remember the words properly, and heard Llywelyn's voice again, first in Latin, and then in Welsh.

For what does it benefit a man, if he should gain the whole world but lose his soul?

Hyw turned to Gawain. He noticed his uncle frowning.

"Uncle, with your help the prince and I will make peace between us until Nos Galan Gaeaf. But what will happen then?"

"We will lay the prince's soul to rest, God willing," Gawain said, keeping his eyes averted.

"Will it be difficult?"

Gawain glanced at him. "If God is with us, we will prevail."

Then God be with us. Llywelyn bowed his head a moment, and when he raised it to look at Hyw, his eyes were determined. *Until then, let us work for peace.*

10

When they heard the clamour at the gates, Cat was kneeling in front of her chest, choosing what to take. She dropped her things and fled to her mam's chamber.

"Quickly," Mam said, and they ran to the main hall where they found Enid. She had finished feeding Baby Gwen and wrapped her soundly for sleep. Aeneus rushed into the hall, followed by four warriors.

"Lady, we are sore pressed at the gates," Aeneus said. "We must make you safe."

Mam hesitated a moment, and then gestured for them to follow her toward the kitchens. Cat was no stranger to war, or to secret escapes from Garth Celyn. She took Enid's arm, careful not to jostle Baby Gwen, and their small group made their way to the centre of the longhouse.

Opening the trap doors to the cellar, Aeneus helped Cat drop down into it. She lifted the wooden ladder into place for the others. Mam held Gwen as Enid stepped down it, and then handed the baby down to Cat before she descended. Three of their warriors came after, making little sound. Before Aeneus dropped through the trap door, he clasped the final warrior's forearm firmly. Aeneus descended and nodded grimly up at him. The warrior's face showed no emotion as he dropped the trap door into place. They heard a scraping overhead, and then light footfalls as he ran from the room. Cat realized he would rejoin the other men at the gate, holding the *Saeson* off as long as he could to cover their escape, even if it cost his life.

Baby Gwen stirred with a small cry, but Enid placed her little finger in the baby's mouth to suckle, soothing her. Aeneus replaced the ladder on the ground as an extra precaution. Mam and Cat each lit a torch from a bundle stored against the cellar wall. Mam pressed one hand on the wall. The release would not be found easily. It had confounded would-be attackers in years past, and Cat was not even sure she could locate it.

"We must hurry, my lady," Aeneus said softly.

Mam handed her torch to Aeneus and placed both hands against the wall. She kept her head bowed as she carefully felt along the wall with her fingertips and palms. Finally, a section of rock scraped aside. Cat jumped back as their flickering torches revealed a small, dark opening.

Mam nodded as Cat handed her the torch and led their way into the darkness. Enid passed the baby through and followed close behind. Cat paused for a moment to return the baby to Enid, as Mam pressed another hidden catch near the opening. The rock swung closed behind them, scraping a little louder than the table had along the floor earlier.

Aeneus lit another torch from the one he held and distributed it to a man behind him. Cat again led the way as their small group started along the dim passage, moving noiselessly. There was a familiarity to their movement—almost a ritual, a disappearing act they had mastered through long years of strife with English siege-masters. Their leather walking shoes barely disturbed the pebbles on the worn stone floor.

The long dark tunnel seemed to stretch ahead of them forever. Cat's mind raced. How many times as a child had she fled in the night, to hide with her mam at dawn? This time, there was no prince to rescue them, and her brother was injured. Would he live? And what of Da—where was he?

In one section, the walls had crumbled to rubble, creating a small opening barely large enough for the taller men to go through. Cat was the only one who would not have to go on hands and knees. With Cat holding the baby, Enid took her own triangular nursing shawl and placed it around Cat's back and shoulders, and then tucked both ends around Baby Gwen in the traditional style. Cat bent only enough to clear the rock ceiling, with Gwen cradled snugly to her chest in the shawl, and felt her way forward with her toes to keep her balance. Finally, the tunnel opened wider again. Enid took Gwen, who sighed and turned a little in her swaddling. Cat had barely felt the baby's weight, in spite of the awkward position.

When they came to the end of the tunnel, Mam touched Cat's shoulder and the group halted behind them. Cat's heart thumped in her chest. This passage ended at the top of the hill outside the castle walls. Always before Hyw had checked to be sure the English soldiers had not discovered it, using his gift to protect them. Mam must wish her to take Hyw's place this time.

But my gift is not the same, Cat wanted to say. Instead, she reached up and groped blindly until her hands grasped a length of leather twine hanging near the top of the low wall. She flattened her palms and pushed up against twigs and brambles. A smattering of old sealing wax flaked into her face as the curtain of thatch covering the entrance gave way. She marvelled again at her mam's ingenuity in hiding the tunnel entrance from prying eyes. Cat pushed the thatch aside, to be replaced later. She stepped through, stopping beneath an overhang of shale.

Late afternoon had turned to night while they made their escape. A sudden fork of lightning split the sky. Cat crouched, drawing her cloak around her. All she could hear was her own hushed breathing and the light patter of raindrops. She looked down at the reflection of the half-moon in a shallow puddle of water at her feet—

—and found herself in a thicket of trees. In front of her, she saw a small mound, and realized it was a man sleeping on the ground. She looked around her, and saw a group of sleeping English soldiers, with their horses tethered near. One man sat awake, his back against a tree, keeping watch.

They must be scouts, she thought, or perhaps a small group sent to capture the women.

She spotted Aeneus crouched in the underbrush, leading their small party through the forest and along the Aber River, straight toward the group of men. The soldier on watch spotted them as well. He stood, waking one of the others with his boot and motioning toward their small party. The group of sleeping soldiers was suddenly awake. The first soldier drew a knife from his belt with a grim smile. Cat tried to cry out a warning—

—and she was back at the mouth of the tunnel.

It was another vision, she realized, but not about Hyw this time. Armed *Saeson* soldiers set to prevent their escape. Surely they had to take another road. She frowned. Something else from her vision played at the edges of her mind: the soldiers had horses. Horses could hasten their journey and help them get Baby Gwen to the safety of Criccieth.

Was this vision sent to her for a reason? Was it to give her knowledge of their fate, or could she influence the outcome? As the others hovered near the tunnel entrance, she gestured to her mam. Quickly she whispered what she had seen. Mam's eyes opened wide in alarm.

"We must not take the path," she began.

"But we have no time," Cat said, and quickly explained about the horses. "These visions, Mam, are they a certain fate? Or can they be changed?"

Her mam's brows knit together, as if she was trying to recall what her grandfather had said and what she had heard in her own childhood. "We must find out." Then she nodded to Cat and took Aeneus's arm to draw him into their circle.

"When Cat first stood here, she spotted a band of men ahead on the path," Mam whispered to him. "They have horses tethered, and only one guard watching. What think you?"

He looked at Cat strangely, and then his eyes became thoughtful, roaming past her toward the dark mountain path ahead of them. "How many men —and how close?" He kept his voice lower than a whisper. "Can you point to where you saw them?"

Cat tried to recall her vision as clearly as possible. "There were eight, I think. As to how close—I cannot be certain now," she admitted.

"How is it that you came to know this?"

"I—" Cat faltered, unable to explain.

"The moon revealed it to her," Mam told him, and they exchanged glances. Aeneus nodded grimly and Mam continued, "Let

Cat lead us, and she will know the place."

"Fear not, Lady," he said. "I will see to the rest."

Cat nodded and willed herself not to think about the implications of what she was about to do.

"This way, Mam," she whispered, and the others followed her, bending low to hide their passage as best they could. When they neared the spot she had seen, she turned back and caught Aeneus's eye.

He took out his knife, placed it between his teeth, and without a word gestured to two of the men to follow him. He waved the other, a younger warrior Cat knew as Ifan, back toward the women.

Cat, Mam, and Enid sank to the ground to catch their breath. Baby Gwen stirred again, and Enid spread her cloak over the baby to feed her. Cat didn't need her gift to know they would reach Criccieth the next day, on the backs of English horses.

11

The ringing of the bells woke Hyw the next morning. Bells marked the daily routine of prayers in the Abbey: *vigils* in the early hours and *lauds* at daybreak. After each, he was soothed back to dreaming by the faint voices of the monks chanting prayers in the nearby chapel. Gawain came to Hyw's room shortly after *terce*, the third prayer of the morning.

"We buried the fallen on the hill," Gawain told him, "but rest easy, Hyw, for your da was not among them."

"Is there no word from him?"

"Nay, but take hope," Gawain put his hand on Hyw's arm. "A villager brought in a wagon of supplies to trade. He told us he saw wounded warriors in the forest on the other side of the River Wye."

Hyw's next thoughts were for the horses, Vox and Cadarn, but Gawain shook his head. Hyw felt some relief that his da's body hadn't been found on the hillside, but he worried for Bran's safety, and for the fate of his sister and mother at Garth Celyn. "What news of home?" he asked.

Gawain had heard nothing, but tried to reassure him by reporting news from the handful of villagers who had taken refuge inside the monastery. Before long, Gawain bade him rise. "We must begin," he said, placing two fingers on the centre of Hyw's forehead. "Close your eyes and call yourself to the cave where we saw the prince."

Hyw's initial attempts failed. The cave he imagined was a pale image, lacking the depth it had during his meeting with Llywelyn.

Gawain showed him how to slow his breathing and focus his mind. After one more try, he was able to feel the cave around him and see the prince again.

They fell into routine quickly, helped by the disciplined life of the monastery. Gawain recommended that Hyw not leave the room until he and Llywelyn found a way to co-exist. The first day was difficult. At first, Hyw would move about the room as he moved about in the cave in his mind. He bruised his knees on the bed, and once even banged his body into the wall.

By the second afternoon, Hyw had nearly mastered the trance-like state and could call the cave into his mind's eye as soon as he closed his eyes. Gawain worked with Hyw until the bells rang *sext* at noon, then returned until *nones* at mid-afternoon, and again until *vespers* at sunset. In between his sessions with Gawain, Hyw rested in his room, echoing what he could hear of the brothers' prayers.

Gawain seemed to have more energy when he returned from the chapel. "It's the prayers," he told Hyw. "Each hour has its own colour and feeling. Singing the hours with my brothers, even in this time of trouble, restores my strength."

Gawain had also been released from manual labour to help Hyw recover. The Cistercians, a new order, were devoted to working the land, and Hyw soon realized Gawain missed the physical and outdoor part of his daily routine. Yet his uncle did not complain, and Hyw took that as his example.

He also had Llywelyn to consider. After their sessions, the prince was often angry. Hyw thought he had seemed aloof or preoccupied when he was alive, and now he seemed to resent his dependence on Hyw. There was a sadness in him, as well. Llywelyn had bound himself to Elinor when she was young, even before they had met in person. The prince had lived a life of strict discipline, especially after the English king had captured Elinor and held her in house arrest for three years before finally allowing them to marry. Llywelyn was almost fifty years old by then, and she was twenty. Elinor was the first person he had allowed himself to trust. Now that she was dead, Hyw could sense a deep loneliness in him.

Hyw said nothing, mindful of his family's obligation, and tried to be patient. He was surprised the prince did not expect him to bow or humble himself.

A warrior is expected to fight and die for Cymru and should be treated with deference by all, said Llywelyn, *and with gratitude by his liege. You are a warrior's son, and I am asking more of you than ever I have of your father.*

Hyw worked to separate his thoughts and actions in the trance-world he shared with Llywelyn from the real world of his physical body. The more he concentrated, the more his mind's landscape seemed to come into focus. When they moved in the cave, his body remained still. Gawain reported that Hyw's lips no longer moved in the physical world when he spoke to Llywelyn in his mind.

At this sign of progress, Llywelyn began training Hyw. They trained every day, the Prince's weapon appearing in his hand as it might in a dream: a sword one day, a bow and quiver of arrows the next. Hyw stood alongside him, matching his movements and trying to learn what Llywelyn knew of fighting. When they took a break for a drink, they needed to wipe the sweat from their eyes and faces. Yet in the physical world, Hyw's face was barely flushed.

"How can this be?" Hyw asked Gawain.

"It must be as the legends describe: the OtherWorld seems as real as our physical life, but exists inside our minds." Gawain shook his head. "I believe few could call up that plane in the way you are doing, Hyw. It leads me to wonder, if we were not so pressed by the English, how far this skill could take you."

Hyw marvelled that he could be one of those few. Unlike Gawain, he wondered how much of this he would recall when he was able to train in the yard again.

Llywelyn would often ask Hyw questions about his life. Hyw told him about fostering in Shrewsbury, about the horses he tended, and about the way he first learned of his gift. He even told the prince about his friendship with James, Shrewsbury's son and heir.

Hyw longed to ask the prince about himself, especially whether the whispers of Shrewsbury's court were true: had he really hugged his cousin with one hand and driven a knife into his body with the other? And how could he imprison his own eldest brother? Hyw dared not ask. Llywelyn offered only advice on how to place his feet, or how hard to pull the bow string.

12

Criccieth Castle rose white and majestic against the morning sky. One of the men pointed out its twin towers on top of the rocky headland.

"No worries, Lady Cat," Aeneus told her. "The wee lass will be safe inside those stone walls."

The path to the gate wound around the mountainside. They dismounted. Ifan and another warrior had been leading the remaining horses to prevent them from returning to the English. The two now took the leads of all their mounts, to leave Aeneus and the other two soldiers free to defend them. Cat offered to take Ifan's horses, but he shook his head.

"The way is treacherous for the horses, lady," Ifan said. "Best that I lead them."

Two Welsh guards appeared, dressed in armour. Aeneus sang out the opening of a Welsh bardic poem. He and the guards spoke for a moment and then one clasped forearms with Aeneus in a warrior's greeting. Then the guards stepped back and waved them on.

Enid tucked Baby Gwen into her cradleboard and let one of the warriors sling it onto his back for the walk along the rocky path to the gatehouse. Cat made the climb nimbly enough, helping her mam and Enid as they needed.

When they gained entry into the courtyard, they were taken to Princess Elizabeth, wife of Dafydd, who had rightfully claimed the title Prince of Wales after Llywelyn's death. The new princess received them in her private solar, wrapped in a light blue shawl that showed off her fair hair and light skin. She embraced each of the women, including Enid and Baby Gwen.

"You have done well to come," she said. "Dafydd left for Dolwyddelan yesterday. You might have passed him on the road?"

"Nay, we passed no one," Mam shook her head. "Has there been any news of my husband Bran, your highness?"

Elizabeth frowned and turned slightly away, rocking the baby. "How strange it is to think of myself as Princess of Wales now. Please, among ourselves, please continue to call me by my name."

Mam took a step toward her. "If I may be so bold, Elizabeth, to put my heart at rest. Will you tell me what you have heard?"

Elizabeth spoke quietly. "Our messenger said—Adara, I am truly sorry. He said all perished with Llywelyn."

Mam went white, and turned her eyes to Cat. Cat moved to support her, feeling the tears coursing down her own cheeks.

"I am most sorry, Adara," Elizabeth said. "You are weak from your journey." She called to her servant. "Make room for Cat with the girls. Lady Adara and the baby will stay here in my rooms. The men will be welcome in the guardhouse." Turning back to Cat and her Mam, she added, "I will have food and drink brought to you. Come, Enid, let us see to Baby Gwen."

Elizabeth herded Enid and the baby from the room along with her own servants. For a moment, Cat and her mam found themselves alone. Mam sat in front of the fireplace and gestured to Cat to come closer.

"He is not dead. I would know. Or you would, surely. Cat, tell me again what you saw."

Cat recounted her vision again, but she had seen nothing of Bran or his fate. For the first time, Cat noticed how frail and thin her mam had become in the past few weeks; or perhaps it was that she herself had grown. Finally, perched on a low stool at her feet, Cat stroked her mam's hand and they comforted each other.

Two of Elizabeth's three children were with them at Criccieth. Gwladys was a cheerful toddler and Cat enjoyed playing games with her. Owain was a serious boy of about ten or eleven, but Cat soon discovered he knew a wealth of information about this part of Wales. He told Cat his older brother Llyw had joined the garrison at Dolbadarn.

A group of six girls in varying ages and sizes shared the nursery with them. Mam quietly explained that these were Dafydd's children by other mothers, and Elizabeth showed great charity in taking them in to protect them during the past few months. Cat noted that Elizabeth was not unkind to the girls, but she did not pay them the same attention as Owain and Gwladys. Owain called them all sisters.

The day after their arrival, Cat rose early while the other girls slept. She crept downstairs and found Owain having breakfast with a few of the other boys.

"How fare you?" he asked, as he grabbed more bread and cheese.

"Well enough," she answered, "but I look forward to working out the stiffness this morning."

He raised his eyebrows as if he wasn't sure what she meant, so she continued, "I will join you for the early exercises today."

"But you are a girl," he said.

"Yes, of course," she said. He laughed then, as did the other boys. Aeneus had always included the girls in the exercises and defence training at Garth Celyn. "Surely your sisters will join us?"

At that, the boys began to laugh in earnest. Before Cat could take them to task, Aeneus walked through the doors. He had already been in the yard, tending his horse and preparing for the morning's training sessions. He smiled at Cat and then turned to the others.

"Share the jest?" Aeneus said to them.

"They seem to be laughing at me," Cat told him.

"She thinks she will be training with us today," Owain said.

"Aye, so she will," Aeneus said. "You boys should always be ready to protect your families, and any woman who comes within your company. But we must also help our women prepare for anything they may face in the days ahead. May it help them against the devil-spawned English," he added with a grim look that sobered the boys.

Cat filed out to the yard behind Aeneus and the other boys, but Owain disappeared. As Aeneus began a series of daily exercises to improve their agility and toughen the muscles of feet and legs, she saw Owain return with his two older sisters. He grinned at her as his sisters joined in the drill, and she smiled back at him.

That night they joked with each other, flexing their sore muscles as they climbed into their shared bed.

"Sleep here," said Margred, indicating a spot between herself and her sisters. She was the eldest, and close to Cat's age. "That way when Rhiannon pulls the covers, you'll still be warm."

The other girls settled quickly, but Cat had a restless night, despite the down-filled quilt. When she closed her eyes, she dreamed of people running and screaming through the halls. Were these prophetic dreams? She wanted to ask her mam, but Adara was impatient for anything but news of Hyw and Bran. Of them, Cat had seen nothing more.

What good was this gift if she could not control it?

Aeneus left the next day to search for Bran and Hyw as he had promised. Criccieth's man would not let Cat and the other girls join in weapons training, as Aeneus had, so they spent their afternoons inside with Elizabeth, Mam, and the other women.

A few days later, while Cat played with Gwladys and Princess Elizabeth tended Baby Gwen, another messenger came. He told of troops that took every Welshman prisoner on the road. With a glance toward the children, he whispered something in Princess Elizabeth's ear that made her face go white. A prickle of fear crept up the back of Cat's neck, for her da and brother, and for Aeneus in his search for them.

Burdened by bad dreams, Cat threw herself into the festive preparations to take her mind off her fears. Princess Elizabeth was determined to give the children all the Christmas cheer that could be had, with their father and elder brother away. Cat decided to make something to cheer her mam. Elizabeth allowed her to look through her stock of woolens and fabrics, and Cat settled on making a scarf of bright Italian red. She embroidered a small tree in one end, with initials for each of them fanning out from the trunk like branches: Adara, Bran, Cat, and Hyw. It took several tries to finish, since her stitches were as loose and poorly formed as ever. She sighed and rolled it up, hoping Mam would find it useful as well as comforting.

At the Feast of St. Stephen's, they sat at the high table with Elizabeth and her children. Cat reached forward to take some roast duck from the platter and glanced at her cup of light wine. Elizabeth always drank English wine rather than Welsh ale and served it on feast days. The liquid seemed to be swirling—

—and she found herself at another table, in a room much more Spartan than Princess Elizabeth's domain. She looked up at the sound of a familiar voice, and on the stairs, she saw Prince Llywelyn.

"For Cymru, let them bring us peace!" he sang. And then his face and voice seemed to melt into the face and voice of her brother Hyw as he sang the line again. Then Hyw seemed to look right at her and smile. She did not see his lips move, but she heard him as if he whispered in her ear.

"I live, Cat, and the prince lives within me." She turned toward him—

—and dropped her knife onto the table with a clatter.

Her mam turned to her, and Cat smiled and took her hands. She could hardly wait to finish so she could take her mam to a quiet corner and tell her the vision. Now she had a proper gift to give her this Christmas season!

13

Gawain worked every day to help Hyw and Llywelyn develop the ability to communicate in a way no one could detect, a way that would not change Hyw's appearance or actions in physical reality. Gawain also cautioned Hyw against bonding with the minds of birds or animals while he held Llywelyn's spirit.

"You may be able to put yourself between the prince and the beasts in time, but for now focus on maintaining the space between you. Let your skills grow as they must."

During one training session, Hyw opened his eyes to find Gawain asleep on the small bed despite the bright sunlight streaming in the window. Hyw hadn't realized how exhausting the work must be for his uncle. He resolved to let Gawain sleep, and worked on his own with Llywelyn for the rest of the day.

When Gawain woke again, it was late afternoon. Gawain looked guilty, but Hyw explained what he had been doing. He couldn't help but smile when his uncle clapped him on the shoulder.

Gradually, Hyw moved more easily in the physical world while keeping his mind open to the prince. Hyw could always sense Llywelyn and hear his voice, but unless he closed his eyes, he was unable to see the prince.

He also discovered they were not restricted to the cave beneath the mountains. In the trance, he "took" them to an open field like the one outside Garth Celyn, and once into a wooded meadow. Llywelyn could also suggest new landscapes for their training, as long as the areas were familiar to Hyw. The prince had only to think of a place, and Hyw could see it in his mind and create it almost as if he was transporting them there.

Once, when Hyw closed his eyes, he found himself on a flat field of green and red squares. It was familiar, but not a natural field. He saw what looked like stone statues surrounding the prince, some upright and others on the ground, broken in pieces.

Hyw blinked: it was the chess set Llywelyn brought back from the Holy Crusades. Llywelyn had kept it in the study where he met with his councillors and nobles. Hyw had often served his father in that study when he was younger, and again since he'd come home. The pieces were carved in stone, each forming a different human figure that might live in a castle. His father had explained the figures and their placement and had begun playing the game with him in the evenings.

Now he and Llywelyn were the size of pieces on the board. Hyw turned to the prince. "This is how you see the world? As a game of strategy?"

Llywelyn stood with his arms folded across his chest and nodded. Showing this board was a gesture of trust, and one not given easily. Hyw stared at the figures carefully. Llywelyn stood in the king's position. Hyw remembered his father talk of a secret move called castling that could only be done if the king-piece had not moved.

Then another piece caught his eye. It had fallen away from the prince and broken into two pieces. Hyw connected with Llywelyn's memories as if the prince had opened a door for him: the grizzled face was Simon de Montfort, Elinor's father and Llywelyn's best friend. Hyw could even hear the knight's laugh booming off the walls at Garth Celyn. Yet de Montfort had died a decade earlier at Edward's hand, before Edward became king of England.

Like you, I fostered with the English, Hyw, and came to appreciate their ways. De Montfort was more a brother to me than any of my own.

Hyw looked up and saw an empty space behind and to Llywelyn's left. It almost seemed to glow. The Queen's position. Elinor had been Llywelyn's wife for three short years, but she had changed the game entirely for him. He could not present her fallen or broken, as he had her father. The space was empty but luminous.

Llywelyn was dressed in black. The stone figures near him shone ebony against the colourful landscape of the chessboard. That meant the prince was not the first to move, but rather the defender of the board. It was easy to guess that the board was Wales.

Few pieces remained around Llywelyn. The castles stood in their spots at either end of the board: Garth Celyn, and a large, imposing stone castle.

That is Y-Bere, Llywelyn said.

One piece in the robes of the councillor or bishop had moved into a protective position a little ahead of Llywelyn. The piece seemed to change shape in front of Hyw's eyes. Once it looked like Gawain, his uncle; then it changed to a likeness of Bran; and once he glimpsed his mother's face as well. He realized the piece represented his family and felt a flush of pride that Llywelyn saw them in this way.

Slowly, Hyw swiveled to face the enemy. As expected, the white king stared back at him: this could be none other than Edward, King of England. Beside him a white knight was poised in his advance, sword raised, grinning. Hyw shuddered and turned to Llywelyn, who answered before he could ask.

Edmund Mortimer.

Hyw was shocked to see other familiar faces in the white army: the face of Dafydd, Llywelyn's brother, crouching as a pawn in front. Several Welsh courtiers crouched with him, identifiable by their coloured emblems and coats of arms.

Their in-fighting serves the English king. Llywelyn's voice held more sorrow than anger.

"It seems they do not know a pawn cannot be crowned king," Hyw quipped, and heard what might have been a snort of laughter behind him. Hyw realized there were no black pawns on the board; in fact, no other black pieces at all.

Now you see the game for what it is. What part will you play, Hyw?

He turned back to Llywelyn. "I will not be a pawn. Even for you, my lord."

The prince studied him and nodded slightly. He unfolded his hands and gestured at the board. *Choose your piece.*

Hyw looked around him again. Then he crouched beside the fallen de Montfort and took the hilt of the knight's sword. With a *zing* he pulled it from the stone and held it high. Instantly he found himself dressed in black like his prince, and under his legs was Aeron, his father's warhorse. Hyw raised his sword, as Aeron rose with hoofs drawn, and found himself and the horse frozen in attack formation. Behind him, he heard the welcome sound of Llywelyn's gruff laugh.

"Have at us," Hyw yelled.

By Christmas Day, Gawain pronounced Hyw fit to make an appearance for the Feast of Saint Stephen the following evening. The abbot had taken in many people displaced by the fighting, and this feast honoured the saint known for his service to the poor. Llywelyn was pleased by the chance to see his people and discover how they fared. Gawain thought it would be a good test for their alliance, since many people would attend, and they could pass unnoticed in the crowd. Still, he hesitated.

"My lord, you will hear of our continued defeat at the hands of the English," he warned. "You must be careful to give nothing away."

The monastery was full of people as Hyw descended the stairs to the common eating area. He felt Llywelyn's anguish at the austerity of the room. Cat had written to him the previous year of the festivities at Garth Celyn. The newly pregnant Princess Elinor had decorated the halls and corners of the longhouse with traditional holly and ivy, along with bits of ribbon and bells, until the whole world seemed alive with the promise of the Christ child. Hyw was glad to concentrate on the stairs so he could not close his eyes to see the prince's face.

Supper was quiet and spare: roots, breads, and mutton stew with few spices, as befits the frugal Cistercian table. As Hyw ate, he looked more closely at the people around him. They were speckled with mud and their clothes were in tatters. Some had old blankets wrapped about their heads and bodies, and many were barefoot.

Their hands, faces, and even feet had been washed clean for the meal, but they sat with slumping shoulders and lowered heads. Hyw felt the prince's grief turn to anger. *Let me up, boy.*

Hyw stood and walked back to the stairs. He moved up a few steps to be visible to the crowd of peasants below. When he opened his mouth, Llywelyn's voice came from it.

> *Open your ears to my words, and*
> *Lift your head from your arms.*
> *Let the old poet lend me his voice.*

He began an old song of the brave three hundred who stood together against an army they could not hope to defeat, to protect their people. At the end of each verse, the poet named a fallen warrior, so they would not be forgotten over time. Hyw had heard the song enough to have memorized the words, but Llywelyn changed the words to praise each of the warriors who had fallen with him at Builth. He created a new verse for Bran and the others whose bodies had not been found, bringing hope to his listeners.

Hyw fingered the cord Cat had tied around his wrist and thought of his sister, and Christmases when they were children.

> *Let the mountains hide their voices,*
> *Let forest and fountain keep them safe.*
> *For Cymru, let us bring them peace.*

"The boy," someone whispered in the crowd. "Look to the boy."

Hyw did not know if they heard their prince's voice in harmony with his own, as he did, or perhaps saw the prince's shape mix with his in the way he had seen figures shifting on the chessboard. But one by one other voices joined with his. Soon the cold stones of the Cistercian monastery rang with their voices.

Shortly after Christmas, the abbot again broke into his stores for the Feast of the Holy Innocents. That night a band of weathered soldiers banged on the abbey door, demanding tribute to feed Edward's army.

Hyw was in the hall with the others when the soldiers clanged in and sat, expecting service from the hardworking Cistercians. In the spirit of the season, the abbot had welcomed them at the door. His concern showed on his face as he entered the hall with them, and Hyw wondered if the English soldiers returned a full measure of seasonal goodwill. Hyw wondered if he should try to fight, so as not to shame his lord. Then he felt or heard Llywelyn's voice, as if whispering in his ear. *Live to fight another day, lad. Yet tarry, that I may listen to their prattle.*

Gawain gestured toward their rooms, but Hyw shook his head and remained seated with the others. Gawain and another monk brought in the trenchers and served the soldiers.

"Ugh," complained one soldier, who looked to be the captain of the rest, as he sopped up the stew with bread. "Sodden tasteless mess. I thought you Welsh crusading went. Brought you nothing back to spice this gruel?"

The abbot shrugged. "We are but simple brothers here."

"Simple indeed," another soldier guffawed. "Simpletons."

"Leave them be," another said. At the man's voice, Hyw could sense Llywelyn bristle. Hyw glanced over to recognize his champion on the hill. From his dress, the man appeared to be a minor English lord. Hyw remembered his name as Stephen de Francton. Hyw closed his eyes to find the prince in full war armour. Hyw placed himself in front of Llywelyn to hold him back.

"Why do you hate this man so?"

He it was who ran me through with his spear. Lucky chance for him, but not so lucky now.

"Yet it was not he who finished you," Hyw pointed out. He remembered the look of remorse on de Francton's face as Llywelyn knelt on the hillside. "He saved me on that day—and you with me."

Llywelyn shook with rage, but made no further move. Hyw opened his eyes again. De Francton was speaking with the abbot, as the captain sloshed back the abbot's ale.

"Ah," the captain said, banging his cup down on the wooden table. He wiped his mouth on the back of his hand. De Francton cringed a little, but said nothing. "Well, good man, have you Welshmen here?"

The question caught the abbot by surprise. "We are all brothers here," he began.

"Aye, but have you Welsh brothers, Father?" The other soldiers guffawed with him at this poor jest. "For you know, do you not, that every Welshman's head will fetch a shilling at Rhuddlan?"

Hyw felt Llywelyn stiffen. *So, the fool lets slip the whereabouts of his king. Let's see what else we may glean from his manly ignorance.*

Hyw understood and slipped to the kitchens to bring more ale for the soldiers. The night wore on, and the men were fully in their cups before they uttered the words the prince had been waiting to hear.

"We took the silver seal from that devil's own pocket, before we sent the body to his cousin's wife," a soldier offered. "It seems he will receive a Christian burial after all. What's left of him."

They mean me! Llywelyn's voice grated against Hyw's ear.

"Aye, and his seal now awaits its companion at Rhuddlan," the captain added. "We hear the babe has one too, and as soon as Garth Celyn falls, we will have it."

Garth Celyn stands! Hyw was impatient to hear more of his family home, but he dared not speak. Instead, he poured more ale and listened to what poured forth.

"Of what use is this silver to the king?" the abbot asked.

"Of no use, I would say." The captain laughed loudly and burped. "Save never to give these Welsh devils an excuse to rise against their betters again. He will march against them within the fortnight."

The talk went on a little longer, before the captain's face fell snoring against his arm. His men left him half sitting at the table and bunked down on the floor by the fire. The abbot showed de Francton to a guest room.

We must learn more of their plans, Llywelyn said in Hyw's inner ear. *Make haste to Rhuddlan. Afterward, if we can get word to Dafydd, we may yet stop this war.*

Hyw continued cleaning tables until he heard the other soldiers snoring too, then made his way to Gawain. "I must go to Rhuddlan."

"I heard them," his uncle whispered back. "We can leave at dawn."

"Nay, Uncle." Hyw laid a hand on his arm. "Not with a shilling on every Welshman's head. I must go. They will not notice me."

"Hyw, I cannot—"

Llywelyn again whispered to Hyw, and the boy reached out to touch his uncle's arm, concentrating. *"Then consider it an order from your liege,"* said a low, deep voice from somewhere inside him. It felt odd to have Llywelyn speak through him in that way, although he had allowed it. Hyw added in his own voice, "It will be fine, you will see. I can pass for much younger than my years. Even Edward cannot countenance killing children. And we—the prince and I—have a plan."

"What will you do?"

"Nay, 'tis best you not know, Uncle. Take my thanks, and I will take your love to my mother when I see her next."

"Tell her she has but to send word, and I will take her and the babes to the Sisters of Light for sanctuary."

With that Hyw continued clearing food to the kitchen. In the process, he gathered bread and cheese in a brown cloth wrapper that would travel in his tunic.

Before Hyw left the abbey, Gawain handed him a cloak. It was frayed but warm, with thick, serviceable lining. "I am due another soon."

Hyw wondered how long that would take, given the scarce supplies of the monastery. He thanked Gawain and drew the cloak around his shoulders. They hugged and moved separately toward the doors: Hyw to the kitchen, and Gawain to his plain monk's cell.

Dawn found Hyw slipping through the hedges to the old Roman roads that led to Rhuddlan Castle, as his mind wandered beyond it to Garth Celyn.

14

On the first day of the new year, as they sat working together in Princess Elizabeth's solar, Cat heard her mam begin humming a familiar tune under her breath. Cat looked up from her attempts at embroidery. It was *Y Calan*, the traditional song of New Year's celebrations. Cat and her family—and the entire court of Prince Llywelyn—had celebrated the Christmas feasts with Princess Elinor and her ladies for the last four years. But the traditional Welsh holidays were always Cat's favourites. Mam shot her a rare grin and touched the scarf around her neck, before she changed the tune and began to hum a more traditional hymn. Cat ducked her head, pleased and embarrassed that her mam had chosen to wear her present.

At dusk, Cat heard the song echoing again at the castle gate, in a chorus of men's voices loud enough to reach them inside the castle.

"We beg your permission, we beg your permission, we beg your permission to sing…"

The sonorous three-part harmony gave Cat a thrill of recognition and a sense of safety, as if their rituals and traditions would continue no matter what threats the Welsh faced. She couldn't help running for the castle door, along with Owain, his older sisters, and the servants. Mam stood to follow, but Cat noticed Elizabeth sniff and take up her embroidery again.

"Will you not come to see the *Mari Lwyd*?" Mam asked, using the Welsh term for the Grey Mare.

"Nay, not I," said Elizabeth. "But it's important to the servants."

"And the children, apparently," said Mam. "I will go and make sure they stay out of trouble."

Mam smiled and touched Cat's shoulder as they went through the doors. Perhaps Elizabeth's English background made her reluctant to take part in the more bawdy Welsh traditions, Cat thought. But at least the princess wouldn't stop the mare, or the luck she would bring the castle once she was allowed inside. The other children ran for the gates as the singers began the third verse, and Cat couldn't contain herself any longer.

She got to the gate in time to hear the last of the ribald insults that accompanied this ritual.

"What's that? Didst thou say thou art a pathetic, pigeon-livered, pribbling pignut?" called a lusty voice from behind the gate. "A mewling, milk-livered, maggot-born miscreant?" A chorus of neighing followed his words. "What's that, my lady? Ah, the mare says she would not have credited thee to speak such truths!"

She saw the castle bard draw himself up and turn red in the face, barely able to control his rage. The man's ample girth and jiggling belly made Cat worry if his rage would do him more harm than it could ever do the mare and her merry men. Up to that point, she had heard him recite the family's genealogy and a few children's rhymes in the nursery. She leaned forward intently to hear how he would fare in the verbal sparring with the mare's merry men.

"Woudst thou try to match wits with me, thou bear-biting, beef-witted churl," the bard began, but a booming voice from the mare's entourage cut him off.

"Nay, not beef, but mare, thou clod-brained cockerel. If brains were beef, thou wouldst not have enough to feed the porcine strumpet who shares thy bed."

The bard balled his fists and hoisted himself toward the gate.

"Grab him!" called the captain of Criccieth's guards. Two warriors took the bard by both arms, dragging him back toward the castle courtyard. "Give him another flagon of ale for his trouble," the captain called. Musicians launched into another tune, and singers on both sides joined their voices in the traditional welcome songs.

The final notes turned from a hoot to a laugh as Criccieth's warriors opened the gate wider for the Grey Mare and her entourage. One of the players led the mare by a long halter, and the pipers piled through the gates behind them.

Although Cat knew what to expect, she gasped at the sight. The "mare" was over seven feet tall. Its bone-white skeleton head and long neck led to a white cloth body. Like a macabre legend, it walked on a man's legs. Harness bells jangled as the head shook its mane of bright-colored, fluttering cloth ribbons. Its long snout clacked at the children as it came through the gate. Owain screamed along with his sisters. Cat ran around the mare with the children and singers, their laughter ringing the stones.

The musicians played and danced once around the courtyard and into the castle hall where servants rolled out barrels of ale. Criccieth's warriors mingled with the four Garth Celyn warriors as well as Dafydd and Elizabeth's guard. Other women and children—the warrior's families, Cat guessed—streamed in behind the players as if called by the procession. One of the warriors tried to offer Cat a flagon of ale, but Mam frowned and bade her drink the less potent ale-and-water mix instead.

The Grey Mare cavorted around the ladies until one consented to dance a few steps. Cat laughed as the bells strung through its colourful mane jangled in time with the music to bless them all with luck and good cheer.

"Who is it?" whispered the girls, trying to guess the mare's true identity beneath the bone mask. "Who can it be?"

"Why, it's Drem, isn't it?" Margred breathed to Cat, pointing to the soft leather shoes on the mare's feet. "He's the butcher's son from town. Already he runs his father's business, they say." Although that meant little to Cat, her new friend's excited eyes told her Margred thought very well of Drem.

A niggling doubt made Cat uneasy. Margred was likely betrothed to another lord's son to form an alliance for her father, Dafydd. Cat thought briefly of Rhys, the young man she was pledged to marry. She had met Rhys several times while she traveled with Princess Elinor and the Welsh court, and thought herself lucky in the match. But being betrothed didn't need to stop them from enjoying themselves on New Year's eve, did it? They weren't doing anything improper.

"She's been eating mistletoe," called the woman leading the mare, and the warriors whistled. Cat saw sprigs of mistletoe sticking out of the skeleton mouth. The "mare" held out its bony muzzle for a kiss, and the older girls screamed and ran away. The mare lowered its head and shook its mane in mock despair. It tried to lay its skeleton head on Cat's shoulder until Margred coaxed it away to dance. When it turned to dance with another girl, Margred grabbed a flagon of ale from a passing servant.

Finally the mare removed its bony head for a moment to reveal the man beneath. Margred held up the flagon. That must be Drem. He grinned at Margred as he took the flagon and tipped it back for a long drink.

The battle of wits that had begun outside the gate continued with riddles and stories as the celebration got underway.

"Can you say the days of the week?" sang one of the players to the children. As Owain began to recite them, the player shook his finger at them and sang again. "Can you say the days of the week—but without naming them?"

The children stared at him and at each other, perplexed. Then the player turned to the adults and asked again, "Can anyone say the days of the week without naming them?"

The cook grinned. "That's a very good riddle, very good indeed. But I have guessed your riddle, if you please." The musicians stopped and the player turned toward her expectantly. The cook continued, "Why, it's the day before yesterday, yesterday, today, tomorrow, and the day after that, isn't it?"

The player bowed to her, and the crowd clapped.

"Your turn, Cookie," called out a woman's voice from the crowd.

"Oh, aye, verra well for you, isn't it? Let me think. Ah! I have in my kitchen a pot the whole sea cannot fill. Can you guess what it is?"

"Your stew pot when you make our supper, I hope," laughed a warrior.

"Nay, 'tis not, as you well know. Guess again. I have a pot the whole sea cannot fill. What is it?" She turned to the musicians and players, since it was their turn first. If they could not guess, the crowd would have a chance.

After a few unsuccessful tries, a musician sang out. "That's a very good riddle, very good indeed. But I have guessed your riddle, if you please. It's a sieve, is it not?"

The cook clapped her hands. As the musicians struck up a bawdy song, the castle doors flew open. A guard entered, followed by another group of people.

"Father Maelgwyn," cried Mam. Their priest from Garth Celyn and a bedraggled group of women, children, and older men entered. The music fell silent and everyone stood still for a moment. Then one of the castle warriors stepped forward and greeted them formally, welcoming them to the castle.

"Time to fetch a proper supper for them, isn't it," the cook said quietly, motioning to her kitchen boys and heading for the castle kitchens.

"Call the Princess Elizabeth," Mam said to a nearby servant, who dashed up the long stairs.

Cat felt as if she was waking from a strange dream. "Welcome!" she cried, as she ran to the priest and gave him a hug, and turned to hug as many of the others as she could reach.

15

Rain and the noises of the forest slowed Hyw's progress. He dared not use his gift to find out more this time, after Gawain's warning. Twice he followed sounds he thought were Welsh voices, hoping to find some sign of his da. None of the sounds led to camps or soldiers. The hair crept up on his neck as he peered at the dark thickets, but he persevered along the path at the prince's urging.

This way. Follow this stream and it will lead you to Rhuddlan.

When Hyw closed his eyes, he could see Llywelyn dressed in his fur traveling cloak, and without thinking drew Gawain's quilted one tighter around himself.

We must make haste.

Once his stores ran out, Hyw picked frozen roots and berries he knew to be edible, wrapping them in the cloth held next to his body to warm them. The stream was frozen, but he melted snow in a skin pouch the same way. A steady drizzle of cold wet snow melted around him as it fell, filling his shoes with slush. Before long, he was wrapped in mud and grime from the road. More than once he consoled himself by remembering he would soon be closer to Garth Celyn. He might at last reunite with his mother and sister.

At dawn on the fourth day of his journey, Hyw saw the spires of Rhuddlan. Sounds of clanking metal traveled across the still valley. Swords rang against armour, reminding him the English occupied the castle. He circled around to the gatehouse. As he tried to dash through the back entryway, someone grabbed him by the scruff of the neck and pulled him backwards.

"What do you think, Thomas? Worth a shilling?"

Hyw heard a short bark of laughter behind him.

"Nay, brother," said another voice. "Probably some village brat. You know the king won't pay for women and children."

"Just need to dip the heads in their own gore," came a third. "I hear they ain't looking too closely. These Welsh women with their short-cropped hair look like men anyways. Good for a tup and a shilling, eh? Boys the same."

"Oh, please, sir." Hyw mimicked the accent of the boys he'd fostered with as best he could and held up the roots from his cloth sack. "Cook sent me for som'at to spice the stew. These Welsh devils never use anything, and the king is plenty sick of bland."

"Ah let him go. He'll be in the kitchens when we need him."

The hand that held him let go abruptly. Hyw lost his balance but managed to scramble upright. One of the soldiers landed a kick on his behind that shoved him through the entranceway, and he ran without looking back.

He'd been worried what Llywelyn might think of his outburst, but he was reassured by the prince's laughter in his inner ear. *Quick thinking, boy. Now follow through and we might get out of this with our skins.*

Hyw followed Llywelyn's directions and slipped into the kitchen. He wiped the road dust from his face and hands with the traveling cloak. In case he needed it again, he folded it and stashed it in a corner by the door.

Two cook's helpers were already starting to prepare the evening meal while a third was setting up a tray of loaves and smoked herring for the breakfast tables. The English cooks would use peasant boys from the castle and villages, especially on feast days. Likely they hadn't looked too closely, and he could pass for a willing kitchen worker.

As he thought, the harried cook called out to him. "You, boy. Take this plate of eels to the high table."

Hyw picked up the dishes pointed out by the cook and followed the other helper into the great hall. Hyw glanced toward the centre of the high table and spotted a figure in purple silks that must be the English king. Edward lounged in his seat, fingers steepled in front of him, staring out over the tables of soldiers. Hyw closed his eyes and noted Llywelyn glaring in the king's direction. Hyw thought it was a good thing Llywelyn didn't have a real sword in his hand and opened his eyes again.

At the tables, people laughed and talked as they cut portions from the main dishes and set them on the thick bread trenchers that served as bowls, to be given to the poor after the meal. Hyw breathed a small prayer of relief that this meal was being served English-style with much ceremony, and several courses carried by many servants. He would never have escaped notice at Garth Celyn, with the simpler fare and more intimate groupings around a traditional Welsh meal.

Then he spotted a thatch of brown hair and a face that gladdened his heart: James, seated at a long table with a group of knights and squires. What luck! If he could get a sign to his friend, he might have an ally to help him discover the fate of Garth Celyn, and perhaps his father. Yet he must tread carefully so as not to give himself away and startle James into revealing his identity.

Hyw stepped up onto the dais and stopped near the end of the high table. He set the plate of eels between two lords wearing silk surcoats. He started when he heard one murmur thanks: Lord Shrewsbury.

Hyw ducked his head into his tunic, hoping his former lord would not recognize him in this setting. Lords and ladies rarely looked at servants, especially in another lord's home. As he hoped, Shrewsbury reached toward the plate without seeing him. The old knight had developed a lifelong habit of courtesy that had caused him to thank his host's servant, but he did not recognize that servant as his former ward.

Just then, James looked up toward the high table and his father. For a moment he merely chewed and watched. Then his mouth fell open and he stared right at Hyw. Hyw moved his hand to his lips in a shushing gesture. He had barely turned to leave the dais when someone thrust a pitcher at him. "Boy, fetch my lord more wine. Be nimble."

The voice made Hyw's blood run cold. It was Robert, the boy who had beaten him on his last day at Shrewsbury's manor—and beaten James as well. As squire, Robert now stood behind Shrewsbury's chair.

Hyw bowed and backed away. Robert moved to help Shrewsbury get a choice morsel for his trencher. Hyw moved swiftly down the tables toward James again. Many times at Shrewsbury they had helped each other escape to play after mealtimes, unnoticed by the bigger boys with table duties. One would touch the other on the shoulder as a signal, and they would leave separately to meet outside or in the kitchens. Hyw touched his friend on the shoulder as he passed, hoping James would remember the game.

Glancing back, he saw Robert's eyes following him. Had he been recognized after all? Then Hyw remembered the wine. Perhaps he could run the wine back to the table and arrange to meet James afterwards.

He filled the decanter and started back toward the dining room. As he reached the door, James appeared. Hyw drew him aside into a darkened recess.

"You didn't write or send word," James whispered fiercely. "I thought—I didn't know what to think."

Hyw whispered back, "Much has happened. I don't know how to begin. And I must return to Robert with this wine before he comes to find me."

James nodded. "We are housed in the wing across the courtyard, nearest the gates. The residences here were recently completed. My father fears the treacherous Welsh—oh, I'm sorry Hyw." James broke off, realizing what he had said. Hyw raised his eyebrows. "Sometimes I forget that my own mother was Welsh."

"You're not to blame for that," Hyw said. James had never known his mother, since she died in childbirth. Hyw had a keener sense of the depth of that loss through Llywelyn, though in a different way. He tried to think of a way to communicate that to his friend, but all he could think to do was lightly punch James' shoulder. "It is what both sides think of the other. Perhaps both are right."

"Can you slip away after the meal?" James looked hopeful. "There are many sheltered spots along the walls where we might talk in peace."

Hyw had come in through the back gate to the kitchens and was not familiar with the layout of Rhuddlan castle. Would Llywelyn know? He only knew one way to communicate with Llywelyn. Dare he take the chance, with James so near? Would James understand? Hyw had to chance it. He took a breath and closed his eyes. He found Llywelyn staring at him, arms crossed across his chest.

Aye, said the prince. *I know this castle well. 'Tis one of Edward's favourite holdings, and he has stolen it from me before. I was forced to submit to Edward here five years ago, to get Elinor back from him. No doubt he has changed it since. Never mind. We will find your friend this evening. Indeed, I would discover more of what Edward has done to the stronghold.*

Hyw opened his eyes again. Llywelyn planned to spy on the king, and his plan might compromise James. James, in turn, was staring at him. "What is it?" James asked. "Why did you stop in your tracks? You look like you've seen a ghost."

"I will explain anon. Tonight. I will find you, never fear." Before he could say more, Robert burst in upon them.

"I would not have known you, had I not seen James follow you here," Robert hissed. "Have you used your devil's craft to hide your shape?"

"He is no heretic," James said, standing up to the bigger boy.

"Let the priests decide."

Robert meant to turn him over to the English priests. Hyw had heard of their trials for heresy. Throw a man in the river: if he floats, he must be a heretic and is put to death; if he sinks, he is no heretic, but just as dead. He thought quickly. If he dropped the wine decanter would it create enough distraction that he could run? Then James stepped in front of him, glaring at Robert.

"And you will serve no master. My father will not have you as squire if you do this. And you will ne'er become a knight."

Robert stepped back from James in something like fear. Hyw felt a glimmer of hope. Then the bigger boy smiled. "But there is one thing they will believe faster than heresy." He shoved James aside and grabbed Hyw by the ear, dragging him back into the hall.

"A spy!" Robert shouted, throwing Hyw in front of the long tables of soldiers. "A Welsh spy in our midst."

16

Cat turned to see Princess Elizabeth sweep into the room, her golden hair down around her shoulders as if for bed. She looked like an angel as she offered Father Maelgwyn and their people sanctuary. The cook brought in plates heaping with cold meats and cheese, and the guards broke out another keg of ale.

As the people were eating, Elizabeth beckoned to Father Maelgwyn before starting up the stairs to her solar.

"Come with us, please, Lady Adara," she said in a low voice. She motioned to one of the serving boys to bring the priest's plate and follow them. Mam held out her hand for Cat to come as well.

The servant set the priest's plate at the table with the women around him. The boy brought wine from a decanter on the sideboard. As the door closed behind him, Princess Elizabeth nodded at the priest to tell his tale.

"We were brought from the castle by Llywelyn's man, one of those I had thought was to accompany you, Lady Adara," he began. "He managed to get us through the gates behind the fighting. He bade us to meet you here at Criccieth, and so we made haste."

"Have you any word of the English troops?" Elizabeth asked.

"The force that attacked was small, and from what I saw, our men held their own. But I fear it was merely a scouting force, with the army to follow."

"Had you any word of my husband, Father?" Mam asked. Her voice and bearing seemed calm and composed but Cat saw her fingers clutched in her skirts. "Or did you meet Aeneus on the way?"

"Nay, we heard nothing of Lord Bran, although I heard your son Hyw was being tended in the Abby Cwmhir. A lad was later dispatched to Anglesey for more men, or so I heard. But we saw no one on the trail here, my lady. Neither Welsh nor English."

Mam nodded gravely and looked down. Cat frowned. He was telling them nothing new, since they had heard Berwyn's story before they left.

"The whole of the north will be at war if the English take Garth Celyn." Father Maelgwyn shook his head.

Elizabeth took a sip of her wine, and they sat in silence a moment. The priest pushed his food around his plate. Cat thought of the warrior who had replaced the trap door for them, and presumably joined the fighting.

"What happened to the warrior who helped you?" she asked.

Father Maelgwyn bowed his head and made the sign of the cross. "He went back to rejoin the fighting and said he would return if all was safe." He looked up at Cat, and she could see the sorrow in his eyes. "He did not return. We waited on the trail as he bade us, but no one followed. The following morning, we came here."

Cat said nothing. She felt her mam touch her fingers and took her hand, but she couldn't calm her fears for her brother and Da. Would Aeneus find them? Would she ever see them again?

After the Garth Celyn survivors arrived, Elizabeth sent her guards through the countryside to warn the people and offer to help any who would fight the English. Cat had taken to walking the battlements in the early hours to dispel her dreams, and she saw the first group of men making their way to the castle gate with grim expressions. That day and the next, many more followed. Some brought small herds of cows with them.

She discovered that these farmers, like the people around Garth Celyn, had fought the English many times. The guards spent their days teaching the farmers to fletch arrows, finish javelins, or curve long shafts of yew to be ready for longbows. Often, the men would train in fighting during the cool of the morning and spend afternoons sharpening weapons and scouring armour. Women from the neighbouring towns came to gather medicinal herbs such as willow bark for pain or moss to pack wounds, weave and sort linens for bandages, or help feed the growing numbers as the people prepared for war.

In the evenings, men and women gathered together for stories and songs near the fire in the outer ward. Cat, Mam, Enid and Gwen, along with Elizabeth and her family, shared rooms in the inner ward. Many of Dafydd's special bodyguards had remained with Elizabeth, including her loyal guards who had come with her from England to Wales when she married Dafydd. These guards slept near the women's quarters, as did the Garth Celyn guards who had come with Mam and Cat. If Cat got up to use the garderobe in the night, she often saw Sir Ifan patrolling the halls outside their rooms.

As January winds turned to heavy rains and sometimes snow, Cat was glad she and the girls had their fireplace, thick wall tapestries, and coverlets. The guards stayed in less fortified timber buildings of the outer ward. Horses and other animals shared one end of the timber buildings where some of the farmers and townsfolk slept. It was not surprising when sniffles and coughs made their way around the courtyard.

Eventually, Father Maelgwyn spotted the girls as they began their training. He had already joined Criccieth's more amiable priest in the chapel and was accompanying him on his rounds to fortify the guards and the people at their work. As they passed by the girls, who were warming up with stretches and exercise, Father Maelgwyn called to Cat.

"What is it you are doing here, Lady Cat?"

"We are training, Father," she replied.

"War is not the work for women," he told them. "Go about your business, ladies."

Cat tried to protest but he was adamant.

"I know you did thus at Garth Celyn, Lady Cat, but it was no more right there than it is here. And now you have no other guide but me, you must let yourself be guided." Cat wanted to say her mam guided her well enough, but the priest believed the male head of the household should be in charge. Without intervention from her father or brother, she could not change his mind.

"Come on," Margred said to her, and the sisters ran toward the castle. Cat shook her head, needing time to think things through. At one time, she might have found Hyw and enlisted his aid. Instinctively, she walked toward the horse pens where she had always been sure to find him. She leaned on the stone fence, watching the shaggy coated horses.

She had never disobeyed the priest, but she had a sudden flash of vision: Margred, her long black tresses streaming, being chased by an armoured horseman with sword raised. Cat could not let that happen! She was not really sure if it was the Sight, or her imagination run wild, but she had to do something. Surely training would make them fit and wary, better able to cope with what they may have to face.

She set out to find Owain then, and a plan hatched in her mind as she walked. By the time she found him lounging with the other boys, she had the details worked out. She drew him aside and explained what she meant to do. At first, he tried to argue, but he could see how determined she was.

"If you don't help me, I will find a way to do it myself," she said.

Owain studied her a moment, and then nodded. "Come with me."

They strolled casually toward the armoury, and he told her a riddle he had heard at the fireside the night before. She laughed, and he said quietly, "That's better. You cannot carry out a devious plan while you look so serious, Lady Cat. Trust me on that. I am the master of mischief in this castle."

She laughed again, glad he was helping her. At the armoury, he swept up a horse blanket from a bench and handed it to her. Then he began to inspect the children's wooden swords and blunted javelins, placing several on the blanket in her outstretched arms.

"What is it that you seek, Master Owain?" asked a voice. Cat turned to see Sir Ifan, the young warrior who had accompanied them from Garth Celyn, with his arms folded across his chest.

"Some of the boys mean to skirmish later, to please my Lady Cat and her friends," Owain replied smoothly, bowing slightly to him. "She is helping me choose the terms."

Ifan frowned for a moment, then nodded and moved toward the javelins. Owain turned to the light daggers then, choosing a few and hastily grabbing belts and sheaths for them.

"Come," he said, and wrapped it all in the blanket as he took it from her. He grabbed a thick shank of rope and tied the package. They made their way out of the armoury and he turned a sharp right, taking her toward the wall. He threw the blanket over the wall and turned to her.

"I will wait on the other side until you arrive. This field is sheltered from the town by the castle wall and should suit your purposes. Now you must gather the girls."

"Thank you, Owain," she began, but he cut her off with a wink.

"If you can beg a round of cheese from Cookie, that will be my reward."

She found Margred and Rhiannon, as well as a few of the other Garth Celyn girls. Owain stayed to help with their practice session and found an old squirrel hole in a tree trunk to stash their gear.

Although Cat could not manage one of the cook's prize cheese rounds later, she did get a quarter piece by saying she was taking the new girls on a walk around the castle to orient them to their new surroundings, which was at least partially true. From the look on Owain's face when she presented him with it, he was as pleased with their bargain as she was with their morning's work. He gallantly shared it with the girls and took the time to walk with them to the path on the other side of the castle where they could survey the town in daylight.

17

Hyw landed hard as Robert threw him down in front of the English knights in Rhuddlan's hall. With the agility he had regained under Aeneus' training, he recovered to one knee in time to see James step forward.

"He's not!" cried James. "Father!"

At Robert's first cry of "spy," many of the knights drew swords, and a gallant few clustered around the king. Edward stood on the dais, arms folded much as Llywelyn's had been moments ago, and glared down at him. Shrewsbury also stood with his fingertips on the tabletop, frowning intently at his son, his squire, and finally Hyw.

"Where is the spy?" Edward demanded. His voice boomed in the great hall. Several soldiers flinched, while those guarding the king moved their swords menacingly.

Fear not, lad, he heard Llywelyn whisper in his ear. *Hope is not lost, where life remains. Show them respect but no fear.*

Robert gestured toward Hyw, who had remained on one knee and turned slightly in a proper greeting to Shrewsbury, his former lord.

"That boy?" Edward's voice was incredulous. When no one moved, the king spoke again. "Are you Welsh, boy?" Hyw could only nod. Edward watched Hyw with narrowed eyes.

Hyw was unable to find his voice. Was he a spy? He had come to Rhuddlan to discover what he could about the English plans in order to help his people. Indeed, in serving one lord he had betrayed another. He was miserably aware of James, kneeling beside him, compromised.

"He serves my father, my lord," James said stoutly.

"And who is your father, boy?"

"Lord Shrewsbury, sir."

The king turned to Hyw again, more kindly this time. "Are you in service?"

In answer, Hyw held the decanter up. He looked toward Shrewsbury, unable to find his tongue.

"My lord king, if I may," Shrewsbury said. "I believe he was bringing me wine."

The king looked astonished. "He is your squire?"

Shrewsbury gestured toward Robert. "I believe my squire asked him to."

"Squire," the king boomed, turning back to Robert. "Am I to understand that you asked a Welsh spy to serve us?"

Robert, who had been mirroring Edward's stance, unfolded his arms and took a step back. His face flushed. "Nay, my lord—" he spluttered.

Shrewsbury took that moment to pick up his mug, gesturing for Hyw to come forward with the wine. "I apologize for my squire, my lord," he said graciously. "His zeal against the Welsh leads him to be ever watchful. These boys have both been in my service four years."

"And you vouch for this one?"

"He has been loyal to me."

"Then may he be so to his liege as well."

"I—I will, my lord." Hyw found his voice. His liege was Llywelyn, after all, and he served as well as he could. He sent up a silent prayer, thankful he could speak the truth, although it might not be the truth Edward heard.

Edward resumed his seat. Hyw stood, keeping his eyes on Shrewsbury, and walked around the dais away from the king. He relied on his training to keep himself erect and pour the wine into the old lord's mug with a steady hand. The soldiers soon lost interest in him and went back to eating. An old soldier cuffed Robert on the ear and sent him sprawling.

"Do not bother your betters with your boyish rivalries, lad," the soldier growled.

On the dais, Hyw bowed low to Shrewsbury.

"So, I find you in my service again, Hyw," the old lord said. "Come to me first thing tomorrow. I would have words with you."

"Aye, my lord." He stumbled from the dais. James stood as well, and moved back toward his own place at the tables. Before they could speak again, another kitchen boy grabbed Hyw's arm roughly.

"Come, Welsh," he spat, "we have work for you anon."

Hyw saw the boy nod over his shoulder toward Robert, as he dragged Hyw from the room toward the kitchens. Robert had recovered himself and was staring at them, his face almost snarling. The older boy would not soon forget the incident.

The kitchen boys kept Hyw busy cleaning grates and all the dirtiest places of the kitchen. All the while they cast insults and well-aimed kicks at him. He was able to dodge most, but his pride was wounded. Robert came to gloat once.

"Make sure he has too much to do to spy on anyone," he growled, handing a copper coin to one of the kitchen boys.

"Welsh devil," laughed the boy, excited to be noticed, lashing out at Hyw again with his bare foot. Hyw dodged easily and the boy fell on his behind as his foot connected with nothing but air. It was little help, though, because Robert kicked him instead and sent Hyw sprawling in turn.

Hyw gathered the last of the plates from the tables as the soldiers bedded down on the floor of the great hall. James had not come to see him before the old lord and his family retired to their wing. Hyw was both glad and sorry. Glad because James would have tried to defend him, and they would have both ended up being beaten—and sorry because they might have stood a chance together.

He closed his eyes, but Llywelyn was nowhere to be found either. Hyw wondered how the prince could hide himself. And whether he might be able to hide someday, if the need arose.

After the cook chased the other boys back to work, they more or less forgot about him. Hyw did the work they set him and said nothing. When the servants had taken themselves to bed, he curled into a warm corner of the kitchen. The cloak he had left there had disappeared, but he had little energy left to mourn its loss. He still had to face Lord Shrewsbury in the morning.

Hyw jerked awake again before dawn and made his way to the courtyard. Rhuddlan was an English castle now, and nowhere was that more evident. There was no ritual shaving while the English held court, or boys ready to help the men shave the hair from body and head. Hyw spotted a vat of cold wash water from the pots the night before and washed some of the grime from his face and hands.

He wasn't sure which direction to go to find Shrewsbury's rooms or how to make his way around the huge stone castle. It was larger and very different from the welcoming wooden structures of Garth Celyn. The stone was cold to the touch and felt menacing. He closed his eyes in the dark. Llywelyn reappeared, and Hyw was glad to find company. He sent his thoughts to Llywelyn as a question.

"Last night I sought you. How came you to disappear?"

I did not think you wished a witness to your ordeal, lad. Llywelyn appeared to turn away. *Many times, as page in an English house, I suffered so. I was younger than you are now when my uncle accepted me as part of his court, and I am glad of it.*

Hyw was a little touched by Llywelyn's consideration. He wanted to know how it was done, though. "It was a neat trick, to disappear."

The prince stared at him and then laughed. *You mean could you do the same if you tried? You know more of this process than I, boy.*

"We both act on instinct then, my liege."

Llywelyn showed him the way to Shrewsbury's rooms, but in the near-dark Hyw almost stumbled into Shrewsbury's new page. The boy slept outside the door. Hyw didn't recognize him. He felt a pang to remember this was his own position a few short months ago.

With a sigh he gave his name to the boy and asked him to tell Lord Shrewsbury he was waiting.

The boy disappeared through the doorway. When he returned, he gestured for Hyw to follow, sneaking glances at him as they went. Hyw couldn't help wondering if the child was trying to see the pointed ears or tail of a "Welsh devil." Yet he said little, more concerned with how to answer the old lord's questions.

Shrewsbury was dressed and ready for him, and Hyw knelt before his former master as custom demanded. For a few moments Shrewsbury looked through some rolls of parchment without acknowledging him. The older man wore a familiar wool tunic over his other clothing. Hyw remembered the soft texture of it, but also the tightness of the weft in its weaving. He wondered if the new page had enough strength to stretch it wide over the man's broad chest, as Hyw had when he'd dressed the lord for training exercises in the yard. It seemed much longer than four months ago.

His knee began to ache with kneeling. When Shrewsbury finally looked up, he did not smile. "So, Hyw, it seems you have found your way into my service again. Or do I flatter myself?"

"My lord, I could do no better." Hyw meant what he said, but felt his face redden.

Shrewsbury finally gestured for Hyw to stand. "Robert is no fool, Hyw, as you and I both know. I wonder why you did not come to me plainly last night."

Hyw raised his eyes as far as the garnet clasp at Shrewsbury's neck, but could neither speak nor look into his eyes.

"I promised your father I would foster you, Hyw, and I will keep that promise. Yet if it is a spy's game you play here, you must know it cannot come to good. Many young men are tempted by gold or glory, but this king does not take treachery lightly. And Robert's are not the only eyes that watch you now."

"Lucky none but my lord can see my soul," Hyw said softly. He was thinking of Llywelyn, trapped inside him, and was tempted to tell the old lord everything. Shrewsbury folded his arms across his chest.

"Many a lord would cuff you for speaking out so, Hyw. Lucky for you I know your ways from my own fosterage in Wales, where I met my first lady, James' mother. Yet know this: God can truly see your soul, and that is as it should be. Be faithful and do your duty well."

"Yes sir."

"If it is your intention to return to my service, know that I will not tolerate any action that stinks of spying. What is in your mind is between you and God, but your actions on this earth reflect on me. I cannot and I will not protect you, if you prove disloyal. Do you understand me, Hyw?"

"Yes, m'lord."

"Then we will not speak of it again." Shrewsbury stared at him a moment longer, before unfolding his arms. "What news have you of your father?"

Hyw felt his chest cave and kept his head down. He could not find his voice. Shrewsbury spoke more softly.

"We had news of Llywelyn's death before Christmastime. I thought your father could not have been far away. Is he also—?"

Hyw felt a lump in his throat, and swallowed it down, but his voice was much quieter than he intended. "I know not, my lord. No trace of him has been found."

"I am sorry to hear it, yet I fear worse. Wars in the borderlands come and go, but this time Edward will stay until it is finished. When that happens, the world may seem a topsy-turvy place for you, and for all with Welsh blood. For my son's sake, and the sake of his dear mother, you may have a place with our guards."

Shrewsbury reached out then and clasped Hyw's shoulder. James' mother, the first Lady Shrewsbury, had been a distant cousin to Hyw's father. They shared bonds of kinship as well as fosterage. She had died birthing James, but as eldest son he would someday be the lord of Shrewsbury. Hyw could think of no better fate than serving in James' guard—but that could lead to fighting against his own people in border skirmishes. Hyw's head whirled with divided loyalties.

Always I have liked this man, Marcher lord or no. He heard Llywelyn's voice in his ear again. *He has honour and kindness in him. I envy him that. You must stay with him, Hyw. He may be useful to us.*

At Llywelyn's last words, Hyw shrugged away, and out of

Shrewsbury's grip as well. Then he knelt again at the old lord's feet.

"My lord," he said, "I could have no finer master than you, and I will serve you in my heart long after I am a man. I know not what I might do, if this war ends as you say. I am Welsh and wish to please my father also. In good conscience, I cannot fight against my own people. But I pledge you this: if I become a knight hereafter, I will never take arms against your son James in battle. I love him like a brother, and will protect him as well as I am able, against all calamity."

The old man considered what Hyw had said. "Your honesty commends you, Hyw, and your bond with my son is well known to me. I appreciate your wish not to fight your own people, but your knowledge of Garth Celyn may compromise you." He paused, stroking his beard. "As soon as I am able, I would get James to Shrewsbury, away from this war. Perhaps you should come with us. Young Robert may win his spurs in the next battle. That will occupy him well, and he would be better served to forget your enmity in service to Edward. I would make you my squire, Hyw. You might then come to Shrewsbury again when this is done and serve me without betraying your own."

"So I will, if you will have me, my lord, and thank you." Hyw was surprised at the old knight's offer, and grateful not to be parted from James again.

"See you do your duty well." The old lord's arm was strong, and he cuffed Hyw on the shoulder. Hyw stood fast, anticipating the cuff he might receive upon knighthood would be much stronger.

That's right, Llywelyn spoke in his ear. *Do your duty, as you pledged you would.* Hyw wondered where his deeper duty lay: to his master Shrewsbury, who offered him a place and the chance to serve James after him, or to the dead prince he carried inside him?

Your purpose here is to find out what you can and get word to your people, Llywelyn reminded him.

Shrewsbury beckoned him to the door. "Come Hyw, let us find James, and try our skills in the yard, before we break our fast with the others."

"What happened to you after you left us, Hyw?" James asked that night. "When you did not send word, I was sore afraid for you. When we saw the prince's head–"

"You saw?"

"Oh, 'twas horrible. And all I could think was that your father may have been nearby. And you—?"

Hyw nodded but could not speak. He longed to confide in his friend about events on the hill, but he could not find words to explain. James patted his shoulder. "You do not need to say, Hyw. I can see in your face how it was with you. Know this: you can confide in me as you choose. I will not betray you. I would die first."

"Nay, never say it James. Have no fears for me, but protect yourself. For I am pledged to give my life for yours—and I am not ready to lie down yet!" Hyw grinned away his embarrassment.

"Come, you fat slug, let me teach you how to dodge the quintain again."

At that Hyw leapt up and followed James, glad for an excuse to run.

18

Cat quickly settled into the routine of training with the other girls each day after chores, explaining it away as a walk or a chance to show the newcomers around. Few noticed the girls in the bustle of activity and people milling about the castle yard. As soon as they got outside the gate, they would meet in their field, choosing a spot on the other side of the wall from the smithy to cover the noise.

Margred naturally led them in warm-up exercises, since she was the most agile and enjoyed the chance to show off a little as the others struggled to keep up. Cat, who had the benefit of Aeneus' tutoring at Garth Celyn, then led them in a series of exercises with the wooden weapons designed to help build their arm and upper body strength. Although Aeneus had never let the girls participate in hand-to-hand combat training, he had encouraged them to throw javelin and lightweight knives at targets. The girls tied planks of wood together to fashion a target, and took turns throwing the javelins and knives Cat and Owain had purloined from Criccieth's armoury.

Owain's younger sisters often joined them, as did several older girls from the Garth Celyn group and a few of the farm women and servants from Criccieth. Cat made a point of swearing them to secrecy, lest the priests discover their activity. With all the extra souls in the castle, she hoped Father Maelgwyn would be busy enough ministering to them to forget the girls—at least for a time. They often returned in smaller groups to begin their afternoon chores. For

Margred, her sisters, and Cat, that meant joining Elizabeth at her embroidery.

One morning the fierce rains and winds of January howled around the castle. Cat sat in the hall at breakfast, chewing staunchly and waiting for Margred. Beside her, Owain groaned.

"You're lucky to be born a woman, Cat," he said. "At least you can stay inside this fine day." He laid his head along his arm on the tabletop.

Cat bristled, recalling Aeneus' words to the warriors of Garth Celyn on wintry days. She repeated them to Owain now. "Do you think the sun will always be shining when our enemies attack?"

"You sound like our captain of the guards," he told her.

She worked hard to recall that he was several years her junior, and calmed herself. "We do not choose the trials that form us." She was quoting her da this time. Owain peered up at her, and she could not resist poking his arm playfully. "Are you going to let mere women show you up?"

"You're not going out in this, surely," he said, more statement than question, raising his head. "You cannot. You will be blown away."

"We shall see."

"You will be alone. My sisters certainly will not join you. I cannot allow it."

Prince's son or no, there were times when his arrogance irked her. Cat said nothing more, pushing back from the table and marching up the stairs to the room she shared with the girls. Owain trooped at her heels.

She burst into their room and shook Margred and Rhiannon awake. Owain leapt onto the bed beside them all, his eyes snapping with laughter.

"Awake, awake," he sang, composing an englyn on the spot:
> "Awake, awake, my sisters here abed.
> Now end your dreams of bliss.
> Do not make the young Cat hiss.
> For her, your moaning dismiss."

"You have little grace and less harmony," laughed Rhiannon, hitting him with the feather pillows. He laughed and pulled her from the bed into a heap on the floor, where he tickled her mercilessly until the servants came in and chased him from the room. By then, the girls were awake and there was no going back under the warm quilts.

For all Owain's teasing, only Margred went with Cat into the gale. After an hour lashed by wind and rain, the two girls had missed more targets than they hit and had fallen so many times their clothes looked and felt like a wall of slush and mud. But their energy kindled against the elements as they stowed their gear in its hidey-hole and raced each other back to the castle.

Margred burst through the doors a hair before Cat. Drenched and laughing, Cat almost didn't notice a man warming his hands by the fire in the inner hall. She thought perhaps he had just arrived. He turned toward them and bowed. The girls bowed in turn but refrained from speaking to him until they could be introduced. Cat thought he looked very familiar to her, and then recognized him as a bard who had travelled with Llywelyn's court the previous year.

"Good day to you, Gwilym ap Einion," she said, curtsying to him. "Pardon our appearance, but we were caught in the weather."

"I am sorry to hear it, young Lady Catrin, but glad to see you here," he responded. He made a strangled sound she thought might have been laughter, but he deftly turned it into a cough.

"May I introduce you to Margred, daughter of Prince Dafydd," Cat said. She stopped abruptly, realizing she did not know Margred's mother's name, and hoped he would not notice as she fully introduced him in turn. As they exchanged greetings, he gazed at Margred longer than seemed polite. Margred made their excuses, grabbed Cat by the arm, and turned toward the stone staircase.

The two girls slogged up to their room to change from their wet things, and Cat all but forgot him as they combed their hair by the fire in their room. She showed Margred how to plait her long black hair the way Princess Elinor and her ladies had preferred. Cat still missed them, but after Elinor died they had asked to return home to resume their own lives. Cat moved back to admire her handiwork.

"You are so beautiful this way, Margred," Cat said.

"Mam says beauty is a curse for a poor woman," Margred said. Before Cat could ask her anything more, she grabbed the bone comb and began to brush Cat's unruly copper locks for her. Rhiannon and the younger girls demanded to learn the new braiding style. By the time they were finished all of them sported the new look, and Margred had mastered it also.

Afterward, Cat and Margred went to Elizabeth's solar, where Cat planned to resign herself to better her skills at embroidery. But the servant making Elizabeth's bed said the ladies had both gone down to entertain "a gentleman"—although the quirk in her mouth told them the girl was not altogether certain he was a gentleman. Wandering bards had a reputation in the Welsh countryside, but a bard of Gwilym's stature and skill had always commanded respect at Llywelyn's court. Cat frowned a little, wondering what had happened to make the girl think badly of the bard.

Margred grabbed her hand and they raced down the stairs again. Princess Elizabeth had joined Gwilym to sit near the fireplace, and they stood to greet the girls. Elizabeth frowned at them as Cat and Margred came to a clattering halt. Mam, holding Baby Gwen, stood too, hiding a smile as she held her free hand out to Cat. The girls came closer.

"It is a pleasure to greet the daughters of the house," he said, bowing to them.

"My husband's daughter," Elizabeth said quietly, her face frozen in a polite smile.

Gwilym turned to her with an encouraging smile. "As we protect all of our children now, may they return to aid us in our nether years."

He smiled at Cat and she liked the twinkle she saw in his eye. He certainly did not seem much like the disreputable wandering bards she had seen come through Garth Celyn, or on her travels with Princess Elinor in past years. As he turned to Margred, his expression changed again. Before he could say anything, Princess Elizabeth spoke.

"Gwilym brings us good news this day, Cat."

"Aye," he said, turning from Margred with what seemed like reluctance, before he smiled at the other women. "I had been across the borderlands these last few months, working out the details of a land settlement for Prince Llywelyn. When word came to us of his untimely murder, I travelled through Builth to learn as much of the truth as I could. I discovered two pieces of information that may interest you.

"First, Prince Dafydd survived the loss of Hawarden and is still at liberty. I have it on good authority that he is safe at Dolwyddelan Castle and intends to prevent King Edward's troops from massing farther north.

"Second, I passed through Abbey Cwmhir, and spoke to a man who claims to be your brother, Lady Adara. He tells me that no trace of your husband was found after the fray. We may surmise that Bran leads the Welsh army against the remaining English."

"And my son? Was there news of him?"

"Aye, Lady. Your son Hyw has taken the northward road to Rhuddlan and come under the protection of his former foster father, Lord Shrewsbury."

"He is with the English?"

"It cannot be." Cat spoke without thinking and ignored her mam's signals. "He would not return to them."

Gwilym turned to her. "I have it on reliable authority," he said. "Yet have no fear. He is not a traitor to his country. Nay, rather, he plans to return with news that may help his people."

She frowned, scarcely listening to her mam's questions. Could the poet be right? Would Hyw betray his friend to save his country?

"—and you are welcome to share our hospitality, such as it is, for as long as you may need it," Princess Elizabeth was saying.

"Winter's bite can scarce be felt with two such early roses to brighten the room," Gwilym said, turning back to Margred and Cat. Gwilym's bow included them both in the compliment, but his eyes never left Margred's face. Cat felt her own cheeks go warm on her friend's behalf, and she wondered if Margred's mam had been right about her beauty.

19

War came upon them swiftly. One afternoon, when Hyw and James were sparring with the other squires, Shrewsbury was called away to Edward's chambers, along with several of the other Marcher lords. When the old lord returned, the boys saw him gesture to his soldiers and they scrambled to prepare to march the following morning.

At dawn a priest gave a hasty blessing, and they formed up in companies. The knights around them were keyed up. These were mainly personal guards, set to meet the bulk of their companies in camps outside the castle gates. Hyw noted many of the more seasoned were quiet or even surly, lacking the enthusiasm of the younger men.

Hyw's heart thumped to the rhythm of hooves pounding the cold ground as he rode out of the gates at James' side. He couldn't help but wonder whether the Welsh were nearby. Where was his da? Would he be with the warriors? Would he have to fight one of his own countrymen—or his own Da? If he did not, would harm come to James, or to Shrewsbury?

Llywelyn spoke in Hyw's ear. *Remember your duty.* Hyw nodded, keeping his thoughts to himself.

He needn't have worried. Shrewsbury sent them as far from the fray as he could. Hyw and James waited with two of Shrewsbury's soldiers on a hillside near the English camp. Around him, he could hear the clanking of arms and men's shouts. Llywelyn whispered again. *If only we had a bird's eye view of this field.*

At those words, Hyw looked up and saw the sky full of black rooks. Then, circling with outspread wings, a huge and beautiful hawk. *Boy, if you use your gift, can we become this bird?*

Careful that James and the other soldiers did not notice him, Hyw closed his eyes to make contact with Llywelyn. "My liege, while I cannot take its corporeal form, I can see through its eyes. Its world can be as real for me as mine own. Or as yours."

Then we must do so.

"But this is what Gawain warned us against. It poses danger for us both."

Llywelyn considered his words. *Always the paths fork ahead of us. The path of green fields and well-trodden ground may also hide a hole to snare the foot of an unwary horse. Its rider then lies face-down in the dust. The path beset by brambles and thorns will breed caution before ever we lay a foot upon it. Thus may a man bravely set out to conquer the way, and more safely reach the end of his journey.*

Hyw understood then why the Welsh lords had followed Llywelyn, even when they intended to fight him. He dismounted to gain better balance, checking his mount's saddle to cover his actions. Mindful of Gawain's cautions, he closed his eyes, placed himself in front of the prince, and threw his mind to the hawk in the sky. He made contact with greater ease than he expected, then felt the shock of wary fear in the bird. At first, he thought the bird was afraid of him, but he sensed it was something outside of their connection. Looking down from the bird's mind, Hyw could see the valley of Clwd below. The battlefield.

Llywelyn, as if looking over Hyw's shoulder, pointed out one Welsh lord or another who had stood with him in battles over the past five years. They watched as the Welsh lords lined up in squares, arms moving to make the sign of the cross on their chests. Row upon row of men crowded together. Where Romans would have linked shields and swords, the Welsh warriors had leather jerkins and lances, and bright war paint on their faces.

No, you fools, Llywelyn cried. *The men don't know this form of fighting. Let them rush and retreat, as they always do.*

The hawk would not go nearer to see the faces of the men who urged the warriors into battle. Then with a roar, the Welsh ran down the hillside. Their lords rode at their sides, streaming proud Welsh colours down into the valley below. The English in their armour rode at them, clanking, from the other side.

As the English swords dove into their lines, the Welsh drove their lances upward. The larger warriors tried to pull the armoured knights from their horses with their bare hands. Then those same warriors were cut down, sharp steel hacking them in two from behind. The battle began to shift. Armour and steel won out over sinew and bone.

The Welsh turned to flee to safety in the hills. Row upon row of their own countrymen stood in their path. The English rode in from the sides and forced them together. Like a wave turning upon itself, they fell to the sword and to their own fear. Llywelyn screamed useless commands. No one heard him but Hyw.

The proud hawk that shared his mind with Hyw was sickened at the smell of sweat and blood. It was held there by Hyw's will, but wanted only to be gone. Hyw tasted copper in his mouth. The hawk would not hunt for prey in this field for many months to come. He felt the bird's disgust at the carrion-eaters, black rooks that dove and plucked at eyes and faces. Hyw felt the pull to flight in himself, but Llywelyn urged him closer.

The hawk shrieked once as Hyw prompted it to circle, slowly drawing nearer. Scores of men lay dead and dying. A hundred—nay, two hundred Welsh warriors lay among them. A mere handful of armoured English knights had fallen. Riderless horses screamed and thrashed, or milled about with fear, banding together in clumps or running wildly across the hills.

Welsh colours trailed upon the ground. English knights on horseback drove Welsh lances into the bodies of the dying. Soldiers hacked at the bodies and flipped something up onto a wheeled cart. Hyw realized it was a cart full of heads and the glint of gold torques that marked a warrior's prowess and skill.

The world blazed red and Hyw felt himself fall into the sun, his wings melting like the stories of Icarus his tutors once told him.

He plummeted downward, his mind full of the sights of war and the screams of his countrymen. Llywelyn's voice was silent.

20

During the following day, Gwilym made no secret of his admiration for Margred. Princess Elizabeth met his hints with that same frozen smile, and Margred grumbled. "She means me to wed a man of more influence," she told Cat at night in their room.

"Would you rather have Gwilym?" Cat asked. "He is a notable poet and often argues disputes of law before Prince Llywelyn's court—I mean, he once did."

"But he's so old, Cat," Margred said, turning away.

"He's not! He can't be more than—"

"Anyway, one old man is much the same as any other. Will you come with us to Market Day in the town tomorrow?"

Cat raised her eyebrows. Margred was skilled at conversation, and this change of subject was more abrupt and clumsy than she had managed previously. Then Cat wondered if it really was a change of subject.

"Will the butcher's son be there?" she asked, teasing. "What was his name again?"

Margred laughed but caught Cat's arm. "You must not mention him! Truly, you must not. Promise me." When Cat nodded, Margred laughed again, a little more light-heartedly, and handed her the bone comb. "Will you braid my hair again?"

On Market Day, it was raining before they left the castle. Mam had asked Cat to buy some fabric and thread, pressing a few pennies into her hand. "That should leave a little something for you, and enough for breakfast for you and Margred," she said with a smile. Cat felt guilty for a moment, wondering what Mam would think of Margred's butcher boy, but she took the money and kept her friend's secret.

Cat covered the beautiful cloak her brother had given her with her old rainproof one, and pulled the hood up over her careful braids, as did Margred. They kept well within sight of Sir Ifan, who accompanied them, but far enough ahead so they could speak privately. Not that they spoke much on the journey to town. Even with the extra clothing, both girls were red-cheeked from the cold by the time they reached the market.

At first it seemed dreary and grey. Puddles dragged at their skirts and plastered their hoods onto their hair. Then the rain stopped for a moment, and the girls were able to throw back their hoods and loosen their fastenings. The market stirred around them. The quiet streets unnerved Cat. She had been looking forward to the voices calling out from stalls around the square, harmonizing to attract their attention and tempt their pocketbooks. But today the sellers showed few wares from their stalls and wagons, and those who were out in the street stepped with silent purpose through the puddles. Margred had to ask the peddler to show Cat her thread when they heard a deep voice chime from a nearby stall.

"Laverbread."

"Ah," Margred exclaimed softly as she turned toward the voice. "I told you we didn't need breakfast at the castle." Looking past Margred, Cat saw the butcher's son beckoning to them with a smile. She wondered why the butcher's stall would serve laverbread, the tasty seaweed rolled with oats.

Margred held her hand out for a penny. He must have known this was her friend's favourite. Perhaps it had been pre-arranged between them? As Margred took the coin and headed for the stall,

Cat lagged behind a little, hoping to give her friend a moment of privacy. The rain dripped from the makeshift stalls to fall in puddles near her feet. A droplet shimmered and coiled in the act of falling. It seemed to expand around her—

—and she found herself standing at the castle battlements. Below her the stones seemed to smoulder with grey smoke. The wind filled her nostrils with the smell of burning flowers, burning flesh, burning torches and the clash and ring of steel on steel. Somewhere nearby she could hear the screams of children, and the frightened cries of men and women. She saw a dark-haired woman running and a man chasing her down, heard the raucous laughter and the screams of what came after.

She saw a man raise his sword and cut the head from a young boy with flaming red hair and then she was screaming his name. "Owain! Owain!" But the wind carried her voice away, up into the air, and she could see it as if the words were flying.

Then it wasn't her voice, at all. It was another sound. "Caw! Caw!" Flocks of jackdaws and ravens filled the air, circling and cawing. One of the jackdaws flew by her, and its yellow eyes bore deep into her soul, and it squawked one word: "Death!"—

—and she felt swallowed in its blackness.

"Cat!" Someone was calling her name and shaking her. "Cat! What happened?"

It was Margred's voice. She struggled as she felt a woman's hand on her forehead.

"She's burning up, poor thing."

"We must get her back to the castle."

Cat frowned. She tried to tell Margred she would be all right. She didn't want to interrupt her friend's plans. Her mouth felt dry and she could not seem to form the words.

Wait—wait! She remembered her vision. She did need to go to the castle. She must find Mam. Cat struggled to open her eyes. But all she saw was the giant head of a raven, its yellow eye staring into hers, and then blackness again.

Cat felt the softness of a down-filled coverlet and smelled the scent of lilies. Princess Elinor, she thought. Oh Princess, save us!

And then she heard singing, and the coo of a small bird. No, not a bird. A child. Baby Gwen, laughing and gurgling, and her mam's voice singing a soft lullaby.

"*Huna'n dawel, annwyl blentyn…*"

Sleep quietly, dear child. Cat remembered the words to the song she had heard long ago, when she was little older than Baby Gwen or Baby Gwladys. Somehow, she knew that her mother, who sang the words, also had them sung to her. And she floated back through all the babies and the mothers of her ancestors, back to the first mother of her line, Aylwen verch Arianrhod, woman of Troy, first Briton to learn the ways of the *dderwyddon* or Druids—

—and she felt Aylwen's hand on her brow and heard her singing.

"*First mother,*" Cat said. "*Why is this happening to me?*"

"*We gained these gifts to help our people,*" Aylwen said. "*Now these gifts are yours. When we are most in need, the gift returns stronger than before. As it was given to my sons and my daughters, so it was given to you.*"

"*Why,*" Cat struggled to speak. "*Why me?*"

"*Because you are my last daughter.*" Cat looked deep into Aylwen's violet eyes and saw that she was weeping. "*You and your brother are the last of our kind. And when you die, you will blaze a trail across the sky for us to follow. But it is not your time. This is the time when you must help us. You must tell what you have seen. You must awaken, Cat. Waken, Cat—*"

"Wake up, Cat," she heard, but it was not Aylwen's voice. It was Adara, her own Mam. "Please wake up."

Cat's eyes flew open, and she saw her mother's face near hers. She reached out, and Mam hugged her. "Oh, Cat," she said, her voice thick with emotion. "I thought—I didn't know what to think!"

"I'm all right, Mam," Cat said, breaking free. "I had a vision. Much stronger than before."

"Of your Da?"

"Much worse." Cat relayed the vision to her mam, recalling every detail. She swallowed bile as she told about Owain, and the raven, and Aylwen's violet eyes. When she had told it all, Mam sat for a moment, staring at the wall.

"Could this be true?" she whispered. "Are we all going to die?"

"Aylwen said to warn them," Cat said, throwing back the goose-down cover and sitting up. For a moment she felt dizzy, and her mam steadied her as she regained her balance. Then she stood. "We must warn Elizabeth."

"And yet, how can we do so?" Mam asked, placing a hand on Cat's shoulder. "How can we tell her what you have seen in a dream, and make her believe us? What I know of Elizabeth tells me she will not be easily convinced."

"There must be a way to prevent what I saw, Mam, and we must find it."

21

"Hyw! Are you injured?"

He heard a voice as if from far away and was surprised to find himself prone on the hillside. He stared up at the overcast sky.

"Wake up! Hyw, are you all right?"

The voice was closer now. James. Hyw's head felt too heavy to raise. He heard James leap down from his horse, and the swish of footsteps as his friend flopped down beside him.

"Did you—" James' voice grew quiet, so the soldiers wouldn't hear. "What did you see? Did you see the battle—"

"No." Hyw struggled to sit up then. James offered an arm. Hyw grabbed it and hung on even after he was sitting on the cold ground. "Your father is right, James. This is not a battle. It's a slaughter."

"Have you seen it, then? Tell me."

Hyw let go of James and plucked a fistful of frozen grass instead, letting the cold sting his fingers. He stared across the hilltop. James laid one hand on his. They sat together for a moment. Then James cleared his throat.

"Your silence tells me all."

Hyw put his other hand over James' hand, linking them like chainmail. After a long silent moment, James added, "I'm sorry for your countrymen."

Hyw was stung into responding. "We are your countrymen

too, or at least we were your mother's. Do you feel no kinship when we are slaughtered?"

James was silent, but he removed his hand and stood, moving to his horse. Too late, Hyw realized what he had said. He jumped up to follow James, but Llywelyn murmured, *Leave it be, Hyw.*

They heard a distant horn. "Come, Hyw," James said, mounting his horse again. "That horn recalls our troops. Ride with me to my father. He must hear more of this."

From the top of a large tent pitched in the encampment, Shrewsbury's standard of three lion heads flapped in the wind. As they made their way toward it, Hyw saw a smattering of soldiers and knights, some in armour, some with bandages over wounds, and some polishing or repairing their equipment. He was relieved to see they'd managed to arrive before Robert and the other knights returned from the field.

Shrewsbury had spread out maps and other parchment upon a makeshift table in the large tent. The lord had removed his armoured leggings and mail for comfort. His dark velvet surcoat hung loosely over his shoulders. Three lion heads with roaring mouths were embroidered on it, in an intricate pattern of gold thread. Shrewsbury stood at his full height, one gloved hand under his chin, staring down at them. He was formidable, and Hyw understood then what it was to be an English lord.

"Father," James said, catching Hyw as he stumbled forward. "Is it over? Do we return to Rhuddlan?"

"A fair question, James." The old lord looked steadily at Hyw as he spoke. "Nay, we march on Dolwyddelan."

They remained camped in the field two days. The old lord had pitched his tents on a sheltered hillside, close enough to the battle to engage quickly and far enough to escape the worst of its sounds and smells. Shrewsbury set James and Hyw to fetch and carry for the squires as they cleaned the blood from blades and armour and made ready for another attack. As he worked, Hyw could hear Llywelyn's questions, pushing him to learn all he could of their plans. Hyw had his own reasons for wanting to know, and he listened for scraps of news. He preferred to stay busy, for whenever he stopped, he was plagued by worries about his mother and sister. He wondered also if his da was alive, and if he would be among the Welsh warriors fighting them at Dolwyddelan.

Knights and squires alike seemed weary and more than a little subdued by the carnage of the battle. Even Robert did not crow over his first kills, although it became known that he would be knighted by the king himself, along with several others who had seen battle on the hillside near Builth.

Learn from those who have survived the longest, the prince commanded. Since soldiers and mercenaries had no squires, Hyw helped one old soldier polish his armour. The man, Alan Acton, came from a border town, so he was familiar with the ways of Welsh and English.

"See the crests and coats of arms?" Alan said. "That be the only means of knowing friend from foe on the battlefield. Once these fellows have their armour on and helmets down, you cannot tell one man from his enemy."

"Whose are the gold lions on a red background?" Hyw asked.

"That's the king himself, Hyw. Three gold lions 'passant guardant.' That means they face you, there, waving their right forepaw, as you see. Anyone who carries those colours carries the king into battle, so to speak."

Hyw noticed the king's lions were shorter than the lions of Gwynedd and had more ruff than the sleek red lions on Llywelyn's personal coat of arms. "Is that on everything the king owns?"

"Aye, that or the rose with gold petals and a green stalk. Those be the king's own, mind you. Our Shrewsbury, he also sports lions, but with three heads instead. He has savvy, our lord. You can see by the grey in his hair and beard. Follow him into battle, young master, and like as not ye'll follow him out again."

Hyw also heard disturbing news as he listened and worked

among the soldiers. Another group had already marched north to take Garth Celyn. At the same time, they would lay siege to several strategic Welsh castles leading through the Eryri mountains, including Dolwyddelan, to cut off any hope of retreat inland. Edward's superiority at sea would prevent the Welsh from sailing over the strait to find refuge in Ireland.

"Some bloody Welsh weasel and his son from Powys are fighting with us, I'm told," Alan told him.

Gruffydd ap Gwenwynwyn and his son. Long have they been the bane of my life, Llywelyn growled inside Hyw. Hyw knew their names from the stories his father had told him. Before Hyw was born, they had tried to assassinate Llywelyn, and then gained sanctuary with the English.

The old soldier leaned closer. "Aye, and they draw point in this march." He grinned, and Hyw realized Gruffydd and his son would face their countrymen first, before the English. The old soldier swore. "Mortimer and his men will no doubt follow, keeping their eyes on those Welshman. Devil take them all."

Llywelyn uttered a soft laugh, but Hyw tried to concentrate on what Alan was saying. After Moritimer's company, Alan expected the troops of Henry de Lacy, followed by the king. Gilbert le Clare would keep close watch as the king's rear guard. Le Clare was the subject of many discussions around the fire at Garth Celyn. He was the scourge of the south, keeping the king's peace with an iron fist.

Shrewsbury's knights would be glad enough to follow the king, Alan told him, grinning. It meant they were cushioned between le Clare's troops in front, and Richard Chester's troops behind to take the brunt of any action the Welsh might muster from the rear. It also gave the more enterprising knights among them one more day to strip the gold torques and other valuables from the bodies of their enemies. Hyw turned his head away and closed his eyes to calm Llywelyn as Alan finished speaking.

Finally, everything was in readiness. After a day's rest and some new booty, Shrewsbury's soldiers were at their peak again. Alan had brought Hyw a young bay gelding as a gift from Shrewsbury. Hyw had kept watch for his father's horses Aeron and Cadarn, but they were not among the captives. This gelding's skittishness showed it had seen battle and probably lost its previous master. He did his best to calm the horse, but he had no will to engage with the beast's mind.

"I'll try to find you a sweet treat later," he murmured in Welsh. The horse turned to look at him almost eagerly. Hyw smiled and patted his neck. Perhaps his former master had been Welsh. "I like a fellow who knows his own tongue."

From that point on, he called the horse *Siwgr*, the Welsh word for sugar. Keeping his voice soft, Hyw mounted without incident. The horse perked up its ears in anticipation.

Shrewsbury raised his gloved hand, and as one, the company rode out.

The January winds blew down from the mountain like the Watchers' wrath. The men broke out cloaks and wrapped themselves, and the horses lowered their heads and plodded along the path that led northward.

Hyw was surprised how slowly the company of soldiers and knights made their way. *These English move like cattle,* Llywelyn muttered inside Hyw's mind. *They need a few Welsh dogs to harry them.*

Hyw and James, at a nod from Shrewsbury, rode ahead to catch sight of the troops passing by. From Alan's prediction, Hyw expected hundreds of troops, but he was sure he could see thousands. Soldiers lined the road in front and behind, as far as Hyw could see. A dozen sturdy horses trundled along beside de Lacy's men, pulling a huge pile of wood of various sizes on a platform. James pointed excitedly at it, and the boys decided it must be meant for the construction of a siege engine. Perhaps a catapult lay below, or was it secured in one of the covered wagons that made their way after it? Soldiers were stationed in front and behind, and made their way slowly along the trail, paced by the tower and horses.

They are foolish to try, Llywelyn told Hyw. *They will soon see why Wales will always be free.*

As they came to a steep hill, Hyw saw the muscles of the horses ripple as they made their way upward, lashed by the whips of the drivers. Some of the older soldiers jumped down and, handing their horses off to the men in front of them, ran back to try to help.

The Shrewsbury standard flew so far behind that James and Hyw had no fear now of losing their place. They jumped off their horses to watch the slow progress of de Lacy's men with the wagon. Twice the platform slithered backwards, the heavy load of wood listing slightly under the thick ropes that held it. Llywelyn laughed softly.

Then de Lacy and his sons rode back to give encouragement to the men. It seemed some of the men were ready to give up, sitting or slumping on the ground. De Lacy spoke to them. Hyw could hear his voice ring across the miles, rising and falling in pitch, although he couldn't hear the words. Then the men cheered, and Hyw could almost see the battle lust rise in them.

Two more horses were added to the team, and two more again. The horses' minds reached out to Hyw, but he resisted. The hawk had been enough for him. He had no wish to learn what other animals thought of war. More men joined the scene as well, and some pushed the platform from behind. Finally, the wagon made the pinnacle. The men broke out in cheers and rejoicing. Hyw could not help but smile at the antics of grown men and grim soldiers dancing around a load of wood like fools at a festival.

Llywelyn, though, was silent.

Screams in the darkness woke Hyw. He startled upright. James stirred and Hyw whispered, "Stay here. I will go and bring back word."

Hyw ran along the path until he slipped in something wet. A soldier behind him brought a lamp.

"Shield that light, man," cried a third. "The devils are upon us."

"What does he mean?"

"The Welsh," cried another. "They attack from the trees, and then disappear."

"Like ghosts."

"Like devils. Like the devils they are."

Hyw searched the darkness with his eyes, something like excitement pounding in his chest. Could his da have been one of the attackers? Before the other man covered the light, Hyw looked down into the gaping wounds of two soldiers on the ground. He recognized the face of one: it was Alan Acton, the soldier who had befriended him. Hyw crossed himself. The poor man.

Fortunes of war, Hyw, Llywelyn said inside him. *That 'poor man' was also your enemy, and the enemy of your people. Yet he treated you with kindness. May he have honour in the OtherWorld, and in the heaven to come.*

"May he have honour," repeated Hyw aloud, crossing himself again and raising one fist to his heart.

"That sounded like Welsh." Someone spoke nearby.

"Nay, 'twas but a Cornish blessing." Hyw flushed with guilt at denying his own language and turned away before the man could raise the light any higher. His guilt turned to anger at the Welsh warriors who had stolen in like thieves in the night to kill the grizzled old soldier. He felt surrounded by enemies on all sides, and his only thought was to make his way back to James. He wiped Alan's blood from his boots and clothes as best he could. And he vowed he would not cry.

22

Cat stood next to the bed. Somehow, there must be a way to prevent what she had seen in her vision. She hadn't told any of them about her gift, other than her mam and Aeneus. Elizabeth may be princess of Wales, but she was English. And the English would surely expect anyone with a hint of such a gift to renounce it. She debated telling Margred, but she wasn't sure what her friend would think of her gift either. What if she found it necessary to tell her priest—what then? Some priests were known to deal harshly with these old ways. She had never considered telling Father Maelgwyn about it.

"No," Cat said out loud. Mam raised her eyebrows. "We need to find a way to tell Elizabeth about the danger without letting anyone know how I learned of it."

"What do we know about the garrison here?" Mam wondered aloud. "We might try to ask the guards how their preparations are going. We are fortunate that Elizabeth keeps the English custom of high table. The captain of the garrison is your da's kinsman, and sits near me. If I show my concern, he might consent to reassure me."

Cat considered what part she might play. Although the girls continued to slip away on their own to practice while the guards were busy training, Ifan often accompanied Cat and Margred on special outings away from the castle. "I'll start with him," Cat said, and Mam nodded.

Word was out in the town that the bard Gwilym was staying at the castle, and on Cat's fifteenth birthday he had agreed to perform in the evening after supper. He was adept at the three bardic instruments—the *telyn*, the long-necked *crwth*, and the *pibgorn*—although his specialty was the *telyn* or harp.

As always, Gwilym began with one of the classical tunes that reminded Cat of Aber Falls with its mists trickling down from the mountains. Cat caught her mam's eye, and Mam nodded slightly as she turned back to the dour garrison captain. He seemed to be explaining something in some detail. Cat looked around her for Ifan. Many of the warriors were moving toward the bard, to show their talent with an instrument or their ability to sing warrior poetry with the master. As Cat tried to catch a glimpse of Ifan among them, Margred stirred beside her.

"I am in the mood for a merry tune tonight," she whispered in Cat's ear.

As supper ended, townsfolk had also begun to trickle into the castle hall, some on the pretext of late deliveries to the castle. The butcher, popular for his voice and his drum, brought mutton for the following day's meal. Cat noticed his son Drem with him, and felt sure that was the cause of Margred's restlessness.

Criccieth's house bard took up the *pibgorn*—he seemed to fare much better with music than with insults—and a tall warrior took up the *crwth*. The butcher brought his drum from behind his back, where he had slung it, and sat behind them. As the music picked up in tempo, Margred grabbed Cat's hands, and began to form a circle with some of the other young women who had arrived from Garth Celyn. Perhaps hoping to show Gwilym up, the bard handed the pipes to another warrior and began a lilting Romany love song in his strong tenor. Gwilym merely smiled and moved his fingers fast and light along the harp strings, harmonizing easily to fill in the chorus of the song.

Margred and Cat clapped and circled their companions, jumping lightly from one foot to the other without ever touching their skirts. As they finished, the musicians turned to another dance song, and the servants quickly moved back the tables to make a dance space. Drem joined the group of dancers along with several other young guards and a few more young women. Cat had little time to be concerned for how close Drem might have been standing next to Margred. She felt the closeness of a young man beside her and stepped aside a little to look up at Sir Ifan.

"A happy birthday to you, Lady Catrin," he said. "I am glad to see you are recovered." She remembered he had accompanied them to town and blushed to realize he must have carried her back to Criccieth.

He smiled at her as he placed his hands behind his back. His eyes were very warm brown in the firelight, she thought, as she turned away in the opening steps of the dance. Ifan's hand warmed her shoulder as the grand circle moved clockwise. She barely brushed his hand as they moved back around the dancing space. She tried to train her mind on Rhys, but she felt Ifan's eyes seek her out more than once as they changed partners, weaving around the room to find each other again.

When they finished, she steeled herself to question him, and found him happy to answer her.

"Welsh warriors train each day," Ifan said. "We have the skill and courage to stand against the English."

"I have seen townsfolk and farmers coming to be trained as well," she said.

He hesitated, as if searching for a way to answer politely. "They have been a boon in helping prepare more arrows and javelins for us," he managed.

Under his bluster, she learned he thought the garrison was small, barely enough to hold a castle of this size. By the time she excused herself to join her mam, Cat understood more about her dream but little about how it might be prevented.

"I thank thee for the honour of partnering the fairest flower in the hall this night," Ifan said to her, bowing formally. She found herself a little breathless. Would he try to kiss her, as she had seen some of the warriors doing to ladies in the hall earlier?

"I thank you for the pretty compliment," she responded,

hoping he remembered she was betrothed. She sidled away before he could respond.

Margred and most of the ladies were still dancing, so Cat didn't need to make excuses to join her mam in the room she shared with Elizabeth's ladies. As they compared notes, Cat's concern grew.

"If the English break through the castle gates…" she began, trailing off.

"We must have a plan in readiness," Mam said decisively. "I will enlist our four guards to help us. We can trust them more than any others."

"I – I am not sure if Sir Ifan misunderstood my intentions," Cat stammered.

Mam considered her a moment. "I recall last winter, when we visited Meirionnydd, you seemed close to Rhys."

"I am," Cat said, without hesitation. "Ifan is a worthy man, Mam, but Rhys is my betrothed."

"Then you must set him right. Mention your betrothal, and make sure he knows you intend to honour it."

Cat nodded, and before long they bid each other good night. She made her way to her room. She found the other girls already in bed, sleeping, but no sign of Margred. Cat meant to remain awake until Margred returned, but she was soon lost to her dreams.

23

Finally, they reached Dolwyddelan Castle. Nightly attacks by the Welsh had done little damage to the vast English forces.

There can be but few men left to defend the land, if so few Englishmen were killed, Llywelyn said. *May God bless those who tried, and keep them safe to fight another day.*

Llywelyn thought Dolwyddelan would withstand the siege for many weeks. It was the castle where the prince had set up his communications, and he was sure his brother Dafydd would have taken refuge there. Hyw could tell Llywelyn hoped the English would give up and leave, as had happened so many times before. Yet everything they heard from the soldiers made them fear for the land and its people. Hyw listened to the snatches of conversation around him.

"Even if bloody Longshanks wanted to give up, le Clare and de Lacy would fight on without him."

"Aye, I wouldn't have the two of them against me for all Christendom!"

"These Welsh will burn before the week is out, mark my words."

"And all Wales with them. They say the would-be prince is inside. De Lacy wants his head, and naught will stop him."

The "would-be prince" must be Dafydd, Llywelyn's brother. He had taken sanctuary with Edward more than once, before he turned on the English troops a year ago, to start this war. Llywelyn fretted.

Dafydd must get word to the pope. He is the Prince Regent now. Edward will have dispatched a rider as soon as he had my head in his grasp. If he gets word of my death to the pope before Dafydd makes a claim, Wales is as good as lost.

The English set up camp around the castle. A messenger rode to the walls to offer what Llywelyn called the usual terms of surrender.

Is Dafydd so foolish to think these English have come so far, only to give up and go away again? He cannot win without help.

Hyw did not mention that Llywelyn himself had been just as foolish a few days before. The determination of de Lacy's soldiers and of their leader seemed to weigh heavily on the prince.

Hyw, I must get inside the castle. I must see my brother and discover for myself what the fool has done.

"How can we, my liege? How can we enter without arousing the English?"

I don't know, lad, but we must think of a way. Our people depend on us now.

On the second day of the siege of Dolwyddelan, a string of packhorses made their way up the steep mountain paths toward the English camp, bringing a load of long white cloaks. Word quickly spread that the queen, Edward's wife, had sent them. Edward had his soldiers and their retainers set out cloaks for all the men. Hyw marvelled at the way the men almost disappeared against the snow. The men sent up a "huzzah" for the queen and her ladies.

Hyw pretended to admire their ruse, while inside his heart sank. Llywelyn grunted, realizing the cloaks would give Edward's troops a clear advantage. *We must get word to Dafydd.* Llywelyn cursed the English again.

On the third day of the siege, Hyw finished polishing his pile of soldiers' armour before James. Saying he wanted to stretch his legs, Hyw walked out of the area and then crept along the outcrop of rock until he came to a spot behind the castle. He crouched low and half-ran up the long meadow toward the next ridge. When he got to the top he concealed himself in a thicket of trees. Looking down, he could see Dolwyddelan in all its splendour: the rectangular tower, its dark stone hulk reaching to the grey sky, guarding the entrance to the Vale of Gwynedd, on the path to Garth Celyn.

Ditches cut into the rock on either side of the castle, and the rough terrain isolated it at the top of the ridge. Llywelyn's grandfather and namesake, Llywelyn the Great, had been born here. Llywelyn himself had fortified the stone keep when he returned from crusades. Llywelyn told Hyw it was a strategic location for the protection of North Wales.

Hyw could see shadows moving behind the battlements at the top of the keep and thought Welsh soldiers must be keeping watch inside. On all sides, a steep drop led from the castle to the valley floor. Edward's vast army of men fanned out along the valley like ants scurrying below him. How could he get the prince inside to see his brother, without being killed by either Welsh guards or English soldiers?

Hyw's eyes strayed upwards. Mountain peaks and ridges rose up on all sides of them. He could see points where the ridges came so close, he could imagine one shepherd hailing another, although they grazed their sheep on different mountains.

Strains of a song crept back into his mind, unbidden. *Watchers now sleep beneath the stone.* Legend said the watchers would rise from beneath the mountain to rescue Wales in the hour of her greatest need. Some said the watchers were King Arthur's men, and they would fight to win back the land for the Britons, as the Welsh called themselves. Foolishness, he thought. How could I believe such foolish stories? And then his hands balled into fists and he raised them to the mountain tops. He stepped out from the concealing bush and screamed.

"Where are you? Can you not see that the stars have fallen? Can you not see the sun plummeting toward the earth? Lightning strikes your halls! Why do you not awaken? Why have you forsaken us?"

His eyes blurred, and he heard himself sobbing. He stood staring up, and had the sense that Llywelyn stood with him, lost in some agony of his own. Then he heard the prince gasp. Hyw swiped at his eyes with his palm to clear his vision and looked back toward the mountain.

What had been mere wisps of cloud around the tips of the highest mountains had gathered and thickened. As he watched, the clouds themselves seemed to rush toward him, descending into the valley like the last rays of the sun. A white mist swallowed the ridges where he had imagined shepherds a moment ago. The mist rolled across the valleys, filling the dips and crevices until it swallowed the king's men. It swallowed the mighty siege equipment. It swallowed the stone castle of Dolwyddelan. And finally, it crept up the meadow to where he stood and swallowed him.

Around him, the white mist blocked everything from view. Where he expected it to be wet against his face, it was dry and light as air. He breathed it in, and tasted nothing.

What magic is this? he heard Llywelyn whisper.

Then he heard a whining. Looking down, he saw two glowing amber points of light in the mist. When the points disappeared and reappeared again, he realized they were the eyes of a small creature, blinking at him. The creature crept to the edge of the thicket where Hyw had concealed himself. Then it crept a little closer, and through the fog he could see it was a fox. It sat, panting and staring at him.

What are you waiting for? Llywelyn spoke within him. *Use your gift, Hyw. You must go with him to get us through the fog, and into the castle.*

"I dare not."

How can you refuse? You asked them to help. Can you not see this creature is your answer?

Hyw stared at the animal and felt himself drawn into its

amber eyes. Although he knew Llywelyn to be a shade with no more life than a prayer in his mind, he placed himself once again in front of the prince as if to protect him. He felt a shock as the curious mind of the fox met his. Unlike any other melding, this one seemed to require no effort on Hyw's part, as his feet seemed to melt into paws.

Then he was running with the fox, back through the camp of men. At any moment someone might see him, stop him, hang him as a spy or as a witch who had called the fog down upon them. But it was as if the English slept where they stood. The fox maneuvered between them, and Hyw went with him.

Finally they stopped and the fox sat on its haunches, panting as before. Hyw found himself standing in front of a section of the castle's stone wall. It was a secret door, like the one his mother could find in the stone when they were forced to leave Garth Celyn.

I have lived here often in the last fifty years, yet I did not know this was here. Llywelyn seemed puzzled.

"Are we dreaming?"

There is only one way to find out.

The fox whined again, and Hyw sensed it would remain to lead them back again. He reached forward and his hand found the hidden latch. The stone opened to him, and he entered.

24

Cat walked up the stone stairs to the battlements of Criccieth and stood in the early light, looking out over the landscape. She had awakened from a bad dream, and in spite of her recent illness she felt the need to walk. She snuggled deeper into her warm cloak, wondering where Hyw and Da were now, and whether she would ever see them again. As she made her way around the wall walk, her thoughts turned to Rhys again. Would he be looking out at another section of the Eryri Mountains? Perhaps standing on the wall walk at Bere and staring at the mountain they called the Giant's Chair?

She made her way slowly to the seaward side. She wasn't thinking about visions, but about the wind blowing across the sea with the hint of January snow. She stopped for a moment and stared down at the roiling waters. The waves began to circle, swirling over and over, drawing her inside—

—and she found herself on the deck of a large ship. She felt timber under her feet instead of stones, and the press of the sea in the breeze on her face. She heard the voices around her and recognized their accents. Irish! Were they raiders? Or English sympathizers come to attack the castle? She looked around her and saw two other ships sailing a little apart from each other.

The sailors were swinging the sail around to catch the wind. She saw them point toward shore and the castle on the horizon. It was Criccieth. Just then a flaming arrow hit the water near them, and someone cried out in a language Cat didn't understand. Then the captain yelled something and pointed upward toward the Irish crest and colours flying there. Two sailors jumped up and grabbed a piece of fabric, hoisting it up a rope toward the mast. A Welsh lion like the one on Llywelyn's crest unfurled under the Irish.

Too late! Huge boulders and flaming arrows began falling around the men, onto the wooden deck of the ship. Criccieth's forces were attacking to prevent the Irish from landing. The sailors began to run, one screaming as an arrow embedded into his arm and the flames engulfed him.

No! Cat tried to cry out. They're friends! She turned as if to tell someone—

—and she was standing alone on the stone battlement of the castle. She stared out at the sea, but she could not see any ships. What if they were on the way right now? She had to tell someone. She turned from the battlements and went in search of her mam.

Mam nodded as Cat told her about the vision and what she thought it meant.

"We'll get Ifan and the others to watch for ships," she said. "How many did you say there were?"

"I saw three."

"And they're friendly?"

"I believe they are, yes." Cat described the lion in Llywelyn's colours that she had seen unfurled against the mast. Mam tapped her fingertips together in thought before she answered.

"This might be our answer, Cat," she said. "While I tended the babies yesterday, Princess Elizabeth's scout reported Bere is garrisoned and not yet under attack. If the English do get through Criccieth's gates, a stout ship could take us around the bay and up the Mawddach river. We'd be a short ride to Bere from there."

Of course, they could escape to Meirionnydd! Cat tried not to admit how much she wanted to see Rhys again, especially because of Ifan's attentions. Then she realized what her mother had said. "Ride?"

"Aye, if the ship is as large as you saw. We can board the horses, and they will take us to the castle."

Now all we need to do is convince the captain not to sink the Irish, Cat thought, as her mam rushed from the room to enlist her remaining guards. That is, if the ships arrive in time.

Elizabeth stood, arms folded one over the other, and looked hard at Cat. "And how do you know the English will attack us?" Mam stood beside Cat, and instinctively reached out and took her hand as they faced their princess.

"I do not know, your highness," Cat admitted. "I only believe—" She tried to think of how to explain without telling Elizabeth about her gift. "I believe we should consider the danger."

"Your garrison is less than half the strength needed to protect and fortify the castle," Mam added. "Every report we have says the English come in the thousands. Castle after castle has fallen before them. How long can we hold them off?"

"They're not at our gates," Elizabeth replied.

"Not yet." Cat shouldn't have spoken, but she couldn't stop herself. "If they have taken Garth Celyn, they will make their way here."

Elizabeth considered for a moment, and then shook her head and unfolded her arms. "What choice do we have? Dafydd is holding the line at Dolwyddelan, and when he has repelled the English, he will rejoin us here."

"Of course, he will," Mam said. "But if they come by way of the sea, as they did five years past, then he—"

Elizabeth waved Mam's words away and paced to the window. Cat almost spoke up. Her mam was right. Dolwyddelan Castle protected the route to the south and west, but it was far inland from the Irish Sea. Cat had heard the stories of English treachery in the bard's songs. The English had captured Princess Elinor on her way to Wales, and kept her prisoner for three years. Prince Llywelyn had tried to fight but they came by sea to Anglesey and burned the crops, crippling the Welsh. In the end, Llywelyn was forced to give up half his kingdom and more to get Elinor back. But Mam shushed her with a gesture, and they waited quietly.

Elizabeth finally turned back to them, her face serious and set. "Very well. I will consider it. We should have a plan of escape. After all, we don't have tunnels like Garth Celyn. I will confer with the captain."

Cat was about to say more, but her mam squeezed her hand. "Thank you, your highness. That is wise and prudent of you."

"I will call him now, if you ladies will excuse me." Elizabeth turned from them. Cat and her mam both curtsied and left her to consider it.

"Come with me to the gardens," Mam said. The snow had melted but the wind played havoc in the garden, swirling their cloaks as they walked. Mam asked in a quiet voice, "There has been no sighting of a ship. How sure are you of what you saw?"

"I don't know, Mam," Cat said. She felt tired and unsure, and wondered if she had completely recovered from her illness. "It was the same as the other times, but—well, we were able to change those times, weren't we?"

"I hope we can change this one as well," Mam said. "No point mentioning it all at once. We will need to find a way to tell Elizabeth without endangering you." Then she turned to look at Cat. "You've grown so much in a few weeks. Sorry I am that this had to happen, Cat, but I am glad to have you with me. You're a real help to me, and to the people here."

Cat felt a flush of pleasure and bowed her head to thank her mam for the compliment. As they came to the entrance of the gardens, they saw two guards holding horses for Father Maelgwyn and the castle priest.

"Heading out on their rounds," Mam said. "The people value their visits."

"Good day to you, Father," Cat called.

He looked their way with a start, and an expression passed across his face that seemed almost guilty to her. She hoped he regretted his decision to stop the girls from exercising, while the news of war came closer with each messenger who rode through their gates. She longed to talk with him about it again, but he often went out these days and left confessions and services to the younger priests in training at the castle. He waved to them without speaking as he mounted. Criccieth's priest mounted as well, and they were off through the gates without looking back.

25

Hyw crouched and crept forward through the hidden door in the wall. Mist shrouded the courtyard of Dolwyddelan castle. The banner streaming out above them was Llywelyn's, with three red lions for the Prince of Wales. It was mid-afternoon, yet all seemed as quiet and still as night. He hesitated as he spotted a guard in the yard. Hyw could see the badge on the guard's cloak, showing a blue lion striding forward on a gold field. He frowned.

The lions of Gwynedd, blue for my brother and heir. This is Dafydd's man. He has not yet changed his colours. The mist seemed to magnify the slight disorientation Hyw felt when the prince spoke inside his mind. If he closed his eyes, he would see the prince clearly. Yet he could not help but stare at the guard, who stayed silent and immobile in the swirling mist. Hyw felt the hairs raise on the back of his neck.

It's just like the stories say, marvelled Llywelyn. *This is truly a gift from the Old Ones, Hyw. Now you must trust them. Push onward. My brother waits inside the castle, and we must get to him while we can.*

Hyw made his way carefully behind the guard, who never moved from his position. Two other soldiers also stood still. One held his hand in front of his face as if he was about to pick his nose. Hyw almost wanted to laugh, but he was afraid a noise might break the spell.

He slipped up the stone stairs to the castle door. The mist followed, swirling around him. His vision narrowed and it seemed as if he saw everything through a small round window in the mist. He could not see the castle's great hall clearly unless he turned directly toward it. Then he was inside. The huge fireplace loomed up, leading to the inset window seats. He made his way by the people in the hall, who did not move but seemed frozen in mid-conversation.

More than passing strange. Llywelyn's whisper sounded as if in Hyw's ear, but Hyw was so taken by the sight of the frozen people that he listened without closing his eyes. *Perhaps they are out-of-time, or we are, as in the old stories. This could be a valuable advantage for us, Hyw, if you could but control it.*

"It is not my doing," Hyw whispered back. "And I know not why the Old Ones have favoured us with this time-out-of-time. But I believe it is as my uncle said. We cannot expect to use this to our personal advantage. It would show disrespect."

Llywelyn remained silent. Across from the door, Hyw spotted a stairwell and moved toward it. Mist drifted with him as he felt his way along the stone wall to the upper reaches of the castle. To his left, he saw another stairwell that must lead to the wall walk, and he knew without Llywelyn's whispered warning that Dafydd's warriors would be patrolling. He prayed the mist held them trapped as well.

To his right was a wooden door. It opened as he neared it, and he stepped inside. A man stood near the fireplace, his back to the door. Hyw watched him rub his hands together for warmth. He didn't understand why this man could move when the others could not.

He is my brother. So again, as in the old stories, the Prince of the Blood is allowed to remain unaffected by their magic. Long ago, before Elinor and Gwenllian, I named Dafydd my heir, and now it seems he has claimed the title. I must speak with him, Hyw, if it can be done.

Hyw nodded at Llywelyn's voice. He closed his eyes and concentrated on the prince's will, until he felt a strange sensation, as if the prince had stepped in front of him. Llywelyn's shadow blocked the firelight, and Hyw craned his neck to see.

Dafydd swung around. He snarled and his eyes glared at them. "You," Dafydd growled. "You are dead, and yet you haunt me. I know you are dead. I heard it from your own man."

Hyw realized two things instantly. First, he realized that

Dafydd could see Llywelyn, standing in the doorway. He wasn't sure how they had managed to give that illusion, or how much was due to the magic of the Old Ones. Still, it felt right to allow the prince to lead this exchange, so he determined not to fight it. Second, when Dafydd referred to "your own man," he had to mean Bran. He almost cried out for more information about his da, but he heard the prince's voice rumble in his ears.

"You speak of Bran ap Maredudd of Gwynedd," Llywelyn said, using formal speech to force his brother to answer, according to custom. "Does he live?"

Dafydd smirked, folding his arms across his chest. "So, you do not keep track of your own men. Lucky are the Cymry that I have taken your place."

"Is it so? And is that why your guards stand unmoving, to let me past?"

"Hah! Of course, if you truly are a shade, my men cannot follow where you go. Whereas your men—well, their loyalties must remain with the living, mustn't they? Like your man, who came to me after you fell."

Now it was Hyw's turn to lay a hand on Llywelyn's arm. He felt Llywelyn's efforts to calm himself. "It is only reasonable that Bran would want to serve the Prince of Wales. What reception did you give him?"

Dafydd's face twisted into a snarl again. "What do you think? I bade him prove himself. He leads the resistance in the mountains."

At this Alan Acton's grisly death sprang into Hyw's mind, but he pushed the thought away to focus on the two princes.

Llywelyn drew a breath and began again. "Brother, I did not make my way here to fight with you or be goaded into it. You see me as I am now: but a shade. I cannot harm you in this incorporeal form. Instead, I come as your ally to help save our people."

Dafydd frowned and inclined his head as if considering what Llywelyn said. Encouraged, Llywelyn continued.

"You are surrounded by the English, but in my presence you have a brief respite. The English have white camouflage and plan to attack with stealth as early as tomorrow. Edward sends a messenger to the pope. You must send a swifter one. You may recall the pope supported my claim as Prince of Wales. Whatever you thought then, use that privilege now, to save our country and our people. Ask for men and arms to help you win against Edward."

Dafydd moved slightly. He kept his head down so Hyw could not see his eyes but unfolded his arms as if open to Llywelyn's words.

"What proof have I to offer?" Dafydd replied. "The pope well knows I sided with Edward over you. Nay, don't deny it. I'm sure that in your messages to and fro, you were careful to paint me a villain and a traitor to you. Why would the pope rally to my side now? I would require a talisman. Have you your royal seal that I might send it to prove my claim?"

"Alas, it was stolen from me," Llywelyn responded. "Edward has it now."

"You know this to be so? As a shade, can you not move among his men as you have mine? And steal it back from them? Or failing that, if I appoint a man to follow you, can you not lead my man to the very spot so we may steal it back?"

"I cannot."

"So, you will not?"

"It is more difficult—"

"You know where it is?"

Llywelyn hesitated. "No."

"What good then in coming here? Why should I do as you ask without a talisman to prove you are who you say you are? Why should I believe you are my brother? You could well be a denizen of the devil come to fool me into betraying my people."

"Me, a denizen of the devil? You sound like the English." Llywelyn's voice grew harsh as he moved forward and rolled up his sleeve. "Here is the scar you gave me yourself when you attacked me on the battlefield, fighting with our brother against me."

"Aye and I would again." Dafydd moved forward as well, and he snarled again. "Even as a shade, you plague me with your status and your pope and your futile stance against the English king. It is your fault I have fallen from Edward's favour. This day I sent a messenger to Edward's camp to offer to join forces with him and win Wales. Instead, he sent me the man's head and with it a note: 'Yours will be next.' Had I your princely seal, I would use it to save this country. If you cannot get it for me, what use are you?"

With this, Dafydd reached toward the dagger on his belt. Llywelyn reacted on instinct, but his hand closed on empty air where his dagger once was. In a sudden rush of wind around them, Hyw felt himself meld with Llywelyn again. *Run!* Llywelyn cried inside his mind.

Hyw turned and ran for the stairwell. As he rounded the door, he heard Dafydd's dagger thwack into the wood near his head. Then he all but fell back down the stairs, leaping to the ground. He whispered thanks to his old captain, Aeneus, for the strictness of his physical training and the strength it gave him to withstand the jump without injury.

Dafydd bellowed behind him. The sound dispelled the mist that had protected them. A guard almost bumped him coming in.

"Help the prince," Hyw cried. The guard stepped around him, looking for Dafydd. Then Hyw was running across the courtyard. Guards sprinted past him the other way, toward the castle and Dafydd's yells.

"He has seen his ghosts again," one guard said to another as they ran. They ignored Hyw. He pushed on toward the wall. His fingers found the release for the secret door and he heard the scrape of stone on stone. He shinnied through as it slammed shut behind him.

26

Cat and her mam asked their guards to watch for Irish ships. Each day the men reported to Adara from the wall walk where they "stretched their legs" with Criccieth's watch. They said nothing yet to Princess Elizabeth. Cat wanted to be present when the ships were sighted so she could claim to see something that proved the ships were friendly to Wales. But she couldn't be sure the banner in her vision had been real, or that the Irish would unfurl it in time.

As the days went by and no ships came in sight, the guards relaxed their vigilance. Cat exchanged glances with her mam and occasionally asked about the ships. She continued to exercise with Margred and the Garth Celyn women in their favourite spot. It was sheltered from the worst of the winds churning up the channel, but Margred's younger sisters claimed it was too chilly for them. Cat and Margred found their exercises warmed them and often removed their cloaks or even loosened their ties during their morning "walks."

"Here, Cat," Margred called, setting up the makeshift target again. "Your turn."

Cat chose three small throwing knives as Margred and the other girls stepped out of range. Their practice weapons were meant for young boys to begin their training, and not weighted with the kind of care the warriors took when they fashioned their own weapons. Cat hefted each one and chose what she thought was the best. She set the other two down and lined up carefully with the target. She drew her arm back, and as she released it, she heard a shout.

"Lady Catrin!"

Cat watched the knife thwack into the target before she turned. Father Maelgwyn and the Criccieth priest had reined their horses on the rise of the hill, and he was staring at her.

"Lady Catrin," he shouted again. "I expressly forbade you from this activity. And you other women—Lady Margred! I am surprised to see you participating in this folly."

The two girls said nothing. Cat was immediately aware that she had caught up her dress in her belt to free her movements, and she quickly moved to smooth it down again. Several other girls did the same, trying to hide their faces from him. One of the other women tried to gather up the target and equipment, but it was too late. Cat felt her mouth gaping open, and quickly shut it, trying to think of something to say.

"We were playing a game, Father," Margred responded, her voice level. She had taken off her skirts in favour of the pair of boy's breeches she always wore and made no move to hide herself now. "There's no harm in it."

"A game?" Father Maelgwyn twitched the horse's reigns and the animal grunted in protest. "I will see you both in the princess' solar within the hour, and at confession tomorrow morning."

He spurred the horse toward Criccieth, with the castle priest following quickly behind him. Margred and Cat stared at each other a moment, and then Margred burst out laughing.

"You should see your face, Cat," she said. Cat laughed as well then, and the other women nervously joined in as they all quickly gathered the target and equipment from the ground.

"We will put it away safe, my lady," said one of the women Cat recognized from Garth Celyn. "You'd best hurry to meet yon priest."

Cat and Margred slipped up to their shared room before going to answer the priest in Elizabeth's chambers. They helped each other adjust their ties and changed into fresh tunics. As Margred brushed her hair, Cat used the jug of water in their room to freshen up. She bent over the basin—

—and she saw Hyw and another boy wading knee-deep in a stream. Each held a bucket, and as she looked into Hyw's eyes she felt herself drawn deeper into the waters. The image dissolved as if a pebble had been dropped into the stream, and it reformed into the snowy grounds of a soldier's camp. She saw Father Maelgwyn handing his horse's reins to a guard and taking a folded piece of parchment from the inside of his gown. He handed the paper to the guard, who looked at the seal and nodded.

Then she saw the other priests behind Father Maelgwyn. They also dismounted and made their way toward a grand tent with a banner flying above it that she somehow knew belonged to the English king, Edward Longshanks. A sudden wave of anger and disappointment rippled through her, and the image changed.

She saw Criccieth as if from the battlements again. The castle was surrounded by English soldiers. Father Maelgwyn stood on the stones with his lantern, waving it. A light answered from the soldiers below. Cat shrank back into the late afternoon shadows. The priest gestured to two guards near him, and they moved toward the pulley that would raise the heavy metal portcullis protecting the castle from the invaders.

No! she tried to cry out. No, you mustn't open it—

—and she found herself staring at the basin of water in her room at Criccieth.

"Traitors!" The words came out of her mouth before she could stop herself.

"Who are?" Margred asked.

Cat was too upset to curb her tongue, and too familiar now with Margred's company to want to hide her gifts any longer. "Father Maelgwyn and the other priest—and more besides them—have met in secret with the English king."

"What? He wouldn't," Margred began. Then Cat was telling her about her gift of Second Sight, and briefly about her connection with her brother Hyw. When she was finished, Margred looked thoughtful.

"How does it happen?" she puzzled. "Your visions, I mean. Is it the water? The songs say that's how Queen Mab contacts her people of the Tylwyth Teg."

"It may be," said Cat. "I gave Hyw a token before he left, an arm band woven with some of my hair as a remembrance. And he gave me a cloak. Perhaps that helps us bridge the distance between us."

"And have you had visions of other things as well?"

Cat nodded and explained about seeing English soldiers and their horses on the trail during their escape from Garth Celyn. She downplayed her vision about the attack on the castle for Margred's sake and spoke of the more recent ships she had seen coming to help them. "The horses had been mere hours away, but the ships haven't appeared."

"Then how do you know if the ships are a true vision, or for that matter this new vision of Father Maelgwyn?" Margred asked. "Would the priest not say your suspicions are convenient?"

"How so?" Cat bit back, and then stopped herself. Could her vision have been influenced by their current troubles with Father Maelgwyn? Cat thought for a moment. "In my vision today, when I first saw Hyw, I saw Father Maelgwyn on his horse arriving to speak to the king. It was the same horse he rode today."

"Do you mean he has betrayed us already?" Margred's face was alarmed.

"It may be," Cat said. "There was something—some quality of light—that seemed different in that part. The second part was more hazy somehow, more like the vision I had of the ships."

"So, the priest's actions may happen on the same day as the ships arrive," said Margred. "The priests were gone for almost a week, and the horses were lathered as if they were hard-rode." She appeared to be thinking it over as well.

Finally, Margred stood up. "We cannot accuse a priest without something more, unless you want everyone to know you are a sage and a soothsayer."

Cat shook her head, standing as well. "Nay, Margred, in these times—"

"Fear me not," Margred laughed, taking Cat's hand. "Yet we must try to find out more somehow. Come. Let us face the music we have made for ourselves and see if we can change the tune."

27

The fox was pacing on silent paws as Hyw sped through the closing gap in the castle's defences. The small animal yelped once and ran. Hyw quickly moulded his mind to the fox, and they sped through the trees back to Shrewsbury's camp.

Almost as soon as the camp came into sight, the fox yelped again and vanished. Hyw felt it torn from his mind, replaced by the terror of falling and blackness. He closed his eyes and stumbled.

Steady, boy, the prince said.

Hyw recovered and stood panting, his arms on his knees. "I am sorry we did not accomplish our goal."

There is more than one way to shear a sheep, Hyw. We know two things from this that we did not know. The first is that your father lives. The second is that he has a following. He would never have gone to Dafydd otherwise. He may be camped nearby.

Hyw raised himself and looked around him at the mountains. Hyw wanted to wave, but stopped himself. He realized if his father was watching, he would see his son among the English. What would happen if the Welsh attacked? Would Hyw in the end be forced to fight his father's men to save his own life? Or to save James?

James! What if James asked for him and no one could find him? How long had he been gone? Hyw ran again, this time back to camp.

He found James seated in the dirt with a pile of armour around him. His friend scowled up at him.

"I thought you were going for a walk in the hills."

Hyw spotted his own pile of finished armour, sitting in the same spot as when he left. He thought about the silent, unmoving people in Dolwyddelan castle. They truly must have been stopped in time. He realized it had only been a few moments since he left to go on a walk, and discover a fox, a castle, and a living prince. He could find no words to explain it to his friend, so he grinned instead.

"I ran. Here, let me give you a hand." For the rest of the afternoon, the two boys worked together to finish readying the men's armour. When Shrewsbury's knights came to collect it, one of the younger soldiers feinted toward Hyw.

"Here's your reward for a job well done, boy." Hyw recognized him as a friend of the grizzled soldier Alan Acton, and he recognized the man's play-fight as a gesture of remembrance where words failed him.

"Gerald, save your fight for tomorrow," another guffawed.

"Why—do you go into battle again?" Hyw took advantage of the younger knight's familiarity to ask, and Gerald nodded.

"May the saints preserve us," said another, shivering. "Not soon enough for me. I like it not in this place. The quicker we put the fear of God into these heathen Welsh and return to our own land, the better, to my mind."

"Fear of God," Gerald snorted. "Fear of Edward, you mean."

"Edward who?" said the first man, settling down on the armour and bringing out his whittling knife and a twig. "Gilbert le Clare, more like. It is his army I will join, after this battle's won. I hear they fare towards South Wales again. The land of milk and honey."

"Aye, and with land—even in godforsaken Wales—you could marry your Sal," said Gerald. The men guffawed and made bawdy jokes about the soldier's upcoming wedding night. The soldier jabbed at one of the jokers with his fist, and Hyw felt his cheeks flame as he guessed what the men meant by the jest.

Ask them which direction Edward goes. Llywelyn's voice was clear enough inside Hyw's head. He turned slightly from the men and closed his eyes to find the prince dressed in full war regalia. *Ask them where the king plans to travel next. We must try, Hyw. If we can get word to Bran, we may yet get the royal seal back for Dafydd.*

Llywelyn must feel desperate if he was willing to try to enlist his brother's help again. Hyw turned back to the men and waited for a break in the conversation.

"You are the lucky ones indeed. Le Clare is brave, but my master will follow the king. Where will he go after the castle falls?"

"Who can say, boy?" Gerald looked at him kindly. "He is the king and can do as he pleases."

"Pah," said another. "Once he has Dafydd in his grasp, he will hang him from the Tower of London, beside his brother's head."

Partly to distract Llywelyn from the comment, Hyw rubbed his head. "That puzzles me. I thought Edward and Dafydd grew up together. That they were allies."

"Nay. This Day-vid was the bait Edward used to hook his war-like brother."

"If that be true, then why does the king remain?

"He means to crush the Welsh now once and for all."

"Aye, he must end the royal line," Gerald agreed, "so there can be no more reason for these Welsh to fight."

Hyw thought swiftly of the baby, Gwenllian. His mother would die rather than see that baby harmed—or killed. He sensed the eyes of the men on him and tried not to show his feelings on his face.

"You may have been Alan's friend, young lad, but I begin to wonder why you are so interested in the king." The older knight had stopped cutting fruit and was staring at Hyw.

He tensed. Just then James' stomach growled. As James made a show of grabbing at his belly, all the men laughed. Gerald reached out to ruffle James' hair. "Time for supper, is it? Enough of your questions, then. A prize for the one who can run the faster down the hill toward yon campfire."

Hyw breathed a small sigh of relief as he led James in the race—slowing enough to let his friend win in the end.

The next day another group of men rode in. They were dressed in hooded cowls, and for a moment Hyw looked for his uncle among them. Then the sun caught the rings on their fingers as they shifted their horse's reins, and in that glint, he realized the men were priests, not simple monks like Gawain. His disappointment grew to fear as the men threw back their hoods. Llywelyn cursed anew, and Hyw ducked his head before he could be seen. Among the group was the priest of Garth Celyn, Father Maelgwyn.

The others are also Welsh. At least one served my brother in years past. Llywelyn's voice was low although only Hyw could hear it. *Bran will know a way to aid our people. No doubt any Welshmen capable of resistance will be with him. We must make contact and warn them. Perhaps he has men inside the castle and can get word to them.*

He directed Hyw up the escarpment beside the stream, and along the nearby meadow. Hyw grabbed a water bucket as he left the others, in case anyone saw him. *Stop here,* the prince said. Hyw could see nothing, but Llywelyn showed him a spot where he believed there were signs of men coming to gather water. He led Hyw over to the hedge. Under some loose branches they found an old pot. It was dented, but not rusted.

Left here for use, but old enough that anyone who finds it would not think it important enough to return for. Nothing but the last man's leavings. Make markings here, as I will show you.

At Llywelyn's bidding, Hyw cleared a bit of dirt and wrote symbols as Llywelyn directed him.

I learned Arabic as a young man on Crusade, and your father knows it well. It was how we passed information to each other after our return, and we have kept that tradition.

"What did I write?"

The words for 'beware' and 'priests.' Hyw traced the symbols in the air and tried to remember them. Then he placed the pot on top so it would not erase the letters. At Llywelyn's bidding he gathered twigs and set them in the form of a fish beside the pot. He used a stone for an eye. *An old trick of mine that your father may remember, if indeed he is here.*

After Hyw replaced the branches to cover his work, he stared around him for a moment. Could his da really be so close? Llywelyn reminded him to run back to the stream for water to take back to the English camp.

The attack on Dolwyddelan began at dawn the following day. Fearing the worst, Hyw and James watched as the soldiers made their way with stealth up the mountain. Again, Shrewsbury would not allow the boys to take part in the battle, and the cooks and stewards kept them busy with chores around the camp all day. Hyw strained to listen, but no sounds of battle carried over the wind.

Hyw was about to try making contact with a hawk or some other bird again when a few soldiers returned and made their way to the camp cook. After a few hasty words, the cook began to move quickly.

"Here boys, you can help." James and Hyw gathered the cook's things and within minutes the camp was rounded up and on the move. They made their way up the hill to the castle.

It was noisy with English soldiers, but Hyw could neither see nor smell blood or signs of fighting. Setting up kept him too busy to ask anyone what had happened. That night, when the men had time around the fire, he and James finally heard the tale.

"We crept up the hill in silence," Gerald said, his eyes glowing in the flames. "The castle gate was open. 'What is this?' our captain said. 'Some kind of Welsh enchantment?' In we came, fearing a trap. But no, there was nothing. Not even a dog in the yard. It was as if they sank into the mountain and vanished." Gerald shivered a little as he told the tale, and Hyw thought it was from more than cold. Yet he could not help but be glad that Dafydd and his people had somehow managed to escape.

Edward's army took up residence in the castle, and the soldiers celebrated long into the night. Dolwyddelan had fallen after only five days of siege.

28

Ifan arrived to escort Cat and Margred as they came out of their room.

"Lady Elizabeth bids you to her solar, ladies," he said. Cat searched for the twinkle she usually saw in his eye since their night of dancing and poetry but could not find it.

"Do you know what it is about, Sir Ifan?" Margred asked for her.

"It is not my place—" he began, but Cat interrupted.

"Nay, Sir Ifan, tell us, that we might be a little prepared," she said.

He looked uncomfortable. "Father Maelgwyn had much to say to the Lady Adara and the princess about your—recent activity."

"He thinks it unseemly." She said it as a statement, and he nodded. "And what do you think?"

"I serve my captain, Lord Aeneus, and would not question his decisions."

"Of course not," she agreed. "But privately, do you agree we should be prepared?"

"I would die before I let any harm come to you," he said, and then added, "or to the Lady Margred, or any of our ladies. Yet these are difficult times. God forbid our enemies should breach our gates. Yet if they do, and aught prevent me from reaching you, if you have the strength to flee from harm—then I think it time well spent."

She nodded, pleased to hear him say so. "Then I am ready to face my priest."

He bowed slightly to them, his mouth twisting in what might have been a smile as he stepped behind the girls. Margred linked her arm through Cat's as they marched toward the princess's rooms.

In the end, they were able to say little in their own defence. Cat was surprised when her mam stood up to Father Maelgwyn.

"Begging your pardon, Princess Elizabeth, but I may be able to shed a different light on this matter." When Elizabeth nodded, Mam went on. "When I was young, we faced a similar threat, and I myself took part in these activities. It was not considered unseemly, but necessary to protect ourselves from the *Saeson*. This we do not talk about, and again I beg pardon, but I myself was grateful for the knowledge to hide well and the agility to move myself from harm's way."

"And, Lady Adara, did you take up weapons?" the priest demanded. His eyes blazed into them. "Did you arm yourself and threaten others?"

Mam looked uncomfortable, and Cat wondered what had happened in her youth to bring the haunted look into her eyes. She shook her head. "I did not learn these skills to threaten anyone, but to protect myself. I still do those exercises in the privacy of my room."

Father Maelgwyn raised his eyebrows and turned away from her, as if disgusted. Princess Elizabeth rubbed her brow and looked at Margred. Cat had not noticed how tired and wan the princess seemed, like Mam looked sometimes when she didn't know Cat was watching. Elizabeth must be as worried about her husband Dafydd and her oldest son, as Cat and her mam were about Bran and Hyw.

"I have been lax, Lady Margred, in protecting you," Elizabeth began. Margred made to protest but Elizabeth shook her head. "When we brought you to us, it was to keep you safe from harm and fear. Although you are not my daughters, I have grown fond of you and your other sisters. But it seems I have not done my duty by you."

She turned to the window, and stood staring out, as if on her own past life. "In our day, a young girl has little say in her own life. You will soon be betrothed, and you will have little say in that."

"It is meet and right—" began the priest, but Elizabeth stopped him with a gesture.

"I do not question it, and my life is testament to that." Elizabeth was talking about her first marriage to an English nobleman, Cat realized, and possibly Prince Dafydd too? They seemed happy enough, but had Elizabeth wanted something else? Someone else? "I see the point in being prepared, and fresh air does the children good. Lady Margred, is this something you wish to do?" She turned to Margred, who nodded. "Very well. This much I can grant you. You may continue, but you must dress appropriately and not masquerade as a boy. And Lady Catrin, you will return everything you have taken." When the girls went to protest, she put both hands on her hips. "You will do this that I have asked of you, as your princess. And if you do, you may take exercise as needed to strengthen yourselves. And may God have mercy on all of us."

"Your highness, I must protest," said the priest. "What if—may God in his wisdom protect us—but what if the enemy does come, and we must close the castle gate? I am trying to protect the young ladies. If they are outside the gate…"

As his voice trailed off, Cat exchanged a glance with Margred. If her earlier vision was correct, why was he warning them now? Did he want to protect them? Or—her scalp prickled—was he planning something much darker? She felt she should say something, but what? She tried to imagine saying, *I've had a vision that Father Maelgwyn will open the gates to the enemies and betray us.* What would the priest do? Would he drag her out to the courtyard and subject her to a trial for heresy, as she had heard another English priest had done?

"I will heed your good counsel as always," Elizabeth was saying. She turned to the girls. "From now on, you will exercise inside the gate, and keep a guard with you at all times." Elizabeth scanned the room, and Sir Ifan straightened a little as her eyes fell on him. "Lady Adara, is this your man?"

"He is Sir Ifan, a member of Prince Llywelyn's *teulu* and loyal to me."

"Sir Ifan, may we—as mothers, and as your Princess and your lady—trust you with the safe keeping of our daughters?"

Ifan nodded and came to attention. "You may, your highness. I will lay down my very life to keep them safe from harm."

"I pray it does not come to that," Elizabeth said. She turned and swept from the room. Ifan bowed and retired to the corner of the room again, already on guard. Father Maelgwyn stared at them a moment, and then followed the princess. Cat couldn't help but think it wasn't the end of the matter. She caught her mam's eye, hoping for a private moment with her.

"Come," Adara said to both of the girls. "Several of the young men have been commissioned to fight with our warriors, should they be needed. You two can help me prepare the crests for their cloaks."

That meant embroidery, and Cat groaned inwardly. But it might also offer her a chance to tell her mam about the vision.

29

Dolwyddelan was much smaller than English castles. Most of the army, including Robert as Hyw was relieved to see, camped outside the gates. Shrewsbury and a select few of his guards bunked in the castle with the other lords, and he kept James with him as squire. Hyw slept with the soldiers in the garrison near the castle gate. He made himself useful there and joined James inside at mealtimes and for short periods in the afternoons, when they could catch up with each other's business.

The English troops began building the next day, and Hyw quickly learned they were putting up a second tower to keep better control of the countryside. A man arrived as if he had been sent for and took control over a number of soldiers and stonemasons. James watched intently until the man—an architect—agreed to explain his plans.

The priests came again. For two days, Edward held council with them and his lords. Hyw tried to get close but the tents were heavily guarded. He worried that Father Maelgwyn had seen him, but the man did not stop or make any sign. Hyw was relieved, but resolved not to try to spy directly again. Instead, he used his old trick of offering help to the soldiers. As before, he heard much while he cleaned and sharpened their weapons or oiled their leather leggings.

"Aye, yon priests come to help us find that heathen Dafydd," said Gerald, who had joined Shrewsbury's personal guard after the siege. "Won't be long now before we know which way the wind blows him."

The priests will know his ways and his castles. Llywelyn made a disgusted sound. Dafydd had controlled several castles in North Wales, such as Dinbych and Caergwrle. Hyw recalled Caergwrle was built near a town called "Hope." Could he have gone there? *His castle there fell months ago,* he heard Llywelyn say. *Dafydd will go to Bere, no doubt. It is the most fortified.*

Hyw was torn between his feelings and his fealty. He wanted to leave for Garth Celyn right away to warn them, and he longed to see his mother again. But Llywelyn would not hear of it. *Not yet, boy. We have much to do.*

With that he led Hyw back to the area where they had left the message. It appeared undisturbed, but as soon as he moved the branch Hyw could see the pot had been moved and the word carefully erased. In its place was a symbol Hyw had not written. Llywelyn laughed.

It is the Arabic for 'friend.' It can be none other than your father, Hyw. Now I am certain of it. We must find him.

Hyw watched from the castle battlements as le Clare and his troops packed up to leave. He could not catch sight of Robert or Gerald in the company, although they must be there. It took most of the day for le Clare's army to head down the mountain to the south. The priests also left the castle under le Clare's protection.

Edward had decided to remain for another week. Some thought it was to get the new tower underway, but Llywelyn had other ideas.

He is sending out spies to discover which way Dafydd has gone. Mark you, my brother has a good chance if he stays hidden and makes his way to Bere. He knows the mountains almost as well as I.

And yet the mountains did not hide you from Mortimer, Hyw thought. If Llywelyn heard, he seemed too preoccupied watching le Clare's departing soldiers to comment.

Hyw ran to the castle keep and found several knights at the table breaking fast. James had served his father and sat at one of the lower tables to grab a bite of food for himself. Hyw slipped over to him.

"When do we leave?"

James shook his head and swallowed a piece of unleavened bread. "Father will remain, and so will I."

"What?"

"'Tis true. He pleaded age and gout, and Edward has given us leave."

Hyw looked into James' bright excited eyes and knew he was thinking about the castle building. At least now James could enjoy watching the architect without hindrance. Hyw tried to smile for his friend. "Do you—have you heard where Edward takes his army?"

James nodded, and a look of concern passed over his features. "Hyw, I am worried for you. He plans to march on all of Dafydd's castles, but the talk is that he moves across the north from Garth Celyn to Criccieth."

It was as Llywelyn thought. Hyw felt a hollow fear in his chest. He tried to hide his eyes from his friend but felt James' hand on his arm.

"You must go, of course," James whispered. "You must get there before them all and find your mother."

Hyw could not believe his friend guessed his heart so well. Hyw felt a pang for deceiving James: it was not mother but father that Hyw would be leaving to find. He steeled his heart: he had to protect James at all costs. He looked into the other boy's eyes. "And you must not help me. Your father would never forgive you."

"Yet I will help you all I can." James set his chin with resolve.

Wait a little, Hyw, Llywelyn said. *Let me think.*

"Give me a moment to consider," Hyw whispered to James. He closed his eyes for a moment and found Llywelyn with his hand cupping his chin in thought.

You need to protect him and his good father. If you run now, it may seem they have harboured a fugitive. It will not go well for them. And you will lose a future ally, once this war has ended. Llywelyn stood and looked squarely at Hyw. *I may know another way.*

It was a way fraught with danger, but Hyw found himself relaying Llywelyn's plan to James. They would offer to go for water together. James would return alone, running, and claim that Hyw had been taken by Welsh marauders. The boys modified it with what they thought might work. They could secure some food from the cook, who was always willing to feed growing boys, and wrap it in cloth as before for Hyw to take along with him. They decided to wait until the following day to try their luck.

Hyw decided to lead James downstream but turn and go upstream once they parted, to make doubly sure the plan would work. *What your friend does not know, he bears no responsibility for,* the prince said.

Later that afternoon, when James went to watch the architect, Hyw used the commotion of armies on the move to leave another message. Llywelyn showed him the Arabic signs that would convince the men to keep clear of the area so the English soldiers would not find them. Hyw looked around him for the last time, wondering if his father watched from the thickets, or perhaps from an unseen cave. He tried spying through the eyes of a nearby jackdaw, but he could not spot any human activity in the area.

Hyw busied himself in the barn for the morning. At dinner, Shrewsbury kept James busy on the dais, but Hyw managed to collect some extra food from his table and from the cook.

He waited for James in the courtyard. James brought two water buckets. "I thought I'd never be done." He wiped his brow with one sleeve. Hyw grabbed a bucket from him as the two boys set out, quickening their pace so no one would find more chores for them.

As they rounded the castle gate, Hyw led them downstream, away from the message bush. They waited until they had gotten well past the castle before they slowed to talk.

"Hold on." James reached into his tunic and brought out a

small flask of watered-down English wine for the journey. Then he slipped off his inner quilted vest.

"No, you will need it yourself." Hyw tried to protest.

"I have another. Besides, I need to know you are warm out here in this snow. Surely it will be warmer near Garth Celyn?"

"I'm sure it will be," Hyw replied. It was still January, but the Menai Strait kept the climate at Garth Celyn milder than in the Snowdon mountains. "I will worry about you, too."

"Me?" James laughed, but his eyes were shadowed. "I have a whole army at my back. I will be fine."

Hyw meant something more than that, recalling the shine in James' eyes as he watched the architect at his work. As Shrewsbury's heir, James couldn't train in a building trade, even if his heart might lean in that direction. Hyw couldn't think of the words to explain his feelings, so he punched James lightly on the arm as they set off again. "I know it."

Since Hyw had explored more often than James, he had chosen the spot for them to part company. He slowed his pace as they neared it, and James brought out his finger weaving. They wound each other a wrist bracelet. The small one Cat had made was barely a thread on Hyw's wrist now, and he could not speak as James plaited his sturdier cord into hers. Hyw touched the bracelet as he looked down into the water of the stream, and thought of his sister and mother, wondering how long it would be before he saw them again.

The boys half filled their bucket and then dropped it on the ground, grinding their feet into the slush and mud around the stream as if a great many men had scuffled there. They were careful to leave a few tracks of their own clearly visible.

"We will meet again Hyw. When all this is over, you will come back to Shrewsbury."

Hyw found his voice then and put one hand on his friend's shoulder. "I will hold you to your father's promise. I should like nothing more than to serve you, when you are lord of Shrewsbury castle."

"It is a pact then."

"Now head you back," Hyw told him, "so I can see you safely around the bend before I go."

James hesitated a moment and threw his arms around Hyw in a quick hug. Then he ran, stopping once to wave. Hyw set out upstream, taking extra time to cover his tracks and hoping James remembered to slow down as he neared Dolwyddelan, so he would not raise the alarm too quickly.

30

Adara released Sir Ifan at the door of her room, and the three women went in together to begin embroidering crests. With no others present, Cat had the chance to tell her mam that Margred knew her secret. Mam made them swear to tell no one else. That gave Cat the chance to turn the conversation to her most recent vision of Father Maelgwyn. Mam digested this news, remaining silent for several moments.

"These are dark days indeed," she said, her low voice resonating with sorrow. Before Cat could respond, they heard a commotion outside the open window. Cat and Margred looked out and saw a group of men dismounting in the courtyard. The men wore chain mail shirts and had swords at their sides, so they must be nobles or *teulu*, although Cat didn't recognize them. She looked for their banner and saw the Welsh red lion walking forward, with some black markings on a red background. The breeze caught it, and she could clearly see three ravens, two above and one below.

"Meirionnydd's banner," she exclaimed out loud. She knew it well, since it would someday be her own. Just then, the tallest man turned and looked up at their window.

"Rhys!"

She ran for the door, leaving Mam and Margred to follow. Cat raced down the stairs to the main hall in time to see Rhys and two of his men enter. Cat had eyes only for Rhys, and the look on his face when he caught sight of her was payment enough for her.

"The lord of Meirionnydd, Rhys ap Cadwgan ap Goronwy ap…" droned Princess Elizabeth's bard, reciting his extensive family history as Rhys and his men swept through the hall. Rhys knelt on one knee before Princess Elizabeth, and kissed her hand in fealty, as his men knelt behind him. Gwilym and some of Criccieth's guards stood behind the princess.

"Welcome to Criccieth, Lord Rhys," said Princess Elizabeth, extending her hands.

"Dolwyddelan Castle has fallen to the English," he said in a clear baritone, and the small crowd that had gathered gave a collective gasp. "We come at your husband's command, Princess Elizabeth, to ensure your safety and join your ranks to defend Criccieth."

She gestured for him to rise. "My husband," she repeated, with a look of relief. "Then he yet lives? Does he send word?"

"He does, your highness, and he bid me deliver this letter into your hands." With that, Rhys handed her a sealed parchment. She inspected the seal and then tore it off with her fingernails, moving to a chair by the window to read it.

Rhys turned to Cat and her mam with a look of eagerness on his face.

"Cat!" he exclaimed. "I mean, gentle ladies." He bowed to Lady Adara first, and then to Cat, and then Margred, greeting them each by name.

Joy and relief swelled in her, and on its heels was fear. He had been her friend when they were children together, when she had visited his castle as Cat from Gwynedd whose father served the Prince of Wales. Their marriage was a good alliance for both their families, since she would own land in the Llyn valley through her mam, to join with his land in the neighbouring realm of Meirionnydd. He was only three years older than her, and they were well matched in interests.

Or were they? Now that she was a seer—and a seer who could not control her sight—would he think the same of her as before? Would he think her strange and unnatural?

As he took a step forward, she took a step back. He hesitated, brushing back a few strands of his dark hair with a look of pure puzzlement on his face.

"Lord Rhys," she said.

"Lady Catrin," he said, bowing to her. Then he stepped back and turned slightly to include her mother in the conversation. "And Lady Adara. We had word that Garth Celyn was attacked in the night. Glad I am to see you here at Criccieth. You are safe?"

"Yes, we were not harmed," Mam told him.

"And the infant, Gwenllian?"

"We fled to bring her to safety," Mam said. "Princess Elizabeth has been most generous."

"The babe is under my protection, and that of my husband, the Prince of Wales," said Princess Elizabeth, barely raising her eyes from the parchment.

"Your hospitality is commendable," Rhys said, bowing to her before turning to Cat again. "I must confess, this is my first visit to the great castle of Criccieth. Would you show me around?"

Cat's tongue was suddenly tied in knots and she turned her eyes to her mam. Mam stepped forward. "We would be pleased to show you," Mam said, as she took Rhys' arm. "Have you heard aught of my husband, Lord Rhys?"

"What is the matter with you?" Margred whispered in Cat's ear. "He's very handsome!"

"What can I say to him?" Cat replied. "What will he think?"

"You mean about your gift?" Margred looked from Cat to Rhys' disappearing back. "Will he not see it as an advantage?"

Cat shrugged. "I cannot tell what he might think."

"Then you should tell him everything and find out. Surely, he will help keep watch on Father Maelgwyn with us. Come, we must at least accompany them." With that Margred followed after Rhys and Adara, leaving Cat to catch up.

At supper, Cat sat on one side of Rhys while Margred sat on the other. Cat could think of little to say, but Margred kept him laughing. Cat glanced sideways at him. He had a clean smell as if he had bathed since the afternoon, and she noticed one of the servants had trimmed his dark hair. Just then, Margred's laughter rang out again, and Rhys joined in. Cat began to resent her friend, and then felt guilty for it. She pushed the cheese-and-leek sausage around on her plate without eating.

"Are you well, Lady Catrin?" she heard a voice ask from her left. "Our hostess has dug deep for these wares, in honour of the Lord Rhys. Does it not please you?" She turned to find the bard Gwilym considering her in some concern. She remembered how he had stared at Margred when they first met. He might understand how she felt better than anyone else at the table.

"It pleases me well, Lord Gwilym," she said, taking a bite of the sausage. "Thank you for asking. How have you been finding your stay at Criccieth?"

Rhys turned to them then, frowning a little as he saw Gwilym leaning toward Cat. "I trust the princess has spared only what she could, with war on our heels," Rhys said. "Lord Gwilym, how long have you been at the castle?" he asked, and soon they were exchanging news, although she noticed both managed to say very little.

After the meal, Gwilym caught her eye, and stood up. "I have a special song this evening," he began, "in honour of Lord Rhys and his people." Gwilym strode to a seat near the fire where he had set his instruments. He picked up the harp, checked its tuning and then began to play.

Rhys smiled as he heard the first notes. "Well known and well loved," he said, loudly enough for Gwilym to hear his approval.

"Another King Arthur tale, no doubt," Margred whispered beside him. "He's very big on those."

"Lord Gwilym is a very well-known poet," Cat began.

"And quite smitten with me," Margred put in.

"I'm sure he is, Lady Margred," Rhys said, agreeably.

"Oh!" Cat tried to frown at her friend but Margred laughed. Soon Cat was laughing too, struggling to hide it behind her hand. Gwilym played another refrain on the harp, letting them quiet down before he began. Then his voice lifted and filled the hall, singing of a woman who fought in a major war to help her people. Cat found herself no longer hearing Margred's chatter but listening intently to the words. Rhys and several other men and women joined in, each voice naturally harmonizing with the other. The woman they sang about had second sight. She carried a message to her people, but they turned away from her. Then the ravens surrounded them, and as the birds descended the woman rose to meet them, changing and dividing until she became three ravens.

"Three ravens," Cat breathed. The song did not say so, but she recalled the banner Rhys' man held when she looked down from her mam's window: the Welsh lion with three dark ravens around it, two above and one below.

"You are thinking of my banner," Rhys said, just as quietly.

"Yes," she said.

"The raven is sacred to us," he said. "Some say King Arthur turned into a raven at his death. It's an old belief in Meirionnydd. Have you heard it?" When Cat shook her head, he continued, "The Lady Modron—you might know her as King Arthur's sister, Morgana—is reviled as Arthur's enemy in many parts of the north. But we see her as the other half of Arthur himself."

"How so?"

"She had knowledge others would not hear, and could not understand, as the poet says. But she led Arthur to his power, and she lent him her power at the end. The power of the raven. So, we carry her symbol: three ravens at the ready, surrounding the heart of Wales."

"This story is important to you."

"It is, my lady." He leaned closer to her, his deep blue eyes holding hers. "Almost as important to me as… well, as you are."

Cat felt her face flush, and she turned from him to listen to the poet. Margred seemed quiet now, and Cat snuck a glance at her to see that she was also watching Gwilym. Rhys was still looking at Cat, and she smiled at him as she turned back to hear the end of the song. She thought through what Rhys had said. He seemed to believe strongly in the legend. Would he believe her if she told him that some legends could come to life?

31

The wind howled across the mountain pass as Hyw made his way toward his home. He was glad of James' extra vest, but the cold bit hard into him as the sun went down. He tried to listen for any sound that men from the castle searched for him or followed him, but he soon gave up trying to hide his tracks. So loud was the wind in his ears that he heard nothing else as he trudged along the path.

Then with a swiftness that caught him completely unawares, something heavy suddenly dropped on him and he fell onto the cold ground. A thick cord net. It covered him wholly, from his head to his feet. He realized he had been captured. The more he struggled, the tighter the net grew. He yelled, but only once. Then he felt a sharp pain on the back of his head, and all went dark.

Llywelyn leapt to consciousness with a start. The darkness around him was absolute. He turned to his other senses—or, rather, the lad's senses. He could feel the warmth and blow of horses where men and beasts huddled together. The smell of men in the closeness of the makeshift hut was not unfamiliar to him. Llywelyn knew the locations of many mountain caches, where gear might be hidden from the elements. Many times in the past he and his men had found shelter from a raging gale in such a place.

For a moment, Llywelyn thought they were returning from a hunt or a diplomatic mission. His kingdom had been hard won and harder to keep. He had waged many campaigns over the years. Some twenty years earlier, he had held more land for Wales than any other Welsh prince. He had traveled often, visiting the far reaches of his homeland to bring the Welsh chieftains into his fold, some willingly and some with persuasion. He had led his men against the English too—many times. His three years with Elinor had been a welcome change.

Then he remembered. A heavy sense of loss poured in on him.

He concentrated on the sounds. Some of the snores around him were familiar enough to bring names to mind, and he smiled at the slight intake of breath that meant Bran slept near. He'd survived. And no wonder. The man slept with one eye open, waking at the slightest sound or movement.

Yet Llywelyn felt a vague sense of unease. Something was wrong, but what? Then he realized he could not sense Hyw. Since they had begun this mad partnership, he had always had a sense of the lad's character. Now he felt—nothing. He wanted to growl and rouse him, but Hyw was not just sleeping. Something else too: Llywelyn could not seem to make a sound.

The lad was his anchor in this new state of existence. If he could wake Hyw, then he had not lost grip on his reason altogether. A line from an old story slipped into his mind: "He found himself in the body of the Other, alone and aware and alive as he had never lived before." The pure voice of the bard in his father's court had sung of a king who traded places for a year with Arawn, king of OtherWorld. In the old stories, OtherWorld or Annwn was always the place of waiting. Certainly, he could do nothing but wait now.

Always these stories had seemed little more than antiques, harmless and beautiful reflections of his ancestors' beliefs. Now they seemed too familiar. Like the king in that story, Llywelyn could feel no physical pain. He was able to take part in training and sports. Yet he was trapped inside the body of a lad forty years younger than he was. And he seemed to spend much of his time waiting, although he wasn't sure for what. He shuddered. Could this be some kind of punishment for not banning the old stories from his court? Or, perhaps, for not believing them?

He was no stranger to the cruelty of fate. For twenty years he had held the balance of power in the Marches—the border lands between Wales and England. The Treaty of Aberconwy robbed him of all but Gwynedd, his ancestral homeland. Even then, he held ambitious men back from trampling the law and language he held dear. Was this to be his reward? He almost laughed.

Then he remembered stories about a magic that could erase the soul from existence. Would that happen to him, if the lad died? What if the force of his soul became lost now? Would all he had done and tried to do be lost with him?

And what of his love for Elinor? Living without her for the last six months of his life had been like descending into the abyss. Dying without her like this was intolerable. More than once, Hyw's laugh or wit or stubbornness had brought him back from darkness of a different sort: a brooding madness that seemed to overpower his spirit. Where was Hyw now? Why could he not feel the lad's presence?

He heard someone stir near them, rustling the straw on the ground.

"Hyw," *someone whispered.*

Could it be Bran's voice? He looked around him but could only see darkness. Then he realized he was trapped in Hyw's unconscious body. If Hyw did not open his eyes, Llywelyn could not either.

"Hyw," *the voice repeated, a bit louder.*

Now he was sure it was Bran who spoke.

"Why does he not stir?" *Bran continued.*

"I did not hit him that hard, sir," *said another voice.* "The English were close by us, following his tracks. He's got a good set of lungs on him. I could not count on the storm to mask the sound."

Llywelyn tried to move or thrash about but he could not get Hyw's body to respond. He tried to call out again. He could hear water in a basin and felt the cool wet cloth as someone wiped Hyw's face.

"He's burning up." *It was Bran's voice again.*

Llywelyn would not allow himself to panic. As he did in preparing for battle, he took stock of the situation. Even when the lad was asleep, he had felt a connection to him. He sensed that Hyw was lost somehow, that they needed to connect again. Perhaps the blow to the head had done some damage? He could think of only one person who could help them now. They must find Gawain. The monk would know what to do.

Llywelyn needed to convince Bran to find Gawain and bring him here. Perhaps I can speak through him, as I did to Dafydd?

He concentrated all his will on making a sound. Finally, Hyw groaned a little. Good, Llywelyn thought. Now to make him ask his father to get Gawain.

"Uhhh—"

"He's trying to say something."

How could he make them understand? He removed all other thoughts from his mind and concentrated on the monk's name.

"Gah—"

It was all he could manage. The effort exhausted him, as if he'd run a mile at his fastest speed. His heart sank as he heard the response from Bran and the others with him.

"Shhh, Hyw. Don't try to speak now."

"What's he saying?"

"I cannot tell. It's the fever talking."

"Bran, I know you don't want to hear it, but what if the boy doesn't recover? Should we fetch the village priest? We could blindfold him and bring him here."

"There's no need for that."

"But the lad—"

"No."

No! The lad must not die. Llywelyn felt powerless, but his warrior's training forced him to think of a plan. He tried to remember the days they had spent with Gawain, and some of the monk's suggestions for communicating with each other. He slowed his breathing and changed the focus of his thoughts to Hyw. Where are you?

Llywelyn fought down through layers of darkness, calling Hyw's name.

Hyw stared through the brackish water. Tendrils of seaweed drifted around him, encasing his ankles and wrists. The light cast dim shadows, like fish swimming in and out. It was peaceful. Hyw floated quietly, not thinking.

He didn't know how long he'd been there. He thought he might have been sleeping, but something had wakened him. Then he saw a figure in front of him: a man. The man was familiar but Hyw couldn't remember his name. He could see the man's mouth moving but couldn't hear any sound. Strange, Hyw thought. He started to turn away, back to the seaweed and shadows. The man reached out then and grabbed Hyw's arms.

Hyw blinked and found himself sitting on the fragrant wild grasses in a field overlooking Garth Celyn. The man sat beside him. He realized it was the prince. For a long time they looked down at the long stone building that Hyw thought of as home.

Flags flapped gaily in the breeze as it blew in off the ocean and whipped up the mountain toward them. Hyw could see the slate roof and the stone watchtower of the longhouse, and almost feel how cool those stones kept the air inside. His fingers twitched to retrace every inch of its rough sandstone windowsills and pillars. In front of the building, the wide, open space of the yard invited men to practice the arts of war. The little church stood guard over the upper courtyard, and around the outside edges he counted the various buildings: brew house, bake house, kitchens, kennels, and stables.

Always there had been people milling about the yard and buildings. Yet today, the yard was silent and still. There were no people in Garth Celyn. No people. A roar like the wind rushed past his ears. He felt pain, as if the hand of a giant had reached into his chest to stop his heart.

"Why did you bring me here?"

This is what it's all about, Hyw. Our home, and the home of our people. This is all it's about. We must stop them. We must protect our people.

Hyw looked at the man then, and knew he was the prince, Llywelyn ap Gruffydd. "You are dead," Hyw said finally. "The Prince of Wales is dead."

Llywelyn stared at him for a moment, somber and thoughtful. *And yet, I am here. You keep me here. I do not begin to comprehend it. Yet I remain.*

Hyw looked back at his silent home. He thought about the soldiers who trained in the yard, and the women inside the hall with their chores, spinning and weaving stories for their spirits along with wool for their clothing. He thought about the men and women who tilled the fertile fields and fished in the sea and hunted on the land where they sat. He saw again the stalks of grass lit like gold in the dawn sun. He breathed in the mist of Aber Falls again and let the spray soak into the pores of his skin. He felt the cry of the hawk vibrate through the sinews of his body. And finally, he nodded.

Without warning, he found himself under the ocean again. He could not breathe. Seaweed tightened around his hands and feet. He began to struggle. With a flash, a metal sword cut through the bracken. Llywelyn hacked the weeds from him, and together they swam for the surface.

32

It was nearly noon when Cat, Margred, and Ifan came back from their field. Ifan carried the weapons for them. It was a small price to pay, but she was sorry to lose them just as she was developing some skill with the throwing knife. Father Maelgwyn watched them from the doorway of the chapel as they made their way into the armoury. Margred waved at him and turned away, almost flouncing past. She must feel the same as Cat about the traitor-priest and his commands.

Ifan set the pile of weapons down and whistled. One of the younger boys came running, eager to be helpful, and Ifan knelt down to explain where to take each set of weapons. Cat was watching him, appreciating his gentleness with the boy, when she heard the shout.

"Ships!" The shout came from the battlements and she whirled, shading her eyes with one hand to look up. "Ships in the harbour!"

Guards began to run for the battlements. The heavy portcullis chains rattled as the gates shut behind them. Ifan stood as if to join the guards but Cat grabbed his arm.

"Get Lord Rhys and bring him to me. Quickly. We will be in the hall."

If he was surprised, he hid it well. He nodded and was gone. Cat and Margred rushed to the castle as Adara came down the stairs looking for them. Ifan and Lord Rhys came through the side doors from the yard, followed by two of his men.

"Go," Mam told Cat. "Tell him on the way. Join us later.

Margred, come with me. We must secure the children and Baby Gwen."

Cat grabbed Rhys's arm and almost pushed him to the doors. "We must not let them fire upon the ships," she hissed.

"What? But they are Irish—"

"There is no time to explain. They are not enemies, and we will need those ships. You must believe me."

He looked at her and then at Ifan who followed them. Ifan's face was impassive.

"Very well, I will try to stop them."

"We must stop them. All our lives depend upon it."

"How do you know?"

"I know," Cat told him. "As Morgana knew, I know."

"She has the message," Ifan finally said. "Will you not hear it?"

Cat glanced at him, and he smiled at her. She thought of the promise she had made her mother that no one else should know, but it was not something she could worry about now. Rhys took her by the shoulders and stared at her face. Ifan's hand went to his sword hilt, but Cat raised her hand to stop him.

"This is—a prophecy?" Rhys looked startled.

"Call it what you will," she said, searching his face. "But we must save those ships."

Rhys let her go then and began to run for the door. Cat followed him, and Ifan kept pace with her.

"Go with him," she told Ifan.

"My duty is your safety, lady," he replied. As they moved from the castle to the courtyard another shout went up, but she could not hear the words. A catapult ground into place. It would not take them long to ready a shot. Could Rhys stop them in time?

They could hear the angry voices from the gatehouse stairs.

"I cannot let you go nearer, lady," Ifan said.

"I must see," she told him. He looked around them and

nodded, leading her up above the battlement to an arrow slit in the stone wall.

"Is that you, Gron?" a voice called from higher up the staircase. The arrow holes were manned, she thought.

"Aye," Ifan answered, putting one finger to his lip. He made way for Cat to look through the bottom end of the long slit. She could see Rhys in the centre of a group of men, arguing with the captain of Criccieth's guard. Some of the men around him looked as ready to fight with Rhys as with the Irish. Rhys's men flanked him, also with drawn swords, facing the Criccieth warriors. Cat realized he was outnumbered by a group of men that did not answer to him.

"You must help him," she whispered to Ifan.

He expelled his breath in what sounded like a sigh, and then motioned for her to stay. "I will return for you." With a glance up the stairs to be sure the men held position above them, he went back down to the courtyard. She heard his voice below, and some of the men made way, but she could not see him.

"We have word that these ships are friends," Ifan told them.

"Word?" the captain scoffed. "From whom?"

"Have you not heard, brother?" Ifan replied, keeping his voice calm. "Lord Rhys has just returned from Prince Dafydd himself."

"So he says," the captain growled.

"I saw the letter he brought with him." It was Ifan's voice again. "It bore the prince's seal."

The commander of the guard was silent a moment, but she could sense a shift among the men. One unclenched his fist, and another put away his sword. Finally, the commander nodded. "My apologies, Lord Rhys, but we have heard much about spies in the fallen castles. We would not count our own among them."

"Your diligence commends you," Rhys replied smoothly. "I would not want to think you would believe without cause. But I can assure you, these ships are a necessity to our princess's safety and to that of the children."

Ifan appeared in the stairs and motioned to Cat. She wanted to stay and make sure the situation was resolved, but his impatience hurried her. They made their way to the yard just as Father Maelgwyn came in sight.

"Lady Cat," he said. "What are you doing in the gatehouse?"

"Why, Father," she began, glancing at Ifan. "Sir Ifan was bringing me to make confession."

"Confession?" He stared at her as if she had not been to chapel already that morning.

"Yes, Father," she continued smoothly. "It is a most urgent matter."

"Now? Can this not wait until mass tomorrow?"

"Oh no, Father, as you yourself will see shortly," she said, "and Sir Ifan also would confess. In fact, his need is more pressing than my own."

"My lady?" She could hear the surprise in Ifan's voice, but he covered it smoothly. "I mean, my lady speaks aright, Father, if you could but spare the time."

"I must freshen up first, Father Maelgwyn, but I will be there with my own confession as soon as Sir Ifan has finished."

The warrior knight looked torn as Cat made to walk across the inner courtyard, but she nodded at him as the priest took his arm. "Come along then, and see you find your words more quickly today." As the two moved into the chapel in the lower tower, Cat ducked out of sight. Rhys finally came out of the stairwell and she stepped up beside him.

"My Lord Rhys, I must explain," she began, startling him. He took her arm and moved her toward the gardens behind the hall.

"We will find a quiet place, and then you must," he told her. "And you can explain how you come to be here, and not in your rooms with the other women."

33

Hyw spluttered and coughed. He tried to open his eyes and the light seared them. A rustle and bump told him someone was nearby.

"He wakes. Steady on, Hyw." The voice was familiar. Hyw's eyelids fluttered again, and his hand came up to shield his face. It was caught in the rough hand of another, familiar one. "Glad I am to see this."

Hyw's eyes flew open. "Da!" he cried, and now both arms seemed to come up of their own volition and around his father's neck. "I thought you were dead!"

"And I you," Bran replied. "If the storm hadn't taken you, I was afraid that knock to the noggin had done you in. You must forgive my oaf for his zeal in bringing you to me."

"Nay, 'twas neither." Hyw would not let go of his da's neck. "You got my messages then?"

"Your messages?" His da looked at him searchingly, and then Hyw saw a strange expression pass over his eyes. "You wrote those messages? How? How did you know the letters to write?"

Hyw opened his mouth to answer when he heard Llywelyn's voice at his ear. *Nay Hyw. Do not tell him about me yet. He is not alone. Let us choose the timing better.* "I—I had help."

"Who? Who was it, Hyw?" Bran stared at him intently, but Hyw could not find a way to answer.

"I cannot say, Da."

"Was it—? Is he—?" Bran left the sentence unfinished.

Hyw had to say something, but he wasn't sure how to form the words to tell his da what had happened. "I saw the words in my mind and wrote them so."

Bran expelled his breath. His voice was so low, Hyw could barely hear him. "I thought perhaps—" Bran tried to smile, but it made him look sad and tired. "I heard the grisly tale of his death, but I could not stop myself from hoping. If we got away, surely he could as well. When I saw the letters under the hiding place—well. I thought it was him."

Bran disengaged Hyw's arms then as gently as possible but kept seated near him. Hyw felt a rush of pity for his da and almost told him everything. He heard Llywelyn's voice again, cautioning him. *A warrior of the new Cymru would not easily understand this thing that happens between us. There will come a time when he will need to know. Let the time be right.*

Bran had already moved to look around them, gesturing to the others. "Welcome my son back to the land of the living."

Hyw noticed the hut fashioned from skins and branches, rising around him. Several other men looked on, one with tears showing at the corners of his eyes.

"Glad I am we did not have to fetch the priest, after all," the man said, pawing at his face with one hand.

Another man moved closer. Hyw noticed the glint of a warrior's gold torque around his neck. "How came you from the English camp in one piece, son of Bran?"

"The English." Hyw tried to rise but fell back against the sheepskin bedding.

"Give it time, Hyw."

"No. We must get to Garth Celyn."

"What says he? Does he speak of the *llys*?" Another familiar voice spoke the Welsh name for the royal court, and Hyw saw a face set like stone, frowning.

"Aeneus!" Hyw again tried to rise. Instead, his former tutor in the arts of war and physical strength came to his bedside and hugged him soundly.

"Glad I am to see you whole again, lad."

"And I you."

"Now I can keep my word to your lady mother. She sent me to seek you, but I was taken on the road. Then came your father to dispatch the *Saeson*. He called me to him to aid in this resistance. Now I am doubly glad I came."

Hyw moved aside then and, gripping Aeneus' shoulders, spoke to him and Bran. "We must make haste. The king will march on all of Dafydd's holdings."

"Is le Clare in charge?"

"He returned to the south. But one of the soldiers showed me the banners for William de Valence. He leads them now. And the king has men from abroad. He pays them silver coins and offers them land if they can take it away from us."

"I know this de Valence." Aeneus nodded at Hyw. "A cousin to the old king, Henry, and fiercely against us."

"What path do they take?"

Hyw turned back to his father. "I am not sure. Criccieth, Dolbadarn, Bere. Those were the names I heard."

Bran looked thoughtful, stroking his moustache. "Roger Le Strange has long sought the castle Criccieth for his own."

"The Marcher lord? Aye, it could well be. They'd be a fool to attack Bere." Aeneus looked grim. "That castle will stand against OtherWorld's hounds. Even Edward Longshanks himself would pose no threat."

"We need more information." Bran straightened and turned to the others. "We must gather everyone we can. Aeneus, when the weather breaks, choose a man, and go in tandem to locate your brother's group. Flush out as many men as you can find—loyal to Cymru all, and willing to fight for Prince Dafydd." Hyw was happy to hear Wales called by its rightful name again: Cymru. "Let the first be a man who hails from Bere."

"Aye, I was born there." The man who teared up earlier had recovered.

Bran and the men conferred. Their voices droned in Hyw's ears. Finally, Bran nodded and turned back to Hyw. "Here, try to regain your strength." He took up an earthen bowl and held it up to Hyw's lips. The broth tasted like nothing Hyw had ever tasted before. Ambrosia, he thought, food of the gods. He remembered the word from the poetry told around the fire in the evenings. That led his mind back to Garth Celyn again. He choked as he remembered his dream.

"There, now. That's enough. Rest, if you can. We must be ready to move out as soon as the wind lets up."

Bran settled a warm sheepskin around his neck, and Hyw closed his eyes.

Hyw was still shaky the next day. He thought he might see Cadarn and Vox with his father, but there were no horses in the camp. Aeneus gruffly told him the English took them all at the ambush. The two men who had shared their hut left at sunup. At noon Bran said they could wait no longer.

Some twenty men broke camp with them. Llywelyn laughed inside him. *It's good to feel the ground beneath our feet again.* Hyw shook his head and looked around him. He had just come from the English camp where cloth and winter gear were plentiful, thanks to their queen and her ladies. He was amazed some of the Welsh warriors were bare-legged in spite of the recent blizzard. Yet none complained or seemed to notice the cold. He heard the rumble of Llywelyn's laugh again. *That is what it means to be Cymry.*

Bran ruffled his hair. "Look at you. You are near as tall as me now. I swear you have grown at least a handspan."

Hyw grinned and ducked his head. He grabbed up some of the camp gear and followed after the men on their way to stash it in a small cavern in the nearby rocks. It wasn't large enough for a man but held the skins and camp tackle easily. The branches that had fortified their hut served a double purpose to hide the stash. Bran handed him a flask to carry.

"Pure mountain water. Keep it full."

Aeneus nodded. "Drink as much as you can. It's from a stream blessed by the Old Ones. Let them protect you from the frost."

Another grunted. "Edward's men share the same stream."

"Aye, but I've heard them curse the very ground as they do," a wizened old warrior grinned. "That should make their ears burn."

"Enough of your blather." A hulk of a warrior carrying a javelin shook his head at the others and turned to Hyw. He heard Llywelyn's voice again: *Listen to this one. See what he hides beneath his cloak.*

Hyw caught sight of a gold torque slung for safekeeping around the man's thick bicep. He had been one of Llywelyn's *teulu*. "Drink you as much water as you can, from any stream you find, boy. May the Old Ones bless you, if they will. If they do not, then bless yourself. You can last three weeks without food if you have to, but no man can stay upright without water. The harsher the weather, the more you must drink to keep the body limber."

Bran sent a man ahead to scout the trail across the mountains. Shortly after they started out, the man returned. The party moved quietly along the ridges and looked down at a knight with two foot soldiers. Englishmen. Without making a sound in the snow, Bran's men dropped them and slit the knight's throat. One soldier lay immobile on the ground, his leg at an unnatural angle.

"I'm from Shrewsbury," said the other soldier quietly, laying down his arms and kneeling. "You know me." Hyw recognized him as a man from Gerald's company who had not gone to the south with le Clare. Bran stared at him, arms across his chest.

"If we know you, then you will not mind aiding our cause."

"I will do all I can, sir."

Aeneus grinned. "Aye, to keep your life intact you will tell us anything."

"Nay, I will tell you truly."

Aeneus leaned closer and set his blade to the man's neck. "See that you do."

Bran nodded. "Where goes the king's army?"

"He split us up, sir. He will attack each castle until he has them all."

"Why? What does he want from us?"

The man thought for a moment. "We had word yesterday that Dolwyddelan Castle has fallen, but Prince Dafydd was not there."

"So, he seeks Dafydd?"

"Aye, my lord. For he believes without a prince, Wales will yield."

Bran pursed his lips at that, but he continued to ask questions. "And how many strong?"

"A thousand men, or more, sir. It cannot go well for you."

Bran looked over at Hyw, who nodded. The man spoke truly about Edward's army, at least. Bran looked back at the soldier, and set his head to one side, as if thinking.

"Why are you pursuing us? It's not as if we haven't all fought this battle many times. Wales wins, then Edward wins. The knights may fight to the death, but we men—we don't often leave each other bleeding in the snow." The man looked embarrassed but said nothing. Bran persisted. "The king's men have never in my recollection crossed the slopes in snow before. Why now? And why are the soldiers stealing our heads from our bodies?"

"The king's bounty," the soldier mumbled. One of the Welsh warriors prodded him with the point of a javelin. "Edward offers a shilling for each Welsh head."

Bran didn't flinch. "And how many have you brought him?"

The man hesitated a fraction of a second, before he began to protest.

Bran turned away. "Leave Edward a message he'll understand." His voice was harsh.

Hyw felt bile in his mouth as he realized his father's intention. "Wait, Da," he said, putting a hand on Bran's arm. "The one with a broken leg cannot join the fighting again. Nor can the other, if he escorts that one home. Is that not enough?"

Bran considered his son for a moment before he spoke. "Good counsel always makes a leader a better man." Then he bent down to the uninjured soldier. "If you are rescued, see that you tell your captains the Welsh showed you mercy. And consider whether that is worth more than a shilling."

34

As they walked in the winter garden, Cat told Rhys as quietly as she could about her visions and the results. She left out some of the details about her brother, concentrating instead on the final three: the ships, the attack on the castle, and Father Maelgwyn at the gates.

For a long moment, Rhys said nothing. Then he asked, "How soon will the remaining two come to pass?"

"I do not know," she said. "It may be that we can prevent them from ever coming to pass. Mam can explain more."

"Your mam knows of your gift?"

"Yes, it is common enough in her family."

"Ah. It is your inheritance?"

"I believe so." She felt miserable now, cold outside and in, and she began to shiver. He noticed her shaking and rubbed her shoulders.

"I forget myself. We tarry too long outside. Come, let us go inside and warm you up."

"Nay, we must be sure Princess Elizabeth has heard of the ships."

He nodded and they turned toward the castle hall. Ifan joined them at the door.

"I am so sorry, Sir Ifan," Cat began.

He raised his eyebrows at her. "I trust my forced confessions were to some benefit," he said.

"More than you know," she said. Rhys looked from one to the

other, but she went through the door Ifan held open for her and up the stairs without another word.

In Princess Elizabeth's solar, Rhys explained his actions in preventing the commander from firing on the ships, without mentioning Cat's role in it. Mam listened with them, but no other ladies were present. The guards Elizabeth had sent to the harbour returned with news. There were three ships in all, with a crew dispatched from one of Meirionnydd's allies in Ireland. They were large merchant vessels with no cargo, but enough room for men and horses. Rhys glanced at Cat but gave nothing away.

"It is Providence," Elizabeth declared, turning to Rhys. "You will know where my Lord Prince would have us meet him, while the English storm Criccieth in search of him?"

Rhys nodded briefly, and it was Cat's turn to be surprised. "He could not trust anyone with the news beforehand, your highness." He looked at the princess, but Cat couldn't help but think the explanation was for her benefit as well. "I was to escort you by land, before anyone could guess our plans. But this will make it easier."

"If we act quickly," she said, and he nodded.

If certain priests do not hear of it, Cat thought. And if there are no more English spies in our midst.

Within a day they were loading horses and chests onto one of the ships.

"Expect your lord, Prince Dafydd, within the week," Elizabeth told the commander and his men. "The other two ships will remain for a time in the harbour, in case they are needed."

The princess had a private audience with the ship's captain, and Cat wondered if she would tell him where they were bound. At least one of her visions had been avoided, but the first one, with the castle under attack and Owain and the others killed, worried her most. She sensed that without preventing both of her other visions, that could still come to pass.

"What of the priest?" Cat asked Rhys, but he shook his head.

"We have no evidence to accuse him," Rhys told her. "I may believe you without question, but I fear it will not sit so with the commander of Elizabeth's guard."

"Or with the princess," Cat added. "Then how can we stop him?"

"We must be diligent, and the answer will present itself." He did not look at her when he said it, and she wondered if he felt as sure as he sounded.

It took several hours to load the ships with food, weapons, trunks of supplies and personal belongings, and finally horses. Rhys was overseeing the horses as Elizabeth, Mam, and the children made their way toward the ship. Gwilym walked near Princess Elizabeth while Ifan accompanied Cat and Margred.

Suddenly she heard a shout and a scuffle, and several hooded men rushed from the gardens toward them. Something glinted in their hands, and Cat realized it was knives. Ifan drew his sword, as did Gwilym and Elizabeth's guards.

"Run for the ships," Ifan shouted. Owain started to draw his sword, but Ifan stopped him. "Take your mam to the ship." He moved between them and the hooded men.

Cat grabbed Enid's arm, jostling Baby Gwen who began to cry. "Come now," she cried, trying to stay calm but almost dragging Enid toward the ships. Owain ran past them with Elizabeth, shielding her from the attackers with his body just as Cat tried to shield Enid. Margred easily passed them both with one sister in her arms and one on her back. Cat did not stop to look back until she had reached the ship, but when she did, she saw Gwilym moving between the men lying on the field. She could not see Ifan. Then she spotted a figure in chain mail lying at an awkward angle on the ground.

And suddenly she was running. Back toward the knot of fallen men and warriors. To Ifan.

"Cat." She heard her mam's voice behind her, but she could not stop. Not until she reached him. Blood pooled around him, and he looked at her dully, as if he didn't know who she was. She knelt near him, ignoring the dark stain on the ground, and took his head into her lap. He tried to raise his hand to her face, and she grasped it.

"Don't move, Ifan," she told him. "You will be all right." She cradled his head with her other hand. She examined him frantically but found nothing until she spotted the deep wound in his thigh. His blood seeped into the ground, covering her skirts, but she did not move even when she heard Rhys's voice behind her. A mist began rising to surround them.

"Call for the priest."

"He is missing, my lord," another soldier said.

"This one over here." Their voices sounded farther away, and Cat realized they must be looking at one of the hooded men. "This is the priest's man, is it not?"

"It is." The voice was that of the commander, gritty and low. "Father Maelgwyn's servant." Now we have him, Cat thought.

"The priest was a spy for the English," Rhys said. "These men must have been set to capture the princess before she could get away."

"That means the English will be close upon us."

Ifan's head moved, and Cat squeezed his hand. "You've done well, Ifan," she said. "We are safe. Rest, now." Ifan's eyes slid away from hers, and he stared up at the sky.

Beyond the mist, she could see him clearly, standing in a field of green grass, the tower of Garth Celyn rising behind him. He raised his arm as if to wave at her. The sun on his chain mail glittered.

She heard the fluttering of wings close overhead and Rhys' surprised voice. "A raven."

But she could not seem to see beyond the glittering that filled her eyes.

35

Hyw blamed the prickly pine branches where they camped for making him toss and turn that night. Every time he closed his eyes, he could see the English army, endless bodies pouring across the field. They seemed as unstoppable as the Nant Peris river flowing over the rocks near their former camp. Finally, Hyw pushed himself up and drew the light blanket closer around him. They had eaten dried meat from their packs, not daring to light a fire lest it lead any headhunting soldiers to them.

He had just stretched his back upright to ease the tension when he heard the owl hoot the first time. It hooted again before he was able to turn toward it. He felt Llywelyn come alert inside him. Responding to the prince's unspoken command, Hyw cast out with his mind. The being he encountered was not feathered, and he pulled back.

Wake your father.

Moving silently in the semi-darkness, Hyw made his way around the men toward his father's form. Bran turned before Hyw got near enough to touch his arm. With a grimace, Bran automatically punched at Hyw, then tried to pull back his arm when he realized who it was. Hyw leapt back in time to avoid the full strength of the blow, but his father's fist felt like iron against his shoulder. He would bear a bruise from the force of it. Bran sat up quickly.

"Hyw," he whispered. "Careful, lad."

Hyw just shook his head and motioned toward the wood.

Together they turned just as the next hooting sounded. Bran rose and took up his javelin. Hyw followed, and his father did not motion him back. Without words or sound, they made their way toward the trees at the far edge of their camp. There they heard the owl-that-was-no-owl hoot again. This time Bran stopped and cupped his hand around his mouth, hooting back in a near-perfect imitation of the night hunter.

Not one man but twenty or more melted out of the shadows toward them. Bran set his javelin point up and at rest, standing with feet firmly planted. Hyw imitated him. The men fanned out behind their leader, who stopped facing Bran. He greeted them formally, giving the names of his ancestors to identify himself. "Dai ap Rhys ap Gruffydd ap Rhys ap Roderic Tewdwr ap Cadell. For Cymru." Although the man's cadence was unfamiliar, Hyw heard the old word for Wales, spoken in their shared mother tongue.

"For Cymru. I am Bran ap Maredudd ap Rhys ap Eineon ap Hywel ap Cadell. Cousin, I bid you welcome." The men relaxed, and the leader came forward to grasp Bran's arm in friendship.

"We go to Dolwyddelan."

Hyw felt Bran's body tighten slightly. Bran considered Dai for a moment, and then shook his head. "It has fallen."

Dai uttered a sound that might have been an oath. "Another fallen. We have come from Carreg Cennen in the south, fallen betimes." Dai spat. "English hounds on our heels. We have left traps and snares on our path to slow them."

"As have we, but as yet we have felt no breath on our necks. The *Saeson* take our heads for shillings."

Dai grunted. "As do le Clare's men." He spat again. "I have lived near two score years, and number my own wife's cousins among our pursuers. This is more than any soul should have to bear. I have seen what I can scarce tell, in the towns and on the roadways where the people flee in vain."

Bran nodded. "You are welcome to our camp. We will share what we have."

Dai placed his hand over his heart, a remnant of Roman times. "As will we."

Bran's small force roused and welcomed the new men. After a brief whispered council, they took up separate sections of the clearing and fell back to a restless sleep until daybreak. As the men shared up what berries and roots they had to break their fast, Dai related some of the horrors of the road. Bran sent Hyw for water, and Hyw was glad to leave them to speak of the unspeakable for a time. He filled skins of water at the nearby creek, reaching out into the woods with his senses. All was quiet.

When he returned, he saw his father sitting with Dai, his shoulders hunched and head down. Llywelyn urged him to Bran's side. *You must rally them, Hyw. Bere must remain our next destination. With both forces combined, they may yet aid in its defence.*

Hyw closed his eyes for a moment. "How can I make him listen to me?"

I know him well, Hyw. You must remind him of the castle. His instinct will do the rest.

Hyw managed to get his father's attention as he handed him a water skin. He took a breath and tried to think of a way to do as Llywelyn had suggested. "Da, what do you know of Bere?"

"Little, Hyw, save what I have seen on trips there in times past. The men say it is still well fortified."

"I know it," Dai looked up at them. "It is held by Cynfrig ap Madog for my lord Rhys ap Cadwgan. I fought with Cynfrig when de Valence attacked some five years past. A good man, with heart. If your forces and mine combine, Bran ap Maredudd, we may yet prove useful in this fight."

"For Cymru." Bran stood, as did Hyw, and they returned to their bedraggled band of warriors.

Bran kept them in the lowlands to make quicker passage through the rugged Eryri Mountains. Hyw had never traveled this route, and he breathed in the fragrant mountain air. *Land of the eagles,* Llywelyn commented inside Hyw's mind. *You'll soon see why.*

They stuck to shadows and treed areas near the Nant Péris River. Bran set the pace over the broken terrain of the river valley. They ran twenty paces, walked twenty in a quick march, ran again, then walked again. The men traveled in silence, stilling their panting breath as much as possible. They could not be sure how long the king's army would tarry to secure each castle, or where they would strike next.

Llywelyn had little more to say, and Hyw was glad of the quiet. During the journey, he'd been too preoccupied to notice any residual effect of his flight through the blizzard and the blow on his head. Now, as his water skin grew lighter and the climb steeper, his head began to ache.

"It's the altitude." One of the men stopped near him during a short break. He was from Dai's group and knew the area. "You'll calm in time. Try this." The man bent forward with his hands on his knees.

Bran stopped near them, concerned. "It is so with several of the men. Yet we must keep up the pace."

"I will try to use the lowlands as much as I can. Water also helps, Hyw." Their guide took a few leaves of an herb from a pouch at his belt and gave a segment to Hyw. "Suck on this." He handed a portion of leaf to the other men as well. Hyw found it bitter at first, but the taste faded.

By mid-morning they passed the small lake at the base of the Yr Wyddfa, the tallest mountain in the range. Their guide's herb had helped ease the pain of his aching head, but Hyw still felt tired and short of breath. He took a moment to stare upward at the mountain. In Welsh its name meant a burial mound, and Hyw shivered.

Bran gestured aside to him, and he was happy to put away his thoughts and search for a likely tree to climb. He would use his gift to check the way ahead. To hide the fact from the other men, Hyw would climb into the tree to act as lookout, then use his gift when he was out of sight.

He steadied himself on a branch and concentrated. It was second nature now to keep the prince safe from any animal minds he might connect to, using the breathing techniques Gawain had shown him. Hyw concentrated, separating a piece of his mind from Llywelyn. He pictured it as stepping in front of the prince, in order to connect another part of himself with a brown eagle. The bird was difficult to control. Hyw sensed it searching for game. He focused his mind on the bird and coasted with it, enjoying a few moments stretched above the trail, staring down at the forest and lake.

The bird rounded in a wide curve. Hyw caught sight of a trail of smoke in the distance. It was far away, a thin streak of grey in the sky, barely enough to make the bird react. Was it a village, or a noble *llys*? Hyw's mind raced to his mam and Cat: were they safe? He forced the bird in that direction until he felt Llywelyn's calming hand on his arm, as if the prince stood behind him, whispering.

We must warn Bran.

Hyw faltered, dropping from the eagle's mind to his own again. In moments, he was standing in front of Bran. Hyw lowered his eyes to hide his feelings.

"I saw smoke, but it is leagues back. More than a campfire, but I could not see—"

Bran laid one hand on Hyw's shoulder and gestured to the men. They rose as one. Their guide took them by a route that avoided the mountain's steeper areas. Even so, the pace was gruelling. They kept it up during the long afternoon, as the sharp rocks stabbed through his foot leathers. His knees and calves ached from the increasing steepness of the path.

The sun was low in the sky before they caught sight of the Desenni valley. It was greening already with spring, and Hyw thought of words he had heard in hymns calling it "the promised land." Bran stopped the group near a brook to refill their water skins and turned to Hyw.

"We may be too far away, but see what you can, before we lose the sun."

Hyw's head pounded now, and he had no strength left to climb a tree. He stood in the shade, staring out across the valley. Far away, towering over the land between them, was the huge summit of Cadair Idris, the giant's chair. He had heard many tales of bards and warriors who spent the night on the mountain, hoping for inspiration, only to discover madness within themselves instead.

As his mind followed his eyeline, he felt rather than saw a small running creature. He made contact: it was a fox. The dappled shadows under the creature's feet told Hyw the path was in shadow, far away on the giant's mountain. He sniffed the air, and felt relief along with the fox when he sensed game. No human scent marred the path. The fox looked up, and through its eyes he saw Bere. Hyw brought himself back to his vantage point reluctantly.

"There are no troops near the castle," he told Bran. He wanted to share some of the experience with his father but wasn't sure how to talk about it. Instead, he pointed toward the path where he had seen the fox. "That way."

"The lad speaks truth." Their warrior-guide from Dai's group stepped near them when Hyw pointed. The man looked surprised. "But to see it from here, he must have sharp eyes. Have you been this way before, lad?"

"Once, but he has a strong memory." Bran responded before Hyw had a chance to speak. The man looked skeptical. Bran handed Hyw his water skin. "Here, son, fill up for both of us."

As Hyw turned away to go to the stream, he saw his father turn back towards their guide. Bran would find some way to explain it. Hyw was tired, he realized, and using his gift taxed him further. He bent to the brook and splashed water over his face and hair, wishing he could explain to his father about Llywelyn.

Give it time, lad. Hyw closed his eyes to find the prince waiting. *You are a strong help to your father. All is not lost while there is yet a Prince in Wales. That castle is a stronghouse, built by my grandfather. If we have any chance to make a stand against Edward, it will be there.*

Fear can keep us alive when all else fails, Hyw. But never give in to despair. These English come and go, but we remain. Our mountains will surely shelter us, until Edward finds someone else to hate.

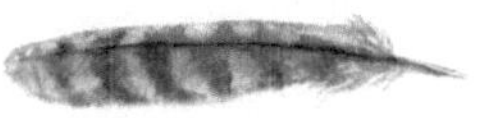

36

Cat accepted her mam's assistance from the ship she could not remember boarding. Margred and the girls stood near, and Owain stood at the ready near his mam. Cat wondered where Ifan was, before she remembered he was no longer with them. Her limbs felt heavy, but her head felt feather-light, as if the breeze off the sea could blow her away. She looked around for Rhys and spotted him checking the saddles. He motioned to his men to bring horses toward the group and moved toward the princess. When Cat saw him look at her, she waved. His nod didn't reflect the easy camaraderie of the past few days at Criccieth but had a kind of deference. Her heart seemed to clench inside her chest.

Then the horses were between them. She helped her mam and Enid mount. When she gained the saddle, Rhys and his warriors were already forging ahead down the road with Princess Elizabeth and Owain between them. Why did he not look back?

She found herself inside the great hall of a castle, with no memory of having seen the castle from the path.

"The horse," Cat said. It was the last thing she remembered.

"Cynfrig has seen to it," Mam told her, with a questioning look. Cat did not know who Cynfrig was.

A man with a kind face and greying moustache took her hand. "You are welcome in this place, Morrigan," he said, moving closer to her to speak quietly. "My Lord Rhys has told me of your feat at Criccieth. It has been many years since one of your kind graced our halls." She stared at him blankly, and he nodded and patted her hand. "You must rest. I will have our Katie show you to your room."

"You are most kind," Cat said. What had he called her? Morrigan? No, she had to correct him. "My name is Catrin. Cat."

It seemed a moment later when she woke, surrounded by quilted softness. She felt the smoothness of the white fabric with her hand.

"It is silk," said her mam's voice, and Cat looked up into her mother's face.

"Where are we?"

Mam looked concerned for a moment and felt Cat's forehead with the inside of her wrist. "We're at Bere. Don't you remember? You must have been more ill than we realized."

She had a sudden flash of the kind man's face and the word "morrigan." It was familiar to her somehow. What did it mean? She felt afraid, but she didn't know what she feared. She felt an urgency to rise and do—something, but she didn't know what. She pushed the quilt off and her mam rose as well.

"How long have we been here?"

"Two days already." Mam caught Cat as she swayed. "Take it slowly. You've barely eaten the last few days, and you've been asleep since yesterday, but I didn't want to wake you. How do you feel now?"

Cat tested herself and looked around. "Better. I think." She dressed with Mam's help and got caught up on the news. Prince Dafydd had come with his eldest son, and she had apparently missed Princess Elizabeth's tearful reunion with her family. Margred and the girls were well, and Owain was practicing in the yard with the other boys.

"And Rhys?" she asked.

"He was here to check on you earlier this morning," her mam told her, smiling.

"He was?" Everything must be fine then.

"And why would he not?" Mam went on. "Nothing stands between you now." When Cat didn't respond, Mam stopped fussing with her hair and looked at her. "Does it?"

"No, of course not," Cat said. But why did she still feel her stomach clench?

In the next few days, Cat found no opportunity to talk with Rhys, even at dinner. They sat in family groups according to the Welsh custom, rather than at long tables as they had at Criccieth. As lord of Meirionnydd, Rhys was expected to serve the others, and Cynfrig and his family helped. Cat sat with her mam, Enid and the baby, and the two remaining Garth Celyn warriors. It was the second evening meal before Rhys happened to serve them.

Mam smiled at him as he and two of the kitchen girls placed the main course of eel and venison in front of them. "It smells tasty," she told him. "Cat should be helping you, Rhys. Then you will know each other's ways before you become hosts together."

"Nay, Lady Adara, I would rather she conserve her health for—what she may need it for," he said, shaking his head. He did not try to catch Cat's eye but turned a general smile upon them all as he backed away toward another table. Cat's smile froze on her face. Was he avoiding her? She watched him joking easily with Margred and Owain as he served them.

"He has great concern for you, Cat," Mam said.

"Perhaps he has too much concern for me, Mam," Cat said.

"Perhaps you should tell him so, then," Mam replied.

Something inside Cat snapped. Enough of this, she thought. If he had reason to avoid her, then he must tell her so to her face. "Perhaps I should do more than that," she said, throwing down her cloth napkin and following Rhys into the kitchens.

"Since I am to be lady of this castle one day, I should offer you assistance in your tasks," she said, moving to the tables.

Rhys stopped what he was doing and raised his eyebrows in surprise. "Nay, Cat—I mean, Lady Catrin," he said, glancing at the Cook and her staff, who had come over to watch. "Your duties are far more onerous than this small task, and I would not have you tax your—strengths."

"I have vast reserves of strength," she said, arranging sliced meats on a plate. "I will admit, what happened as we left Criccieth cast a pall on my spirits, but I did very little. Others did a great deal, while I was merely a witness."

"I beg your pardon, Lady Cat, but I know well what you did," he said, stopping her with one hand. "And I know very well that you were taxed by it."

"I was weary from the voyage, but I am rested now," she told him.

"Perhaps you would take a breath of fresh air with me so we might talk about this together," he said, glancing around them. "Just we two."

She looked around to see a gaggle of kitchen staff staring at them. Cynfrig's grey moustache twitched, and his wife held her hands over her mouth. Cat could not tell if they were upset or—could they be—laughing?

"Aye, Rhys, lad," Cynfrig said, his voice strained. "Take the lady for a quick look at the garden under the moon. We can easily finish what you have begun here."

"Can we indeed?" his wife said, turning away quickly in a fit of what must have been coughing. Then she turned back again. "Aye, I suppose we can."

Cat let Rhys lead her from the kitchen and into the yard at the side of the castle. "Here we grow the fine roots and herbs you tasted in tonight's meal," he said, loudly enough for the others to hear. As the door shut behind them, he turned on her. "What do you mean, you were weary from the voyage? You sat and stared at the water without speaking for most of the trip."

"I did?" she asked.

"You did. And I should know, for I tried every way I could to coax a response from you."

"Every way?"

He pulled her to him. "Nay, not every way. Not with your mam hovering so close." He kissed her. She felt the softness of his lips against her mouth, and the sudden cold when he pulled himself away.

"I beg your pardon," he said. "I did not mean to—I know what you are, Cat. And I know this cannot be, now. You are meant for a higher calling."

"What do you mean?" she said.

"You are the morrigan," he said. "A woman of power. My da had such a woman in our home before the last great war, and I know well what it means."

"What? What is it that you think—"

"I know. I know you cannot marry as other women, or birth children. You must keep your power pure."

"Fie," she said, stopping him. "I know not how you do things in Meirionnydd, but we have no such prohibitions at Garth Celyn. My own mam is a woman of power, yet she loves my da just as other women love their husbands. And she gave birth to my brother and to me, and two other children who died in infancy, just as other women's children die."

Rhys shook his head. "Nay, I am sure it cannot be so."

"It is so," Cat said. "I am here, standing in front of you, to prove it."

Rhys cupped her face in his hands. "Yet I saw you release the young warrior's soul."

"I—I don't know what I did," she said. "I saw Sir Ifan standing in the field outside our home, and I knew he was free."

"You released him," Rhys said. "How can we live as normal man and wife, when you have the power to—the power of the raven?" They stood looking at each other for a moment, and then Rhys turned and disappeared down the dark garden path.

37

Hyw could see the men grow more hesitant the closer they got to Bere. The lush lowlands were surrounded by stark, rugged mountains. As they climbed the craggy slopes to a rock-cut road that stretched ahead of them, the setting sun threw long shadows over the ground. The low howl of the wind through the craggy mountain face made his hair stand on end.

"Gwyn ap Nudd," one of the men murmured. Hyw recalled the name of the legendary king of the Tylwyth Teg. The wind made him think of Nudd's huge baying hounds, said to have the power to drag a man's soul to the OtherWorld. Another warrior behind them on the path made the hooting call of an owl. When the superstitious one jerked around, fearful and wide-eyed, several laughed. Llywelyn laughed with them.

Take heart Hyw. The English soldiers know that legend, as do their masters. Our stories may shelter us here better than the rocks of the castle itself.

The guide took his sword and held it hilt-up toward the valley. He moved it from side to side, using the sun's rays to send a signal toward the castle walls. He repeated the motion three times.

Hyw was standing near him in a thicket. Before long, they

spotted an answering flash that seemed to come from within the mountainside. He squinted until he found the spot where he saw the fox. That rocky slope must hide the great castle.

Their guide nodded down at him. "They know we come, and we are friends. But in these times, you cannot be too careful. We will still need the password, you will see." He pointed to his own temple. "Lucky we are that this is still in one piece."

Hyw could sense Llywelyn's hope rising within him, and almost feel the prince's laugh rumble inside his own chest. *Wait until you see it, Hyw. The English king can try his tricks, but he cannot win here. Would that my grandfather could know his stronghold would stand for us, e'en today.*

An eerie mist dampened the air around them as Hyw and the others followed their warrior-guide over wooden bridges that crossed several deep, rock-cut ditches and culverts. He stopped and spoke quietly into the mist, as if giving a pre-ordained password. A man holding a javelin rose up in front of them, appearing from between the rocks as if by magic. He waved them on, and stood aside as they gained the high-walled path.

When they rounded the last curve, Hyw felt dwarfed by the cavernous stoneworks that led into the castle yard. He felt as if the rock cliffs and slanted pathway pushed them into the inner courtyard. Then the dusk grew rosy in a blaze of setting sun, and colour flooded the castle courtyard as people bustled into view.

Hyw saw townsfolk, women and children, and warriors of all ages. Several wore the traditional Gwynedd warrior garb of a red tunic over chain mail, and Hyw realized some of Llywelyn's army manned the castle. He spotted the dark hair and eyes of a familiar face, and caught a glimpse of the red sash that marked the warrior's privilege. It was Emrys, Hyw's childhood friend, still as wiry and thin as he had been at Garth Celyn.

Before he could wave, a grizzled warrior came toward them. He was short and muscular, but his air of confidence and authority marked him as a leader. His arms opened wide to them. "Welcome to our fortress, Bere." He hugged each man to him in turn. The man's deep-set eyes were troubled but kind. "I am Cynfrig ap Madog, constable here for many years, and glad to be named your host. We ration against the future, but such as we have, we will share with you. Gather you all inside, and dine with us, and with our own Prince of Wales."

Hyw was confused for a moment, wondering how Cynfrig had guessed his secret. He closed his eyes almost out of habit, and saw Llywelyn laughing at him. *Nay Hyw, he speaks of Dafydd. My brother is here. We've made it.*

Too tired to question further, Hyw allowed himself to be led to the castle by his father. They entered together, handing over weapons and washing their feet in keeping with the old customs. Hyw saw Bran run a hand along his chin, rough from quick shaving with his knife on the road. His father would look forward to proper morning rituals again.

Then they were pushed along in the stream of men. Hyw saw several of their companions greet friends, hugging wives and other relations who had taken refuge in the castle. Women sitting in other groupings rose hesitantly to their feet and peered at their group. Some of these women fell still and looked down at their own hands. Even as he felt sorrow for them, he hoped Dai or the others would bring them news of their loved ones to ease their minds.

He didn't realize until the last minute that the constable had led his father toward Dafydd's own family group. Hyw hesitated, but Dafydd made no outcry against him. If Llywelyn's brother remembered him from Dolwyddelan, the only sign he gave was a slight pause as he brought a leg of mutton to his lips, and the narrowing of his ice-blue eyes. Bran made to pay homage to Dafydd, but he waved them off graciously. "We will speak later. See to your wife and children, Bran."

Then Hyw thought of it no more, for at the next table he heard a cry. Up sprang his mother, Adara. The blush of joy on her face lit the room, just as the setting sun had lit the rocks outside. She flew into Bran's arms. Then she turned to Hyw. He was aware of his mother's smallness and hugged her to him.

"Hyw, you're a man in truth now. How tall you have grown."

He grinned down at her. As she turned back to Bran again, he spotted his sister Cat coming toward them. He hugged her to him. "Glad I am to see you, Cat."

"And I you."

She seemed older too, and a little sadder, he thought. He wondered how bedraggled he must look, and how different he would be after a few months away. She hesitated a moment longer, and then turned to greet her da.

Adara turned back to Hyw then. "You are too thin, the both of you," she scolded. "And here we sit, warm and well fed." She broke down then. Bran crushed her to him for a long moment.

"I feared you were dead," Adara mumbled into his chest.

"And how could that be?" Bran's voice was husky. "No one could ever capture this black bird but you, milady."

Hyw thought he glimpsed a shine in his da's eyes as well. Then he noticed Enid the nursemaid beside them, waiting for her turn, and he hugged her with one arm as he kept the other around his sister.

"Where is Gwenllian?" he asked.

"She is asleep, the dear child," Enid said. She knelt and rocked a bassinet beside her. He could only see blankets from where he stood. He didn't want to disturb the babe, but Llywelyn urged him closer. *You see how she has grown anon. Would I could hold her but a moment, though I would not disturb her.* Hyw reached down and stroked the babe's sleeping head, to let Llywelyn feel the softness of her hair and skin.

Finally, Bran set Adara back on her own feet. Cynfrig and his wife brought out more plates of food for all the men, including Hyw's company. Hyw noticed cheese and mutton, along with jugs of white milk. Still blushing, his mam pushed him to a spot near her and added to their plates from her own, beckoning Bran to her other side.

Hyw paused, noticing the easy familiarity of the family gatherings in the Welsh hall. What a contrast from the formal gathering of the English, where the king and his favourites sat on a raised dais apart from rows of knights. Here there were no tablecloths, elaborate fixtures, or cleverly-dressed dishes, but plain food, well-made and nourishing. He tried to imagine King Edward and his wife serving their guests before they ate themselves, as Welsh custom required. He could not imagine the English, even the kindly Shrewsbury, without servants and squires to serve them.

Then he noticed his father's hand shaking as he picked up some of the food. Bran turned to Adara and pulled her to him again, as they sat at the table.

Cat took the opportunity to scramble around them and sit beside her brother. He turned to her, showing her the braided threads he still wore around his wrist. "See, here is the band you made for me long ago. Do you remember?"

"You've added another in with it, here."

He thought of James, and the day they had parted. It seemed much longer than weeks ago. "Aye, that was done with the help of a good friend. It keeps yours in good repair. Always you were in my heart, Cat. This wristband kept you near."

"It did indeed, Hyw," she said, and the look on her face made him wonder if she would say more. Instead, she passed a few morsels of meat from her plate to his. "After supper I would show you around this gloomy place. The wolves howl always here. Have you heard them?"

"It's not wolves, child," Enid put in, "but the wind, howling through the rock face of the mountain."

"I heard it as we came." Hyw gripped her hand. "That very wind and its mournful howl may yet keep us safe from harm." He made up a story for her then, of a sleeping giant knocking the English soldiers off the mountain with his snoring. Before he was finished, Gwladys and young Owain and some of the other children gathered near as well. Lord Rhys also came near, although he remained standing apart.

"Good it is to have you and Da with us again, Hyw," said Cat, laughing at the end of Hyw's story.

"Aye, he has all the warrior's graces." Adara's shining eyes reminded him of all the bardic tales he had heard played and sung by warriors in Garth Celyn, where a man was expected to be as adept at musical arts as he was at combat.

Sure enough, before they had finished the meal, a warrior bard began to sing and play the harp. Cat whispered to remind him this was Gwilym ap Einion, and he pretended to remember the bard from his time at Garth Celyn. Five years ago, he realized. A beautiful young woman came to sit near Cat, and she introduced her as Margred, daughter of Prince Dafydd. People gradually cleared their places, feeding their leftovers to the hunting dogs that shared their space.

Bran rose to follow Dafydd, gesturing to Dai and a handful of other men. They would confer about the war, and Hyw longed to be with them. Above the heads of other groupings, he spotted Emrys watching the men as well. Their eyes met, and Hyw grinned, as did Emrys. He was seated with Dai's group, so he must be related to the warriors they had met on the trail.

Then Adara called his attention back to her. He found himself giving his mother an account of the battle at Dolwyddelan. He hesitated to recount their capture of soldiers, finishing, "We found Dai and his companions as we made our way here."

Adara took his hand gently. "Glad I am you have come back to us at last." He welcomed her touch and the chance to feel Cat warm against his side. Dafydd had been at Dolwyddelan. Had his mam and Cat been with him there?

"Yet how did you come to be here, Mam?"

"We were attacked at Garth Celyn, and we fled to Criccieth, where Princess Elizabeth gave us her protection. Then Lord Rhys came to us, with messages from the prince to commend us to his protection at Bere."

"Does Garth Celyn still stand?"

"I know not. We thought it best to bring the babe to her uncle. After that, we did not plan."

Hyw could see the sense of bringing Gwenllian to Dafydd. *Aye,* agreed Llywelyn inside him. *My brother would never harm the child. Gwenllian is safest with him.* Then Llywelyn asked the question that Hyw realized he should have asked. *Does your mother carry Gwenllian's seal?* Hyw turned to Adara and asked quietly if she still kept the baby's royal seal. She nodded, glancing at Dafydd's table with a gesture that told Hyw to keep this to himself.

So, things were not as cozy as they seemed, perhaps. He looked over at Llywelyn's brother, who was seated with his wife and seven children. Surely Dafydd would have been safe with Edward too, Hyw thought, since they had been friends.

Edward must hate him worst of all now, Llywelyn said softly in his ear, *because in the end, my brother could not kill me. And now he is Wales. You must help him if you can, Hyw, just as you have helped me.*

38

After supper Cat took Hyw by the hand. "Come and let me show you the castle, before it becomes too dark to see," she said, leading him up the stairwell.

"I will," said Hyw. "And who better to tour it with, since you will be its lady one day."

"I suppose I will," she said. Cat had been so dazed by Ifan's death when she first arrived that she had not really taken it in: this would have been her home for the past two years, had her marriage to Rhys gone forward. If she had married, she would not have been there when the unthinkable happened. Cat had a sudden flash of Princess Elinor, smiling and holding out her hand in welcome. Of Elinor's peals of laughter, bringing smiles to the room full of ladies—especially after she understood enough Welsh to catch the clever puns in the songs Cat sang to her. And how quickly the princess learned the harmonies for those songs. She was quick in all her movements, and in her expressions of love for anything and everything from her new country, including Cat. The princess passed along her beautiful gowns to Cat, and fussed over Cat's red hair, bidding her own maid to brush it.

Elinor was twenty when she married Prince Llywelyn, and three years later she came of child for the first time. Cat could still see her mam's pale face when she examined the princess. Mam had squared her shoulders and forced a smile as she made the happy announcement. But Cat had clearly seen what came before, and she was old enough to know what it might mean. When the princess asked, of course, Cat had to stay. Cat would not let herself regret her decision now.

Besides, this castle might still be hers, one day. She looked back across the battlement, smiling at the guard who waved as he walked his rounds. Bere was built oblong, almost triangular, to fit its rocky plateau. One D-shaped tower overlooked the castle well.

"One of the warriors told me these waters grant the powers of sharp sight and strength," Cat told her brother. "He and many others drink from it before leaving the castle."

"So, I will as well," Hyw said. "Quite a bit grander than home."

He meant their longhouse at Garth Celyn. She felt a small pang, thinking of the guard who had helped them escape. How many had died there before the English took it? For a moment they stood together, saying nothing. Cat had to force herself to remember why she'd taken him away from the others.

"There is something else, Hyw," she began. "I'm not sure how to explain. When you left, I had no gift to speak of."

"That never mattered—"

"I know, but after you left, I found I was able to connect with you."

"Connect?" he repeated. "What do you mean?"

She explained her visions, and how she had known he was alive, and about the treachery of the priest Maelgwyn. "After a time, I realized it happened whenever I looked into some kind of liquid, whether a cup of ale at supper or a raindrop. Now I think I see you because of this bracelet I tied to your wrist." She took his hand and pressed the rough wool.

"You used a lock of your own hair," he said.

"Perhaps that is why. Yet something puzzles me. More than once I saw you with the prince, almost as if you were one."

He went pale and took both of her hands. "You saw?"

"What does it mean, Hyw?"

He told her what had happened on the hillside at Builth, about his bonding with Llywelyn and their travels together.

Cat took an involuntary step back in shock. "Our former

prince? And he is with you now?" She searched his face but saw no trace of the former Prince of Wales.

Hyw nodded.

"What does he tell you?"

"Many things," he said. "He knows more of this castle than we do." Hyw pointed to the large D-shaped tower guarding the path at the southern end of the courtyard. "Those walls are ten feet thick. If the English manage to get in, this is where the people should run."

She huffed, almost like a laugh. "How does it work? Does he speak to you?"

"He speaks inside my head, and I can see him if I close my eyes. Come. He says he will show us the castle."

They made their way to the rectangular keep. They took turns peeking out the archer's portals, careful not to disturb the bows and arrows set ready in case of attack.

"These rooms along here—we can rest or sleep here during an attack," Hyw told her as they continued.

"Or tend the injured," she added, and then wished she hadn't said it aloud.

Inside it was strangely quiet, as if the building stood in its own enchanted world that no threat could penetrate. Everyone was still listening to the bards. Cat touched the decorated tiles on the walls, stained glass windows, and lovely stone carvings of armed soldiers and heraldic battles as Hyw reported what Llywelyn told him.

"This is truly the most magnificent castle I have ever seen," Cat breathed. She could not imagine herself as its lady, any more than she could see herself as Rhys's wife.

"Prince Llywelyn says he brought back many of these items from the Crusades," Hyw said, still appearing to listen to his inner voice. "The same place he learned how to speak foreign languages and the strategies of chess."

Wall hangings of legendary battles flickered in the torch light as if they were alive. On one wall, the great King Henry crowned their own Llywelyn as Prince of Wales, only a few decades earlier. Cat wondered what the prince must feel when he saw it now, but she did not ask Hyw.

"Look there," she said instead, pointing to another wall where

Gruffydd ap Rhys of Deheubarth led his troops into the field to win his glorious victory over the English at Crug Mawr. As Cat looked away, Hyw asked her what was wrong, and she told him of her concerns about Rhys and the legend that had caused a rift between them.

Hyw was silent for several minutes when she had finished. "Your gift is of immense value to us now, Cat," he finally said. "Are you sure there is no truth in what Rhys says? This is Meirionnydd's legend, after all."

"There cannot be." Cat was adamant. "If there was, how could you or I be here to discuss it today? Besides, I only have the second sight. In the legends, the morrigan—whatever she is—also transforms into a raven and commands the spirits of the dead. I'm fairly certain I won't be sprouting black feathers anytime soon."

Hyw shot Cat a look. "Yet I have been able to communicate with many animals, including ravens and hawks."

She considered that. "Have you ever shifted shape with any other creature?"

He did not answer right away. "I have been able to allow Prince Llywelyn to—I'm not sure how to explain it. He sometimes appears through me." He told her of the fox at Dolwyddelan, and how it seemed that he had become a fox himself.

Cat nodded, thinking of her vision. "Then do you think you will someday be able to shift into another form?"

Hyw shrugged. "Our uncle mentioned it."

Cat told him of Aylwen, their ancestor, who had told her they had stronger gifts because they were born in a time of need. Hyw said nothing, but she could tell by his face he was considering it. She thought about the morrigan legend again, and what it might mean for them.

It had grown dark while they explored, and in one torch-lit hall they could hear men's angry voices echoing off the castle walls. Cat recalled Da and the other men who had left with Prince Dafydd. Hyw shook his head and she led the way back to the main hall, where they rejoined Mam and the others to listen to bardic songs. Then Owain came to collect Hyw, since he was to share a room with the other boys inside the castle. In spite of her pleasure at seeing her brother again, Cat found herself tired enough to willingly bid him goodnight as she and Margred went up the stairs to their room.

The next morning, Cat poured wash water into her basin. She saw her reflection in the water—

—and she found herself in the castle courtyard. The crash and whump of swords on armour deafened her as arrows sped by. The people ran, screaming. She saw Prince Dafydd surrounded by English knights.

"You we take, and your wife and children, since the king demands they not be harmed," said a large armoured man she somehow knew to be de Valence. "But these others—" He turned with a savage grin and nodded at his sergeant. The man took his sword and moved to Da and Mam. Enid cowered behind them, holding Baby Gwen. The armoured man raised his sword to her mam as another soldier held her da back.

"No," roared Lord Rhys, running at the man in fury. His hands were tied but raised toward de Valence's throat. Suddenly he stopped, his eyes searching. He found Cat's face, and half-smiled. She didn't see the arrow in his back until he fell.

"No!" She reached toward him—

—and she was staring at her own reflection in the basin, a look of horror on her face. "No," she cried aloud.

"What is it?" Margred grabbed her.

"It cannot be," Cat said, staring at her. Margred glanced at her sisters and drew Cat from the room.

"Calm yourself, Cat," she said. "We will find your mam. She will know what it means."

Adara listened to the girls and turned to Cat. "Your da and the others have been arguing about what to do. The prince wants to wage war, but Rhys and some of the others want to avoid it as long as possible. Your vision may be more important than you know. I will make sure your da hears of it, Cat."

"What can we do?"

"I have a thought," she said. "It would seem the simplest way would be for Dafydd and Rhys to part company. Each will get his wish, and your vision will be averted. Rest easy now. If this can be prevented, we will find a way."

39

The next morning, Hyw woke at dawn.

"Psst." He looked up at a young man's face, and realized it was Emrys. His friend's dark eyes snapped with laughter. He gestured for Hyw to follow. Hyw got up, careful not to disturb those still sleeping. In the bustle of the castle courtyard, he waved at his father just as Bran sat down for his turn at the ritual shaving. Other men had already begun their daily exercise, and Hyw and Emrys ran to join them.

"You can train with us today if you wish it." Emrys strapped on his sash. "I serve here with my uncle and his men."

"Who is your uncle?"

The other boys giggled but Emrys shushed them with a gesture. "*Ust.* He is not to know, is he? My uncle is Cynfrig, constable of this castle. But now my cousin Dai has returned, perhaps I may serve with him."

Hyw agreed to train with them, and the boys began with basic agility much the same as Aeneus would at Garth Celyn. Then Emrys turned to him. "I know you spent some time with the English. My da says you cannot defeat an enemy unless you learn his strengths and weaknesses. We would know all we could of those *Saeson*. What can you show us of their moves?"

Hyw thought for a moment, recalling his early days in training before he went to foster in England. "They are different and not so different. They prize their steel and armour well. It is difficult to show you how they train without the—the pieces in the yard."

"What do you mean?"

Hyw tried as best he could to describe the quintain, and the wooden dummies set up for practice with sword and mace. Emrys nodded. "Aye, we have something like it," he said. Hyw thought back to the days before he had gone to foster at Shrewsbury, to contrast the English use of wooden swords to the moves Aeneus taught during field practice. Emrys stood and grabbed two javelin sticks, handing one to Hyw. "Show me how those English move, if you can."

Hyw hesitated, until he heard Llywelyn's voice. *Nay, lad, show him. May it help save his life.*

They skirmished, using the sticks as swords. Hyw struck lightly so as not to break any bones before the battle to come. Emrys, however, knew no such qualms, and played hard. Hyw took a bruise on his arm, and at the next skirmish he also played harder, turning back to front and striking low with the sword at Emrys's feet.

Emrys went down. Around him the others had taken up similar positions with each other to learn what Hyw could show them. As Emrys tumbled, all stopped and went quiet. Hyw wondered for a moment if he had managed to set this group against him so soon, and if he would have a new enemy as powerful as the bully Robert had been in Shrewsbury's court.

But Emrys was not Robert. At sixteen, he wore the sash proudly. He had already seen battle and what the English could do. He got up and dusted himself off. "That was a clever move. Show me again."

By the next day, most of the boys had taken just such a tumble. Then, working as a team, Emrys and Hyw worked out a way to predict the move and leap up over the stick before it struck.

Cynfrig watched them work the move through. He called them over to show some of the other men. Hyw and Emrys fought hard with sticks, and each of them in turn made and sidestepped the blow Hyw had shown them. The men nodded, and soon groups of them began to use the new skill as they had seen the boys do it.

"You have used your time well, I see." Hyw turned to see Bran beside him. His da's eyes twinkled as he stroked his newly-trimmed moustache, and Hyw felt a rush of pride. "It is well that the young teach the old, in this war. Many things have changed, and we must change with them. While there is life, there is yet hope." He tousled Hyw's hair. "Now, before your head swells out of your hair altogether, show me this move."

Llywelyn laughed inside Hyw as they prepared to skirmish with Bran. *Now you know why he is my captain.*

Hyw descended for supper in the castle hall along with his father. Emrys nodded toward him, as did several of the other boys as they made their way to their family table. Hyw saw someone sitting with them in a white robe.

"Uncle Gawain!" he exclaimed, and caught his uncle up in a huge hug.

Now we will hear the news, Llywelyn remarked, and Hyw did not need to close his eyes to know the look of grim anticipation on the former prince's face.

His uncle's normally calm face was clouded throughout the meal, and even Cat's harmonizing with Gwilym on his favourite hymn as the evening progressed did little to brighten his spirits. As Gwilym moved into a longer ballad, Aeneus moved to their table touching Gawain's shoulder as he sat with them. Adara finally leaned closer to Gawain.

"What news, brother?" she began in a low voice. "I know you spoke with Prince Dafydd this afternoon. I bid you, speak freely. What news of home?"

For a moment Gawain was silent, his eyes focused on his hands as if searching for direction there. Finally, he looked up at her and spoke. "I was sent hither by my lord Abbot," he began. "The abbey at Aberconwy is no more. The English king claims our allegiance, and bids us move to Maenan. My lord can do aught but agree, save send me to warn the prince his ancestral lands are gone."

"Gone," Bran said. "How can it be?"

Gawain was silent, folding his hands in his lap. Bran made a noise of disbelief. Hyw heard Llywelyn make almost the same sound.

His mother made no sound, but when he glanced toward her, he saw tears streaming down her face.

"It cannot," Aeneus cried. Adara quickly shushed him, and he went on in a lower voice. "What of the garrison at Garth Celyn, or the men of Ynys Môn?"

"The *Saeson* were merciless," Gawain said, his voice scraping against Hyw's ears. "They ran down all that moved for their shillings. Some of the women and children managed to reach the abbey. I cannot say they were the lucky ones."

4⊙

The next few days went by in a whirlwind. Cat could find no reason to smile, after Gawain's news. Her uncle kept mainly to the chapel except for the evening meal, where he was often silent. She had asked him about the morrigan legends, and he said he would make the time to tell her as soon as he could.

The girls and women were able to exercise freely at Bere at the north end of the courtyard while the warriors practiced farther south. The Bere warriors trained any men and women willing to fight for Cymru. Cat sought out Bronwen, a childhood friend, and bade her join her and Margred. The girls spoke little but worked hard at the exercises set for them by one of the Bere warriors.

"Yours were much tougher," Cat whispered to Margred. Bronwen was impressed when she heard how the girls had formed their own practice at Criccieth.

Cat found throwing knives helped ease her mind. Once when she was lining up the target, Cat felt as if someone was watching her. She let the knife fly and felt the satisfying thwack as it hit squarely in the centre. She turned in time to see Rhys watching her, but in the next heartbeat he looked away. Margred saw as well and put an arm around her as they returned to the back of the line for their next turn.

"Is aught amiss between you and Lord Rhys?"

Cat straightened her shoulders. "Lord Rhys is reconsidering the wisdom of our union."

Mam, who had joined them, heard and pulled Cat out of the line. "Why would he do so? Was it because of Sir Ifan? Did you have feelings for him?"

"Nay, Mam," Cat began, surprised. "Not like that." Cat poured out the story then, telling her mam about the legend and the morrigan who once served Rhys' family.

"I knew her," Mam said. "You know your gift is no problem for you as a woman, don't you?" When Cat said nothing, Mam gave her another quick hug. "You have concerns."

"The legend connects Arthur and Morgana," Cat said. "It speaks of a combination of brother and sister."

"Ah, I see," her mam said. "You think perhaps you and Hyw make two sides of the morrigan." Mam thought for a moment and shook her head. "I also have gifted sisters and brothers who married happily. Your Uncle Gawain took his vows as a monk, but the rest have families."

"But how can I answer Rhys' concerns?"

"Only he can do that," Mam said.

By then it was time for them to join Princess Elizabeth and help her greet some of the townsfolk and farmers who were arriving daily to seek refuge within the castle walls, as word of the English moved down the valleys. Cat and Margred listened for news of Criccieth and those left to defend the castle. Although Margred never said so, Cat suspected she worried for the butcher's son Drem more than her other friends from the town.

Elizabeth, Mam, and the girls welcomed and cared for the women and children, especially those who were pregnant or in need. Most afternoons, Hyw went with Emrys and the other boys to help the Welsh survivors carry their wares, along with oats and other grains in barrels, back to the castle longhouse to feed the people pouring in from surrounding areas. Twice Cat joined the people working in the fields, pounding meat into strips and smoking it for storage and travel, or helping in the cookhouses. Bronwen sometimes came with her and saved a few choice tidbits for Emrys.

"See how she loves me, poor thing," Emrys joked, but Cat could sense the longing in both of them and thought of Rhys.

Cat was on the way to the north exercise yard when Rhys stopped her. After greeting Margred and Bronwen, he asked her to walk with him a moment. His tunic sleeves were rolled up and the glisten on his skin showed he had already been practicing, so he must have been watching for them. She waved at the other girls and fell into step beside him.

He drew a dull grey cloth from beneath the cloak he had slung across one shoulder. She unrolled it to find a set of three lightweight throwing knives. The hilts were burnished with one small green jewel set cleverly in scrollwork, and they fit her hand.

"Be careful," he cautioned her. "They are deadly sharp."

She held one up to the sun and saw it was tapered to a fine thin edge. He touched the leather sheath that held them.

"This sheath belonged to the morrigan," he said. "She was my teacher for a time, and I saw her use her knife more than once. It fixes to your leg with the point inside your boot and seemed to work very well for her."

She was tempted to give it back to him then, but he placed his hand on hers as if he knew what she was thinking. "Please, Cat. If we are separated, I must know that you are safe. I have worried about your safety since Gawain gave us his news. When I saw you in the practice yard, I decided to have them made especially for you. I believe the sheath is special and will help keep you safe."

His eyes blazed into hers and made her think of the kiss in the night garden. Perhaps he remembered also, because he dropped her hands and moved past her to the castle without a backward glance.

41

It was well past noon when Hyw heard a warrior's shout. "They're coming."

He ran with the others to climb the low retaining wall around Bere and strained to see through the light mist that always seem to hang over the lush valleys. He still thought of it as the giant's breath, and felt a shiver run down the length of his back.

Emrys jumped onto the stone wall and mimed a fight. "With some of those moves you taught us, Hyw, they should be more afraid of us than of the giant who breathes down on them now."

All the boys laughed then, the tension broken. Hyw marvelled at the way Emrys could lift their spirits and make them feel bold, even in their fear. *A leader in training*, Llywelyn said softly in his ear. *If he survives what comes, Emrys would be a good candidate for the prince's teulu.* It was a high compliment.

"Look there!" The boys looked where Emrys pointed and spied a flash of metal. With a flush of excitement and fear, they leaned against the wall. Each tried to be the first to see, and the first to point out English troops to his friends. It began with the metallic flash from moment to moment through the thick trees and undergrowth. Then soldiers began to march into the lowlands and muster in groups. Hyw had no need of his gift to track them. By mid-day, the lowlands were full of English banners.

The clouds that ringed the mountain darkened and belched out rain, covering the plain with a muddy mixture that showed the outline of the army clearly. The king's white camouflage coats were useless against the giant of Cadair Idris. Hyw looked for the siege engines the English had taken with them to Dolwyddelan, but in truth they had no need of them. He heard the men guess at the size of de Valence's troops. Camped beyond arrow range, fanning out in the valley, their numbers filled every inch of the Desenni plain.

"There can be nothing left now, of food or game," one man said.

"That will be the end of them, then." Emrys laughed. "How can they remain, without food?"

The man guffawed. "*Saeson.*" He spat. "What do you think they eat?"

"Rat?"

"Sheep droppings." He made a rude gesture and some of the other men huffed a grim laugh at his antics.

"Best stay out of their sights, Gron." Aeneus folded his arms across his chest and stared down at the field of enemy soldiers, unsmiling. "Names will not help you. Hunger makes fierce foes. Who knows what it will do to them? I hear they have mercenaries among them."

"Them I have seen. They dig under the ground and eat the bugs."

Gron launched into a bawdy song, and Aeneus turned away in disgust.

About mid-afternoon, a roar caught Hyw's attention as a younger knight with a banner no one recognized led a hundred or so cavalry and soldiers out of the ranks. After a short flourish, they swarmed toward the Welsh castle. Hyw remembered Edward's words as they left Rhuddlan: any man, no matter his rank, could keep the land he won in this battle. Hyw had seen the hard greed in their eyes as they prepared for the journey.

At first his stomach tightened with what Llywelyn called battle-fear. Hyw felt his hands form fists without waiting for direction from his thoughts. Then, as they reached the base of the rocky cliff, the horses faltered. Emrys laughed a little too loudly. "You see! The fools. They need mountain goats to get up that cliff."

"Or good Welsh ponies," Hyw added.

"Look closer." Emrys cast him a sideways look. Hyw did and noted the line of Welsh breeding in the sturdy horses, realizing his friend suspected their countrymen of aiding the English. "Devil take them."

As Emrys spoke the words, several horses slid backwards. One shaggy mount lost its footing on the rocks and went over backwards, falling onto its rider. Hyw gasped as the horse reached out to him in panic. Vox and Cadarn flashed into his mind, but they were gone. He quickly built around his mind a battlement like the one surrounding Y-Bere. Yet he felt as much as saw the horse flounder, struggling on top of the still form of the armoured man. Had Emrys summoned the horned god from OtherWorld? Hyw made the sign of the cross and felt Emrys make a similar sign beside him. He turned in time to see his expression of horror reflected on Emrys' face.

A few of the horses and some foot soldiers pulled themselves up the cliffs nearer the castle. A volley of arrows from the battlements rained down. The shafts seemed to hit their mark with extra force. It was as if they were drawn by the pull of the valley floor, Hyw thought, or perhaps blown by the giant's breath. Then he noticed half-formed pieces of the siege engines on the valley floor and wondered if these were the same ones the English had dragged to Dolwyddelan. They were of little use on the giant's mountain.

Horses and men fell and pulled back. Twice more the English knight and his followers charged, until he fell back for the final time. Hyw could see the knight bowed over, with an arrow protruding from his shoulder.

Later that day, under a flag of truce, some men on foot dragged off the fallen soldiers. Hyw wondered if they would recover or be buried by their countrymen, never to see their own lands again. He heard a rumble on Cadair Idris, and his skin prickled as he imagined the giant laughing at the tiny men on the field below.

The next day, a rider came to the castle, holding a white flag. Bran went down the path to speak with him, along with two other men from Cynfrig's garrison. Aeneus and the other warriors kept watch from the battlement, javelins at the ready. After a long conversation, the knight rode off again and the men returned to hold conference with Dafydd.

Rumours were rife through the castle most of the afternoon, as the people waited to hear news of the rider. When Bran and the others finally came out of the meeting room, it was as if the whole castle went quiet. All eyes turned to them.

Dafydd came out last and looked around him. "The English know we cannot be beaten. They sent their Lancelot to tell us so." He laughed.

Several others laughed, and then began to cheer. Dafydd let them enjoy the moment. When they had quieted, he went on. "It is right that you know the truth. They will not back off this time. They will starve us out."

"Let them try." Aeneus stood defiantly at the back of the room. "They will need to return to their fields this season, same as us."

Yet too many are not English soldiers, Llywelyn reminded Hyw, in his inner ear. *These men will not drop their swords to take up a plough unless they are given a piece of Welsh land to tend.*

"Nay, their mercenaries will stay," Dafydd echoed the comment. "They can wait us out and trap us here in this stone castle like sheep." Around the room, people shifted. Like many, Hyw had always preferred his *llys* to these stone castles, built to defend Cymru against the English. A handful had already begun complaining they would prefer mountain caves to the cold stone under their feet. Gwilym the warrior poet looked thoughtful.

Dafydd went on. "Lestrange wants me. He offers you the chance to depart this castle in peace, with eighty English pounds divided among you."

A murmur buzzed around the room like a wasp swarm. Lestrange's offer meant surrender.

Aeneus' voice boomed across the room. "They would have our prince? Never!" The room erupted around him. Hyw was dismayed to hear angry voices, as if some disagreed with Aeneus.

No, Hyw heard Llywelyn inside him. *Dafydd must not surrender. He is Wales now. They must not let him.*

Hyw closed his eyes and found Llywelyn seated in front of a chessboard. This was no time to think of games, Hyw thought, but Llywelyn gestured at it. *How many ways can players jump positions?*

Hyw let out an exasperated breath and looked at the board. The white nearly overwhelmed the few remaining black pieces, leaving Llywelyn's king guarded by only one knight. "The knight can jump other players. And I know of a move called castling where the king moves two squares, and the rook jumps across to take its place."

And we have a squire who could take the prince's place, Llywelyn suggested, removing the black king from the board. *Dafydd could flee with the children, while the English remain behind, thinking to capture their prize.*

Hyw recalled taking the knight's position during their training. It was only weeks ago but seemed longer. "My great-grandfather had the ability to change form, but my skills fall far short of that. And I would not put you in jeopardy."

It is too late to fear for me, Hyw. But did not Gawain say that your gift was stronger than any he had seen? Whatsoever you can do to save Wales, you must now do. I charge you to attempt it, no matter the cost to either of us.

Hyw stared at Llywelyn until Dafydd's voice roared out across the hall, startling him into opening his eyes.

"Think you well on this offer, friends. It may be the only way to save you."

42

As the English settled in around them, Cat helped her mam and Cynfrig's family ration their dwindling stores of food. The castle was full of people from the surrounding towns and farms. The food they had gathered, which had seemed so plentiful as they had carried it into the castle, scarcely seemed enough to last the week.

As she served a platter to their family table the next morning, Hyw touched her hand. "I need your help," he said. "This morning, if you can make time."

When she had finished her chores, they made their way to the battlements. Unlike the previous day, Aeneus kept only a few warriors for the watch, strategically placed along the wall walk.

"Most will spend this day in the practice yard, readying for the signal," Aeneus told them. "After yesterday, the *Saeson* will need to rethink their strategy. But their archers will be watching. Mind you both return to the keep."

"The girls will be with Elizabeth and Mam this morning," Cat whispered. Hyw nodded, and they made their way to the room Cat shared with Margred and her sisters. Hyw looked uncomfortable in the small bedroom, as if he had grown too large for it already. He stood at the window, opening the heavy wooden shutter just enough to see out without being seen. She moved impatiently and finally he began.

"Do you remember when you asked me if I had ever used my

gift to become another creature? Would it surprise you to know I've tried?"

She shrugged. "I know the stories of our great-grandfather as well as you. Why shouldn't you see if your gift is as strong as his?"

"Nay, I care not if it is." He went on without waiting for her to answer, tapping his temple lightly. "My liege has asked me to do this thing. For his sake I have tried, but I cannot."

"It will come," she told him. "You know our gifts grow with time and use. What you cannot do now, you may do in a year, or ten years."

"I need to do it now," he said. "In a year or ten, Prince Dafydd may be a prisoner or worse. I must help him now."

"What, would you change into Dafydd himself and go to prison for him? Or into a horse to spirit him away?"

"Nay, but something of smaller size and more spirit," he quipped, drawing her to the window and pointing at a pair of hawks flying together against the grey clouds, just above the castle battlements.

"I don't understand." Cat stared at the hawks, wondering if Hyw meant to fly Dafydd away like Pegasus, the winged horse from the old songs.

"I cannot tell you all just yet, Cat, but if I can manage this thing, I will make sense of it, I promise you."

"But how can I be of service in this task?"

"These powers you have, as a morrigan," he said, "can you call them to you?"

"I do not know. Water plays a part, as you know." She thought of Ifan's death again, and the infinite sadness that enveloped her then. Her powers had seemed such a part of her that she did not fully realize what she had done until Rhys told her what he had seen. Could she call that power to her? Did she want to feel it, ever again?

"And if I did," she said aloud, "how could it help you accomplish your task?"

He shook his head. The look of discouragement on his face made her want to say something more to reassure him.

"Our uncle Gawain may have wisdom to offer," she suggested. "You said he helped you connect with our prince when you began this strange journey. He has some knowledge of the morrigan, but he has not had the time to tell me. We should ask him for his thoughts on all."

"Lucky we are that he remained with us," Hyw said, brightening a little. "Let us find him."

"He has been at chapel every day since he arrived."

"Then let us give him a reason to come outside and enjoy this fine April weather with us," Hyw said, and they started down the stairs together.

Cat asked a passing servant and discovered her uncle was in the chapel. She persuaded Hyw not to disturb the monk's prayers, especially with the English so near. They sat watching, and Hyw gave an audible sigh when Gawain finally crossed himself and stood.

At their insistence, he walked with them through the courtyard as they began to explain. Gawain stopped at the castle well to talk with a group of worried farmers and people from neighbouring towns, reassuring them as he filled his flask. She made an impatient gesture.

"The warriors say this water helps them," he told her. "Perhaps it will be useful to bolster their spirits in the coming days."

She felt guilty for her impatience but joined her brother in pressing Gawain to walk with them again. They made their way to the chapel garden, where Gawain began plucking weeds. Hyw half-sat on the rock fence nearby as he explained their situation. Unable to be still, Cat stood in front of them, shifting from her heels to her toes.

"So can the morrigan—if that's truly what I am—help him?" she finally broke in.

Gawain straightened up and brushed the dirt from his hands. "In truth I know but little of the morrigan," he said. "The Irish have many stories, and some have crossed the sea to us. Like the crow or the raven, she was thought to follow warriors during wartime. Many believed she could predict which side would win and might be convinced to tell them. Yet if a warrior saw her washing his clothes, he believed he would die in the battle. Did she then cause it, or did his own thinking defeat him?" Gawain shrugged. "But Geoffrey of Monmouth writes of a Morgana le Fay, who had healing powers to protect the land and its sovereign."

Cat did her best to listen, but she didn't want a history lesson. She needed to know how it might connect to her, here and now. She could not help but interrupt. "Your pardon, uncle, but much of this I knew. And yet—if I am a morrigan, it would be right for me to protect Prince Dafydd."

Gawain shrugged. "Or Prince Llywelyn, who resides in Hyw. In the old stories, Morgana placed King Arthur into an enchanted sleep to help him to Avalon."

"But I cannot see Llywelyn, let alone give him a sleep tonic."

Hyw sat upright. "Wait," he said. "Some have seen the prince, even so." He scrambled to his feet in front of her and stood for a moment with his eyes closed. Something shifted in the air around him, and for a moment she saw the tall form of the Prince of Wales shimmer into view. "My lady." She heard a deep voice almost in echo with Hyw's and knew it must be Llywelyn's. Then all disappeared again, and Hyw stood where he had before.

Cat gasped. "How did you do that?"

"It is difficult," Hyw admitted. "I must—step aside of myself, as it were, and allow Llywelyn to speak through me. It first happened the day we met the fox of Dolwyddelan, but I cannot manage it for long."

"I wonder," Gawain said, leading them to a spot further away, where they would be sheltered from sight by trees. "You have the gift of foretelling, Cat. I recall that some with this gift may connect their minds with the minds of others close to them. Can you reach Hyw?" Gawain asked. "Can you see the prince as Hyw does, from inside his mind?"

Cat closed her eyes and tried to reach out to her brother, but she saw nothing but blackness. She shook her head.

"There is much talk in the morrigan myths of the powers of three," he said. "And we are three, together. We can but try."

Gawain put two fingers on her forehead in the space above her eyes, and two on Hyw's in the same spot. He nodded, and all three of them closed their eyes. For several minutes, nothing happened. Gawain removed his fingers. He bid her cup her hands in front of her and poured water into them from his flask. Water from her own well.

"Breathe slowly, Cat, as you do when you sing. From here." Gawain laid a hand on her belly, and when he felt her breathing change, moved his fingers to their foreheads again and closed his eyes. She stared at the water in her cupped hands, and heard him begin to sing softly, a song she had never heard before, of the mountains and the watchers.

After a few moments, she began to see a dark form as if through a mist. "I see him!"

Gawain nodded, and dropped his hands. "You each astound me. I have heard stories from our grandfather of powers like yours, but never thought I would see it in my lifetime."

Cat told him of her ancestor vision then, and he looked thoughtful.

"So, might we coax your powers to help both princes, then," he said.

Cat and Hyw tried again, and Gawain gradually moved away from them, as he had when he first taught Llywelyn and Hyw to connect with each other. Cupping the water again, Cat welcomed the mist rising around her. She pushed into and through it to reach the image of the prince.

"My lord," she said, her voice echoing as if they stood in a cave. She looked around her, and they were in a sort of cave. The mist was steam rising from an underground stream that began to trickle in the background. Hyw lounged against a rock at the edge and grinned at her.

In this world, what we think becomes real, the prince said with a smile, and she heard his voice as clearly as she had the day the messenger came to Garth Celyn.

Gawain tested them, taking her aside and asking her to describe the prince's clothing or some other detail to check with Hyw. After the third such grilling, Cat threw her hands in the air in frustration. Droplets of water sprinkled her face and hair.

"What could my seeing Llywelyn possibly have to do with

helping Hyw change into a hawk?"

Gawain turned and looked out at Cadair Idris. "It is something my grandfather once said. Hyw carries a heavy burden in holding the prince's soul to this world. I believe what is stopping him from testing his true powers to their limits is the very thing that allows him to accomplish it." He turned to Hyw then. "When you make contact with the animal, you are doing no more or less than you have always done. But to make the final shift, that will require you to let go of this world and find the body of the animal inside yourself. Yet Llywelyn anchors you here. You must find a way to trust that the prince will follow and accept the shift to a new form."

Hyw looked miserable. "I have sworn fealty."

Cat finally understood what Gawain wanted from her. "So, you want me to help Hyw separate himself from the prince."

Gawain nodded.

"But how am I to do that?"

"I know not, Cat," Gawain said. "I believe it must be something that comes from you, and honestly."

They got no further that morning, and Cat found herself returning to the problem throughout the day.

"What's wrong?" Margred finally asked her, as they prepared for bed. Cat shook her head and said nothing, unwilling to discuss her brother with her friend any more than she already had.

After a night of tossing and turning, Cat stood at the window, opening the shutters the barest crack to look out at the sky. She thought about how Hyw might look outlined by the low clouds, if their plan worked. Her brother had always been more comfortable on the hills than inside a castle, or even in the *llys* at Garth Celyn. Cat stared out for a moment, and then turned and almost ran from the room.

She caught Hyw and Gawain as they entered the hall. "Now is our best hope," she told them, almost dragging them with her to the battlement. It was early, and only the lookouts manned the wall.

They found a sheltered spot and crouched on the courtyard side of the walk, out of sight of both English and Welsh. Hyw sat cross-legged in front of her.

Cat held out her hands for water from Gawain's flask. As soon as she focused on it, she found the connection to her brother's mind. She rode the mist deeper, until she could see the prince. He stood with his arms folded.

"My liege," she began, "you said anything we think here becomes real. Please, allow me to serve you." When he nodded, she hesitated a moment and then held out her hand. A goblet appeared in it. She swirled the dark liquid inside it. It smelled of honey and strawberries, of the mist of *Rhaeadr Fawr* and the gold of sunlight on the hillside near their home. She mixed the waters of her own well into it. Finally, she offered it to the prince with a shy curtsey.

"Will you take this drink, your highness, and allow it to help you sleep?"

Sorcery, young Cat, he said, his voice rising in a question.

She hesitated again. Was this not what she feared most, when her gift first came to her that day in church? That it might be a thing of sorcery and darkness? So long ago that seemed now, although it was only a few short months. She thought of Owain, whose life she saved, and of all the tall Irish ships of their allies. And she thought again of Ifan, waving to her from the green fields of Garth Celyn. The voice of her ancestor, Aylwen, echoed in her mind. *We have gained these gifts to help our people.* All the while she stared into the eyes of the shade she had known as the last Prince of Wales.

"It is the gift of a true heart and will not harm you," she told him, certain of the truth in her words. He reached out his hand and took the goblet.

When the prince closed his eyes, Cat opened hers. Gawain was crouching beside her as before, and she realized he had been singing the same song, almost under his breath. Her brother sat with his eyes closed a moment longer, and then opened them to look directly into hers. Gawain let his hands drop, but his voice grew louder. For a few moments, nothing happened.

Then Hyw cast his eyes upward. A hawk soared near them, adding its cry to Gawain's song. Hyw made a sound like a moan and began to shimmer as he had when the prince appeared earlier. She heard a grinding noise and a loud crackle. Hyw cried out, and his arms stretched to the side, his bones stretching and thinning. He drew his legs up and they seemed to shrink into his body. His clothing fell around him. Red and brown feathers sprouted from his flesh. He cried out, and the cry became the shriek of the hawk. She and Gawain ducked at the wind from flapping wings all around them. They looked up in time to see a great hawk, wings outstretched, where Hyw had been. For a moment he faltered, as if hanging on a current of wind. And then he flew.

43

Hyw, exhausted after his ordeal, relied on his sister and uncle to help him to their family table. Cat scrounged what she could for him from the platters as the voices droned around them. People were abuzz throughout the supper hour. Listening to the talk, Hyw realized the English had sent another rider with another offer: less money this time. And it would be less every day, this one said, until the Welsh gave in or were starved out of Bere.

The meal was barely finished when Dafydd called for Bran again. Hyw settled beside Cat and their mam, listening to the bards amid the people's continued murmuring. From time to time an angry voice broke out, yelling defiance against the English or arguing with a neighbour. Hyw heard no clear agreement among the people, and it left him uneasy. The bards switched to warrior tales, and soon many of the defiant voices chimed in with harmonies that shook the walls of the castle hall.

In spite of his tortured muscles, Hyw found himself strangely alert. He noticed Cat often looked toward her betrothed, Lord Rhys, but the two said little to each other. Cat had seemed happy with the match, but he wondered how the war affected their relationship. Hyw reached out with his arm, almost surprised to see it rather than a feathered wing, and placed it around her shoulders.

The torches had barely been trimmed when Bran returned and gestured for Hyw to come with him. Hyw stood, finding his feet carefully, and almost stumbled as he made his way to his father.

"Are you ill, Hyw?" Bran asked.

Hyw shook his head. "Tired only, Da," he said, his voice almost a squawk.

His father looked at him a moment longer, and then nodded. "The prince would have a word with you," he said in a low voice. "Answer well, and truthfully. I will be outside, if you need me. You have only to call."

Bran led the way into a room at the end of the hall. *Tywysog* Dafydd was seated at a round oak table. His fingers were spread and touching, and he nodded. With that, Bran turned and left the room, shutting the door behind him.

Hyw stared into a pair of ice-blue eyes. Dafydd remained seated at the table, with his fingers steepled in front of his mouth. His hair and moustache shone auburn in the firelight. The muscles bulged on his biceps, and his shoulders were square under his light tunic.

Dafydd gestured to the seat. Hyw stumbled again and nearly fell into one of the large chairs that ringed the table, making everyone equal in importance. This was where Llywelyn had met with the other Welsh princes. Hyw thought of Arthur, the great king, who was known to have listened well to all of his counsellors. Every Welshman was raised to believe in those traditions of equality for everyone, equal service and equal reward, and it was ingrained in the laws they fought so hard to defend. Hyw had a right to sit in that chair, but at that moment he felt small and insignificant.

Never think it, lad, he heard inside his mind. *You have brought us this far. You will see this through. You are the one Dafydd must listen to now, and you are the only one who can make sure he does.*

Hyw nodded and sat up straighter. Dafydd shifted forward and held Hyw's eyes. Hyw stared back, willing himself not to flinch. Dafydd raised his eyebrows as he reached forward to take a sip from his goblet of spiced ale.

"Your father tells me you lived with the English at his bidding. I thank you for your service. It seems you have used your time there well, if Cynfrig's tales of the practice yard can be believed."

"I've done my best to share what I've learned."

Dafydd smiled a little and filled a goblet for Hyw. Hyw swirled the liquid. It was spiced Welsh ale. He could smell the flavour of it. He had been allowed a mug on saints' days and holidays and knew it would taste sweet and strong. He took a sip.

"Are you comfortable with us?" Dafydd asked.

"Yes. Very much."

"Really? It surprises me, since you've been with the English for so long."

"I returned to my father in October."

"Yet you were not with him in January, when last we met."

Hyw looked at him steadily. *There's little point denying it,* he heard Llywelyn advise in his mind. "Your words are true. I was with Lord Shrewsbury."

"And Edward." The words were soft, but the ice in Prince Dafydd's blue eyes seemed to harden, if that were possible. "How was the king?"

In his mind, Hyw heard Llywelyn expel his breath, almost in a hiss. *Even now, he cares about the English king. Even now.* Hyw remembered hearing Dafydd had been friends with Edward since childhood and had spent time there during the attempted English invasion earlier in Llywelyn's rule. He thought about his own complicated relationship with James and wondered how he would feel in Dafydd's place. He also remembered Dafydd's face on the chess piece Llywelyn had shown him many months ago: the face of a pawn. Looking at that same face now, Hyw could see the shadows under his eyes.

"In truth, I saw the king but little," Hyw said. "He seemed hearty, and his wife appeared to dote on him."

"That is well. And was she beautiful?"

Hyw thought for a moment, not sure how to answer truthfully. "The king seemed to think her so." He told Dafydd as best he could about the English king's expression as he looked upon his wife, and how his voice seemed to soften when he addressed her.

Dafydd threw back his head and laughed. "A passable answer indeed, Hyw. You have certainly seen them together."

Good work, lad. He was testing you, and he found you sound. Hyw felt a small flush of pride at Llywelyn's words.

But in the next breath, Dafydd's hand smacked the table with a loud thud. His face changed, and his laughter became a snarl. "Yet somehow you brought the spirit of my brother to me at Dolwyddelan. And before I could wring the truth from him, you vanished. Now I need to know everything you know."

Hyw started at the sound and fury of Dafydd's words. Through it, he could also hear Llywelyn's calming voice like a whisper in his inner ear. *Steady. It's just bluster. Let him wind down.*

Hyw took a deep breath. "You are my prince, and I will tell you anything you wish to know." Hyw answered Dafydd's questions about the English army, its strengths and weaknesses, its horses and weapons. Finally, Dafydd's shoulders slumped forward.

"You were with him—when he died?" Dafydd meant his brother Llywelyn, Hyw realized, and nodded. "I hope he did not suffer overmuch."

Hyw did not know what to say and was glad to hear Llywelyn's voice in his inner ear again. *Tell him I did not.* By the catch in Llywelyn's voice, he could tell the prince was moved. As Hyw repeated Llywelyn's words, Dafydd looked into his eyes. "It was much less than Edward had planned for him."

"Could—could you not send to the king again and bid him stop this slaughter?"

"On the grounds of our childhood friendship? Or because my wife Elizabeth was his choice for me? Or because I had tried many times to kill my own brother for him?" Dafydd laughed bitterly. "Even if he would listen to me, I would not. I am Wales now, and I will take my duty as it falls. Believe me, it would do no good. Edward has a taste for our blood now. I know him well. He is the predator, and Wales is his prey."

His manner and tone changed, and he seemed more desperate than cynical as he continued. "I must take back Garth Celyn, and I will take as many men as I can into the mountains with me to plan our attack. Has my brother anything more to tell me?"

Hyw closed his eyes and found Llywelyn stroking his moustache. *Tell him he must not let them catch him, or his children. Or mine.* Hyw nodded and opened his eyes again, to find Dafydd staring into them. The living prince's eyes were bright and intense, and he held Hyw like the glint of the knife holds the deer. As he had at Dolwyddelan and on the battlements with Cat and Gawain, Hyw felt the pressure of Llywelyn's hand on his shoulder. He closed his eyes and shifted slightly to let Llywelyn through. When he opened his eyes again, Dafydd drew back, startled.

"He is—within you?"

Hyw came back into himself, and Llywelyn receded once more. Dafydd continued to stare at Hyw strangely. "These are the old ways," he said. "You and your family, I have heard you all bear such gifts?"

Hyw felt a moment of fear, wondering if he had revealed too much. "Be assured, Prince Dafydd, your brother means you no harm. Nor do I."

Dafydd sat back and held Hyw's eyes again. "I should fear you, Hyw ap Bran, and the spirit you carry. Men follow me, but I can see in their eyes that they long for my brother. It would be an easy thing for you to help him regain his hold over them."

Hyw tried to protest and heard Llywelyn's voice echo inside him. Dafydd held up his hand. "This war is very different than any other battle with the English we have fought. Edward's hatred leads him, and I am not sure we will survive it. Though your claim might seem fantastical to some, it would be welcome to many. You could divide the people just at the time they need to rally most."

"My lord—" Hyw began. Then Dafydd laughed again.

"I have watched you carefully in the days you have been with us. You hide my brother from the others and make no attempt to reveal your gift. That leads me to think you can be trusted, and my brother knew it. I could not be there to protect him on the field when he was ambushed. Indeed, I am sure he would not believe that I would protect him. Yet I am glad to know his spirit continues. I would ask you this: continue to hide my brother, for his protection. Swear it."

"I swear."

"Tell my brother this: I will take his baby with my family into the mountains, with the majority of our warriors, to move in force to retake Garth Celyn. To cover our escape, Lord Rhys and his steward Cynfrig will stretch the talks with the English. They will hold off the English as long as they can, and then relinquish this castle and accompany their people to safety at the abbey.

He leaned toward Hyw before he continued. "Hyw ap Bran. Your father and mother are set to accompany me, along with my family. Because you carry my brother's spirit in the world, I would offer you the choice. You may remain with Lord Rhys, and earn your place with Cynfrig and his men. Those who continue with us to Garth Celyn will tread the more difficult path. We will find our way blocked by soldiers. We face hardship and endurance and most likely death before we retake Garth Celyn. Think well the path you choose."

Hyw closed his eyes for a moment, and Llywelyn nodded at him. *My brother speaks true, Hyw, and I will do no less. You have made a place here, and these are men to trust your back to. You must make your own decision.*

Hyw opened his eyes and stared for a moment without seeing either of them. "I may have a plan that will best serve you and help all of us."

44

Cat stood in front of Rhys' door and raised her eyebrows at the warrior who stood guard. His face did not change as he reached back and pushed open the wooden door for her.

Rhys was alone, washing up for supper. He turned as she entered. His chest and arms were bare and glistening with water. She had seen him so during practice in the yard, but in the closeness of his rooms she felt herself flush. His muscles were tightly corded and his shoulders were broad, tapering down to a flat stomach. He smiled slightly as he picked up a cloth to wipe the water away.

"I am sorry to disturb you." She found it difficult to begin.

"Your thoughts are always welcome, my lady," he said, reaching for his shirt.

"If that is true, then you will agree with what I have to say," she said, seizing the opening. "You believe me to be a morrigan, and you seem to have experience with someone of my nature. I would know more about how to use my gift, in order to offer what help I can in this war."

"Surely your mother advises you."

"She has some understanding of it from family lore, but you and Cynfrig have worked with a morrigan. You know more about the nature of my gift." She warmed to her topic now, sure of her decision.

"Cat, Cynfrig and I will stay to negotiate with the English. If aught goes wrong—"

This was what Cat had hoped to hear, because she needed to be in the castle when Hyw put his plan into action. "I must stand with you. Is it not what your own morrigan would have done? My gifts cannot serve you from across the mountains. I must be here, with you."

He looked uncertain, but she could see he was thinking through the wisdom of her words. She went on, pressing her advantage. "If there is a battle in our future, as surely there must be, you will be victorious only if I am with you."

Finally, he nodded. "Very well. I—I would rather have you with me, where I can be sure of your safety. And I will marry you, Cat, to give you the full benefit of my protection." He looked away from her again. "But protection is all it can be."

She folded her arms across her chest. "We have been promised to each other since childhood. I have known you in my heart since my princess first brought us together as playmates. And now, even as our enemies surround us, we have found each other again. Is that truly all you believe we can have between us now?" She held his eyes until she saw the deep blue grow in intensity. *We shall see,* she thought, and nodded.

Her goodbyes to Margred were tearful, but they vowed to see each other again once the war had ended. She shook Owain's hand to wish him well and was surprised when he planted a kiss on her cheek.

Their goodbyes were interrupted by Cynfrig's bellow. "We cannot surrender the castle, my liege. Honour demands that we stand and fight for you and drive these *Saeson* from our land by the Grace of God."

She was still holding Owain's hand, as she looked down to see Cynfrig kneel at Prince Dafydd's feet. Rhys stood near them, undecided. She recalled her vision of Owain slain at Criccieth, and of Rhys and the others cut down in the courtyard of Bere. Owain had become like a little brother to her, and she had grown to care about all of Elizabeth's children. She had to make them understand.

"If I am the morrigan, then they must believe that I know the outcome of this battle."

"Pardon, Lady Cat?" Owain said, and she realized she had spoken aloud. Instead of answering, she squeezed his hand once and let go as she moved past him.

"My lords," she called out. She could feel the flush creep from her neck onto her face as all turned to her, but she kept moving through the room towards them. "You must listen."

Rhys stepped up and opened the curtains of an adjoining alcove. "My lords, would you draw inside to give this lady audience?" He bowed toward Cynfrig and the prince, and Cat ducked her head toward him gratefully. When they had seated themselves at the window seats, they turned toward her expectantly.

"Speak you as the morrigan, returned?" Cynfrig asked.

"The morrigan?" Prince Dafydd's tone was full of scorn.

"If you say I am, then you must believe I know the outcome of this war," she began.

"If she speaks of what she has seen, my lord," broke in Rhys in careful tones, "you must grant her leave, whatever her words might impart about the coming fray."

Dafydd considered them, and finally nodded. "Speak your leave."

She told them of her visions in as much detail as she could, beginning with Owain's death and moving to the scene in the courtyard that had come to her only days before. "You must believe me, my lord. I would not wish harm to you or any of your children, who are as dear to me as my own family now. But I beg you, do not change your course for some ancient sense of honour. Why must it always be kill or be killed? Why can we not live, to fight again another day?"

Dafydd considered her for a long moment, and then dismissed her with a wave of his hand. "Leave us. We will discuss it further."

She left them, hoping they might heed her words.

When she could avoid it no longer, Cat came back to her mam's room. She entered while Hyw was explaining his decision to join them in recapturing Garth Celyn. Hyw had planned to explain Llywelyn to their mam as well. Perhaps it was the looks on their faces, or the connection she now had with her brother, but it seemed clear he had already done so.

"I'm proud of you, Hyw." Mam hugged him.

"I hope you will feel the same of me, Mam," Cat said. "I have decided to remain with Lord Rhys and his people, to offer what help I may."

"Are you sure?" When Cat nodded, Mam reached out her arms and hugged Cat as well. "You have both grown up so quickly," she said, her eyes shining with unshed tears.

"May God keep you safe. And Lord Rhys, of course," Hyw said to her.

"You think little of my own skill," Cat chided, pulling up her skirt and extracting one of Rhys' knives to show him. He examined it carefully.

"He appears to be paying close attention," he told her. "The emerald matches your eyes."

"So I see," she said, wondering a little. She felt a flush creep along her throat as she looked again at the emerald. Had Rhys meant to send her a message of hope with it? She turned slightly to replace the knife in its sheath.

"It is a fitting gift for your skill and position," her brother said, "but I hope you never need to use them."

"Before we take our leave, there is one more thing we must do," their mam said. "Fetch your da, Hyw, and do not tarry. Cat, we must find Elizabeth and the children. Come."

45

Hyw and Bran found them again in the receiving room, along with the prince and princess. Hyw saw Margred and Owain, as well as several of the warriors, including Aeneus, Rhys, and Cynfrig. Emrys waved and grinned at him, taking Bronwen's hand. They had been married the previous Sunday along with several other young couples. Hyw wondered if some announcement was coming.

Mam reached forward and enfolded Hyw in a warm hug. Cat held out a package wrapped in cloth.

"I made it for you, Hyw."

He unwrapped it to find the red tunic and sash she had sewn. "Can it be? The stitches seem straight!" he marvelled. She punched his shoulder to break the tension.

Their da reached out his hand for the sash, and Hyw gave it to him. "I wish we had time for a proper ceremony," Bran said.

"This means more to me than any pomp or ceremony by priest or lord, Da," Hyw told him. Bran half-smiled and drew him toward the prince.

Prince Dafydd nodded to them and stood, clearing his throat. "Our enemies dog our heels, as well you know," the prince began. "Yet we will take the time to honour the old ways, and one of our number who has earned his place among us. We can present it again, properly, when we arrive at Garth Celyn."

There was a murmur of appreciation among the small band as Bran drew Hyw to him. Hyw's throat tightened and his chest seemed to swell as his da unfolded the red sash, draped it over Hyw's shoulder, and tied it at his waist. Then Bran turned to the others, holding up Hyw's right arm.

"My son," he said, and the pride in his voice hit Hyw like the warm sun through a cloud. "Warrior."

Bran then gathered Hyw to him in a fierce hug. He could hear the sounds of his friends clapping and calling around him. Bran's mouth was close to Hyw's ear as he whispered, "I am proud to call you son—for all of your abilities, not just the skill that makes you fit to wear the sash." Hyw choked back the tears that threatened to spill over, and as he drew back he noticed Da's eyes glistening as well.

"Welcome, warrior," the prince said, and raised a mug Elizabeth handed him. "I drink to your future." Aeneus clasped his forearm in Roman style, as Llywelyn had taught his bodyguard, and then hugged him as well. Emrys slugged Hyw hard on the arm and then circled his shoulder with the same hand. Finally, the prince called out.

"Though I am loathe to call this moment to an end, friends, we must depart. Go you to your preparations, as my wife and I will ours. We will greet you one last time in the dining hall."

As they made their way from the room, Hyw drew Cat aside in the stairwell. "This wristband cannot last for much longer." He pulled two chains from his pouch and handed her one. She fingered the scrolled locket before popping it open. "A lock of my hair," he told her. He held open his empty locket, and she used her knife to cut a lock of hers for it.

"As long as we have this, my gift will connect us," she said.

"I will keep it with me always," he said, placing the locket around his neck and under his tunic. "Next to my heart, as you will always be."

A few hours later, under the cover of darkness, Hyw and his family joined the people in the courtyard. Lord Rhys and the people of

Meirionnydd also waited there, and Cat squeezed Hyw's hand once before moving to join Rhys.

Emrys pushed through the crowd to his new wife Bronwen, who threw her arms around him. He would remain with Rhys, Cat, and a handful of Cynfrig's warriors at the castle to negotiate the settlement. Bronwen would travel with their people toward a holding in Meirionnydd, and if all went well, she and Emrys would be reunited in a few days.

Dafydd and Bran began moving their group towards the gate. The princess and her children, including Margred and the other girls, walked with other families who had determined to accompany their men into the mountains, on their way back to Garth Celyn. Aeneus had burned Bere's wooden bridges a few days before so the *Saeson* could not cross, but the men had placed boards over one ditch so the people could get away safely. Emrys moved back to the small group that included the warrior-poet Gwilym ap Einion. Hyw was grateful he would stay to help them bargain with the English.

As he marched with his people along the mountain path, Hyw felt something prickle along his skin almost like vertigo. It took him a moment to realize it was silence. The people sang while walking, while working, even while marching to battle. Tonight they dared not, lest their voices waken the English troops. The silence and the dark made his stomach clench.

Then he heard a groan of wind, as if the mountain giant wept to see them leave. Some of the townsfolk stopped, huddled together. Hyw hesitated. *Let me speak to them,* Llywelyn said. Hyw ran ahead, drawing near to the frightened ones.

"I remember the story, as I have heard it told," Hyw began, keeping his voice low as he repeated Llywelyn's words to them. "On just such a night as this, as the Greeks poured forth from the great horse of their treachery, Brutus and his people stole away in silence from Troy. It was to this land and to these mountains that Brutus led his people. When the Tylwyth Teg heard his story, they bade the giants make room for the people here.

"This night we cannot sing lest we be discovered. This sound we hear is the giant Idris, singing for us. He sings to the soldiers below, camped on the plain. They cannot hide from him. He sings this song to bolster your hearts, to cover your flight from this land into his own. You must believe he will shelter you, and keep the English from you."

He moved up the line to repeat the tale. As he neared his mother and Gawain, she took his hand. "We shall miss your stories, Hyw. Can you stay a while longer?"

"Until sunrise," he promised her, untying his red sash and handing it to her. "Keep this for me, and be assured I will return for it."

She smiled at him, and he made his way past her to the front of the line, where he found his father and the other warriors. It was easier in the cool darkness to use his gift. His mind seemed to reach naturally into the thickets and bushes as they passed. Here a hare scurried for cover, and there a meadow mouse kept her home. Through their eyes, he sensed the roots and dips that might have tripped someone unfamiliar with the territory and passed the information back to the people behind him.

As the sun rose, Hyw pulled away from the group and watched them trudge along the path in silence. They could see for themselves now. When he had walked past the last of his people, he began casting with his senses until he found a hawk flying near. He found a safe place off the path to leave his clothes, touched the locket around his neck, and closed his eyes. He watched Llywelyn take the goblet Cat had given him, swish the liquid, and drink. Llywelyn smiled at him and sat down to close his eyes in sleep. Hyw recalled their circle of three, seeing Cat and Gawain's faces around him as he had on the battlements. Only then did he reach out to the hawk. A gust of wind blew against his face, and he heard the hawk's shrill cry in his mind.

He raised his arms and his bones seemed to thin and twist. He heard the grating of bone on bone and intense pain gripped his body. He felt a moment of panic, but he knew he must not fight this sensation. The pain would pass. He let himself grow light and strong as he lifted off the ground into the wind.

He glanced to the side and spotted the tip of a wing with mottled brown feathers. It took him a moment to realize it was his own. He was no longer one with the mind of the hawk; he was the hawk. Beyond his own wingtip, he could see the hawk he had spotted from the ground, now flying beside him. They soared for a moment, almost circling each other. Then the other hawk dove, leaving Hyw alone in the grey sky.

When he looked down, he could see the people walking along the mountain path. He cried out, and a woman turned toward the sound. Part of him, the human part, recognized her as his mam and he circled above her. She waved, and he flew on.

As he drifted on air currents, he passed over the English soldiers camped below. He could feel the mind of the hawk inside himself—a mind caught in the instant changes of wind and sound and smell. Before he realized he was hungry, his hawk instincts drew his eyes toward the rabbit in the grass below him. Then he saw Bere. He remembered, and with a wing thrust he turned himself east toward it.

46

Cat scanned the skies, watching every bird that circled the battlements. She had seen what it cost Hyw to change as their plan required him to, and she worried that he could not accomplish it without their circle of three. She tried to recall the song Gawain had sung and opened her mind to connect with him. For too long, she felt nothing but her own fear.

Finally, she saw a large red and brown hawk soaring toward her. Although she couldn't see his face or detailing clearly against the grey sky, she could tell it was him by the feel of his mind, like a familiar presence in her peripheral vision. She saw the bird shimmer a little as it moved awkwardly toward the wall walk. It shrieked, and the sound became a cry of pain. The claws pointing toward the wooden platform became a man's bare feet. She heard a grinding of bone on bone and a low moaning as he settled. Flapping wings became arms as feathers became flesh. And Hyw lay, panting, where the bird had landed.

She knelt beside him, giving him a chunk of bread and her skin of well-water to wash it down. She closed her eyes and probed into his mind, finding Llywelyn still sleeping. Gently she hummed the song she had been singing earlier, and the prince opened his eyes and gave her his teasing half-smile. *Do we yet live?* he asked.

"You do, my liege," she answered. "And welcome."

When she opened her eyes again, Hyw asked her the same question. She answered him by ruffling his hair and making the face that always made him smile.

When her brother had recovered, she helped him dress in the clothes Dafydd had left. She'd stuffed the shoulders and waist of the tunic, and helped him drape Dafydd's tabard loosely over it, with the coat of arms clearly showing. She darkened his hair a little with bramble tea. Rhys had contributed a gold torque similar to Dafydd's and a crown, which he said he found in a castle vault. Then she stood back to survey her brother.

"It will do from afar," she said, critically.

"It had better," he said, looking through the battlements at the path far below, where the English company could be seen making their way toward the castle.

Hyw stood in borrowed clothing and watched the soldiers haggle with the warriors. He was himself again, but he felt more than himself. He stood between the battlements, where he could clearly see Rhys with Gwilym, Cynfrig and Emrys on the path, as well as Cat standing off to one side, trying to stay out of the soldier's sight behind them. As Hyw expected, the English captain pointed toward him.

"They will not accept that Dafydd is here without some kind of proof," Hyw had told Cynfrig and Emrys earlier. "They will expect a trick. When they ask you, tell them the prince will wave to you to prove he is there in truth. Then turn and wave, and I will do the rest."

Emrys turned and waved at Hyw. Hyw stood, straightening his tabard so they would see Dafydd's crest, and waved back. He turned his head, hoping the gold of the crown and torque would flash in the sunlight.

Time slowed for Cat as the English captain stared, rubbing his beard with one hand. It isn't working, she thought wildly. She and Rhys stood behind Cynfrig and Gwilym, letting them handle the negotiating. She felt Rhys grope for the sword under his cloak and wondered if they would have to fight their way out. Lucky, she had brought her water skin. Staring down at the water inside it, she tried to make contact with Hyw. She could feel his presence, but she could not enter his mind to send him a message.

Then she thought of Llywelyn. She saw the former prince, standing as if behind Hyw. Her brother said they communicated in thoughts, like silent speaking. She frowned in concentration, focusing her thoughts on them. *Help us. The English captain does not believe the ruse.*

Llywelyn touched Hyw on the shoulder. Cat broke contact and looked up at the battlements. The difference was subtle. Hyw suddenly stood taller and more regally than before, and his hair shone more like Dafydd's than it had. The crown caught the sunlight. Was that the same one she had found for her brother? she wondered. Or was it Llywelyn's conjuring? More importantly, would it help the *Saeson* believe that Hyw was Prince Dafydd?

Finally, the captain nodded. He gave Emrys and Cynfrig a pouch. Cynfrig checked it. That would be the payment for surrendering the castle, and a letter of safe passage, she thought.

As part of the bargain, the English soldiers were to give the Welsh a day to clear the castle before they entered. Cynfrig and Rhys believed they would not wait, so they had agreed to send the people on their way the night before. Now, the little negotiating party began to move toward the road, away from the castle. Cat was drawn along with the others. If all went well, they would join the people who had already escaped before the English knew they were gone.

Hyw would remain where he was, on the battlements, to lull the English into believing Prince Dafydd remained in the castle. She dared not wave but tried to send her thoughts again to reassure him as they made their way into the mountains. The path grew quiet around them and they barely stirred the grass as they passed. Even the giant seemed to be holding his breath.

"Here," someone called. "Up here."

Hyw wiped the sleep from his eyes and stood. The position

of the sun told him it was late afternoon. So, Cynfrig was right. The English had not waited, but were even now storming the castle in search of Prince Dafydd.

In search of him.

Hyw looked down and saw soldiers streaming through the gates. He cast around him and for a moment he panicked. He could not find a hawk, and could not bring the shape into his mind. Could he shift without one? Could he take the form of another bird?

He heard voices at the bottom of the stairs. It was time. He shrugged off his borrowed cloak and clothing. He closed his eyes and raised his arms.

Nothing.

Steady on, lad, he heard Llywelyn say behind him. *Think of the circle of three.*

Hyw could hear pounding footsteps on the stone stairwell but shut his mind to them. Llywelyn began humming the song Gawain and Cat had sung and he focused on it. He imagined them standing with him, singing. Llywelyn drank from the goblet and sank to the floor, asleep.

Hyw reached out for the hawk.

As he let the scent and rush of wind flood through him, he recognized the first man rushing toward him from the stairwell. It was Robert, the bully of Shrewsbury's court, in full knight's armour. His face glistened with sweat and his breath came heavy and panting. And then Robert saw Hyw and raised his drawn sword high to rush at him.

"It is a trick!" Robert's cry of alarm rose like the crash of arms on armour.

But Hyw could not —would not—stop. He felt feathers grow from his skin, and his bones knit and press into the shape the wind loved best.

Robert stumbled a moment as his mind tried to grasp the transformation before him. His face became even more distorted with fear and hatred. "Sorcerer!"

As he took to the sky, Hyw saw Robert suddenly pull a bow and arrow from his shoulder. The arrow zipped past Hyw, almost knocking him off balance. Robert swore, and took a second arrow from his quiver. Hyw struggled against the wind, aware of the young knight setting his feet and drawing back his bow for another shot. Then a second figure trod the wall walk behind him, knocking the bow from Robert's hand.

"Why are you wasting arrows on this bird?" the second man said as Robert's second arrow flew wide. "Where is the prince?"

Hyw circled to identify his benefactor. In the human part of his brain, he knew it was Stephen de Francton. The man had saved him twice. Robert was arguing with him but other human shouts caught Hyw's attention. He circled once more as soldiers picked up the cloak and fought over the gold ornaments. Deep inside him, he heard the rumble of laughter, but he could not tell if it was Llywelyn's or his own.

And he became one with the wind, letting it turn him toward the mountain.

By dawn the people had traveled far into the mountain range. With the hawk's keen eyesight he had easily found his clothes, but he had to run all night in his human form to catch up. Behind them, Bere sat solidly in the rock of Idris, the mountain giant. The English army looked like a dark patch of blight on the once-lush Desenni valley. Like locusts, they would soon have their way and depart. How long would the castle remain? For a moment, he thought he saw Idris himself heave a sigh. Hyw rubbed his eyes and saw the mountain again.

Hyw started toward his mam and da. He could not see his sister anywhere. Cat and Rhys must have found them in the night, and split off from Dafydd's group to take Rhys's people to the safety of Cymer Abbey. Hyw passed Prince Dafydd, who carried one of his sleeping children on his back. The way seemed easier along the mountain plateau, as they followed a path worn by sheep and cattle.

Hyw heard a wavering sound and realized someone had begun to sing. He recognized the clear tones of his mother's soprano, and heard the rich harmonies slide into place as one voice joined another.

The song was a hymn of thanksgiving. He and Llywelyn joined in as he found Adara, and their voices warmed him as the light snow began to fall around them.

Author's note: Castell-y-Bere fell to the English in April 1283, after the longest siege of the war. The English paid £53 to the castle's constable, Cynfrig ap Madog, for the castle's surrender. But Dafydd ap Gruffydd, the last true Prince of Wales, once again escaped their grasp. Cynfrig and the Welsh who held Castell-y-Bere melted into their mountain, never to appear again in the written annals of history.

LAST OF THE GIFTED
WATER SIGHT
MARIE POWELL
BOOK TWO

1

Meirionnydd, North Wales, April 1283

Mist circled the mountain like a massive fist. Squinting upward, Cat could barely make out the legendary giant's seat near the top of Cadair Idris. The fog surrounded her, obscuring Rhys who climbed behind her, but she drew it around her like a cloak. They needed stealth. Below them, the valley was full of English mercenaries, hunting for Welsh heads. It didn't matter that only a handful of warriors remained. Women, children, any of them would satisfy the wretched king.

"Not much further," Rhys murmured.

She hadn't had a vision since they'd fled Bere castle. Not when she stared into the rain that morning, not through her reflection in the stream they crossed earlier, not even in the waterfall when she cupped her hands in it to drink. With English soldiers camped near the lake, Rhys had agreed to show her a stream farther up the mountain so she could try again.

Her foot dislodged a chunk of slate. It clinked down the side of the mountain, disturbing the mist blanket as it went. Her breath caught. She glanced back toward the gulley where they had left the others.

Rhys loomed behind her out of the mist. His features held the usual stoic calmness, but the heat radiating from him made her wonder if the anger still boiled inside him at the loss of his castle. He had given it up to save them. His people. Her.

"You are the morrigan," he said. "If you see not, it may be there is naught to see."

She tried to smile at his wordplay. "I'm no legend," she muttered, but he only raised his eyebrows. He thought of her as a wise woman, like his Irish nurse, whose gift of foretelling could predict and prevent their doom. But Cat was Welsh. Her gift came as it chose. She forced herself to breathe out, slowly. For his sake, she would find a way to will it to herself.

She reached for the rocks and climbed, one step, then another, feeling her way with hands and feet as she went. She had tucked away her pretty leather-soled shoes so she wouldn't slip on the smooth slate. Her feet were used to their freedom, but the jagged edges caught at her toes, and her calves ached from two days of hiding and backtracking on a route that should not have taken them one.

"There," he said as their feet finally found the firmer ground of a small plateau. They could hear the roar of the stream. She drew a long breath and tried to smile again. He took her hand and led her to a large tree, pulling her forward to stand beside him. The mist had cleared a little, and she could see a fork in the rocky streambed.

"Look there." He gestured toward the ledge where the rushing water parted. "Those stones will hold you."

She stepped onto a large flat stone and crouched down. The rocks slowed the water enough that her pale, sombre face stared back, waving in the ripples. She must see what was facing them. She chose a calm spot near an eddy and fought to remember the songs to call her gift. She could hear her uncle's voice in her memory as she stared fixedly at the liquid, whispering the words, not daring to sing aloud.

Nothing stirred. Cat rubbed her forehead with one hand and sat back on her heels. His hand rested on her shoulder, warm and supportive even through the fabric of her cloak.

"The first thing we must do is get our people to safety. Focus on that now, Cat."

Of course, he would say that. He was raised to be their leader, and he always put his people's welfare above his own. Cat longed to help him more than anything else. If only her gift would cooperate.

A water beetle skimmed across the clear surface of the stream. She followed its path, staring at the ripples it made, when her surroundings began to dissolve—

—and she could feel thudding all around her. Hooves pounding toward her on the flat dirt. She shrank back into the dark stone of the abbey walls, sheltered in its shadow. Familiar voices screamed and cried out, somewhere nearby. Rhys drew his longsword from its sheath and sprinted toward the riders. He swung around as the first horseman flew at him and lunged up toward the armoured man. Cat saw the man flinch as Rhys thrust. The bite of steel tore open the knight's throat. The horse screamed as it careened past Rhys. He whirled but the second horseman was already bearing down on him. Rhys threw his sword and the force carried the knight off his horse.

Then the third was upon him. Rhys leapt upward again, his bare arms outstretched as if to drag the man from his saddle. The knight's sword flashed as dust and churning hooves covered the scene. Then the horses passed. The dust cleared. She saw a crumpled form on the grass—

—and Cat was crouching by the stream again.

"No!" She twisted up and threw her arms around him, unable to speak.

"What?" he asked, holding her tightly. "What did you see?"

She stared at Rhys. The violence of the vision stopped her voice. How could she tell him? She had clearly felt the abbey around her. The abbey would offer the people shelter. Food, shelter, rest. What they all needed. And it was the place they must go to collect the relics. But if they went, it would end his life.

"Tell me," he said.

She drew away from him. *Tywysog* Dafydd—the man who would be Prince of Wales—had sent Rhys on this errand. The House of Aberffraw would fall, and all of free Wales with it, if Dafydd could not rally the people to him, as his brother had. Many said the relics had helped Prince Llywelyn keep the people on his side: the Cross of Neith that marked him as their leader in the eyes of the Church, the Crown of Arthur that marked his true heritage, and the Coronet of Wales given by the English king to mark Llywelyn as the Prince of Wales in the eyes of the world. Now these relics would gain Dafydd the support he needed for a final stand against the English. And it was up to Rhys to get the relics to him.

"Tell me what you saw."

Cat's heart thumped.

"We must not go," she said. "You must not go." And she told him all of it. He listened, his blue eyes intent on hers, drawing the words from her. When she was done, he said nothing for a moment, a muscle flinching once in his jaw belying his calm.

"And the people?" he asked. "Were they safe?"

She heard their voices screaming again, and slowly shook her head. His face fell for a moment, so fleeting she wondered if she'd imagined it, before he regained the stoicism she had come to expect from him. Always in the past, her visions had held hope, a way to change the fate that would surely bring them defeat. But there were so few Welsh warriors left now, and the enemy had so many. How could she change this vision?

"My visions," she began, and faltered. "What do you think of your morrigan now?"

"Your visions give us a chance."

"And yet, I wish I had not seen it." She folded her arms across her chest, falling back into their old argument. "I wish you had married me at the castle, if it would prevent me from seeing such scenes."

"I would do nothing to disrupt your visions. You are a woman of power, and you must keep your power pure." He started to put an arm around her shoulder, but she shook him off.

"It may have been so for your Irish nurse, but it was not so for my own mam, and for the other women of our family. Mam married and had children, but her gift remains strong."

He shook his head. "How can we risk it? Your visions may be our only advantage now."

Each time they argued, it ended the same way. If her mam was here with them, maybe she could convince him. But Mam was half a world away, caring for Prince Llywelyn's only child. Cat turned away from Rhys but his arm came around her shoulders and drew her toward him. His quick response surprised her, and she let herself be drawn.

"Do not think you will get away so easily. Once the English return to their own land…" He bent his head to her and waited until she raised hers to meet him. Then he kissed her gently, as he had in the garden at Bere, and this time she responded.

When he drew back, the blue of his eyes had darkened, and his voice was husky. "I know your value, Cat, and not only as a morrigan. We will be man and wife, if you still will it, but we two must wait until our people are safe."

She swallowed and pushed away from him. "Yet we cannot go to the abbey now."

"We cannot take the people there."

Something in the way he said it made her turn back to him, but she could not catch his eye. "You cannot go," she said. "That much is clear enough."

"And yet I cannot tarry." He looked at her then. "If your vision happens with the people there, then there may be a way to forestall it and secure the relics. One warrior on his own would make better time."

A chill spread through her, and she returned to her vision, seeking a way to stop him. "It was only you I saw," she said. "The English soldiers came for you."

"It is not clear why the English would attack God's holy church, unless they knew of its earthly treasure. If that is true, I have no choice but to go."

"You cannot go. You must not go. There are others you can send—"

"None the abbot will trust."

"What of Cynfrig?"

The old warrior had been the steward at Bere castle, trusted by Rhys and by Prince Llywelyn himself, before the prince was murdered six months ago. Had it even been six months?

Rhys was shaking his head. "Cynfrig is loyal but he has a wife and children. I cannot endanger him."

"What of Emrys?"

"With his new wife already pregnant?" He shook his head.

Who else could they send? Most of the warriors who still stood with them had gone with Prince Dafydd to retake their ancestral home at Garth Celyn. Who else had she seen as she watched from the shadow of the abbey's walls? Only Rhys and herself—

And then she realized. The abbey had been sheltering her.

Not Rhys, but her.

She must go. And he must not. It made sense. Her family had been with Prince Llywelyn when he hid the relics there. Her vision was telling her she must go to collect them, alone. Fear shuddered through her. Rhys responded by holding her again. She put her arms around his waist, looking up into his eyes. And she knew he would not let her go, if he thought she would face danger. How could she hide her intention from him? Yet she must.

She shifted away from him and squared her shoulders. If she must do it, she would need to act quickly.

"What has happened?" he asked. "Did you have another vision?"

"Not vision," she said, shaking her head, "but reason. You must see the people to safety before anything else."

"On that, I must rely on you and Cynfrig. I will leave you in his charge. He knows the land as well as I and can guide you all to the safety of a nearby holding. A place where the people might be safe for a time."

"You must see to the people first."

Rhys held her eyes and nodded. Yes, she thought, looking away. You must see to the people. And I must see to our future.

As they returned to the path, Cat spotted Cynfrig's youngest child already scrambling nimbly over the rubble on the mountain path. The boy had been well warned, so instead of his usual jubilance, the loudest sound he made was his panting as he caught his breath on the plateau. He was soon followed by his mother Haf, and finally the elder steward himself. As the mist cleared, Cat was able to spot the homespun cloaks of a handful of farmers and their families following at intervals on the mountain path. Below them, the army of the English king blanketed the valley like locusts. Cat wanted to lean into Rhys, to reassure herself, but now was not the time.

"In times past, we might have waited out the spring," Cynfrig said, "trusting the *Saeson* to get sick of our mountains and return home to take up their ploughs. But these sell-swords have no such concerns."

"They will not cease their search for Prince Dafydd," Rhys agreed. "We must get the relics to him without delay."

Only the three of them knew of Rhys' errand, but every Welshman knew of the enmity between Dafydd and Llywelyn in life. With the three relics in hand—Cross, Crown, and Coronet— surely the people would believe Prince Dafydd had his elder brother's blessing at the end, and follow him to defeat the English.

She shifted restlessly, watching Rhys step forward to help a farmer and his family up the path. She knew Rhys would want to speak with his warriors in person before he left for the abbey. With luck, Emrys, the other warrior travelling with them, would be bringing up the rear with his pregnant wife Bron. That would give Cat a small head start. As she expected, Rhys and Cynfrig reached into their meager stores and shared them out with the women and children. She noticed that Cynfrig halved his portion with his wife and son, while Rhys gave most of his to a young farmer and his family.

Cat had to get to the abbey first, and this might be her only chance. She went to Cynfrig as the one person who might help her.

"Often you have called me your morrigan," she said, drawing him aside. "If you believe it truly, you must help me now." As quickly as possible, she told him the main points of her vision.

"Did you see me in your vision?"

As Cat searched her memory, she caught sight of his young son, watching them almost forlornly, and shook her head. "The abbey only offered me its protection. It must be me who goes."

"But Rhys will come after you," Cynfrig told her. "I will not be able to prevent him."

"Then you must delay him at least half a day," she said. "It will take me that long to get to the abbey."

"Only that long?" Cynfrig rubbed his moustache ruefully.

"You know how fast I am. I will take the fox path, and I will rejoin you with the relics before nightfall."

"I cannot guarantee Rhys will not discover you gone sooner than you wish it."

"Then send him by the fox trail, if he tries to come after me. I will return that way to the holding and so meet him on the trail." She watched the older man's face, but he still hesitated. With a glance toward Rhys, who was lifting a child over the rubble onto the plateau, she took Cynfrig's hands in hers. "We need him now, more than ever. This way we will have Rhys, alive, and we will have the relics with no one the wiser. If you believe as you say, then you know I must do this. It is the only way."

Finally, he reached into his pouch and put a small package of dried meat into her hands. "God's speed," he said, and moved past her to block her from Rhys' view.

Cat thanked him and moved swiftly up the path toward the fox trail. She touched the locket around her neck that held the twist of hair binding her to her brother Hyw, wishing for the thousandth time that she had his gift instead of her own. If only she could transform into an eagle or a hawk, she could fly to the abbey and back before Rhys noticed she was gone.

The road forked and she looked longingly down the pony path to the holding where Rhys and their people would travel later that day. Then she set her mind and turned to the shorter trail that would take her to the abbey. She had wasted too much time already. She prayed that Cynfrig would keep Rhys focused on his people, so he would not look for her until it was time for them to say goodbye. She willed that she would be on her way back by then.

2

Hyw circled over the treetops surrounding the silent tower of Dolbadarn Castle. Catching a wind current, he rose effortlessly to the top of the mottled slate-and-rubble stronghold, rising some eighty feet above the eastern tip of the lake. The ever-present rain clouds parted to let the mid-morning sun peek through for a moment. He drifted downward, barely moving the tips of his long, red wing-feathers. Training his sharp eyes on the castle courtyard far below, he saw the glint of sun on steel. *Saeson.* English. Knights in armour, and with them the soldiers of King Edward's army.

Flying lower, he trained his eyes on a man walking the castle's defensive inner wall. The lone soldier paced the length of the wall and back, staring at the countryside around him. His posture was slack and his footfalls heavy, not like one wary and at war, but more like one lost in dreams of his faraway home in England.

Good.

The hawk part of Hyw saw the enemy as fat and complacent, ready for plucking. The other part, the human part, recalled his father and the other Welsh warriors, waiting for word of what he could discover at Dolbadarn. Wait, he told himself. There may be more to see. He flew to the west tower, spotting two soldiers inside, playing at dice. Better. These men expected no trouble from the remains of the Welsh army.

Hyw folded his wings and perched on the tower, staring down at the English practicing in the castle yard. Five—no, six men. A small stack of armour leaned against one wall. The castle barns stood open and empty of horses. The knights and soldiers must have left the castle. A few sorry-looking cows milled about near the barn. The animals were too large to interest the hawk, but the human part of him salivated. A cow, even as thin as these, would have been more than welcome to Prince Dafydd's handful of warriors with their wives and children, now refugees in their own land.

Hyw soared off again, past the main entry, alert and watchful. He spied the portcullis, open for the return of the troops that would be searching for Prince Dafydd and their company. New wood on the entryway told him it had been rebuilt during the months since Dolbadarn had been taken. It held a barbican like the kind he'd seen in Shrewsbury: an elaborate maze of gates for defence. The English had already been busy. Farther inside the courtyard, he noted the wooden stairs still attached to the second-floor entrance of the tall round tower. The English had made no attempt to secure the inner courtyard, no doubt trusting the portcullis, which could be lowered in one blow by the lone guard walking the hoarding, to defend the castle.

Hyw rounded the corner, still scanning the ground, and flew into a wall of black and grey feathers behind the castle. Crows and jackdaws wheeled like a dark writhing blotch against the sky. The ravening birds circled, ducked and dived at each other and at him. Hyw flew past them a little and then turned back to follow. The birds squabbled and flew, squabbled and flew, as he glided behind, letting instinct guide him.

Then he saw it: a mound of burned and decaying bodies. The castle's former inhabitants. The English had thrown Welsh bodies into a pile to burn them instead of burying them. But the deed was only half-finished, and the birds and animals had done the rest. He could taste the acrid stench all around him. Wings spread, Hyw hung suspended in the air. The world stood still.

Barbaric. He heard the voice in the back of his mind. It was the prince. Hyw closed his eyes to see the former Prince of Wales inside his mind. Llywelyn appeared to stand with arms crossed, as he had stood so often in the royal court of Garth Celyn. When the prince had been murdered on a hill near Cilmeri, Hyw had saved

Llywelyn's spirit from oblivion by taking it within himself.

But Prince Llywelyn should be sleeping inside him now.

Instead, Llywelyn stared back at him, his dark eyes full of grief. Grief that changed to concern. *Steady, lad.*

The feathers of his long wings poked Hyw like a thousand quills into his flesh. No! His eyes flew open as he tried to fight the change that would leave them both plummeting toward the hard earth far below. No! He spread his wings wide and tried to push against the air currents, but he felt himself falter. No! He shuddered once and tried to take charge of his wings again. The prince, his sister Cat, his family. They were counting on him. He must get back to give them the news of what he had found at Dolbadarn.

For *Cymru!* he thought desperately. But it was too late. Looking down, he saw long pale feet where his talons should be. With a grinding crunch, his bones twisted and reshaped. The hawk's shriek became his own scream as he plummeted into the mass grave.

The jackdaws screeched and pecked at him as he fell, a foreigner in their world of wind and sky. Instinctively Hyw bent his knees and raised his arms to protect his head, turning away from the birds. He took the impact on his side, sinking deep into the gore of decay. Something bumped at his back and he turned to find a hand reaching for him, white fingers curling as if beckoning him to hell. He swooshed it away in a thick wave of viscous gore that returned and clung to him. It splashed at his body, filling his nostrils with the stench of death.

The tepid pool of dead flesh and blood and bone shocked him back to earth. He gagged on the smell of burnt hair and rot, even as he tore his way through it. He thrashed and clawed at the blackened bodies that blocked his way. Everywhere he turned there were more. He wanted to scream but could not find his voice.

Get us out of here, boy. Hyw's hands found something solid, and he clutched at it, pulling himself forward. He ripped at a pile in front of him and it gave way in tattered clothing and bone. Finally he heaved himself out, clear of the gore, and ran from it. He saw the trees at the edge of the forest and ran toward them until he stumbled over a tree root and lay there retching and shuddering.

Steady. Llywelyn's calm voice resonated in Hyw's mind.

Hyw wanted to regain the shape of the hawk and fly them as far away as he could, but his strength was gone. He shivered, the cold assaulting his naked body. As he wrapped his arms around his torso, he felt a roughness like sand and snatched his hands away again. The gore was already drying on his skin. The smell of rot and bile assaulted his human nostrils. He gagged but couldn't find the strength to retch again.

The prince rasped an oath. Hyw didn't even try to close his eyes. He had no wish to see the expression on Llywelyn's face. *I was the one excommunicated, not my people. How could they have been left like this?*

A muffled call caught Hyw's ear. He rolled over to see the faint glimmer of torches flare up, high on the castle walls. It must be the soldier he'd seen, calling to others inside the gates.

Changing the watch.

Hyw closed his eyes then. Llywelyn crouched at the ready.

"How is it that you were awake?" Hyw asked, thinking the words rather than saying them. The prince shook his head and gave a slight shrug. Hyw sucked in his bottom lip, considering the situation. It had taken his sister and uncle days to find a way to get Llywelyn to sleep inside him, so he could manage the transformation.

It seems you can manage well enough until you realize I am with you. Llywelyn responded as if he could hear Hyw's thoughts.

"Do you mean you've been awake before?" How had he not realized it?

The prince looked away from him. *Time enough for this later. We must move, lad. Now.*

"Did you see—?"

I see only what you see. And your eyes are closed.

Hyw felt the barb and opened his eyes again. He could not stop himself from shaking and the stench of the pit still filled his nostrils. He heard rather than felt the rain as it began to fall around them. If only it would be enough to wash the filth from his body. He rolled away from the trees and back, trying to clean some of it off himself before he sat up.

We need shelter. Clothing to protect us from the night.

"We have none," he told the prince, without closing his eyes again.

Aye, we do.

Hyw snapped his eyes shut and stared at Llywelyn. Comprehension dawned, and with it, horror. "No!" he said aloud. His voice sounded like a croaking whisper to his ears.

You must, Llywelyn persisted.

Hyw recoiled. Go back to the pit of bodies? "No. It's easy for you. You can't smell anything or feel anything—"

I share your senses. Get up. We can't stay here.

Hyw shook his head. Feathers would cover them well enough. He tried to change again, but he still he had no strength for it. He had served Llywelyn, doing his bidding as best he could these many months. He had transformed his life and his body in service to his prince. But this time, the prince demanded too much. He could not take clothing from the dead. Could not wear the cloth those decaying bodies wore. He shuddered again.

These, who served me well in life, will not protest to serve me yet in death.

"Would they have been so willing, had they known it would bring them to this?" Even as he thought the words, Hyw wished he could recall them. This uneasy state between them always seemed easier for the former prince. Hyw wanted to do his duty, but with Llywelyn inside his head, he was never free of it.

Hyw slapped the earth with one hand and pushed himself upright. The worst of it was that Llywelyn was right. If they didn't move, they would be caught. And he had to get the former prince back to his brother, Prince Dafydd. Dafydd would need every weapon in his armoury, including his brother's spirit, to protect the people from these English invaders. It was nearly May. They had only six months left to rally the Welsh and win this war, before Llywelyn's ghost must be laid to his final rest on *Nos Galan Gaeaf,* or All Hallow's Eve, as the English called it. If they did not succeed, the prince's soul—and perhaps Hyw's sanity—would be lost forever.

The cold bit into Hyw, and the rain made his skin pimple with gooseflesh. He pushed himself up to a crouching position and crept back until he stood looking at the pile of bodies in the fading light.

These are my subjects, Llywelyn said. *Let me through, and they will not fail me.*

Several times over the past few months, Llywelyn had guided them in body and mind. Hyw stood aside now and let the prince take control. He saw himself picking through the mass until he found a cloak that had been thrown aside, a little way from the man who had once worn it. But when the prince tried pulling the leggings from another, Hyw could not stomach it. He stepped in front of him again.

"Nay, my liege. I will cover myself well enough with this."

The prince nodded and seemed to step back in Hyw's mind again.

Hyw flung the rough cloak around his shoulders, put one arm through a rip in the fabric, and fastened it with crude string at the waist, creating a tunic. He willed himself not to feel the scratchy wool or think of the bodies in the pit again. Creeping low so the guards would not see him, he circled around the pit to the safety of the forest. He wished again that he could return to hawk form, but he was only a man. He looked down at his feet; he'd gone barefoot often enough. He willed them forward.

Hyw followed the riverbed, careful to keep his footing, to fool the dogs and trackers of the *Saeson*. His heart pounded in his chest, but he tried to tell himself it was from running. The English were always combing the forest for easy targets. He had no wish to add his head to some mercenaries' pile for Edward's shillings. And he had Prince Llywelyn to protect as well. Hyw repeated his mental prayer that his uncle Gawain could lay the prince's soul to rest at *Nos Galan Gaeaf.*

Your family's magic may save my soul, Llywelyn railed, *but what of my people? We must settle them before the autumn equinox. When your sister returns, she must find all who are scattered and bring them home again.*

Hyw tried not to think of Garth Celyn, which had always been a beacon of home to him. Or Cat, who would be far away with Rhys and his people now. Da would be waiting for his report, and they would rejoin Mam and Baby Gwen shortly. Hyw trudged along the shallow stream, his mind drifting from Llywelyn's ranting to memories of the Aber near Garth Celyn. Would that he could swim again in the pool beneath the waterfall. He and Cat had spent hours with Emrys and Bronwen and so many other friends there. Where were they all now? Were Emrys and Bronwen still alive? He banished that thought and focused on his feet as he slogged through the rushing water. The rocky streambed had scraped his feet clean. That only made him more aware of what still clung to his skin and the stench that gagged him whenever he tried to change into his hawk form again.

The bank curved and finally the river widened. He could stand it no longer. Without stopping to remove his make-shift tunic, he ran a few steps and arced his body into the chilly water. Llywelyn's voice finally fell silent. Hyw broke the surface, spraying water from his mouth, and turned on his back. The fast-running current tugged at him so he let it carry him downstream, alternately floating and swimming with it.

The pull of the current lessened as he found a pool in the stream, and he turned onto his side. The late April sun dappled the shoreline. He let the peace of the moment envelop him. How easy it would be to cease the struggle, to sink into the dark water, to let them both rest.

A movement in the bushes on the bank caught his eye. He shifted so he could tread water, watching the figure move from clump to clump until he recognized the green cloak. She'd hidden her dark tresses beneath a boy's cap, but the cloak was unmistakable. Margred.

Hyw was mildly annoyed to see a bow slung over her shoulder. She'd been hunting again. He could not see what his sister Cat found to like in Prince Dafydd's eldest daughter. He'd overheard the Princess Elizabeth telling her to stop this unseemly activity not two days ago — and Margred's retort that Elizabeth was not her mam, which seemed to slice through that lady's heart. Whatever Margred's rebellion, she should surely know hunting was dangerous with the English occupying the castle and the surrounding woods. They should all be in hiding.

Besides, Hyw could have told her there was nothing here to hunt. He stared at her, unable to find his voice. *You must be civil and greet her*, Llywelyn said in his inner ear. Hyw almost stepped from the stream to reveal himself to her, but he would have to explain his own presence there. Before he could decide, she had glided into another section of the forest. Llywelyn huffed in Hyw's head, and he closed his eyes to see the prince standing with his arms crossed.

She is comely, lad, but her father has need of alliances. The heat rose in his cheeks, but he did not reply. Llywelyn had no need to warn him off. Or perhaps he did. Had he been watching Margred? He would have to keep a tighter rein on himself, both inside his mind and to the outside world.

But when he opened his eyes again, Margred was gone.

She must have some reason for her actions. And she may need your help, Llywelyn whispered. Hyw finally struggled toward the bank. He was far from the place where he had entered, but the tunic, though cleaner, still stank with the memory of decaying bodies. The cold, still-dripping fabric shocked his skin. He wanted to find his da and reclaim his own clothing, but Llywelyn pressed him to go after Margred. Hyw was furious with both of them, but he kept himself in check. After all, he had to watch for others that might be following them as he waded from the stream. He started after her, pressing water from his hair and clothes as he went.

3

The rocky shale shifted under Cat's feet and brambles grabbed at her clothing as she half-ran along the treacherous path. A stiff breeze moaned and caught at her clothing until it threatened to push her over the narrow edge, and she hitched her skirts further under her belt. It had been over a year since Cat had seen the abbey, and then she had gone with her family on horseback. She knew of the fox trail only because she and Rhys had run this way to get away from the others, and they had sat talking for what seemed like hours on the ledge of the mountain, listening to the giant moan. How young their former selves seemed now. She soon stopped trying to wipe the sweat from her face, and she barely paused to drink from her water skin. She didn't touch the food the old steward had bid her take. Later, she thought. On the way back, I'll eat.

The sun crawled overhead, and she could only hope the people would move even slower. Finally she drew near the River Mawddach, but it, too, caught at her feet to slow her down. Her thighs and calves were on fire with every step. She followed the river for at least another hour before she saw the austere stone walls of Abbey Cymer, named for the meeting of the waters. She pushed herself to a sprint, letting her mind focus on her argument to convince the abbot to give the relics to her.

White-robed monks worked the fields around the abbey, oblivious to the English threat — or perhaps because of it, to show them God's work would be done in spite of the king. One lean form in particular caught her attention. It was her uncle Gawain, her mother's brother. Here she would find an ally in her quest.

She ran towards him. "Uncle," she called out, panting a little and waving madly.

He was herding a few sheep toward the stream. At the sound, he tensed and swung around, his crook at the ready, before he recognized her. Then he dropped the tool and took a few steps to close the gap between them, taking her into his arms as he did when she was a young child.

"Well met, Catrin." His voice held a warm welcome, but no hint of his usual ready laughter. "How is it that I find you here, alone? Do you know how dangerous—?"

"I found you, it seems," she broke in, catching her breath. "But I have come in haste and in need of your assistance."

"What's happened?" His eyes narrowed in fear and concern.

"No, nothing to mam and da," she assured him. "Dafydd must have the artifacts and has sent us to claim them."

Gawain raised his eyebrows and looked past her down the path. "And where is Rhys?"

She tugged him toward the abbey, and he began to follow as her tale unfolded. "There's no time," she said. "I must return with the artifacts so we can be on our way before the English soldiers come." He grew more concerned as she told him of her vision, shaking his head, and finally he drew her toward the abbey.

"Come, we must tell the abbot."

"Surely not?" she asked him, unsure of how the holy man would react to her visions. "I mean, not about all?"

"You make it difficult for me, Cat. I cannot counsel you to say aught but the truth, and yet…" His frown deepened. "It may be enough to tell him of Dafydd's need. Abbot Cadwgan has not held himself away from the world entirely. He has always counselled working together, tempering the old ways with the new, for the betterment of all. And he has long been a supporter of the House of Aberffraw. We must hope that he will support us now."

In spite of his misgivings, she followed her uncle into the nave.

"Nay, I must disagree, Lady Catrin." Abbot Cadwgan's voice was gravelly, as if scoured by the stones along the confluence of streams that marked the abbey grounds. Determination gleamed from his eyes. "The relics are here, they are safe, and so they will remain."

"But *Tywysog* Dafydd needs the relics now, Father, to rally the Welsh people to him. He sent us—me to collect them."

"Did he?" the abbot asked. He had shown Gawain and Cat into the chapter hall, which was empty at this time of day. Although she knew the abbot had championed the acceptance of women generally, he seemed uncomfortable in her presence. "We hold many here for safekeeping, for our sister abbey and for the House of Aberffraw. If he did indeed send you, then you must know what to ask for."

"The True Cross, the Crown of Arthur, and the Coronet of Llywelyn," Cat answered without hesitation.

The abbot drew back, his eyes almost fierce as he stared at her. "You know the words, yet there is something you are hiding from me." She tried to look back at him squarely, but in the end she looked away and touched her locket again.

"I have known her since she was a babe in swaddling," Gawain put in. "She was gently raised, and it has made her deed this day all the more daring, and the more difficult."

Cat kept her eyes averted, wondering if what Gawain had said was still true of her. The abbot sighed and his voice softened as he spoke again. "We must trust each other, child." She was staring at his hands, and he steepled his fingers. "I understand what *Tywysog* Dafydd wants, Lady Catrin," he said finally.

"The prince is in hiding, as you know, Father. I must take the relics back to Lord Rhys, and he will take them to the spot for the exchange."

The abbot's hands broke apart, and she stepped back. "I still do not understand why Rhys did not come himself, why he would send—"

Before he could finish, the door flew open, and Rhys all but burst through it, closely followed by a monk almost the same age. Cat couldn't stop a rush of relief at the sight of Rhys, and she noted the same relief in his eyes. Then panic flooded through her. He should not be here. Must not be here.

"Pardon the interruption, Your Holiness," Rhys said as he came to a stop on one knee. The abbot gave his blessing automatically before turning to the monk who was still trying to prevent him from entering.

"All is fine, Brother Mark. You may go about your chores." When the younger monk had quietly closed the door behind him, the abbot turned to Rhys again. "Well, young man," he began.

"My Lord Abbot," Rhys broke in. "I mean no disrespect to you, nor to Him who protects us. But a threat approaches that will not accept these stones as a deterrent."

The abbot drew himself up. "With God to protect us, who should we fear?" Cat could look at him fully while his attention was on Rhys, and she let herself be impressed by the strength of character in the lines of his face. "Who would dare to disrespect the sanctity of God's holy church?"

"Truly, we must fear God, but we must also fear Edward," Rhys replied, "and most especially fear his men. Where the king may have scruples, his servants have shown none. We must secure our treasures, all three, and you with them, Father."

"Whither can we go that would be as safe as here? As we did in the last uprising, we will garrison your men here, and gladly accept their help to secure us all."

"In those days, we had a garrison. We have only a handful of warriors with us," Rhys told him. "The others guard our people as they make for the nearby holding." He glanced at Cat, and she could tell he was trying to find the words to warn the abbot of the coming danger.

"For the young, the answer is always in fighting, but there are other ways," the abbot said, crossing himself. "I have seen much over the years, young Rhys. It may seem to you that today's horrors trump all others, but what evil men do to each other in times of war remains more constant than you or I can know. Come, I must say a mass and we must all pray for the safety of our people."

"Father, there is no time."

"For this, we must make time." He turned away then, refusing to discuss it further. Cat's stomach clenched, but Rhys reached into his tunic and withdrew a wrapped package. The abbot unwrapped it slowly and examined the object inside. "This is the seal *Tywysog* Llywelyn received for Gwenllian from her dying mother's hand."

Rhys nodded. "We lost Llywelyn's own seal with his body at Builth. His brother and heir, *Tywysog* Dafydd, bade me keep this one safe to show to you, if need arose. Now Dafydd holds all that is left of the House of Aberffraw and would call the faithful to him to stand against the invaders. He must have the relics to do it."

"Yes, I suppose he must." The abbot stared at the seal, and spoke softly, as if to himself. "Young and old must work together if we are to prevail in difficult times. Yet I cannot help but feel there is more danger in taking the relics out of the abbey."

"Had you seen the carnage done over the past few months," Rhys said, "you would not be as sure of their safety, here or anywhere."

The abbot went to a cabinet in the wall and gestured to Gawain to join him. As they conferred, Cat felt that strange grey foreboding that sometimes came over her and stepped closer to Rhys. She had to find a way to convince him now.

"You must go," she whispered. "Back to the holding. To protect the others." And yourself, she wanted to add. "I will bring the relics to you."

"Nay, my duty is here." His eyes probed hers as if to be sure she was truly safe.

"I told you of my vision, Rhys." She looked at him squarely. "I saw you slain."

A look of impatience passed over his face. "Always we have found a way to change the futures you see."

"And I believe this is the best way to save you and the treasures."

"You have warned me, and so I will change it. Or we will change it together. But you must be safe, so I can prepare for the rest." His eyes seemed a deeper blue than she had ever seen them, and she could not look away. "Please, Cat, go back now to join the others. They will be at the holding by now, and Cynfrig and Emrys will keep you all safe while I meet with Dafydd."

"Nay, Rhys. If you stay, I stay."

The abbot turned back to them. "With what you have told me, if the relics are not safe within these thick walls, how can you hope to keep them safe outside it?"

"I pledge it on my life," Rhys said, his voice pitched low and steady with the force of his conviction. Cat had a sudden image of the body lying crumpled on the grass in her vision. As if she had bidden it, a commotion broke outside, and Brother Mark threw open the door.

"Riders," the monk cried. Cat heard a sound and turned in time to see the abbot reaching out as a panel in the wood clicked open.

"How many?" Rhys' voice was sharp.

"Many!" Brother Mark shook his head. "Bearing an English pennant. They did not stop—"

He was interrupted by cries from the courtyard, punctuated with a sound of steel drawn from scabbards and the thudding of horse's hooves. Rhys rushed past the monk and out of the room.

"No!" Cat's vision rose to choke her. Too late.

"Wait," Gawain called out, but Cat was running after Rhys.

4

Hyw tracked Margred through the brush at the riverside. He was determined to find her quickly so they could return to his father with the report of Dolbadarn — not to mention getting his own clothing back. He twitched in the itchy fabric. He had not gone far when he heard men's voices and shushed Llywelyn's running commentary to listen. The voices were faint but unmistakable. He immediately crouched and made his way toward the sound.

Several men were watering horses, still wearing their armour. English troops from the castle. Hyw dropped lower into the shelter of the bushes, heart pounding, and schooled his breathing. He counted seven men, but twice as many horses. Scanning the area, he saw at least three more men on the shore. Their voices ebbed and flowed just beyond his hearing.

Using his gift of empathy, Hyw located a marten hiding at the water's edge, waiting for the men to leave. He listened through the marten's ears to their words.

"I'm telling you, there was a whole village of them. And you heard the king's promise—a shilling a head."

"Low-hanging fruit." The gruff laughter chilled Hyw's blood.

"No," a third voice interrupted. "We are not going to stoop to killing women and children for blood money, nor will the mercenaries if I have any say in it."

Hyw recognized the voice, but he couldn't quite place it.

"The king has his eye on other game that will bring us a far greater prize," the voice continued. "Prince Dafydd is hiding in this area, I am sure of it. We didn't catch him at Bere, but he cannot have gone far."

Murderer! Hyw closed his eyes to find Llywelyn in his fighting stance, sword raised above his head. He had recognized the voice at the same moment Hyw did. Stephen de Francton! The English knight had thrown a spear at an enemy on the hillside at Builth — and that enemy had turned out to be none other than Llywelyn, then Prince of Wales.

But de Francton was also the knight who had taken a delirious boy to a nearby abbey, shortly after the boy had unknowingly captured the prince's soul at the moment of his death. If the knight had not done so, Hyw would not have survived to bond with Llywelyn.

"Stay, my liege," he told Llywelyn inside his mind, without uttering a sound aloud. "The time will come when you can avenge yourself, if you still wish to do so. But that time is not now."

Hyw was aware enough to hear a slight rustle, as if an animal shifted in the trees above. Llywelyn sensed it as well and dropped his sword. Hyw opened his eyes and looked up into Margred's face. She was well hidden from the English soldiers, but he knew they would soon be checking the area. It would not be safe for long. He jutted his chin toward the woods behind them. She nodded and disappeared into the branches.

She was lithe, and he marvelled at her agility as he tried to track her progress through the tree branches above him. It was something they had all done as children. He had used the trees as concealment many times, before his transformation made it easier to search from the skies. He met her as she climbed down, leaves still in her hair and a combination of mud and moss smeared on her face for concealment. He gestured for her to follow and led her some distance away. Then he stopped and listened for any unnatural sound before speaking.

"Did you think to use your arrows on them?" he asked, keeping his voice quiet.

"Not on a group so large as that." She scoffed. "I was waiting for a man alone."

He raised his eyebrows and said nothing.

"I am a good shot," she said. "But even had I missed, it would have caused confusion among them."

He considered it a moment. Such an act might cause enough confusion for a hidden bowman to get away. It might also steer the soldiers away from the place where the Welsh hid, especially if it were two or three bowmen who could move with agility through the trees. It was dangerous but had sense in it for those with skill. He nodded at her.

"Come," he said and turned to make his way back. She stopped him.

"Wait. You think it a good plan? Then should we not go back?" She moved her head in the direction of the English soldiers.

He shook his head. "It will be a good plan. A few well-placed bowmen might take their minds off our warriors, and let the people pass by these woods safely, if we time it well." He gestured again for her to follow. "My father waits for word. Every minute we tarry now will put him in more jeopardy, especially with the English so near."

"But you must tell them it is my plan."

He stared at her for a moment. "Would it not be best if you tell them yourself?"

"Me? But—"

"Who better?" He gestured for her to follow and continued through the trees.

Hyw was almost as glad to see his own clothes as he was to see his father safe. Bran cast a look at Margred, but he said nothing about the rough cloak Hyw wore or the fact that he was human and not hawk when he arrived. Bran held the bundle out to Hyw.

"Clothing?" Margred's voice held a hint of laughter. "Why are you changing your clothes?"

"I—uh," he stammered.

"His mam wants him to be presentable," Bran answered smoothly.

Hyw grabbed his clothes and started to untie the tattered

cloak of the dead Welshman. Margred made a startled sound.

My niece is a lady, and a maid, however she dresses, Llywelyn whispered fiercely in his inner ear. *Move apart a way, into that bush.* Hyw's neck flushed but he did as directed. He heard his father's voice behind him.

"Lady Margred. You are far from camp, it seems."

"I sought our supper."

"I would applaud you, but we have more need for stealth than supper in these woods, my lady," he said. "If the English soldiers saw you, you would be taken and questioned."

"They had no hope of seeing me," she scoffed, but Bran cut her off.

"You do not know them, but they would not be gentle. And once they discover who you are, they would use you against your father."

"I would never tell—"

"They would get the answers they seek. Have no doubt."

The quietness of Bran's voice was chilling. Hyw had not anticipated the added danger for Margred, and he was certain she would not have. Straightening his tunic and breeches, Hyw returned to them. Before Margred could argue the point further, he launched into his account of the castle. He tried to recall every detail, from oil and tinder set near the trapdoor, to the lone soldier on the hoarding.

"There were perhaps a score of soldiers in the woods as well," Hyw added. "We came upon them at the stream, watering their horses. Armed, and with arrows aplenty."

"And how did the two of you come upon each other?" Bran asked.

Hyw recalled how he had spotted her from the stream. He could not explain, even to himself, why he had let the current take him as he had, but Margred had saved him from himself by her appearance. He did not want to admit what had gone through his mind, if only for a moment. Yet he would not have it seem—to her or to his father—that he had gone swimming instead of scouting for their people.

"I saw the soldiers from the trees a moment before I saw Hyw watching from the path. We made our way hence to tell you."

Hyw was relieved that she had spoken first. When she looked at him for support, he added, "I overheard them talking about hunting Prince Dafydd."

"You could not have overheard them from our hiding spot," Margred said. "I could not, and my ears are sharp." Hyw could not tell her that he had used the marten's ears, so he shrugged.

"You were there as well, Lady Margred?" Bran's face was grim, but she nodded as if she hadn't seen his scowl.

"I believe there is a way to sow confusion—"

"Confusion indeed," Bran said, cutting her off. "I feel there is more to this story, but I will hear it at the camp. We tarry here too long already. We must get back and make our report to the prince."

With that, Bran gestured to them to follow, and jogged off toward the camp where they had left Dafydd and the people.

Hyw marveled a little that Margred ran beside him, as easily and silently as he and his father ran. Llywelyn reminded him that Cat had mentioned their training sessions at the castle, but Hyw had not realized the girls had been so serious about it. He wondered if he should be worried about her, but instead, he found himself more than a little impressed.

Bran slowed near a shadowed area in the slate mountain that had once been an ancient hillfort, a series of small caves that now sheltered the warriors' wives and children. Near the mouth of one, he stopped and made a sound like the hoot of an owl, repeating it twice. Shortly after, a man appeared and gestured to them. They joined him and moved farther into the caves to find Prince Dafydd with twenty or so warriors from his and Llywelyn's hand-picked bodyguard.

Bran spoke for them, telling first of the countryside blackened from fires that had ravaged the fields and woodlands. Even as a hawk, Hyw had seen little game. The warriors nodded and shifted restlessly. Like Margred, others had gone out hunting, and like her, most had come back empty-handed again.

"Too many of us are freezing and hungry and tired," one man

was grumbling. "And now the *Saeson* put fire to the countryside."

"The fire will have scared away the game, but like us, the animals are creatures of habit," another warrior said. "They will be searching for new homes even now."

Unless their new homes are in the bellies of the Saeson, Llywelyn said in Hyw's inner ear.

"Unless they feed the English soldiers," the first man responded. The near-echo made Hyw raise his eyebrows, although Llywelyn couldn't see it. "We must find a place, and soon, or meet a similar fate."

"I do not think you would provide the same sustenance, Cadarn," Bran put in softly, gaining a grim laugh from some of the warriors near him.

"Even so," said another, glancing pointedly away from Dafydd. "As our prince knows, we were allowed to bring precious little from our stores at Bere. We need to replenish our supplies soon."

"If our grain for bread, and now even the roots and herbs that might have stretched our stores in a soup, are but smoke in an English fire, we are in a sorry state indeed."

"You are right." Prince Dafydd's voice rumbled around the men as he stood staring past them as if he could see the distant mountain and austere Dolbadarn Castle.

He could work from strength if he took back this castle first, Llywelyn whispered.

"And yet," said Dafydd, turning away as if rejecting the unspoken idea, "Dolbadarn is more detour than boon. We must retake my brother's *llys* at Garth Celyn."

He still thinks to best me in some way, Llywelyn fumed. *He could never take the easier or better path. You must persuade him to use what he has at hand.*

"Dolbadarn could become a strong base to keep the people safe as we call more troops." This time it was Bran who echoed Llywelyn's words. Before Prince Dafydd could refuse, Bran began the report on Dolbadarn castle, drawing it and their proposed route in the dirt.

As Bran spoke, one of Margred's sisters came to fetch her and the two girls whispered together. Margred had not been able to detail her plan, Hyw realized. He wanted to reassure her that he would broach it for her and credit her with it. Before he could find the words, Bran called him over to correct the castle outline he was drawing in the dirt.

"How many men, here?"

"I saw three, one watching and the other two inside the tower."

"Watching closely?" Dafydd's blue eyes raked Hyw sternly.

"They had no fear. Two played at chess, I think."

"But one man is all they need to sound the alarm and lower the portcullis," Dafydd said, his arms crossed over his chest. "I held that castle after our eldest brother was released from Llywelyn's imprisonment. It is well fortified and difficult to breach."

"For the *Saeson*," one of the men guffawed, and this set some to arguing the relative value of Welsh and English soldiers.

There is another way in. Llywelyn's voice was gruff. *You know of the tunnels at Garth Celyn. Your Mam's family set a similar tunnel in the caverns under Dolbadarn for my grandfather's use when he built this castle.*

One of the men was describing how to climb a rock wall, like the one on the eastern side of the castle. As Dafydd considered the idea, Hyw went to his father and in a low voice reminded him of Llywelyn's tunnel. But when Bran broached it to Dafydd, the prince was skeptical.

"I held this castle five years, and heard naught of it," Dafydd scoffed.

Because we did not trust you with it, Llywelyn remarked in Hyw's inner ear.

"Yet it is there, in truth." Another voice spoke, and Hyw looked up and found himself staring into the eyes of Aeneus, former head of Llywelyn's personal guard and his mam's confidante. "For one who can find the way."

"And who can do that?"

"The boy will know, and his Mam, since it was his Mam's family that built the tunnels."

The wall will open, but only to one who can find the catch. The prince's voice was low and gruff, as if the words were pulled from him. *My elder brother rose against me and I brought him here. Since your grand-mam had closed the tunnel at Garth Celyn, I bade her close this one as well.*

"Why would you do that?" Hyw asked him, without speaking the words aloud.

I had no wish for him to escape and try to kill me again. Those we left to guard him had no inkling of it. And I confess, that witchcraft—beg pardon, Hyw—but it holds no attraction for me, however I may find myself beholden to it now. Llywelyn had not mentioned his modern dislike of their ancient gifts since he and Hyw agreed to work together some months earlier. *Your Mam will know of it,* Llywelyn went on, *as Aeneus has said. He knows all your family's secrets.*

Dafydd stood without speaking for so long, Llywelyn clicked his tongue with annoyance.

"It seems we must climb over the rock or under it," Dafydd finally said. "Yet neither suits me well."

Bran stepped in to continue with his plan and gestured to Hyw to show them where he and Margred had spotted the English troops. As Margred looked his way, Hyw had a sudden wish for his red tunic and sash. Had she been at his ceremony at Bere? It had been a simpler ritual than usual, but her father had made Hyw a member of the prince's guard there.

And our colours would be a pretty target for the English here. Llywelyn's gruff voice sounded inside him again. *This is no time to impress a maid, lad—if you have not already.*

Again, Hyw's thoughts had escaped his control. He wondered if he could be developing feelings for Margred. He glanced sideways at her, and she took it as her cue to step forward.

"I was safe enough in the trees," she put in, "since they could not raise their heads with their helmets on." That gained a laugh or two from the warriors, so she continued. "A few of us with arrows could easily confuse their progress."

Prince Dafydd considered the idea and nodded, pointing to three of the warriors.

"And me, Da," she said quickly. "I can show them where the soldiers are."

He frowned at her, and the men hesitated. Margred moved toward them, shouldering her bow.

"Don't worry," she said, "I'll keep your men safe."

It was a bold move, and Hyw held his breath for her. Then one of the men grinned at her, and another laughed as they all began to move away with her among them. Hyw released his breath slowly as he watched her walk off with them, silently agreeing with Llywelyn's voice in his ear. *Her bravery puts the men to shame.*

5

Cat ran as far as the abbey courtyard before her fear rooted her. The riders careened toward Rhys but he stepped forward, as he had in her vision. He held his sword drawn and at the ready.

She could see the vision again in her mind's eye: Rhys cutting down the first rider, fending off the second, and then—No! She could not let it happen. She must change the outcome. The jewelled throwing knives Rhys had given her were stowed in the sheath strapped to her calf. She rustled her skirts and withdrew two of the knives. She held them lightly, flipping the first to hold the tip between her index finger and thumb.

It was almost over before she had time to set her throw. She heard the scrape of Rhys' sword and the thunder of the horse's hooves. When the first horse screamed, she forced her mind back to the scene. Rhys whirled but the second horseman was nearly upon him. Where had she seen the third rider? Her hand flew forward and released the knife.

The man came into view, and he jerked in the saddle. She saw the spurt of red blood. Had her knife struck home? For endless seconds, Cat could not move her eyes from the Englishman, reeling in the saddle. Her hand came up to her throat, but her mind blanked. His sword clattered to the ground as he fell out of sight behind the horse. Rhys took up the fallen English sword as he rushed past to engage two other men on horseback.

The English were everywhere. The younger monks had thrown

their reserve to the wind and were doing their best to fight, even as the abbot called out for peace. The world reeled around her. Had she really hit the English knight? She felt the answer in her gut and almost doubled over. Then Gawain seized her by the arm, pulling her into the abbey.

"Rhys," she said, unable to finish. Had she saved Rhys? Or was it all for naught? She struggled to get away from Gawain, but he held her fast.

"He will join us." Gawain rushed her into the darkness of the abbey nave. He balanced a pack under his other arm. "We must secure the relics."

Cat let Gawain pull her through the back doors of the abbey and into the woods by the stream. They ran until they could run no longer, and then lay in the grasses, hiding from the English pursuers that were sure to follow.

Her uncle tensed and looked up. He was peering over the long grasses. She scrambled up to look as well. They watched as four—no, five—horses galloped by, bunched close together around a man in white, seated in an awkward position.

"They have taken the White Abbot," Gawain whispered. It seemed impossible. Only moments before she had been negotiating with Abbot Cadwgan, and now he was bound and powerless. For a moment, the world seemed to flip upside down.

More horses galloped by and she craned her neck. There was only one man she really wanted to see in the throng, and bound would be better than what she feared. Rhys. Does he yet live?

"I do not see him." Gawain's words startled her, and she realized she must have said Rhys' name out loud.

The horse holding the abbot suddenly shied and the holy man was nearly thrown. Gawain went suddenly still beside her, and Cat saw the horse raise its head up twice and then step calmly into place beside the English soldiers. Her uncle must have used his gift. Gawain had an empathy with horses similar to her brother's. She reached up and touched her locket again. If only Hyw were here now, he could change into a hawk and bring them news of Rhys. Or turn into a lion and defeat these *Saeson*, once and for all.

One of the horsemen looked around him on the road, and Gawain pulled her down into the grass again. Cat's fear roared in her ears and she put one hand over her mouth to muffle her gasping breath. They lay still for a long time, listening to the horses' hooves clop on the packed earth of the roadway.

After a long moment of silence, she half-rose to check, but Gawain laid a hand on her arm. He placed one finger over his mouth without speaking, and she nodded. Sure enough, another round of thumps beat the ground as more horses rode by. They lay without moving for so long that her eyes began to droop.

Without meaning to, she drifted off, dreaming herself back into the abbey. She stood before an ornate door. Pushing against it, she felt it slowly open, and followed its momentum into the room. A monk stood with his back to her. She recognized Brother Mark's dark hair, and touched his shoulder. "Have you seen Lord Rhys—" But when he turned to face her, his eyes were pure white in his pale, bloodless face.

She jerked awake. Gawain clapped his hand over her mouth.

"Did I scream?" she asked softly, when he released her.

He shook his head. "You moaned, but I could not take the risk. Beg your pardon, Catrin."

"Did you see him?"

Gawain, knowing she meant Rhys without needing to hear the name, shook his head. "We must find the others."

"We must go back and look for—"

Gawain shook his head again and kept his voice at a whisper. "If he is alive, he will find us. If we go back to search for him, we take the risk of bringing the English to us, and so endanger him more." He laid a hand on her arm as she started to protest. "You must trust his instincts now, as I do."

She searched his face for a moment before she nodded. She put her knife back in its sheath. He grabbed her hand to pull her up and they crouched over, using the grass as cover while they ran. After what seemed like an eternity, Gawain tapped her arm.

"There," he said, pointing down the field.

She saw the brush move, and a figure stumbled into sight. Rhys! He was limping, and his clothes were caked with mud and blood, but he was alive! She pushed past Gawain and ran to meet him.

Rhys hugged her fiercely. "Are you injured?"

Her laugh was muffled in his tunic. He took both her arms and looked at her carefully.

"I am fine," she told him. He dropped his hands from her shoulders, and she shivered with sudden cold. Then it was her turn to inspect him. "The blood—is it yours?"

"Some of it."

Yet you are alive, she thought. He had already tied a strip of fabric around his thigh to staunch the bleeding, and the cut was shallow. She turned his arm over and saw another cut on his forearm, streaming with bright red blood. She set to work cleaning it with water from the flask on her belt.

Gawain caught up with them as she did so. Through the bush came Cynfrig, holding up another man as they made their way back toward the wooded stream. It was Emrys.

"Bronwen sent me." Emrys grinned sheepishly.

"Where is she?"

"At the holding," Cynfrig said, as he helped Emrys settle on the ground. "Our people are safe enough for now. I meant to come alone to help but my stubborn nephew would not hear of it."

Cat expelled a breath of relief at knowing Bronwen and her unborn babe were out of danger.

"I am glad of your stubbornness," Rhys said.

"And glad I am to see you safe." Cynfrig hugged Rhys to him. Although the older man barely came to Rhys' shoulder, Rhys hugged him back just as fiercely.

"And the others?"

Cynfrig moved his head slightly. "I did not see."

"But you are injured." Cat moved toward Emrys.

Emrys waved dismissively. "Cynfrig has made it worse with his linens."

The older man grinned at her. She examined Emrys and saw the old steward had torn a piece of his own tunic and tied it above Emrys' wound.

"The abbot," Gawain said, more as a statement than a question.

"Aye, they took him," Cynfrig said. "But he was alive when we saw him last. Edward's army moved in force. We could not prevent the mercenary scum from entering the abbey. We saw them bring the abbot out and ride off with him. After that, most of the soldiers broke off and rode after them. It was all we could do to get ourselves to safety. So the English have the Cross of Neith?"

"Nay." Gawain patted the travel pack slung around his shoulders, but his eyes were hooded. "The abbot believes this is more valuable than his own life. That the power of God's word alone is enough to stop these invaders."

The abbot must have stayed behind to help them get away. Cat took a closer look at the modest brown pack and could see the sturdy quality of the worn leather. This must contain the relics. Her hand began to reach out of its own accord toward the pack, but Gawain chose that moment to look up again.

"What of my brothers? Do any remain in the abbey?"

"The abbey was overrun with *Saeson*," Rhys said, shaking his head. "They rode out as soon as they had the abbot. I trust some of the brothers were taken prisoner with him."

Gawain said nothing. Cat crossed herself, recalling the spectre of Brother Mark in her dream. And when they watched from the roadside earlier, she had seen only one white-robed man on the horses that rode off with the abbot.

Emrys was resting easy and seemed little interested in their talk, so she gathered a strip of cloth from the kit she always carried at her waist to finish bandaging Rhys' wound. Her mind turned again to her uncle's pack and its contents. Many still believed that piece of the True Cross offered the Welsh divine protection. Arthur's crown had been passed down the Aberffraw family line for centuries, and it was said to be thrumming with the power of old traditions. She had seen the ornate coronet King Edward's father had given to Llywelyn, and wondered if Arthur's crown would have more jewels. She itched to ask if Gawain would open his pack to let them see the triad of treasures, but she busied her hands with the bandage instead.

"They must have taken the abbot to one of their strongholds," Rhys said. He didn't continue, but she knew the *Saeson* would stop at nothing to discover the whereabouts of the relics. If the enemy held these items, they could leech the fight from the people without resorting to swords. She crossed herself again, praying for the abbot's safety as she tended Rhys' wound.

"It is a surety where they will take the White Abbot," said Cynfrig. "To King Edward."

As Cat finished her bandage, Rhys flexed his arm. "Then we must get him back."

"Nay, the abbot bade me promise I would keep these safe," Gawain said. His face was drawn and worried. "I must take them to Abbey Conwy." Cat hadn't thought of their home abbey near Garth Celyn for too long. Her uncle must be homesick for it as well, she realized.

"You must not, Brother Gawain," Rhys was saying. "The way is not safe, and the English are too many. I have been charged by Prince Dafydd to bring the relics to him, that he may rally the people to fight against the English king."

"Then I will come with you to the prince, and we may guard these together, with force and prayer," said Gawain. "Where is Dafydd now?"

"He is gathering forces, and we must also join him as soon as we can," said Rhys. He averted his eyes, and Cat realized he had never said the actual meeting place. He had been cautious with any information, and she wondered if Dafydd was afraid of more betrayal.

Cynfrig grimaced. "I hope the prince had an easier way than ours. And your family with him, Lady Cat." All eyes suddenly riveted on Cat.

"I…" she stammered, glancing around to be sure Emrys was out of earshot. "I have seen nothing of the prince or my family, nor how they fare."

"Your visions will come as we need them," said Rhys, reassuringly. "If you have seen nothing, it bodes well for them."

"Aye," said Cynfrig, his face drawn into more wrinkles than usual. "And we will soon be able to ask them, when we get these relics back to our new leader. May they have the intended result and help to secure our land."

6

As Hyw prepared to go with the others to gather supplies, the prince stepped in front of him.

"Have you heard from your sister or Lord Rhys?"

"No, my liege," Hyw responded.

"We shall have to send you in search of them soon." Dafydd stood a moment with his hands crossed over his chest. "Tell your shade that I know he is responsible for this scheme to take Dolbadarn. Let us hope his prescience pays off." The prince brushed past before Hyw could respond.

Your shade! Llywelyn's arms were folded across his chest. *Is that what he calls me? Why will he not accept my advice? Always he went his own way. Trying to help him may yet prove to be a mistake.* Hyw wished Dafydd would accept his brother's advice more easily, but their animosity lasted even after death. The two brothers were too similar in their anger. But Hyw tried to guard such thoughts from the former prince, whose frustrations with their situation were always close to the surface. At least Hyw knew he had made the right choice in approaching his father first.

As Hyw turned, Bran stopped him with a small smile. "Thank our liege for the guidance." At first Hyw thought he meant Prince Dafydd, but quickly realized his father referred to Llywelyn's spirit.

"I have strict orders from your Mam to send you to her, as soon as you are free," Bran continued, with a firmness that brooked no argument. "And you should perhaps check with her on the location of the tunnel entrance."

Hyw looked for his mother in the caves with the other women and found her preparing Baby Gwenllian for travel. *The child has grown*, Llywelyn said with pride. *Would that I could hold her.*

Hyw sensed the prince's grief keenly. Llywelyn and Elinor had spent only four years together before the princess was taken in childbirth, and Gwen was their only daughter. Hyw reached down and swung the babe up into the air to make her laugh, and then held her to him and sat on a nearby rock ledge. He closed his eyes a moment and turned to the prince, who stepped forward to hold his daughter in his arms. When they changed places again, Hyw could see tears in the former prince's eyes.

Adara smiled at him, seeming to understand the depth of what had transpired, although she never asked for the details. She motioned for Rhiannon, Margred's sister, to watch the baby, and Hyw handed the child to her.

Adara took his arm to walk with him a ways apart from the other women. She was a little thinner than he recalled, but she glowed with spring and seemed only a little older than Margred or Cat. He realized it was her gift, and it would sustain her as she prepared for the May Day rituals.

"You look well, Mam." He knew she liked it when he called her Mam, instead of using the English words he had learned while fostering at Shrewsbury, training to become a squire. "Will you bring in the May this spring?" He had attended many times when he was young, and even now he could recall his mother dancing in the moonlight with a crown of bees around her.

"I must," she said, "wherever we find ourselves. Do you know where we will be then, or what Prince Dafydd has planned?"

"We may have found a sanctuary for you." He told her of Llywelyn's plan. Taking a cue from his father, he drew her a plan in the dirt, and she helped him trace the route from it to the mountainside where the others should wait. She also went over the location of the latch in the armoury of the castle, and Llywelyn agreed as she spoke. When they had finished, Hyw tried to smile at her but could not help looking toward the trees, anxious to return to hawk form. The look on his mother's face caused him to leave his desire unspoken.

"The gift you have is a powerful one, Hyw," she said. "My grandfather had the same power of shifting form. He was always staring at the trees and woods, as you do. And like you, he could take any shape."

I recall him well, said Llywelyn, his voice like a whisper in Hyw's ear. *He brought us information on the movements of Edward's troops that won many battles. I did not know of his power, but as a spy, he was unparalleled.*

Hyw knew his uncle Gawain had done his best to guide him in the use of his powers, but he wished he had known his great-grandfather. Hyw could barely imagine the secrets his ancestor could have shared.

"Was there one shape that he preferred?" Hyw could not help but ask.

Adara pursed her mouth. "He did not say. He seemed to love them all. My mother spoke of him as a hawk, like you, and also as a horse. For my brother Gawain, it was always horses that kept him connected to the earth, although he never tried to change his form to one."

Hyw wondered what the world might be like as a horse. His gift had found him in Shrewsbury's stables, while he was a page, and his first connection had been with the horses. As he focused on the animal's powerful chest and legs, his body began to expand.

Adara shook his arm. "Nay, Hyw," she said. "Stay with me as you are." He focused on his hands to keep his form. But he discovered a reluctance in himself, almost a distaste for the shape of his own hands. Glancing sideways, he caught her frowning at him.

"You must beware, my son," she said. "Our grandfather used his power rarely, yet even more rarely did he speak or interact with us, his grandchildren. Mam—your nan—told me once that his power lay heavy on him when he was young, and he liked it too well. Had he not tethered himself to our grand-mam, he might have taken a beast's form altogether."

"You mean, not return to the form of a man at all?" Hyw was surprised to hear the wistfulness in his voice. Adara stopped then and turned him to face her.

"I see the look of him in you," she told him. "It is there, in your eyes. Of late, since we left Bere, I have feared it. Stay with us, Hyw. We need you now, more than ever before. Tether yourself to someone."

"You are my tether, Mam," he said. "You and Cat."

She searched his face, as if she could see a different answer there, and then hugged him to her briefly. "If that is true, then be with us, as much as ever you can, and only make the change when it cannot be helped," she told him. "Your gifts are strong, but you have equal strengths as a man, Hyw. Remember that we need you now. If we do not work together we will surely perish—us and all our people with us."

He could see the urgency in her face and stopped himself from looking at the woods again. He was not convinced that he could help as much in his human form, but he did not want to worry her further. "Ease your mind on that account, Mam. Whenever you have need of me, I will be here."

She stared into his eyes a moment longer and seemed satisfied with what she saw. "Come, let us get back to the others," she said. "Rhiannon will be fuming that I have left her too long as a nursemaid." As she turned, she glanced sideways at him, and he caught her smiling.

"What?" he asked.

"I saw you come back from the woods with her sister Margred earlier. You could surely not find a better match in our company."

"It's nothing like that," he said, trying not to show his embarrassment as he gave her his arm again. "She is Prince Dafydd's daughter. And we are at war." His mam said nothing more as they returned to the group of women and children.

Llywelyn reminisced about the feats of men who had fallen in the last war. Hyw carefully shrouded his thoughts, and let his mind turn, as it often did, to James, his foster brother from the time he spent at Shrewsbury's English court. After the English took Dolwyddelan castle, James had helped Hyw escape to warn Bran and the Welsh. Hyw had promised James' father that he would never take arms against James, if they should meet on the battlefield as enemies. What would he do if he found Shrewsbury and James at Dolbadarn? How could he protect his friend without betraying his prince?

Hyw jogged behind his father and the other warriors, along the pathways of Llanberis Pass and up the rocky crag to the castle. They had slathered themselves in the mud and a crude dye his Mam had made from woad leaves. She said it would help them blend into the afternoon shadows, whispering to Hyw that it would also help with his transformations. Knowledge of what awaited them at Dolbadarn clenched his stomach long before he caught sight of the round tower rising above the lake. He tempered his gift to connect with birds in the surrounding area, using their sharp eyes to watch for English soldiers without changing his shape.

Bran signalled everyone down, and Hyw crouched a little behind the others so he could slip away to transform at his father's signal. Bran had found them a place near the mouth of the tunnel to wait, but not so close that Hyw would be noticed. His da now turned to give him an encouraging smile. Hyw took a deep breath to ease the tension in his stomach and shoulders. He moved his mouth in what he hoped was an answering smile and slipped off the path.

The hawk's form called to him and he barely stopped to stow his clothes. Always before, he had waited for Llywelyn to fall asleep before he began the change. But the prince stood with his arms crossed.

If your powers rival your great-grandfather's, then what you may see is invaluable. And I can guide you more if I am conscious than if I am prone.

"I've given my word to serve and protect you," Hyw responded, without speaking aloud. "When I give myself to another form, how can I be certain that I keep you safe from it?"

I am the protector of Wales, boy, Llywelyn's voice rumbled. *You must know that I can protect myself from this OtherWorld magic.* Hyw frowned but Llywelyn would not be swayed. *If you mean to serve me well, then you must share with me everything you see.*

Hyw opened his eyes. Still uncertain, he raised his arms and stared at his fragile skin, covered with the blue woad his mam had devised. Something ancient stirred under his skin, and he reached into his memory for the songs Cat and Gawain had sung to help him in the past. The sound brought a bird form into his mind, and it beckoned to him. He imagined covering his arms with bright plumage as his mouth curved and hardened. Spreading his arms higher, he burst into feathered wings. His heavy bones lightened and disappeared as he took flight.

He circled the spot where his human form had been, marvelling at how painless it was to assume the hawk's form and how swiftly he could glide through the trees. His mother's woad was working. After an initial cry that might have been terror or exhilaration, Llywelyn remained largely silent. Hyw dared not close his eyes to see how his prince fared, nor think about the change back. Instead he focused on the task of finding his way into the castle to open the tunnel.

Swooping over the wall above the portcullis, Hyw flew around the windows of the tall, round keep. The tunnel entrance was inside the lowest floor, accessible only through a trap door that led into the keep's massive armoury. He kept his eyes sharp for the movement of humans inside. Finding an unoccupied room past the second tier of arrow slits, he landed on the stone ledge. The room was empty, and he opened his wings to glide into the building.

From the landing he glided down, past the guard who leaned lazily in the keep's main entrance, staring out at the courtyard. The guard yawned loudly, and Hyw held his breath as he circled above him, but the man merely called out an insult to someone who must have been practicing nearby. Hyw continued down the stairwell and through the open trap door into the darkness below.

With no windows, the thick stone walls of the armoury protected it from attack even by catapult. The trap door offered a small slit of light, enough for his hawk's eyes. He glided past the makeshift wooden ladder that stood against the opening, and landed softly, his claws silent against the dirt floor.

Now he had no choice. Muffling his moans, his body writhed and crackled as it fought to return to its human shape again. The woad had eased the change, but the cold of the uncovered floor shocked him and his aching muscles seized against it. As he lay panting on the ground, goosebumps prickled his arms and legs like the remains of shredded feathers. He quieted, listening. There was no shout of alarm. So far, so good. Llywelyn stirred inside him. He was sure there would be a torch or lantern, but he dared not look for it, praying the darkness and the remains of his mother's woad might hide him as he sought for the tunnel.

On his hands and knees, he crept forward as Llywelyn directed. When he reached the wall, he scraped his fingers against the rough stone but could not find the catch.

Hurry, Llywelyn whispered. Hyw fumbled across the same area over and over, scraping his fingers raw. Would it be easier to fly back to the other end of the tunnel and approach from inside? Surely the guards would not hear them? *Nay, the catch was not set from that end,* Llywelyn told him. *We deemed it safer to have only an exit in case of attack, but not to open ourselves to one. It must be found, Hyw.*

At the prince's direction, Hyw moved back to the ladder and stood to measure out the steps, heel to toe, as he moved to the wall again. Still nothing. Then he walked back to the trap door, and again to the wall on the other side. He felt along the wall—and found nothing. Again at Llywelyn's order, he moved around the wall, counting steps, circling the ladder that remained partially lit by the sunlight far above them. He examined the stone wall of the armoury, feeling for a catch at his shoulder. Once a shadow moved across the ladder, and Hyw paused as the guard's footsteps crossed the room and returned to the castle doorway. When they heard his muffled voice yelling insults again, Hyw relaxed and continued his slow progress.

Try higher on the wall, Llywelyn growled. *More at my shoulder height than yours.* Again Hyw slowly circled the room, scraping his fingers against the uneven rock surface. A hole? Merely a flaw in the mortar. A ridge? The seam of two badly fitted stones.

Finally Hyw stepped aside to let Llywelyn take over his body. He watched, as if over Llywelyn's shoulder, as the prince scanned the room, no doubt harkening back in his memory. Then they moved toward the dark shape of the wall, counting steps again, this time using a measure a little longer than Hyw's own foot. He could not feel his fingers under Llywelyn's control, but knew he was searching the wall as Hyw had done. The moments ticked by in darkness, interminably, as they stood facing the wall. Finally he heard something click, and a scraping of stone as the doorway opened.

"Huh?" The guard had also heard the sound and held a lantern into the trap door opening. His voice quavered a little. "Who's there?"

Frantically, Hyw scrabbled deeper into the shadows and at the same time sent his senses outward into the room. Nothing larger than a sowbug snuffled through the chinks in the stone wall. There was no help other than what he himself could devise. Gesturing in his mind for Llywelyn to prepare, he focused on the hawk and began to step forward into the change.

Then he felt Llywelyn's hand on his arm. *Steady, lad*, the former prince said. *We must get through the tunnel and open the second doorway. It was made to aid escape, not invasion.*

Hyw nodded but could not call his mind back from the escape of wings so quickly. He struggled against himself and focused on his human hands to stop the change, but his mind soared toward the light from the windows in the room above them. As if he had called it, a small black tern winged through the upper window of the keep. Hyw's consciousness settled as lightly into the bird's as a butterfly might settle on his hand. He felt the bird's joy and almost laughed as they fluttered together around the guard's head. The guard stepped back with a curse, nearly throwing the lantern at the bird. The tern screeched back at him, flapping its wings. Hyw led the tern toward the open doorway and out to safety.

The guard swore and expelled a shaky breath. "A bird in the house is an ill omen." Hyw could almost see the man cross himself. He heard the lantern creak and a second set of footsteps moved toward the trap door as the guard called out. Hyw strained to hear their voices but couldn't make out the words.

"'Ere, Ralph," a second voice said suddenly. "Yer losin' yer mind in this hole." Another muffled sentence, and two sets of footsteps returned to the doorway together.

Well played, Hyw. He was listening so hard to the guard's fading chatter that Llywelyn's voice in his ear nearly made him jump. *Let us hope we can find the next latch more easily than this one.* Hyw said a silent prayer as he felt his way into the dark tunnel.

7

By the time Cat had finished tending Rhys and Emrys, the sun was lower in the sky. Rhys said little but she could tell by the tension in his body that he wanted to be on their way to Prince Dafydd with the relics in Gawain's pack.

Cynfrig was keeping watch for other men from their company who had also survived the English attack, and finally a small group had gathered. They had volunteered to help Cynfrig when he went after Rhys, but that meant leaving the women and children at the nearby holding with little protection, so Rhys addressed them first.

"We have few warriors to spare, and the people will have need of you now. You must assist those who are wounded and return swiftly to the holding." Then Rhys turned to Gawain, jutting his chin toward the pack he carried close to his side. "Brother Gawain, I welcome your blessing and company on the road to rejoin Prince Dafydd."

Cat noticed he didn't mention the relics in front of Emrys and their other companions. Finally Rhys turned to her. "Cat, will you go with Emrys? I am sure Bronwen would appreciate your assistance now."

"Bron has Haf and many other women to help her," Cat said. She turned to the steward to add, "Doesn't she, Cynfrig?" Cynfrig said nothing, so she turned back. "Besides, after you get to the prince, you will stay to fight for him, will you not?" When Rhys lowered his eyes, she knew she had been right. "At least, I may be reunited with my family there also. And we have my uncle as chaperone."

She softened her decision by offering a warm goodbye to Emrys, and thanked the other men for helping him return to Bronwen. Since Emrys was not from the area, Cynfrig and Gawain offered to walk a ways with the party of warriors to help them find the path they needed. As soon as they had taken a few steps, Rhys turned to her again.

"Will you at least remain with your mam after we get there?"

"Of course," she said, but this time it was she who turned away. "And in the meantime I would have a way to defend myself, even with your sword for protection." She glanced up to find a question on his face. "Avert your eyes."

"What?"

She gestured to her skirts, and he gave a slight shrug as he shifted to look at the nearby trees. She rummaged under her skirt to find her sheath with the two remaining daggers, and quickly moved it to a spot around her waist, fixing it to her belt. As she finished, Cynfrig and Gawain returned from seeing the others off.

"Do not start," Cynfrig said, holding up a hand to Rhys. "I stay for the relics. It is my duty as much as yours."

"Only because I made it so."

Cynfrig continued as if Rhys hadn't spoken. "And of course, Cat must go with us." The old steward patted Rhys on the back. "Mab helped us often enough in similar circumstances."

Mab, Cat remembered, was the name of Rhys' former nurse, the Irish morrigan. Cat touched her sheath. Rhys had had the throwing knives forged for Cat, but the sheath that held them had been Mab's. It was a testament to his faith in her gift. Cat thought suddenly of Ifan, the young warrior who had taken care of her when they were in hiding at Criccieth so many months ago. Ifan had become a friend and had given his life protecting her and the others from a sudden attack. The past swallowed her present as the sharpness of his loss flooded her again. She had held Ifan's hand as he lay dying, until she found herself standing with his spirit in the mist. The mist held them in a strange compulsion, and she moved through it to lead the young warrior's spirit safely home. She shuddered back to reality and crossed herself, dreading the time when she would have to use that aspect of her gift again.

"Lady Catrin may help us in our duty now," Cynfrig was saying. "A morrigan and a holy man among us can only bring us luck. The three of us form a triad at your back."

"I see my words have no effect on any of you." Rhys turned away from them, brooding. Cynfrig nodded at Cat, but she couldn't find the words to respond. He stepped up to her left side, so she walked between him and Rhys. Gawain followed with his pack as they began the trek to bring Prince Dafydd the relics. Her uncle's white robes would be easily visible, but he could not be convinced to change to regular clothing.

"I must trust in God's plan for me, as for all of us," was all he would say about it.

The place they were headed was more than a day's travel from the holding. The lateness of the hour meant they would need to spend one night, perhaps two, in the open, so they kept a lookout for shelter. It was nearly May, and the sky was cloudless with the promise of a warm evening. Cynfrig nodded to her, clasping his hands behind his back.

"Have you—seen anything of note, Lady Cat?"

She shook her head. She had tried a few times as they crossed streams, but nothing else had come to her. She couldn't shake the feeling that her powers were waning, but she didn't want to admit that to Cynfrig.

Rhys spoke from her other side. "She will tell us when something comes to her, and then we must be wary."

"We should always be wary," she said, looking down at the path.

"Aye, so we are, so we are," Cynfrig assured her.

They set up a makeshift camp near a small, crumbling well that Gawain told them was a shrine to a holy woman. He sat against the edge and took off his pack. With shaking hands, he unbuckled the top and reached into the pack, checking the contents with great care. First, he took out Llywelyn's jewelled coronet, and in his other hand he brought out the crown said to be the legendary King Arthur's. Involuntarily Cat reached out, and Gawain put the simple ring of gold into her hands. A shock of power ran through her body. It thrummed! Just as people said it did.

Yet when she handed it to Cynfrig in turn, he turned it over in his hands as if disappointed. "It's almost too plain, isn't it?" He handed it back to Gawain.

Cat wondered if he really could not feel it. Perhaps she had been imagining it, or she had some special connection with it through her gift.

Y Groes Naid was smaller than she remembered. The gold and jewelled Celtic cross was a reliquary hiding a splinter of wood from Christ's True Cross safely inside it. Llywelyn had worn this reliquary around his neck on great occasions, like Baby Gwen's christening. Was that really less than a year ago? Cat could feel the relic's power even without touching it. She and the men instinctively knelt and crossed themselves when Gawain held it up. He set it down reverently, and led them in a fervent prayer for their protection and for peace to return to their beleaguered country.

"By God's grace," she echoed when her uncle had finished.

Finally, if reluctantly, Gawain replaced the relics in the bag. Moving around the well, he gathered a few large, loose stones and began to pile them around the pack for safekeeping. Then Gawain sat and leaned his back against the area, and the pack effectively disappeared from view.

Cynfrig had packed some hard-tack for them, and they shared it with thanks, since they dared not hunt or light a fire. The old steward pulled a flask from inside his tunic as well.

"To fortify us on our journey," he said with a wink as he handed the flask to Cat. It turned out to be strongly spiced Welsh ale, and she was glad of it.

Cat's need to prove her value to Rhys and Cynfrig tugged at her. She still had not seen a vision of the prince, or one that might tell her whether they were taking the safest path. She shifted to sit beside Gawain.

"Uncle," she began, "I know that we can call on our gifts by breathing and focus."

"And through the old songs," he reminded her.

"Yes. All that I have tried, but to no avail. My gift comes when it wills, and it seems as if I have little power to command it."

He frowned. "Are you concerned that you cannot see your family?"

"I – I had been focusing on the prince," she admitted. She had not thought of her mam and da, nor of Hyw.

"Ah," he said. "How have your visions happened for you in the past?" When she shrugged, he continued. "Do you recall your first vision?"

"It was of Hyw, as he watered horses in a stream," she began. Later she had seen Aeneus, her mother's friend and their protector, and often she had seen her friends Owain or Margred. She had once seen a vision of Irish ships when she was thinking about Rhys. Her most recent vision of Rhys was perhaps the most powerful one she had seen.

"Wait," she said. "You are saying I must focus on those close to me, rather than the prince himself, or the English and their soldiers?"

"It could be," Gawain suggested. "Perhaps your visions come to you through friends and family, rather than through your enemies. After all, Prince Dafydd was your father's enemy when you were young." She raised her eyebrows, and he continued. "Your father was always loyal to Llywelyn, but Dafydd betrayed them both for Edward's favour many years before Edward became the king of England."

Cat went quiet, thinking this over. Gawain watched her as he continued.

"Or perhaps you are chasing away the visions in your anxiety to be of service. You have always had a vision when it was most needed. Perhaps Rhys is right, and when we are truly in danger, then your visions will come to aid us."

"Thank you, uncle," she said, kissing him on the cheek.

Before she could stand up to test her idea, Cynfrig dropped to one knee and laid his palm on the ground. His expression turned grim. Then Cat could feel it: the rumble underfoot. Horses. Rhys moved his shabby cloak down to cover his sword and gestured to Cynfrig. But it was too late. The riders were upon them.

Cat's breath caught in her throat as she saw the banner carried by the first rider—the same sigil she'd seen when Cynfrig negotiated the fate of Bere. The *Saeson*—the English—had found them. Why hadn't she foreseen this? A tremor went through her, a combination of exhaustion and fear.

Fear? She raised her head a little higher. She'd been raised at the Welsh royal court, with spies all around and family secrets to keep hidden from friend and foe. She could almost hear Mam's voice: Never assume what others may or may not know. Say only the truth, or enough of it to turn the conversation to your side. Rhys nodded with his chin toward Cynfrig and the others, but she drew in a deeper breath and moved to Rhys' side, ignoring his frown. The time had come for her to prove her value.

One rider reined in, and the horses behind him slowed to a stop. Several of the riders drew swords, but the first remained still, his hands crossed over the reins. Their leader. His richly coloured surcoat bore King Edward's colours. Holding his seat easily, the leader raised his visor to stare first at Rhys, and then at Cat. His eyes lingered too long on her face and form, and she flushed. She did not move away when Rhys shifted to stand a little in front of her.

Cynfrig was already speaking, proffering a parchment. "We have safe passage from King Edward. I am Cynfrig ap Madoc, and this my kin and his lady wife."

Wife? She steeled herself, but Rhys didn't try to contradict him. No doubt they hoped to protect her, and looking at the armoured soldiers surrounding them, she was glad of it.

"And I am Brother Gawain of Abbey Conwy." Gawain stood slowly and held his arms open in front of him as the English captain crossed himself. Cat noted that his action spread his white habit so that he continued to shield the stones that protected the pack of relics from the soldiers' view.

"I would say 'well met,' Lord Cynfrig," the leader said, in Welsh, "but it isn't really so, is it? You may recall me, as I do you. I am Stephen de Francton, late of Shrewsbury."

His name was familiar. De Francton caught her eye again as he took the parchment Cynfrig was holding out. Cat shifted uneasily, stepping farther behind Rhys. She heard a rustle as de Francton unrolled the parchment, and she felt a flush of relief. At least the man could read. Their guarantee of safe passage for surrendering the castle would prove its worth now.

She frowned. She understood English well enough, but de Francton seemed fully fluent in Welsh. Then it came to her. This was the man her brother Hyw had named in the murder of Llywelyn, their former liege and prince. And this de Francton had also been there when Rhys and Cynfrig made their bargain: the freedom of their people in return for the castle and Prince Dafydd. What must have happened when the English found the castle empty?

"Came you by this honestly, would you say?" de Francton asked. There was an edge to his voice and she was glad he was still speaking Welsh so she could follow the nuances.

"We gave up a fortified castle for this and some few English pounds," Cynfrig was saying. "Far less than the castle was worth, and we would do far more, to keep our freedom."

De Francton straightened, looking at Rhys now. "You are lucky we found you, and not the Gascons. Or the Castilians. They make no distinction between peasant and prey."

For a long moment, de Francton stared from one to the other, again stopping at Cat. Rhys moved forward, but de Francton backed his horse deftly to keep her in view. She could not name his expression, but it was neither admiration nor approval, and it prickled her skin to gooseflesh.

Cynfrig reached out a hand for the return of the parchment. De Francton ignored him.

"We made this bargain to find Prince Dafydd," de Francton said, slapping the parchment against his own gloved palm. "And I think you know that we were not satisfied. So why should we keep faith with it now?"

"Why would you not?" Cynfrig asked. "The prince stood on

the battlements when we left the castle, as you could plainly see. As for what happened afterwards, that is a matter between you and Prince Dafydd."

"What, did some Welsh magic spirit him away?" Unexpectedly, he turned to Cat. "And you, Lady? Perhaps you can shed some light on his whereabouts?"

Startled, Cat met his eyes. Did he know the truth of her brother's gift? Of her gift? Mam's words came to her again. *Never assume.* Rhys moved his arm toward his sword, where it hid beneath his cloak, but she placed her hand on his elbow in what she hoped was a wifely gesture.

"Any light I can shed is what you can see for yourself," Cat said, straining to keep her voice as smooth as she could. "The prince is not with us."

"Are you saying he casts a dimmer light for you than for me?" De Francton scanned them, flicking his eyes over their tattered cloaks and road-worn clothing. "From the look of you, it would indeed seem that your Prince has abandoned you."

Cat's anger sparked and she raised her chin, letting the feeling seethe inside her. It was not Dafydd that had brought them to this state, but this man and his English king, besieging them for more than a year. Nay, a hundred years, and more. Why could these *Saeson* not go back to their own land and leave Wales alone? But before she could speak, de Francton added, "And your brother? Where has he flown?"

A chill doused her anger as a cloud might cover the sun. Her brother Hyw had dressed as the prince at the castle and then escaped by transforming himself into a hawk. That was his gift, as the Sight was hers. For less than that, the English priests could brand them both as practitioners of the dark arts. Cat held very still.

"So the lad is your brother," de Francton continued. "I thought as much. You are as alike as any who shared a womb."

She must be careful now. "And yet he is two years my senior. May I ask how you know him?"

"He did not tell you?" de Francton smirked. "I saved his life. Well, no matter. Perhaps I shall tell you the whole story of it someday. For now, we have more pressing matters. Tell me, if I find the lad, will I also find the prince?"

So, he only sought to provoke her into giving away information, like any courtier, and yet not as skillfully as many she had known. Cat let out her breath in a chuff.

"You think well of us, to believe we may keep company with the Prince of Wales."

"Your prince remains the most sought-after prize in this God-forsaken country."

"And yet I do not know his whereabouts, or my brother's. My place is with my husband."

"That is unfortunate. As soon as we find the prince, we can leave you all in peace."

"Then may I wish you well on your return to Shrewsbury." Letting anger push her forward, Cat reached out for the parchment. "Pray you, if you see my brother, give him our greetings."

As he handed the parchment to her, de Francton held his end a moment too long. Cat braced herself, never taking her eyes from him. Finally, the Englishman broke eye contact, and she felt the parchment in her hand. She quickly handed it to the side, where she knew Cynfrig would be waiting. The steward's cloak rustled as he slipped the king's letter back into its folds.

The move had shifted her cloak and de Francton paused, his eyes on her belt. A look of shock passed over his face. She reached instinctively to it and found the two little knives sheathed there. She moved to cover them with her cloak again but it was too late.

"It would seem you are missing something," de Francton said. Looking her in the eye, he reached under his cloak and held up a small dagger. Its emerald jewel caught the light, and she realized he must have seen the matching jewels in the pair she still had. "Perhaps this is the match? I found it in the shoulder of one of my own kinsmen yesterday. My cousin, also late of Shrewsbury. A fine swordsman and solid rider; now he will return home sooner than I, though in a wooden crate." He eyed her, coldly. "So, what think you? Is this yours?"

Cat froze. The third rider. Guilt flooded her, and she heard the voice of Father Maelgwyn, the only priest and confessor she had known. He had proven to be a turncoat for the English, but she could still recall his sermons on the wages of sin. *As ye sow, so shall ye reap.* She tried to shake off the idea. They were at war; she had done what she had to do, to protect Rhys. But she had not thought about the man she targeted with her knife. Had she really killed him?

"Nay, my lord." Rhys spoke quietly, his deep blue eyes seeking hers, to reassure her and warn her to remain silent at the same time. "It is mine."

"And you are mine," de Francton said.

Cat's attention snapped to de Francton. He would take out his ire on Rhys now. She had thrown her knife and killed a man, and Rhys had claimed the deed and its consequences. Her sins compounded and she fought down a wave of sickness that threatened to overcome her.

"I would run you through and let my men keep your heads for the king's gift," de Francton went on, switching to English. She had no need of nuance to follow his meaning, and he spoke loudly enough for his men to hear as well. "But I do believe Lord Mortimer will give me a great deal more than that, if I return to him with Rhys ap Cadwgan, Lord of Meirionnydd."

8

Hyw stood aside to let the warriors file by him into the tunnel mouth. Aeneus went first: he would lead them back to Dolbadarn's armoury, find the makeshift ladder, and climb up into the tower itself to dispatch the guard. Bran went next, pausing to pat Hyw's shoulder and deftly hand him his breeches before disappearing into the tunnel. One by one, the others followed. When the last had passed into the tunnel, Hyw sealed the entrance and pitched them into darkness.

Their plan hinged on stealth. Hyw could hear the rustle of the men breathing, their feet making almost no sound against the rough slate floor of the long tunnel. They kept their bearings by placing one hand on the shoulder of the man ahead. For a moment, Hyw let himself envy Margred and the handful of warriors with her in the trees, lying in wait for the English. Her band would join the rest of the Welsh forces later, at the gates of the castle.

Hyw channelled his sharper hawk's eyesight, but had to focus to resist the urge to change. When he closed his eyes, he could see Llywelyn also crouching, his expression tense, as if the former prince moved through the heavy darkness with them. Finally, as his chest felt like bursting with the tension, a dim glimmer appeared ahead. Then the armoury came into view, and finally he was out of the tunnel.

Hyw waited as the men climbed up the ladder. They moved together as a practiced unit, without the need to speak or even look at each other. When the last man had a foot on the ladder, Hyw pushed against the wall portal. The man glanced back as it scraped shut behind them, locking the armoury again. Hyw ran his hand over the wall but there was no telltale sign that there had ever been a door.

He took up an English spear from against the wall and followed the others up the ladder. He entered the keep in time to see Dafydd and the other warriors making their way up the circular stairway of the keep to the wall walk. Aeneus must have already given the all-clear.

According to plan, they would overcome the guards there and secure the portcullis. Hyw tried not to look at the still form of the guard in the corner. Had this been Ralph, or the second man? Hyw gulped down his bile and turned away as he followed the rest through the keep and into the castle yard.

Dolbadarn was strangely empty. The hairs on Hyw's neck tingled until he realized what was wrong. No children shouting at play, no horses neighing in the courtyard, no women singing as they worked. He had not noticed the lack in his hawk form. The stench of neglect and the coppery smell of dried blood clung to the stones. He gulped again and tried not to breathe as their party stepped out into the open.

Hyw heard a shout and the metallic scrape of a sword being drawn from its scabbard as an English guard rounded on them. Bran lifted his javelin to deflect the steel, and Hyw lifted his as well. As the guard swung, Bran turned the javelin point around to stab it into the man's neck, between armour and helmet. Blood spattered stone around them, and Hyw felt it splash across his arm and shoulder.

He heard a clang near his ear and turned to find Prince Dafydd's sword meeting that of an English soldier. Hyw jumped back as he realized the English sword had been aimed at his neck, and Dafydd moved forward. With a few quick strokes Dafydd left the English knight, unmoving, on the ground. Hyw swallowed hard at the bodies around them, as the prince straightened to wipe the blood on his sash.

"Be sure there is no one left," Dafydd whispered to Bran and the others. "We must bring our families to safety—"

But before he could finish, Aeneus hooted twice, giving the alarm from the wall walk. Horses' hooves thundered on the packed dirt in the field. Hyw heard a thud and the rattling whoosh as the portcullis, cut from its moorings, came crashing down into the stone floor of the entranceway. Bran touched Hyw's shoulder.

"You all right?"

Hyw nodded, and Bran gestured for him to follow as he ran toward the keep. As they mounted the stairs, his father all but pushed him toward an arrow slit. "What can you see, lad?"

Hyw counted twenty knights and mounted bowmen returning from the mountains. The Welsh were almost evenly matched against them.

But we have the advantage of being inside the castle, Llywelyn said in his ear. *We can use our enemies' stockpiled defences against them.* Hyw realized how well Aeneus and Bran had used the information he brought them to take the English by surprise. *But none must get away to group against us, or worse, to warn Edward's army. What of the horses? Can you steal the mounts out from under them?*

Hyw felt for the horses' minds, but the animals were focused on home, food, and rest. His focus split as he tried to reach them without turning into one of them. One armoured knight held the reins tight on his big black charger, and Hyw winced with pain as the steel bit into the animal's mouth. Focusing on the pain, he entered the horse's consciousness. The charger balked, and the knight struggled to regain control, lashing the animal with his spurs.

As the others struggled with their mounts, Hyw heard Aeneus whoop the signal somewhere behind him. The Welsh would be shooting a volley of arrows from one side of Dolbadarn's battlements. Then half of them would change position to shoot from the other side, hoping to confuse the English into thinking they had a larger force inside the castle.

His da clapped Hyw on the shoulder, bringing him back from the minds of the horses far enough to cup his hands and shriek like a hawk. Hyw tried to look for Margred among the Welsh warriors hiding outside the castle, as they ran forward with an ululating war cry or dropped from the trees to fall on the English from behind. Several of Edward's mercenaries fell—including, Hyw noted, the knight on the black charger. But before Hyw could harness his gift to connect with it again, the riderless horse thundered off into the surrounding woods.

He turned to the other mounted English soldiers and found he could interfere with their horses if he focused on one at a time. He made one bump and bite the horse beside it, and both mounted bowmen found themselves on the ground. Then he was distracted as a group of horsemen charged toward the castle walls. Hyw saw the glint of metal as they bent low, raising their shields. He managed to connect with a heavily armoured horse near the centre of the charge, and it bucked sideways into another.

Aeneus signalled the two men nearest him. They unleashed a volley of arrows taken from the armoury. Another charger snarled at the horse nearest it, and Hyw concentrated harder to expand his reach. The two large animals reared at each other. One crashed sideways to the ground, pinning its rider.

Hyw heard one of the mercenaries shout: "Hold! Fall back!" He looked up to see one man pushing another aside as the two raced back up the hill and were lost from sight in the surrounding bush. Aeneus and some of the others yelled in triumph. They lowered themselves on thick braided ropes from the wall walk onto the narrow path, javelins strung at their backs.

A rider raced toward Aeneus, sword drawn, but Hyw was able to spook the horse into a misstep. As the rider tipped, Aeneus turned and thrust with his javelin. Hyw sought to calm the rearing horse. With his mind full of horses, he felt a sharp pull in his bones and had to force himself not to change to horse form. Instead, he stretched his mind toward the frightened animal on the battlefield, which responded to his probing by clomping both feet back on the ground and shaking its mane. It slowly turned and cantered toward the other horses Hyw had reached earlier. A small band of horses was forming, as if waiting for his instructions.

Bring them back to us, he heard Llywelyn say, as if the former prince were standing close behind him. Hyw took a deep breath and sent the horses a mental image of the waiting barn and the familiar smell of hay. One started back toward the castle. After a moment, the second followed, but the third, still spooked, looked back to where

Aeneus had left its rider, slain. Hyw tried again to send another soothing message, careful to show only horses and the warmth of the barn. One of the other horses nickered, and finally the spooked one turned to follow them toward the castle.

Good lad, Llywelyn rumbled.

Hyw opened his eyes and nodded at his da. "I see no Englishmen."

"They must have gone to ground." Bran stared out at the field through the arrow slits in the direction the men had disappeared. "And the horses?"

"Coming," Hyw responded. Bran shot him a look of appreciation. His father's praise was much less obvious than Llywelyn's, but it meant as much to Hyw. They went to the gate together to meet Aeneus, who was leading the captured horses. Bran sent some of the men to crank up the portcullis. Aeneus began his report through its bars.

"I count at least two who are not among the fallen here," he rasped.

Bran turned again to Hyw, putting his hand on Hyw's shoulder. "None can escape to tell Edward we have re-taken Dolbadarn," he said quietly.

"The hawk will find them," Hyw said to his father, and Bran nodded.

"You must take another warrior with you," Bran started to say, but Aeneus shook his head.

"We don't have enough men as it is," he barked. "I will make do, as I always have. And Hyw will have my back if I need it." Aeneus nodded in Hyw's direction. "Find them, lad."

Although Aeneus knew of his gift, Hyw had no wish to be seen changing by him or by anyone. Many of their people were suspicious of the old ways, led on by Edward's English priests. Hyw nodded at Aeneus and moved away, crouching near the old mews to transform. Hyw barely gave a nod to Llywelyn as he moved into his hawk form and took to the air.

The bird's sharper eyes made it easy to spot the two soldiers camped near the stream. Two English men. Was one of them James? No, but one was younger. Possibly a knight and his squire. Hyw settled his mind. If they got away, these two could reunite with the king's forces and bring ten thousand soldiers down on the small company guarding Prince Dafydd. Hyw knew that, but for a heartbeat he faltered. The spectre of James, his foster brother, rose in his thoughts. The look of pure delight on James' face that day, so long ago it seemed, in Shrewsbury's stables. James had stumbled on Hyw—not grooming a horse, but communing with it. How much it meant to tell someone about his gift and have them accept it. More than that: to enjoy it with him. But James was English. The enemy. Like these two men.

Hyw's stomach clenched as Llywelyn silently directed him, as if the prince had reached out and pointed right at the men. Did the animals feel this when he directed them with his mind? Focusing on the hawk's instincts, he banked on an air current to fly them back towards Dolbadarn. Everything was easier in animal form, but he also recalled the danger his mother had mentioned. He focused on his da, circling until Bran looked up, tapped Aeneus on the shoulder, and gestured upward. The two warriors stood close a moment before Aeneus nodded, his mouth set in an almost straight line as he gestured for Hyw to lead on.

Hyw let the wind currents do the work, moving his wings only enough to keep his balance in the air. Aeneus ran effortlessly and silently below him. Hyw felt for a moment that they were one, somehow. He, the hawk, Aeneus, even the prince riding with and within him, sharing the sun and wind that was Wales.

When Hyw saw the English soldiers at the stream again, he gave a mewling cry and circled them. Aeneus heard and went on alert, dropping to all fours and taking out his dagger in one movement. Aeneus slipped through the thicket and set upon the first man before either knew he was there.

Hyw saw the spurt of blood and his own talons jerked, as if he had done the deed. How many have I killed this day? he wondered, but for once the prince's voice was silent. Blood splattered the face of the other man, who ducked. It was his fatal mistake. Aeneus lunged forward to finish him as well. Then the warrior wiped his dagger and began gathering the soldier's gear. Aeneus looked up then, but Hyw circled away from the scene.

The motion took Hyw in a wide arc, and below him he could see lines of smoke. The main bulk of the English army. Somewhere in their camp, he might find James. What if James had been one of these men? But he could not let his mind go there. As he circled, he could see Dolbadarn castle, where his father, no doubt, would be standing. And farther around, the caves where his people lay in hiding. He loved his family and his people, and he loved the land below him. Surely his duty was clear.

Hyw circled once more, but his heart continued to pound. Finally, he let the wind fill his feathers and the sky fill his eyes.

The wind carried Hyw past the scent of war and death, until he could feel the breath of the ocean in it. He neither knew nor cared how far he flew, heedless of Llywelyn's voice in his ear, keeping pace with the sun in the sky. In this form he could not see Llywelyn, but he could sense the former prince inside him, and his pledge to serve was a weight inside his chest.

Hyw caught movement in his peripheral vision and turned to spot a group of squires, practicing archery.

They are English, Hyw. See the banner, there. You must get closer to find out what you can about their movements.

Yes, Hyw thought, circling lower. Then he spotted a shock of brown hair and heard a peal of familiar laughter. James! Hyw tried to call out his friend's name, but the hawk shrieked instead. James looked up, shielding his eyes, but he did not wave. Instead he looked away again, back to the group of knights-in-training with him. Of course, he wouldn't recognize Hyw in this form—would not even be aware of this new aspect of the gift.

You must find out where they are going, Hyw. Check the riders, there.

Hyw ignored Llywelyn's demand and rode the air currents down to land in a nearby oak tree. Hidden in the foliage, he watched his friend. James was taller, and his hair had grown longer. He carried himself with the same easy grace that Hyw recalled so well. When

Hyw had gone back to Shrewsbury's service a few months earlier to discover news of Edward's plans, it was as if their friendship had never been interrupted. James had even helped him get away again.

Now James seemed confident, even happy, with his new companions. Hyw was uncomfortably aware of the changes in his own appearance over the past year. Would James recognize him? Hyw had to change back to his own form and find a way to make contact.

No, Hyw. You cannot—

Hyw launched himself toward a lower branch, closer to where James was standing, flexing his bow. Peering down the field, Hyw could see the arrow squarely in the centre of the target.

"Good job, lad," an older man was saying to James. Another squire gave James a playful slug on the arm. It was a small gesture of camaraderie and friendship, but it pierced Hyw like a barbed arrow. James had made new friends. Of course he had. After all, James would need allies to survive when he took his place as Lord Shrewsbury. And Hyw wanted him to do just that. Didn't he? Yes. He wanted his friend to thrive, not merely survive. It was good.

Then why did Hyw feel this tightness in his chest?

He must find a way to make contact with James. Hyw flew past the group, looking for a place where he could make the painful change back to human form and find clothing. At that moment, one of the other squires pointed at him.

"Look there, James. A more fitting target on the wing."

James raised the bow and Hyw shrieked again, fluttering in mid-air. For a long moment, James held the aim. Then he shook his head and lowered the bow.

"It wouldn't be right."

"Well, if you won't try it, I will." Another squire raised his bow.

Move, lad! Llywelyn shouted, and Hyw scrambled for purchase in the air. Then he was flying away from them, his wings beating the air. He heard the arrow zing, stirring his feathers as it flew past.

Too close! Take us back to camp.

Hyw was only too glad to follow those instructions. He tried to feel chastened by the former prince's running commentary as they flew, but he felt a strange elation to think it hadn't been James who shot at him. No. James had lowered his bow.

As Hyw neared the caves where the rest of the group sheltered, the first person he saw was his mam. He shrieked and she looked up, shielding her eyes from the sun for a moment before she waved and stood. He hung effortlessly in the air to watch her gather the other women and children to her. She understood his signal. He imagined her leading the other women and children to meet his father and the handful of warriors who would come to take them to Dolbadarn.

The horizon drew him again, and for a moment he let it. Then he felt a stirring inside him, and at first he wasn't sure what it was. Apprehension? Was there somewhere else he should be? He dipped his wing and looked toward the ground. He recalled his mam, his da, his friends. They were trapped in that world. What would befall them if he did not return?

Hyw let the wind carry him toward the caves, his people, his daily life. Finally, he spotted his mam again, scanning the skies. A momentary guilt gnawed him at having been so long away, mixed with a strange gladness to see her watching for him. He circled until he knew she had seen him. He spotted the bundle of clothes where she had dropped them, so he could dress again after his transformation, and drifted toward it.

He blinked, and the world came rushing at him. The crack of his strong hawk bones as they elongated into human form startled him, and he jerked backward as he transformed. Pain filled him. He struggled against the sharp stabs in his legs and arms and body until it overcame him. He lay on his back, the hard ground awkward under him. Struggling to raise his head, he stared for a moment at the long pale foot, ending in short fleshy toes. Unnatural.

Human.

Steady. He heard Llywelyn's voice in his ear, and the world came into focus. He drew himself up and slowly regained his feet. The blue of the woad his mam had prepared for him was gone now, and the rough wool of his tunic and leggings burned his skin as he shrugged them on. When he saw his mam, he walked toward her.

Adara hugged him. He held her small frame tightly, determined to set the day's business behind him.

Hyw walked beside his mam on the way to Dolbadarn. His legs felt awkward and he let Prince Dafydd's son Owain and the other boys take turns scouting ahead. Margred and the men had returned from the woods to join them, rather than proceeding on to the captured castle. Margred's idea, of course. She fell into step beside them and Adara quietly stepped back to let them walk together. Margred began to tell him about her foray into the woods, and he could hear jubilance in her voice.

"I suppose you had a chance to use your bow, then?" The anger in his voice surprised him. He couldn't shake the sight of Aeneus killing the two English soldiers. The image of James' face and willing smile forced its way into Hyw's mind. Even when he shook his head he couldn't clear it, so he turned on Margred instead. "And did you have your chance to kill one of the hated *Saeson*?"

She stopped and faced him with her hands on her hips. "They are the enemy."

Hyw knew she was right. He should have been glad to see those soldiers die. He had only done his duty, hadn't he? He should want to kill them himself, and he shouldn't begrudge Margred her wish to do so. He turned from Margred and started walking. For a few moments he walked alone before he heard her footsteps beside him again.

"If you must know," she said, "we were able to lure the English into chasing us instead. We led them as far away from the castle as we dared. They were still hunting for us when we turned back. We made a laughing-stock of them without firing a shot."

Boy, you may owe the lady an apology. Llywelyn's voice was grave.

A mix of shame and relief flooded Hyw. She might understand if he told her what he was feeling, but he couldn't find the words to begin.

"And yes, that was my idea!" Margred finally growled at him. He shifted to look at her, but she skipped away and headed back to her sisters. He could hear them laughing behind him as he turned back to the path. His mam was still walking with another woman, now several paces ahead on the path. He was alone with his thoughts.

When they reached the castle, Dafydd's wife Elizabeth took charge of the kitchens with the few servants who had remained with them. The English had left them well stocked, and their first order of business was to feed everyone. Hyw walked toward Margred, but when she saw him, she stalked away to join the warriors celebrating around the fire. He had to show her that he supported her as a warrior and a friend. Before he could go after her, Dafydd began breaking apart the high trestle table the English had left behind. Bran and Aeneus joined him, and at Bran's gesture, Hyw stepped up to help.

The prince and his wife served the evening meal themselves in Welsh fashion, as the people sat in family groups of three. Margred sat with her sisters, and none of them looked his way. As the meal wore on, Hyw found himself laughing as his mam and da told stories about their shared history. Gwilym, the warrior poet, had found his way back to the group and entertained after the meal. Hyw felt mild surprise at how quickly they all seemed to feel at home again in Dolbadarn.

We are an itinerant court, Llywelyn commented. Hyw recalled the nomadic nature of the royal family, moving from castle to estate, from one *llys* or court to another, throughout the year. *And Dolbadarn was always ours.*

But Dafydd had an extra purpose in his actions that evening. As Gwilym strummed the final chords to an old song, the prince stood, motioning Bran nearer to him.

"Now must we act," Dafydd said. "We must call the remaining lords to us. You were steward to Llywelyn. Which lords swore allegiance to him, November last?"

The last time the Welsh lords gathered had been to answer the archbishop's offer of land to Llywelyn if he would surrender. Only six months ago, but it seemed so much longer. Hope ran high then. Llywelyn had defeated the English at Menai Strait after they broke the truce. But now…

They will come, Llywelyn assured him. *I named Dafydd as my heir. Once he has the relics, he can reunite Wales, if he can withstand Edward's pull.*

Bran began a list, reading it to Owain and the other messengers to be sure they knew which lords maintained which areas and where they might be hiding.

"Say only Llanberis," Bran cautioned them, using the name of the nearest village. "Any Welshman would know *Tywysog* Dafydd holds his court here at Dolbadarn, but if the *Saeson* should intercept the message, they may think of the town."

Dafydd sent his cousin John to find Rhys, who would be waiting with the relics at their agreed rendezvous point. After John had left the castle, Dafydd sat back with a satisfied air. Gwilym stood and raised his goblet.

"To the fallen," the bard said, and at Dafydd's nod, Gwilym began to sing. "Heavy snow has covered my heart, frozen like all Gwynedd by this untimely frost …"

It was a new song. Gwilym sang of the land, lamenting all they had lost. Hyw's mind conjured the battlefield where he had watched *Cymru's* fiercest warriors cut down by mounted English knights and their hired mercenaries. When Gwilym praised "the brave prince," Hyw thought he meant Dafydd, but at "the Lion cut down, claws unsheathed even as he hit the ground" it was obvious the poet meant Llywelyn. Hyw saw his mam place her arm around his da's waist. Bran leaned against her, his head down, and Hyw knew he was deeply moved. When Hyw closed his eyes, he saw Llywelyn standing with his arms folded. The song had every man in the room conjuring an image of Llywelyn in that moment, but Hyw could see that the prince had a look of concern on his face.

Look you to my brother, Llywelyn told him gruffly. *This tribute does me proud, but it will serve to bring the contrast between us back into the men's minds at a time when Dafydd can least afford it. I won the land by force, but I held it by reason and judgment. They must see past my brother's temper to his skill and wisdom, or they will never accept him as their leader. May Cat and Rhys be successful in their quest and rejoin us soon.*

When Gwilym finished singing, no one spoke. The last tone of the harp resonated as Hyw looked toward the living prince for his reaction. Dafydd's face was an angry grimace as he pushed back his chair. As Dafydd stormed from the room, Hyw prayed his sister would soon deliver the relics and join them inside Dolbadarn's thick stone walls.

9

Cat's heart was beating so fast she could barely hear as Rhys stepped back and drew his sword. Cynfrig did the same, and the two seasoned warriors circled in front of her and Gawain, swords out toward the enemy. One of the guards pulled out a bow, but de Francton held his hand up and his men stilled.

"Such manners, and with a holy man present," de Francton said loudly in English, no doubt for his men's benefit. "We have no desire to harm you."

"If you know who I am," Rhys said in Welsh, his voice strong but pitched so low she saw de Francton lean forward a little to hear him, "then you also know my prowess, and the cunning of my steward." Rhys moved his chin toward the men on horseback who surrounded them. "I could take them with me to hell, and still have room for you."

De Francton raised his eyebrows and switched to Welsh. "And yet, if you truly meant to do it, we surely would be there already."

"You are right. We could fight, or we could agree to come with you willingly."

"And what must I ransom for this boon?"

"Only that you let my wife and the brother go free," Rhys said. He had not hesitated to say the word "wife," Cat noted with some surprise.

"That I cannot do," de Francton responded. "But I can guarantee their safety— if, as you say, you come without a fight. I

306

have no desire to see you harmed, when you could prove useful to my liege lord." The two men stared each other down. "Think hard on it, my lord Rhys. Believe me, your wife is safer with us than facing the mercenaries."

"Surely not, if she travels with a monk?" Rhys asked. "Surely even the mercenaries would honour a safe-passage from your king?"

Cynfrig deftly reached his free hand into his tunic for the parchment, and thrust it at Gawain. Cat risked a look at her uncle. Gawain held the king's letter in front of the pack he cradled over his arm. She had not seen him take it up, but she knew what it was: the pack that held the relics.

De Francton pursed his lips. Cat went cold: this captain was no fool. What if he killed Gawain? Or opened the pack? Would he even know what the relics were?

"We are not uncivilized men," de Francton said. "We have priests and holy men aplenty with us, and I'm sure your White Monk would feel at home in our company. Far better than with the Gascons, I assure you. And we will make your wife quite comfortable. Besides, it will be nothing for my men to find her again. Especially if I bid them follow her." He looked over at his men then, and she saw him nod, passing a signal to someone. "And some of them are more familiar with this land than you may expect."

She turned her eyes in time to see two soldiers move with practiced ease toward the bush beside them. She had heard the English king recruited Welsh to their side, and had seen her own priest seduced to serve their enemies. These soldiers must also be traitors. Cat's anger burned inside her. Could she do nothing— think of nothing—to save Rhys? Or Cynfrig—or her uncle Gawain? What good was her gift to them now? This gift from her ancestor had forged a link with the ancient Druids. The words she had sung and heard sung so many times came to her mind, legends of the founder of the Welsh lineage, Brutus of Troy. These were the songs and legends that all Welshmen had heard from birth, but these men would ignore their wisdom.

"Go you to your deaths, traitors to Brutus," she called out in Welsh to the men who had begun to melt into the bush. "If you know who I am, then you know what I am! Die at the hand of those who keep you, before cock crow tomorrow!"

"Morrigan," Cynfrig said, a trace of fear in his voice.

One of the traitor Welshmen stopped and looked back at her in horror. At his terrified expression, she faltered. She turned to see de Francton staring at her too, although the look on his face was more guarded and knowing.

"So," de Francton said, making the sign of the cross. His men followed suit, although their bewildered looks showed that they hadn't understood the exchange. De Francton switched to Welsh again. "I had wondered why you kept her close. But know that your superstition will not save you from my lord and his Christian king."

"She is more Cassandra than Medb," Rhys said, his voice almost pleading. Cat tensed as if she had been punched in the stomach. Medb was an Irish legend, the morrigan who foretold the death of warriors before battle. But Rhys saw her as Cassandra, the mad seer who prophesied the sack of Troy, although no one could understand her ravings? Had his belief in her been a lie all this time? Cynfrig moved closer to her.

"Don't worry, lass," he murmured. "Our Rhys has a silver tongue."

Rhys did not look at her or at Cynfrig, but moved his sword deftly to call attention to it. He spoke loudly in English. "Spare her, and we will give up our swords."

"Done," de Francton answered in English. He seemed pleased with himself and Cat's stomach churned again. "Disarm them."

One of the guards dismounted and took their swords. Another reached for Gawain's pack but Cat intervened.

"This pack is mine." She looked defiantly at de Francton as she reached for it. Gawain's eyebrows twitched as he passed it to her, but she continued. "Thank you for carrying it for me, uncle, but I must take care of it now."

"Yours?" De Francton was leaning towards her. "And what, pray tell, is in it?"

Her mother's training rushed to the surface. Englishmen often held strange notions about Welsh women, and she could play on that if she trod carefully. "Items that are not intended for men's eyes," she answered.

The guard refused to back away, and de Francton narrowed his eyes at her. If he took it from her and opened it, all would be lost. Cat expelled her breath in what she hoped sounded like frustration. Knowing Gawain had wrapped the relics in cloth and hoping they were well hidden, she made as if to open the pack for their inspection.

De Francton half-laughed and she stopped rummaging to look at him. He held up a hand and shook his head at the guard, speaking English. "We certainly wouldn't want to separate a lady from her—necessary items." The guard backed away with an odd look on his face. Then de Francton pointed at the sheath on her belt. "But those, we simply must have."

Cat shouldered the pack and began to untie her sheath, but the guard ripped it from her as soon as she had loosened it enough. He handed it to the captain.

"This," de Francton almost whispered in Welsh as he tucked the third knife into it and pocketed all, "can be our little secret." Cat's hand instinctively went to her throat, where she found the necklace that tied her to her brother. The metal warmed in her hand as she forced herself to breathe slowly and evenly.

Then de Francton switched back to English and raised his voice again. "It seems that we have had a misunderstanding. I am pleased to have you join our company, Lord Rhys. It would not do to leave you, gentle lady, nor your husband, nor Lord Cynfrig, nor the esteemed holy brother, to the ferocity of the mercenaries who roam your fair land at present. It wouldn't be civilized of me. You must all join us at the castle."

"You are very kind, Sir Francton, but—" Cynfrig began.

"Come now, there can be no 'buts' between us." De Francton smiled but his eyes were cold. "You must all be our guests this night. I insist. I am sorry we don't have horses for all of you, but certainly the lady may ride."

With that, one of the guards lifted her and de Francton deftly caught her up in front of him on the big war horse. She was startled and had to clutch the pack to prevent herself from dropping it. She tamped down the terror that threatened to overwhelm her as de Francton pulled her against him. Rhys stepped forward but two guards held him back. She managed to nod reassuringly at him and held her face as expressionless as she could.

She could only watch as de Francton's guards crowded around the three men, herding them to follow on foot even as he turned his horse around to lead the way.

Cat felt shivers down her spine as de Francton led them into the great hall of Bere castle. Rhys, Cynfrig, and Gawain marched behind her, and she wished she could at least turn and see their faces for reassurance. Was it really only days ago, the last time she was here, pleading with Dafydd and his advisors to give their castle up as a ruse to help the prince—and her family—get away? Now the stone seemed to ring with derisive English voices, their words and accents unfamiliar to her. There were almost no women in the hall. These were the English lords and knights who had taken the castle, a fighting force of the enemy. But she would have been mistress of this castle, had the English remained behind their own borders. Keeping her head held high, she marched past them.

De Francton spoke first, but he had switched to English. She was distracted by the noise in the hall, and his words came too fast for her to follow what he was saying. He was speaking to a big man seated in a high chair. Cat took a steadying breath. This could not be the king, since no one had bent a knee or called him "your highness." Lord Mortimer, perhaps?

She stole a glance around them as the others were herded up to stand beside her. The room had changed much in the few days since they had sheltered there with Dafydd and Elizabeth. The tables were littered with rolled parchment and jugs of ale. She looked sideways at Rhys. His expression was stoic and immobile, as always. He was lucky his swarthier skin and moustache hid the burning cheeks that so often betrayed her. They weren't bound by ropes or chains, but the guards were too close for her to speak to him easily. Then he caught her eye, and she saw a calm determination in his that reassured her. He had a plan. She would do her best to follow his lead.

A guard placed a hand on Rhys' shoulder as if to make him

kneel, but Rhys barely moved. Then another guard joined and together they shoved Rhys forward toward the seated man. A robed man standing beside the chair leaned over to say something in what sounded like French, but she couldn't quite hear the words. A priest or holy man, no doubt. Then they both turned to Rhys.

"Aye, my lord," Rhys said. He must have heard what the robed man had said. She felt a moment of pride that he had spoken first, letting them know the Welsh were an educated people. "I have pledged to serve you to secure the safety of my wife and kinsmen."

Her stomach fell. Even as a ruse, how could Rhys pledge his loyalty to these invaders? She moved as if to stop him, but her guard grabbed her back roughly. Cynfrig turned his head and gestured for her to be quiet. A guard cuffed him, and she subsided.

"These two will stand as pledge to your honour," the robed man said quickly. She knew the term well. The English meant to keep her and Cynfrig as hostages to make sure Rhys kept his word. She could feel herself pale. The English were famous for blinding or maiming Welsh prisoners at the slightest provocation.

"As you will it, of course," Rhys said slowly. "Yet there might be a better use for them. My steward has more knowledge of these mountains than even I do, and my wife is gifted in healing."

It took Cat a moment to realize he meant her. De Francton looked at her, a tight smile on his mouth that did not reach his eyes. Would he betray her, and tell Mortimer of the knife? Or expose her gift? She tried to look calm and serene, as she imagined a healer would look. At his continued silence, she grew cold, wondering what game he had planned for them.

"…if you think it wise, my Lord Mortimer," the robed man was saying.

So the big man was indeed Baron Edmund Mortimer, the one Hyw blamed for the murder of their former leader, Llywelyn. And Rhys had pledged them to his service! She wished she understood more of his plan.

"Your word that your men will treat my people gently is all I require to remain steadfast," Rhys told them. "This Dafydd and his brother have taken the bounty from our land and the food from our mouths in taxes these many years, and we would gladly free ourselves from that yoke."

"And become yoked to my service instead?" asked Mortimer. His booming voice made her realize how imposing he was.

Rhys bowed low. "Even if your lordship held a whip, I believe it would be the better fit. And with so many to help in the harness, surely we will dispatch the work more quickly."

Mortimer stared at him for a long moment. Rhys remained standing with his head bowed, a perfect submissive vassal. Finally de Francton broke the silence with a small laugh.

"These Welsh are all poets."

Mortimer half-smiled, showing his teeth, and the men and women around the room laughed along with their leader. Rhys straightened from his bow, but Cat could see his shoulders remained tense.

"How many men have you?" Mortimer boomed.

"Twenty fit to fight, and more once we gather the farmers to us," Rhys responded, without hesitation.

Mortimer made a dismissive gesture with his hand, and Rhys turned to nod at her and Cynfrig. De Francton glanced her way, and she worked to make her face neutral again. They had only six warriors in total, and Emrys was wounded. All the rest had gone with Dafydd. The farmers and their sons would fight if he asked them, but that only gave him ten at the outside. What was Rhys thinking? Cat's mind raced.

10

It took the better part of a week for the various lords to gather at Dolbadarn. The first were the fallen lords of Ceredigion. Hyw watched from the gate as the guards greeted Lord Hywel ap Rhys Gryg, who arrived disguised as a beggar. Dafydd and Aeneus came in from the exercise yard to greet Lord Hywel, and Hyw noted their deference in spite of the older man's tattered cloak.

"Truer Welshman never was nor will be," Aeneus told Hyw with a grin. "Twas he who led the battle against the old king, this Edward's father." Hyw had heard the bards sing of it many times. Lord Hywel had served with Llywelyn since the very early years of his leadership and had been granted a *llys* in the western lands of Carmarthen.

When Hyw closed his eyes, he could see Llywelyn beaming in agreement. *That cunning got him past the English, and it will yet keep us all alive.*

"Your mam will want to know he is here," Aeneus added. "Lucky you are that you will have a chance to hear his stories, while I must keep watch. Listen well, and you may yet survive this war."

Adara came quickly when Hyw gave her the news.

"We all have our ways of staying alive," Lord Hywel said later in the main hall, bowing deeply to her and then hugging her to him.

"Let us help with that by sharing what our enemies have so kindly left for us," she said, offering a flatbread platter with pieces of meat and stewed roots beside a flagon that Hyw knew would contain good Welsh ale.

"You do the *Cymry* proud." Lord Hywel's hands shook as he gestured for the two of them to join him in a traditional grouping, and Hyw wondered how long it had been since he'd eaten. "Please, share with me."

"Of course," Adara said, gesturing for Hyw to sit down, although neither Adara nor Hyw took any of the food for themselves. As Lord Hywel ate, he told them how he had convinced an English chaplain to spare his life and even give him a slab of cheese to see him on his way, never knowing he was aiding the lord of the *llys*.

"There are good men among us all," the nobleman added, soberly. "This chaplain shamed the mercenaries, when they looked for easy trophies for their shillings. No doubt that chaplain will not last long in this war. May God have mercy on him."

A few days afterward, Lord Hywel's sons arrived. The following day, Lord Pyrs Wyndod and Lord Hywel's brother raced their horses through the castle gates together, as if fearing pursuit. Each lord had a few warriors in his bodyguard, and *Tywysog* Dafydd greeted them all warmly. But Hyw couldn't help noticing the tension between these Welsh lords and Dafydd.

They are among the few who never strayed from my side, Llywelyn offered in his ear. *The same cannot be said for my brother, who ever showed his love for Edward over me.*

Hyw recalled a tale he had once heard about how these lords had supported their *Tywysog* Llywelyn through an attempt on his life that had been blamed on Dafydd.

"Aye," said Lord Pyrs as he clasped Dafydd's proffered arm. "I serve Wales."

"As do we all," Dafydd replied smoothly.

Yet they check for treachery, Llywelyn grunted. Clasping forearms had been an old Roman trick Llywelyn taught his bodyguard to be sure their adversaries concealed no knives in their sleeves at a peace talk.

"The mantle of prince comes with a heavy burden," Dafydd went on, "and I would not take it up but with a sure hand and steady heart."

Pyrs stood looking in his eyes a moment longer, and then released him. "For *Cymru*." The men around him repeated the vow and relaxed. Dafydd had passed his first test.

For two more days, Hyw would spot Dafydd at the window, as if keeping watch, but only a handful of lords arrived to join them. There was no sign of Dafydd's cousin John, nor of Cat and Rhys, nor of the relics. On the second night, as Hyw made his way to Adara to sit next to her and his father in a traditional grouping for supper, the prince stood with his cup raised as if in salute, and his bitter voice filled the room.

"We began with seven thousand men. We had no need of my brother's *teulu*, but we made them welcome. Some say his men numbered one hundred and sixty." Hyw tried to avert his eyes, but the prince caught sight of him, straightened, and continued as if talking to Llywelyn. "Where, pray tell, is that hundred-and-sixty now, when we need them most?"

The best of my men are already here, Llywelyn answered, his voice tight with anger even in Hyw's mind. *And if Garth Celyn has fallen, the rest are dead.*

Although they had made a point of taking down the English trestle table, Hyw noticed Elizabeth still preferred to sit in the English manner: at a long table, with her children arrayed around her, and Margred and her sisters nearer Dafydd at the far end. Margred had covered her hair with a silk veil that made her look more feminine. Hyw wondered if it had come from the cedar chests upstairs in the bedrooms, left by the previous inhabitants of Dolbadarn. He tried to smile at her, but a memory of the bodies in the marsh behind the castle caught him. He turned away, shuddering. He was glad Dafydd had the warriors bury the bodies shortly after they took the castle. At least his mother and Margred—and the others—hadn't had to see them. Hyw crossed himself, wishing again that they had a priest with them to say a mass for those souls.

A grizzled warrior seated with Aeneus stood then. "The lords of Dinas Bran fight alongside the rightful House of Aberffraw. Let fear swallow the English invaders at our approach."

Dafydd stared at him a moment too long. Before the tables began to fall silent, Elizabeth stood beside her husband and placed her hand alongside his on his cup, raising it a little further. She murmured something, and Dafydd's voice suddenly boomed.

"A toast to Gruffydd Fychan for his strength and courage—and to all the men who fight by our side. Let the bards sing our praises."

On cue, Gwilym picked up his harp. When the cheering died down, Dafydd sat heavily on his chair and Elizabeth perched beside him.

"My lord, let me go to the king in person and entreat for you." Elizabeth raised her voice so all could hear, and laid both of her hands on his arm in a comforting gesture. "I can make Edward listen. If we can form a treaty with him again, then our lands will be at peace."

She was ever his soft spot, Llywelyn said softly in Hyw's inner ear. *You know the English king forced her to marry my brother, but Dafydd was smitten from the first moment he saw her. He won her over, as only my younger brother could do. It was partly for her sake that I forgave him, even after he tried to kill me. But that was too many years ago now, and she has made him a better man. I wonder if Edward regrets that decision, when he thinks on how well they fare together.*

"My lord, I have seen much strife in these past few years," boomed a voice from the darkness. Lord Hywel ap Rhys Gryg stood to his full height to address the company. The elder warrior-lord had chosen to dine with his sons in Welsh fashion, seated among their men. When he stood, he towered over them, and his height and broad shoulders dwarfed the room, gaining him the attention of all present.

"Many now seated here have swayed in the cold wind Edward has brought to our land." Several of the others, including Dafydd, looked away at his words. Only a handful of lords had kept their faith with Llywelyn in the previous battle with Edward, some five years before, and all knew Hywel ap Rhys Gryg was one of them.

"I commend you for regaining a foothold in this castle," Lord Hywel continued. "But we are backed against the wall. It is easy to forget in the sunshine of spring and your strong heart, my liege. But our fields are burning, and this time the English are barely seen among Edward's paid demons. They hunt our people down and slaughter us like animals. Not only my kinsmen have fallen to their axes, my liege, but farmers and villagers. Women and children are cut down as they run. But still we fight. My sons and I will fight on the side of a free Wales as long as I am able to stand, as always I have done."

There was a general cry of "Hear!" and "*Cymru!*" among the listeners. One of his sons held up a flagon, and the father took a long draft of Welsh ale before continuing.

"It is a bitter taste for you, my liege, but your wife speaks with sense. For the sake of our people, you must let her bid for reason and peace. She may yet prevail and prevent Edward from sweeping us into the sea. I beg your leave to accompany the Princess Elizabeth to Edward. My sons will join me, but we will leave our captains and the bulk of our force, what is left of us, at your disposal. Even if we do not succeed, if we fail to convince the king, I pledge to return your wife safely to you. And whether you fight here or at Garth Celyn, we stand with you."

At those stirring words, another cry of "*Cymru!*" went up from all. Hywel's two grown sons stood up as well and the three seemed as tall and firm as giants among the warriors. Dafydd remained silent until the cheering stopped, and then he rose to his feet again.

"I thank you for your counsel, Lord Hywel," he began. "As you are aware, I am well acquainted with the excesses of the English soldiers. These actions began a year ago, and we stopped them then." A murmur trickled around the room at Dafydd's reference to his own actions at Hawarden Castle that had started the war during the previous spring. The prince's face clouded, but he straightened his shoulders.

"Very well," Dafydd continued. "My good wife may match wits with her cousin Edward. She could have no better sword at her side than yours, Lord Hywel." Again the cheers went up, and again Dafydd waited before continuing. "We, in the meantime, will not lie in idleness for Edward's answer. Only yesterday a messenger brought word that Garth Celyn is held by few troops now, as Edward sends his men after me. We will gather to us as many strong men as we can find in the fields and the villages, as many as are willing, to retake Garth Celyn and our heritage."

There was a silence at these words, and Hyw could hear a shuffling among the people around him.

It may be that the people can best be rallied from our own capital at Garth Celyn, Llywelyn said softly in Hyw's inner ear. *But if Elizabeth can sue for peace, then my brother must swallow his pride and take the best ending he can for the sake of the people, even if our own llys is lost to us.* Hyw whispered as much to his father. Bran nodded even as he stood. Behind them, Aeneus and others from the former prince's *teulu* also rose to their feet.

"Aye, we know Garth Celyn's secrets better than the English ever could," Bran called out. "When the time comes, it will be there as it was here, at Dolbadarn."

"And we will fight like ten men apiece," boomed Aeneus, "to wrest our home back from the *Saeson*."

"I know you will, my friends," Dafydd replied. "With men like you behind me, we cannot help but succeed."

"Yet my lord, surely we must let the lady Elizabeth sue for peace in good faith," Bran went on. "If there is a hope for peace, we must take it."

"Yours is a good plan, my liege," Lord Hywel said. "Our enemy seeks the Prince of Wales, but cannot find him—or us. We are not idle, but we are cunning. Let us bargain from this strength. And if the *Saeson* do not want peace, we will have this stronghold at our backs, even as we retake our homeland."

For a long, hushed moment, Aeneus, Hywel, and Bran stood quietly while Dafydd deliberated.

"It is well said," the prince finally agreed. "Let my lady have her turn as peace-maker, and we will pray for her success."

This drew an excited reaction from the crowd, not quite as loud as for Hywel ap Rhys Gryg, but definitely a cheer.

And now my brother shows his mettle, said Llywelyn, pride thickening his voice in Hyw's head. Hyw looked at the expectant faces around the room, noticing a few still in shadows with their heads bowed, and said nothing.

Bran and Hyw accompanied Lord Hywel in escorting Princess Elizabeth to her meeting with King Edward. It was arranged under the flag of truce at a neutral location, but Dafydd feared treachery and demanded that Bran take Hyw as an added precaution. Bran was reluctant to agree.

"I can also keep watch for Cat," Hyw argued, gaining an ally in his mother at those words.

And keep watch on Elizabeth. If aught should happen to her, who can say how my brother would react?

At that Hyw doubled his efforts, adding Llywelyn's suggestions out loud to convince Bran. Finally, Bran nodded tersely, and before he could change his mind, Hyw darted away to round up horses for the trip.

As they travelled, Hyw used his gift to reach out to the birds around them without changing shape, often choosing the familiar hawk as his eyes. He found Edward's army easily. The king rode out to meet them with a small party of about a dozen riders, all heavily armoured. Hyw bade the hawk circle closer, trying to be more gentle but needing to see the crests on their cloaks and helms.

The hawk showed him a familiar sigil and Hyw felt a surge of joy: Shrewsbury! Hyw scanned the soldiers for James. Hyw couldn't tell from their armour what members of Shrewsbury's guard attended the king, but he took it as a good omen that Shrewsbury was among those chosen for this parley.

He reported as much to Bran when they stopped at the appointed meeting spot. The king's men had set up a white tent, and Elizabeth went inside with Lord Hywel and his sons. As he held the horse's reins, Hyw watched the king's guard, and one squire in particular seemed to stare at him. Could it be James? He was at the far edge of the king's company, and Hyw toyed with the idea of making contact. He could transform into a hawk and fly nearer to see...

Before he could finish his plan, the tent flap flew open. Lord Hywel and his sons escorted Elizabeth out, moving quickly. The king's men drew arms, as did the Welsh, and for a moment the forces stood opposed. The king exited the tent, and Elizabeth turned to face him. Her back was straight and she held her arms folded in front of her proudly. For a long moment, they stared at each other.

Hyw had drawn his sword with the others, but now he glanced again toward the squire, who was facing him, sword drawn. A scene came back to him: he had gone to Lord Shrewsbury to make his case for service, and the old lord had asked him about allegiances. He had answered easily: "I pledge you this: if I become a knight hereafter, I will never take arms against your son James in battle…" Hyw lowered his sword.

Llywelyn boomed in his ear. *Hyw, you cannot do this. Even if it is James, you cannot turn your back on your own people, any more than he can. And think of James: it would be an affront to Edward if he lowers his sword as you have.*

Hyw tried to ignore Llywelyn's ranting. He moved his cloak aside and returned his sword to its sheath. Across the field, the squire's sword flashed. Hyw held his breath. If it was James, he dared not risk his position or his father's. And yet, how could James draw a sword against Hyw?

The sword wavered.

Then Elizabeth was crossing the field, and Hyw raced to hold the horse's reins as she mounted behind Lord Hywel. Bran and the other warriors fell in after them. Hyw looked back as he scrambled onto his own mount, but the squire had turned toward his knight as if for orders. Lord Hywel raised his gloved hand to signal the Welsh to ride. As Hyw tightened his knees against his mount's side, he found himself hoping it had been James, and that somehow this war would end so he could see his friend without a battlefield between them.

11

"Get them swift horses," de Francton barked, and two of his men rushed past Cat toward Bere's stables. He turned to Rhys. "I will see to you and your steward. If you truly have twenty men," he said curtly, stressing the number slightly as if he knew it wasn't true, "they will need to bring their own mounts." Rhys only nodded in response.

Then de Francton turned to Cat, although his words were still directed at Rhys. "And of course, I will safeguard your wife until your return."

Rhys took an involuntary step toward Cat before a guard grabbed his shoulder and held him back.

"I must reassure my wife," Rhys said, struggling.

De Francton continued as if Rhys hadn't spoken. "We have no time to rest, if we are to be true allies."

Cat tried to move to Rhys, but de Francton stepped in front of her, touching his belt, where he had placed the sheath.

"If you keep your pledge, all will be well," he said in Welsh again. "If not, I will take this token to Mortimer and explain how I came by it." Before either of them could respond, de Francton's tone hardened. "And all of my men had best remain among the living at daybreak, or your holy man's eyes are forfeit."

He referred to her thoughtless words against the two Welshmen. Cat felt goosebumps on her arms and rubbed them. De Francton expected some response from her, so she nodded.

"Do not count yourself in the clear, Lady Catrin," he went on.

"I serve my Lord Lestrange, who is away at present. On his return, I may find it necessary to reveal what I know to him. I am sure he will see the sense of our arrangement, if I am still disposed to plead your case." De Francton turned from them, gesturing to one of the guards. "Get them on their horses and be ready." They could hear the ring of his boots against the stone courtyard as he walked off.

One guard gestured to Rhys and Cynfrig as the other took Cat's arm. She feigned stumbling and Rhys caught her, pulling her towards him before the guard could force her away.

Rhys bent toward her, holding her even as the guards pulled them apart. "Fear not," he whispered in her ear. He didn't have time to explain more before he was pulled away, but those words told her he would do all he could to protect Dafydd and her family.

As she passed Cynfrig, she caught his disapproving look as he whispered in Welsh, "Once a morrigan speaks a man's death, it is fated."

"I meant only to scare them," she whispered back.

"Quit talking," said the guard, and before he could push her again Cat raised her hands in a placating gesture. Cynfrig said nothing more, but her cheeks burned again. No doubt Rhys' nurse would never have spoken such words unless she had used her gift. Cynfrig could understand Rhys lying outright to their captors, but not her attempt to frighten them? Was it fine to lie about everyday things, but not about their gifts? Or—her anger froze—was it because she had used a morrigan's curse? Some said when the morrigan foretold a warrior's death, that man's soul belonged to the morrigan. Might using such a gift harm her as well, in some way?

Cat looked for her uncle, who might know the answers to her questions, but two monks in drab brown clothing were escorting him away. Her shoulders drooped as she followed after de Francton. Her foolish words had not only endangered them all, but she had put herself in de Francton's power. Cat touched her locket, wishing her brother and her mam were here.

Guards pushed Cat toward an upstairs chamber. De Francton stood aside, gesturing for her to enter. She looked around her. Rich tapestries hung on the walls and tables and chairs in all shapes and sizes sat around the large hearth that gave warmth to the room, but she barely registered them.

"I trust you will feel comfortable here," he said.

She nodded, but knew instantly that it was the wrong response. He narrowed his eyes at her and she shifted so the table was between them. From the corner of her eye she watched de Francton, but he reached out for a pitcher and poured a goblet of red liquid, holding it out to her.

"This may fortify you after the journey."

"Thank you," she said, bowing her head but making no move to take the goblet. He made an impatient noise and took a sip from it himself.

"It is not poisoned." He placed it down on the table. "Please, make yourself at home here, Lady Catrin. After all, this was your room, was it not?"

She looked away in confusion. These had been Princess Elizabeth's rooms a few weeks ago. Cat had slept with Margred and the other unmarried girls in a common room farther down the D-shaped tower. Then a thought struck her. If she and Rhys had been married last year, as their families had planned, she would have been the lady of this castle. These rooms would have been hers. De Francton was staring at her as if he expected an answer.

"Of course," she said. "I am only surprised at your consideration."

"I don't want you to feel that you are a prisoner here," he responded, bowing slightly. "As I said, your cooperation makes you an ally."

Cat glanced at the door. "So I am free to leave?"

"Leave this room? I would not advise it," he told her, a serious look in his eyes. "Your guards are from Chester, and have little patience with the Welsh. In faith, I can barely control their actions myself."

From the east-facing window, the heavy wooden shutters had been thrown open to the sun, and she could see the courtyard far below. Far enough to keep her confined, even without bars. Cat couldn't breathe for a moment and rested her hand on the table.

"Of course," she said, struggling to keep her voice calm. "And if you would show yourself a man of your word, then you will not harm me or my husband, or any of our party?"

His fist clenched at his side. "I have guaranteed your safety, and I will show you that my intentions are sound."

With that, he turned on his heel and left the room. She could hear him speaking to the guards, and knew without looking that they would remain at the door. She paused for a long, breathless moment, in case he came back in or sent in a guard to watch her. When she was sure no one else was entering, she snatched up the pack and almost ran with it into the curtains surrounding the bedchamber. Time pressed hard on her as she fumbled to find a hiding place, first under the bed, then beside it, and finally under a pillow near the headboard. Still not satisfied, she took the pack out again and held it close to her.

She fought the draperies as she made her way out to the solar again, smoothing them behind her, but no one else had entered. She made herself breathe slowly, in and out, and shifted her legs to hold her steady. Gradually, when no one else came, she began to look around the room. Rich tapestries adorned the walls. Cynfrig's wife and the other ladies must have been responsible for the scenes of hunting dogs, hawks, and forests with plentiful game. On the far wall, they had brought to life the legendary giant Idris on his chair. Cat had reason to thank that giant and his moaning winds for masking their earlier flight from Bere. Surely he would not fail her now.

Only a week ago, her mam and the other women had been seated on these chairs, spinning and mending, giving their counsel and laughter to Dafydd's wife, Elizabeth. She thought back to when Princess Elinor and her ladies had visited this castle—Elinor had slept in this room. Cat had stood in that corner, singing Welsh songs to help the princess learn the language. It seemed so long ago, yet it had been less than two years. Before they could even discuss plans for the wedding, Elinor had disclosed her pregnancy and asked Cat to remain with her for one more year. If the princess had lived…

Cat abruptly turned toward the table. She noticed the goblet de Francton had offered her. The liquid was dark and red, and she leaned forward, focusing on it. She was self-conscious at first, but she recalled her uncle's suggestion: think of her family and those close to her. What would happen to Rhys? She calmed her breathing, hummed the tune of the old songs, and focused on him. But the red liquid remained still and would not stir even when she moved against the table. What of her mam? Nothing. Her da yielded the same result.

Cat sat slowly on the chair, holding the pack in her lap. She could feel the pull of the relics inside it, especially the Crown of Arthur. Could it help her focus her gift? She dared not remove it and hold it openly, but she opened the top of the pack and reached her hand inside. Arthur's simple crown was almost warm to the touch, vibrating under her fingers. Instinctively, she reached up with her other hand to touch her necklace. She took a deep breath, held it, and released it slowly, humming an old song as she did so. She stared at the still liquid, breathing evenly as she imagined her brother's face—

—and she found herself standing on the hard-packed ground of a castle courtyard, her brother in front of her. Hyw glanced to the side and she followed his eyes to find her mam, glowing with health and vigour. Mam held up her May Day garlands as she readied for the rites of spring. Around Mam, other women herded children from the keep into the courtyard. Beyond them was a round stone tower. Cat turned and saw Hyw again. This time she followed his gaze to Margred, who stood with a sullen young man Cat knew from somewhere, but could not place.

She knew suddenly where she was. It was Dolbadarn, the castle at Llanberis Pass. This was the place Llywelyn had imprisoned his traitorous elder brother long ago. Cat had visited it with Princess Elinor and her retinue several times over the years. There was the round tower, and there were her father and Aeneus, ready to accompany the women. Dafydd and Elizabeth were standing near as well, smiling together.

Then she heard hoof beats, as if many horses rode together. Her brother tensed, and her da drew his sword.

"We will be better off," someone shouted.

Da moved in front of Mam as she tried to herd the other women and children back into the keep. At the head of the army that bore down upon them was a tall young man who reined in and tried to turn his horse away before she could see him clearly. But there was only one man it could be. Rhys! He had led the English right to the prince's hiding place—

—and Cat reeled out of her vision back into the room where de Francton had left her.

"No!" she cried out but the vision was gone.

"There, now," said a cheery voice. Cat started almost guiltily, snatching her hand out of the pack and shifting around to face the door. A young woman bustled in, her prominent apron spoiled with splotches that could be food, proclaiming her to be a kitchen girl.

"There now, Lady Catrin," the girl said again, her face drawing in with sympathy. "Of course you're upset. Sir Stephen can be a scary one, but he in't half as bad as some of the others. Lord Mortimer scares the life out of me, I will tell you. Well, no need to fret now, ma'am. They've all gone and rode off on their travels, haven't they? And Sir Stephen says from tomorrow I'm to be your maid, and help you with your things, ma'am."

Cat moved the pack protectively. How could she hide the relics from a maid whose duty it was to help her dress? To make the bed? She drew the pack closed and tried to settle it beside her without attracting the girl's attention.

"If you like, you can stay sitting there, ma'am, and I will bring your meal to you. I'm sorry to be so late with it." The girl set down an embroidered cloth with a flourish and placed a wooden platter on it. "It won't take a moment. Sir Stephen says you are to be well treated and no mistake. I don't mind saying I was glad to hear that, I was."

The girl helped Cat drape a cloth over her dress.

"How—How do you come to be here?" Cat asked.

"Pure luck, my lady," the girl said. "It's much nicer than slaving in that hot kitchen, or following around behind the soldiers." Then a blush crept into her cheeks. "Oh, you mean—here? Well, it was an easy choice. My young man—most of our village, truth to tell—came along to serve with Sir Stephen, and I couldn't let him go alone, could I? And now we have a proper kitchen and a larder filled to bursting. Of course you would know all about that, wouldn't you?

They say you and your young lord were the ones that filled it."

Cat felt trapped in some kind of nightmare as the girl continued to talk non-stop, arranging choice bits of smoked fish, mushroom, cheese, and laverbread. Still reeling inside, Cat moved the pieces around the plate in a semblance of eating, unable to escape the vision of her family under attack. Rhys could be leading them toward Dolbadarn even now. But if he knew the prince was at Dolbadarn, could he find a way to lead the English away? She had to get word to him somehow.

"I thank you for this bounty," she finally managed to say, "but I am tired from the journey and have no appetite at present."

"Of course you are. Will you rest for a time, ma'am? Can I help you with your dress?" The maid moved toward the bedchamber. "And do your hair and—"

"No. Thank you, but no." Cat was firm. "The bed is already made. I can manage." At the girl's crestfallen look, Cat softened her tone. "As you said, you will be my maid tomorrow. You must have other duties that need tending today?"

The girl dropped into a movement resembling a curtsey. "Thanks ever so much, ma'am. I confess, I have never been a ladies' maid, so I am not sure what to expect. But you are right, I must still help in the kitchens tonight after we are done here."

"You may leave me to finish your chores," Cat began. "I'm sorry, I've forgotten your name."

"Agnes, ma'am."

"Very well, Agnes." Cat placed her hand on the tray. "Leave this tray for me. I may want more of it later."

"They told me you Welsh ladies was far easier to please than our English ones." With another awkward curtsey, the kitchen girl buzzed out of the room, and Cat jumped up from the table. She had to get to a message to her brother. But how? No, she had to get a message to Rhys. If she could tell him what she had seen, he would help her find a way to stop it from happening. At the very least, he could work to avoid the part he had played in the ambush.

She almost ran to the window. Looking down, she tried to orient herself, and realized she was near the top of Bere's D-shaped tower. The farthest tower from the gate, of course. She saw the men far below, milling about in the courtyard. Even if she could get out, and make her way to the barns for a horse, she still had to get out of the gate and across the bridge before anyone saw her. What about the servant girl? Would she carry a message to Rhys? Could she be trusted?

Cat's restless pacing took her back to the door again. She could hear a woman's voice. She moved closer, listening. The guards' low voices rumbled outside, punctuated by the talkative kitchen girl. Was she telling them everything that had happened? Cat's hopes fell. The girl couldn't be trusted. Unless Cat could find a way to slip a message through? Perhaps the girl could be an unwitting carrier. But how? Cat shook her head in frustration. She made her way back to the window again, more quietly now so they wouldn't hear her and realize she wasn't resting.

As she turned to pace back to the door, she stopped. Bells at the nearby church called the monks to prayer. Cat stared straight ahead, unseeing, at the table and her untouched food. She focused on the area around Bere, recalling the church of St. Michael's where her uncle Gawain was no doubt shuffling into the chapel with the English monks. He was her last hope. If they were willing to feed her so lavishly, surely they couldn't refuse a request to feed her soul with spiritual comfort from a holy man?

Cat almost didn't recognize Gawain. When he came through the door a few hours later, he was wearing a brown homespun habit, instead of his usual white one.

"Uncle!" She hugged him even more fiercely, wondering what had happened to him since they had been separated and knowing that he probably wouldn't tell her.

"Lady Catrin," he said. With an arm around her, he moved them toward the window. "I hope you are being graciously treated here."

She was a little confused by his formal tone. He hadn't asked her about the relics or her visions. "Yes, of course, I—"

"I was pleased to hear you called for me." Gawain interrupted her, holding up one hand in a small gesture to stop her. He jutted his chin at the door for extra emphasis, and then toward the window. "I am glad that you wish for spiritual counsel. I have been concerned about you—since Lord de Francton's revelation."

A wave of guilt washed over Cat again. He meant the death of the English soldier by her knife, of course. She had forced the memory away so she could deal with de Francton and their captivity, but it flooded back now. Gawain was a monk, not a priest, and could not take her confession, which was just as well with the English listening. But he was still a holy man, and her spiritual health would naturally be his concern. She crossed her arms, struggling to rein in her shame as she turned toward him. "I was—shocked—as well, Uncle."

He nodded, seeing the warring emotions in her face. "I am instructed to remind you that you may have a priest if you wish it, and there will be full services on Sunday."

She read caution in his eyes. Even the comfort of confession would be denied her, if she wished to protect Rhys and her family. Her uncle's actions clearly showed they were being spied upon by the English. She had to play for time so she could think this through. Obviously their conversation could be overheard, and the English were listening. Could the English also see their actions? She had a momentary flash to hiding the pack with the relics in it. Surely they could not see past the curtains around the bed! Hairs pricked at the back of her neck and she squelched an urge to look around the room for peepholes or other devices she had heard mentioned in the *chansons* their Welsh bards had learned for Princess Elinor. But this was Cat's own castle—or it would have been—and Rhys had never mentioned anything of the kind.

"That will be most welcome," she said, trying to play along without really being sure of the rules of the game. "But uncle, you are more familiar to me than any priest or holy man here. I am very grateful to our captors for allowing you to visit me, to provide your welcome guidance."

As she mentioned captors, he looked again toward the door. "Lord de Francton especially bade me reassure you that you are not a captive here. Rather you are an honoured guest."

She nodded, trying to signal her understanding of his spoken and unspoken message. "Of course. And you, Uncle? Are you being well treated?"

"My brother monks are most generous in their humility." He plucked at the brown garment as he responded, making a disgusted face, and she had her answer. "But tell me more of how you fare, Niece."

She understood that he was asking about the relics as much as about her and held his eyes as she nodded. "They have not harmed me in any way," she answered, inclining her head so he could see that she understood him. "But I had hoped for your counsel, Uncle."

"I would be pleased to pray with you for guidance, Lady Catrin." They turned from the window, and he took her hands in his as they took seats together at the table. She took it as a reminder to continue being cautious when he added, "Perhaps we should include a prayer of thanksgiving for our deliverance."

While he said a suitable prayer, her mind raced. She had to warn Rhys about her vision, but if they could be overheard in this room, then even if they allowed him to stay here with her—she could feel her face flush a little—they could not speak openly. She had wanted Gawain to help her think of a plan to avert the vision, but how could she tell him now? Unless she could find a way to say it in code—and she recalled Gawain' own stories.

When Cat had turned fourteen with no sign of a hereditary gift appearing, Gawain consoled her with stories of her Aunt Cadi, who had never received one. He felt closer to Cadi than to any of his sisters, he confided, and they had developed many secret games together—including a way to pass messages their siblings couldn't understand. They used the form of the triads, but made up groups of their own, so that only every third word contained the message. Of course, they had to be subtle or the others caught on, at which point they would change the game so one of the other words was the correct one.

"Amen," she said with him as he ended the prayer and helped her up. "Thank you, uncle. I was thinking earlier today of my Aunt Cadi. That prayer was one of her favourites, was it not?"

He frowned at her as if mystified. "You may be right." He

took a seat across from her at the table.

"My mam and her sisters were ever playing tricks on you," Cat went on, taking his hands so he would look at her, "Mam, Aunt Enid, Aunt Cadi."

He frowned a little and moved his head to one side. She nodded. Understanding lit his eyes. "They certainly were quite a triad." She nodded again, sure he was with her in the rules of the game now.

"I long to see Mam again," she began, trying to think of a way to convey her message. "Do you recall when you told me to try to envision my family in my mind's eye, whenever I am homesick? I have found that this works well and offers me much comfort."

He regarded her steadily, eyebrows raised. "I am glad to hear it."

"If we were at home now, they would be bringing in the May."

"Yes, the May Day itself will soon be upon us. Your Mam was always the leader in that dance, as I recall."

"And she will be again, even now, in spite of our castles that have fallen in recent months: Garth Celyn, Criccieth, Dolbadarn." He sat up a little straighter and listened to her more intently, and she continued talking to cover the message. "I can only hope to see them again soon, in happier times and circumstances."

"I am sure you can see the truth," Gawain replied, and she nodded.

"This is certainly one of my favourite holidays: *Nos Galan*, St. David's, and *Calan Mai*." She used the Welsh words for New Year's and May day to emphasize her meaning. "For myself, I am glad to be here with you, but I fear for all: you, Cynfrig, Rhys. My husband has chosen a most difficult path and I can only hope he fares well on it."

"You have no reason to fear, Cat," Gawain told her. "Would it ease your mind if I could find Lord Rhys and offer him a blessing upon his return?"

"Yes, uncle, that would be my very wish. I only wish it could have been before he left," she said, and he patted her hand reassuringly.

"I am sure God will return him safely to us, and I am sure Lord de Francton will agree that a blessing will only ensure the outcome."

She shivered a little, recalling her last encounter with de Francton, and glanced at her uncle. "Yes, he is a most gracious host."

12

Hyw swung the javelin pole so its weight balanced in one hand, and then the other. He struck the stake in front of him on the left, feinted right, then ducked and crouched low to sweep it across where a man's ankles might be. Aeneus' gruff laugh behind him made him turn.

"Good lad," Aeneus said. "If you have only one weapon, use it well. And keep the element of surprise with you."

Dolbadarn's wide courtyard gave them ample room for daily exercises, and Aeneus kept them training every spare minute in preparation for the battles ahead. Llywelyn coached Hyw as he worked, and Aeneus noted his improvement more than once. The exercise kept worry at bay, and Hyw began to enjoy the feeling of his human muscles again.

As Hyw turned to ask more advice, he caught sight of Owain rushing toward them. The prince's son still carried the wooden sword he had been using with the other boys, and his face was pinched with concern. Something must be wrong. Hyw was on his guard instantly. Aeneus turned with a growl to see what had caught Hyw's attention. Owain pulled up beside them, winded.

"What is it, boy?" Aeneus asked.

"My sister," Owain said between ragged breaths. "Margred— she's gone. She rode out this morning without permission."

Hyw frowned. Margred could not be thinking of hunting now, with the English so near? But why had she taken a horse? The Welsh had only the handful of horses he had managed to call back from the woods around the castle, and it was no easy task. Each one would be needed if the English discovered them.

"Slow down." Aeneus put his hand on Owain's shoulder, and the boy stopped talking to catch his breath. "Did no one raise the alarm?"

"We knew it not until the horse came back without her," Owain said. The boy looked miserable. "Mam said not to disturb Da while he is in meetings with their lordships."

"And you want to get her back before your da finds out." Aeneus abruptly turned Owain around and strode toward the castle door with him in tow. "From which direction did the horse come?"

Hyw followed them, uncomfortably realizing he'd been more concerned about the horse than the girl's safety. If she was taken by the English… He could not finish. He knew she could be headstrong. Still, she wasn't foolish. Why would she do this?

As they neared the gates, Owain pointed toward the west. Hyw nodded.

"I will find her."

Aeneus glanced back at Hyw. "Your da won't like it. I will go."

"You know I can get to her faster."

Nay, Hyw. Llywelyn's voice burst in, gravelly with concern. *You must let someone else go. We are needed here. Dafydd needs—*

Hyw closed his eyes and confronted Llywelyn, speaking only in his mind. "Prince Dafydd will not listen to you, my liege. This I must do." Then he spoke aloud, so Aeneus could hear. "It will not take long."

As Aeneus narrowed his eyes, Owain spoke up. "I would go as well. She's my sister."

"Nay, young Owain. One of you lost is all we can spare. And your father would never forgive me." But the warrior clapped Owain on the back in approval before he nodded at Hyw. "Fear not: Hyw will find her."

As Hyw sprinted toward the gates, he spotted a horse being brushed down by a warrior. It was the bay Margred had admired the previous day. That must be the one she took. Hyw connected with the animal briefly without slowing down. It held an image of Margred in its mind as she took one path and sent the horse another way. She was clever, Hyw gave her that. Unencumbered, the bay had managed to elude its pursuers and return home. He thanked the animal for sharing the fearful memory.

He kept running down the path and out of the castle. He would go as far as he could before he started the change. He had promised Adara not to transform unless it was needed, but Margred was too far away now for him to find her without transforming. She could be injured, or captive. Or worse. There was no time to make woad or gather supplies. Briefly he felt for Llywelyn inside his mind.

"She is your niece and your subject," he told the former prince, feeling much more but unable to put it into words.

Do what needs be done, Hyw, Llywelyn whispered resignedly in his ear. *But do it quickly.*

She was running. Hyw recognized Margred's tunic and breeches through the trees. Lucky it was still spring and their foliage hadn't reached full growth. He kept pace with her easily from above. Something was different about her. He watched her almost lazily, spreading his wings to touch her with his shadow. Then he realized she was not alone. Three men ran close behind her. His heart rose to his throat and he uttered a shriek before he could stop himself.

Her speed and agility kept her ahead of her three pursuers, but they were too close. He trained his sharp eyes on them, circling behind them. One pointed in her direction as if he heard something. She would need help, and soon. Too soon for him to return to get Aeneus or the others. She may have confused them briefly by sending her horse back to the castle, but they had realized her ruse and were close on her trail again.

He had chosen the red kite's form, but now he needed something faster. He turned to face the English soldiers, recalling the peregrines from the hunting mews at Garth Celyn. He felt Llywelyn with him and turned his mind to flight. Bird to bird. He concentrated and his bones began to grow tight and dense. His speed increased and the sky was a roar around and inside him. He could see a break in the trees where the men would come through, and set himself at them.

His talons flashed. Llywelyn's strength joined his and together they hit one running man squarely in the back of the head. The man was knocked aside and hit the ground hard with a cry. Hyw flew past and circled back. The other two men had stopped running after Margred, and turned toward him. One was trying to draw a bow, and the other reached for him as if to catch him. He was too fast for them and sped past, raking them with his claws. The bowman dropped his bow, and the arrow flew sideways into the first man as he tried to rise. As the other two ducked and turned toward their companion, Hyw flew upward, out of range through the trees.

He spotted Margred's clothing again. His peregrine vision recognized the colour of her clothing to be human, and not forest. She had gone to ground, well hidden behind a ridge of rock and trees. But she had no mount to carry her away from them. He looked for a branch to land on but urgency pressed at him. An old tale came back to him of a bard who had changed forms in mid-air from bird to animal without breaking stride. Could he manage it? If his plan was to work, he must use all his energy to help Margred.

Knowing he had Llywelyn's support, Hyw concentrated, searching his mind for the smells and warmth of the stables at Shrewsbury. Llywelyn whispered, *Home.* Hyw shifted to the stables at Garth Celyn, searching for the former prince's favourite horses and locating in memory where they had once been stabled. The chuff and blow of the animals, the thunk of hoof on wood. The broad chest, the strong back, and finally the elongated head. Breathing in, he let the bird fly free and willed the equine into himself in its stead. Hooves hit the ground before wings gave way to mane and tail.

In the end, it cost him less than the change to human form often did. His hooves beat softly on the forest floor, and he made his way through the trees to Margred. She heard him, and sat up, ready to defend herself. He stopped, and blew a quiet puff of air through his long muzzle. She stared at him.

Now, he willed her with his eyes and his body. She looked behind her, and he knew she was listening for the men chasing her. He flicked his ears up, but heard nothing. He gurgled a sound through his throat, like a chortle. *Now.*

Finally she rose and came toward him. She shifted to his left and placed both her hands on his shoulder. Her hands were warm and firm on his skin as she pushed him a little away from her. Then she rocked back and he shifted, following her movements until she could slip onto his back. Her hands pulled at his mane and her knees dug into his sides, urging him toward safety.

As they neared the place where he had left his clothing, he stopped. She might have tried to press onward, but he wouldn't move. As if she understood without words, she slid from his back. He had left his clothes behind a rock, and he clomped slowly off the path toward it. She waited, not looking at him but away, down the path.

He was tired now, and could not stop the transformation coming over him. *Let go then, lad*, Llywelyn whispered. Hyw felt the anguish of releasing the animal's shape, and the pop and crack of his bones as they compressed down into human form again. His hide seemed to hiss as it dissolved into skin and shrank to fit along his torso, legs, and arms. He tried to stifle his cries at the pain of it.

When it was over, he lay with his stomach pressed against the cold, sharp rock. He had never transformed more than once and could not remember holding another form for so long at one stretch. Llywelyn stirred inside him and he closed his eyes. The former prince looked drained as well but nodded reassuringly.

Never have I seen such marvels. You have done it, Hyw. My niece is safe. Now let us return and see what her father has been up to.

Hyw opened his eyes again to find Margred staring at him with a combination of fascination and horror on her face. He wondered why she had not run away at the strangeness of it. He was too tired to be embarrassed at his nakedness, but he sensed neither fear nor revulsion in her.

"I thought at first that you had been sent to save me," she said softly. "I had never seen a horse with blue-grey eyes." As if jogged out of her daze then, she took off the waterskin she carried and left it beside him.

She turned away to let him dress. He was pleased to see that she waited for him on the path. She turned to look at him squarely as he drew near to her. "How did you—"

"It is an ancient gift," he said.

"Like Cat's sight," she said. "She told me about her abilities, but not about yours."

"We don't discuss it outside the family."

"Are all your family so gifted?"

"Not all."

"The others must be so disappointed," she said simply.

He felt a rush of relief that she accepted his gift and himself along with it. He cleared his throat to hide his emotions.

"Some would say we are cursed, and they are the lucky ones to escape it." As he handed the waterskin back to her, he noticed her cap had come off. "You cut your hair."

She immediately reached up to finger the limp locks hanging around her shoulders, and he flushed. It had once flowed in black curls around her face and down her back. It looked like she had hacked it off with her hunting knife.

"I like it," he added quickly.

"Safer to travel as a boy," she said.

"An English boy," he said. He touched his own hair, which had grown longer since his return from the English. He had begun to braid it again, but the braid was not as long as the ones Aeneus or Emrys sported.

"It's long enough," she told him, as if he'd spoken the warriors' names aloud. Then she shook her head. "I thank you for your help, but you must know, I will not return to Dolbadarn. Not until I can bring the people of Criccieth with me."

Llywelyn began to argue. *You must return me to Dolbadarn. The needs of the people must come first.*

Hyw shook his head, more at Llywelyn than Margred. "Why?"

"I was born there," she said. "In the village, not in the castle. You have your family, and Cat has the people of Meirionnydd. But what of the people of Criccieth?"

She has her father and her sisters at Dolbadarn, Llywelyn persisted.

And what of the people of Criccieth? Hyw let it play out. The English had invaded the northlands like an incoming tidal storm, as he knew from the hushed stories of the men around the campfire. Welsh heads rolled as they killed everyone—including women and children—for Edward's promise of a shilling a head. He recalled Cat's stories of how they had fled before Edward's armies, first from their home at Garth Celyn, then from Criccieth, and finally from Bere.

"There will be no one left there to lead home," he said gently.

She turned away from him and shook her dark curls. "There are always some who survive," she said. "This is not the first time the English armies have made their way to our doors. I know where the survivors will be hiding. They need us now more than ever before. You warriors," she scoffed, tapping her foot on the ground. "You are supposed to be fierce, but I can convince no one to return hither to help those who are stranded. So there is nothing left but to go myself."

"I could go," he said, even as the former prince inside him sputtered in protest. "I could check for those in hiding. If they are able to travel, I will change back and lead them to join us. We could use more warriors for our cause." He was speaking as much to Llywelyn as to Margred. The prince responded first.

If any are fit to travel, they will find a way to join with us, Llywelyn argued. *We cannot spare the time to seek them, especially when you are most likely to find the injured by travelling back to the scene of a battle.*

"If there are injured, I could convince my father to send a small force back to help them," Hyw said aloud.

"You will convince no one," Margred said, and for a moment Hyw wondered if she knew about Llywelyn, until her next words made her meaning more clear. "All of them must go with my father to win back Garth Celyn. Even you. Criccieth is the opposite direction, and I cannot let you divert our forces." Her voice was strained now, as if she was holding back tears. "Besides, if the people are in hiding, only I know the likeliest places to look for them. I must go myself."

She is brave, came Llywelyn's grudging voice inside his head.

"You misunderstand," he said, to both of them. "I could go, not as myself, but as a hawk."

He saw the look of realization dawn on her face, and with it a gleam something like greed.

"Aye," she cried. "Aye, you could go, but not as a hawk. As a horse, you could take me with you. Then as a hawk you could lead me to them. Then we could find food and bring it to them. Why, as an ox you could pull a cart-load—"

"Wait, my lady," he said, a little horrified at the idea of becoming a heavy ox to pull a cart at her whim. Was this why his family had kept their gifts secret, known only to a few, for so long? He had to find a way to convince her that what she asked was not the right of a leader or the daughter of a leader. "It is not like the songs by Taliesin. You have seen with your own eyes what it costs me to return to human form. Each time it takes something from me that I cannot get back."

Margred stared at him, her dark eyes changing from hope to despair. Even Llywelyn's voice was silenced.

"The hawk is easiest for me, or the horse," he finally said.

"The horse," she said. "Quickly."

13

It was dark when Cat heard a clatter in the courtyard. She had only meant to rest a moment. She woke with a start, struggled off the high four-poster bed, and raced to the window. Only a few torches lit the courtyard of Bere castle, but she could see horses and men milling about. She couldn't tell if Rhys was among them. She shook her head, still half asleep. Likely Gawain wouldn't be able to speak with him tonight anyway.

Then she heard the bells ring compline: the priest and monks would be awake and giving their final service of the working day. Perhaps the men would be taken to the service? Unable to go back to sleep, she lit a candle and looked around the room. A flush crept up her neck as her eyes lit on the curtaining that surrounded the bed. Would they bring Rhys here to sleep?

The scene of de Francton holding her jewelled knife flashed before her eyes. She had caused their capture. Worse: her reckless throw had killed a man, and sent his unshriven soul to hell. Why would Rhys want her for his wife now? The rustle of wind through the curtains played on her imagination. The slight flicker of the candle flame made ghosts move in every corner.

Cat shivered and shook herself, stumbling forward to the little table. The earlier meal had been cleaned away, but there was a pitcher with some hard biscuit. So the maid must have returned. Cat fought a touch of panic and raced back to the pack that she had hidden under her pillow. It was there, and she picked it up. The last thing she wanted now was to try to sleep again.

She finally returned to the same chair she had sat on earlier, held the pack in her lap, and placed the candle on the table beside her. She poured a drink for herself, but she had no stomach for the biscuit. The clattering of hooves and voices of men in the courtyard filtered up to her through the window. She swirled the cup, watching the liquid slosh the edges. The candle flame guttered in the wick, but no visions danced in front of her eyes.

De Francton sent Agnes early the following morning to rouse Cat and help her dress. Cat kept her pack near but the maid paid little attention to it, preferring to rummage through Elizabeth's neatly packed chests. They had barely finished Cat's hair when de Francton knocked on the door.

"I trust you slept well, Lady Catrin," he began, dismissing the breathless girl with a wave of his hand.

Cat schooled her nerves. She had to find out what had happened to Rhys and Cynfrig. "As well as can be expected, my lord," she told him. "It is always more difficult without my husband nearby."

"Ah," he began, drawing nearer to the table. "I hope we can remedy that before long. I don't mean you harm, you know. We are neighbours. I hail from Shrewsbury. My people have done business with the Welsh for many generations. In truth, I don't have anything against your—erhm, skills, if we can call them that. My lady wife birthed her second child with the help of a witch."

"And did they drown her or punish her for her troubles?"

De Francton ignored her remark. "We have great respect for the old ways, although we may not follow them ourselves. And I sympathize with your plight. It is very becoming in a wife to miss her husband so. Lord Rhys is indeed a lucky man."

"I count myself the lucky one," Cat said, taking the opportunity he opened for her. "Will he be joining me this morning?"

"I would like nothing more than to rejoin you two." He spread his fingers and half bowed to her. "But I am afraid I have need of him and his skills again today."

"I take it you were not successful in finding the prince yesterday?"

"Rest assured, we will find him."

"Or he will find you first." She wanted to recall the words as soon as they were spoken, but it was too late.

"Whether we find him, or he finds us, the outcome is certain." De Francton set his jaw but continued smiling. "We are aware of the number of men that might still be with him."

It chilled her to hear him speak of hunting Prince Dafydd, especially since her family was among those de Francton mentioned. Cat moved toward the window to hide her thoughts.

"Look down into the courtyard," de Francton continued, "and you will see the number of fighting men we have."

"And is my husband among them?"

"He is."

Cat willed herself to remain calm. Rhys must have spent the night in the guardhouse with the other men. An unexpected disappointment flooded over her and she drew her shawl closer. "And when you find the prince, then you will let us go?"

"I would think you would want our protection then, my lady, more than ever. Nay, your husband is important to our cause. It would have to be a miracle to cause me to release Lord Rhys from his pledge."

Unbidden, an image of the True Cross came to her. The cross and crowns together. She still heard the faint buzzing in her ears from the power of Arthur's crown. If only she could hold it again, perhaps she would know what to do. What if she held it now? Or Llywelyn's coronet. A reckless thought came to her. What if she gave de Francton back Llywelyn's coronet? It had been given to Llywelyn by King Edward's father, making it the least of the triad for the Welsh. Surely the relic and Arthur's crown together would be enough for Dafydd to rally the Welsh resistance to him. Could they trade the coronet for their freedom, and accomplish their mission?

"What if you found the relics?" Her heart beat faster as she spoke the words aloud. "Would that be miracle enough?"

"Would it, indeed," he said, but she couldn't tell if he meant it as a statement or a question. He narrowed his eyes at her. "If you had them, yes, it would certainly count in your favour."

She recoiled. Did de Francton think she would bargain with him? Rhys and Cynfrig would be aghast if they knew she had even mentioned the relics. "And do you even know why they are important?" she said.

"A relic of the True Cross, with the Coronet of Llywelyn, and the Crown of Arthur?" His voice was greedy with glee. "Your countrymen were quick to tell us of their value. I certainly put no faith in such trinkets, but King Edward and his Lady Queen are convinced that such legends will mean the loyalty of the Welsh. That is why we took Cymer Abbey, and what we sought in vain there. We questioned the abbot, but he said nothing."

The White Abbot. He had been a severe man, but she did not like to think of him at the mercy of these men, or how he might have been questioned. De Francton had called the relics "trinkets" and her confidence slipped.

"Who am I to doubt my betters?" de Francton went on, lightly. "You Welsh are mired in romantic notions. If such relics could bring your nation to its knees in front of my king, why... It would be worth more than gold to me." He brought his face close to hers, his voice suddenly serious. "What do you know of these relics?"

She raised her chin. "No more than any loyal countryman." But Rhys... If Rhys were here, surely they could think of a way out of this. And at the same time, if Rhys were free, couldn't he use the relics himself to rally the people against these *Saeson*? Her mind raced with possibilities. Could she trick de Francton into thinking she would give him the relics, but keep them for Rhys? Perhaps only the coronet? Could she bargain with it and keep the other two? If Rhys could break free of this pledge, they could use the power stored within Arthur's crown alone to draw the people to them. She could almost see it happening.

"Come now, you must know something." His voice was almost jovial, as if he was teasing her, but his eyes were unreadable. "With your gifts? If you could take me to the relic and the crowns,

I'm sure we could come to some kind of agreement."

"I?" Cat stubbornly shook her head, trying to think. "Of course, I could not." She glanced back out the window. Her breath was shallow and her mind raced. She must be careful.

"You could not?"

His voice was low and strangely gentle. This man had helped to kill Llywelyn; yet Hyw said he did it unwittingly, that de Francton did not realize he threw his spear at the Prince of Wales, and that he had rescued Hyw afterwards out of guilt or remorse or both. Her stomach clenched as if she stood on the edge of a precipice. In the old stories, if your faith was strong, the faery bridge would appear as you took the first step. If she could trust him…

"Then perhaps I should question your husband further?"

Cat felt a roaring in her ears. She let out a breath and pulled back. Whatever he seemed, he was the enemy. He must not guess that she now held the very relics he sought.

"You have given your word that my husband will come to no harm."

He raised his eyebrows. "And I can assure you, I am a man of my word."

Another story came to her: if she spoke only the truth, she would not betray herself to her enemy. Her mind calmed. She schooled her face and turned to stare back at him. "Prince Llywelyn was the one who hid the treasures," she said. "Neither Prince Dafydd nor any other would have been privy to that secret."

"Yet, if you could perhaps divine where these relics are, I would escort you and your party back to your countrymen myself."

She pretended to consider his offer. "My—skills—could prove useful."

"Indeed they could. And what of the prince? Could you divine his location?"

"I may be able to divine the location of many things, under the right circumstances."

His mouth twitched and she knew she had him. Perhaps there was a way to keep her latest vision from coming true. This time he hesitated before continuing. "And what might those circumstances be?"

This is what he had wanted all along. She strove for control and held still, as if considering his words. She must convince de Francton to take her in place of Rhys, or at least to reunite them. Then she could direct de Francton's search away from Dolbadarn and the prince—and her family. She had the advantage of her earlier vision, but if she could get de Francton to take them away from the castle's fortifications, they might find a way to escape.

She drew in a breath to steady herself. Then she sighed and gestured at the room. "Alas, I must be near a body of water, such as a swift stream or lake."

"That can certainly be arranged, Lady Catrin." If he was surprised at her words, he hid his emotions well. "I am glad to see you are willing to do what is necessary to save your husband."

"Of course," she added, "I will need to prepare. And I will need more suitable clothing."

He bowed to her and turned to leave. When she heard his voice in the hall, calling for Agnes, her legs began to shake and she reached for the windowsill to steady herself. Then she took a deep breath, straightened her spine, and channeled her memory of the regal Princess Elinor.

Cat stood at the window, listening to the noises in the courtyard as grooms and stable boys prepared the horses to ride. It was simple. All she had to do was steer the English troops away from Dolbadarn, protect Rhys, and keep de Francton's belief in her craft as she did so. And somehow let Rhys know her plans. Of course. Simple.

A moment later the maid sang out and stepped through the doorway. Agnes held up a sturdy green sleeveless overtunic. "I found this in the chest, ma'am."

Cat set aside her doubts. So far, her ruse was working better than she had hoped. Perhaps this could even provide them a chance to get away so they could finally deliver the relics to Dafydd.

"It should do for this day," Agnes prattled on. "Sir Stephen—may fortune find him—says you are to have the best we can offer. He's already sent a man to find the pillion."

Cat forced her mind to think. A pillion saddle would require her to ride behind a man, presumably de Francton. That would mean no chance of escape. Even if they let her ride behind her "husband" Rhys—her heart quickened for a moment—carrying both of them would burden the horse. She made a show of feeling the smooth linen and held it out to see the breadth of the skirt. Its wide folds would cover her legs modestly, whether she rode astride or across the saddle. She felt a small flutter at riding in the midst of a group of English soldiers, but Princess Elinor and her ladies—her own mam among them—had managed well enough. Cat straightened her shoulders. As Agnes moved to help her dress, Cat raised her hand, palm-up.

"I can manage, Agnes, and I thank you for your help. But tell Sir Stephen that I will not ride pillion."

The maid raised her eyebrows but Cat stood firm, offering a smile that she hoped would win Agnes over to her side.

"There was a pretty bay palfrey in the courtyard when we arrived," Cat said, "and that one looked to be a good fit. Pray ask them to saddle her for me."

"Saddle, ma'am? Not the pillion?"

Cat nodded and gestured for Agnes to move. "As you say, we Welsh ladies have our differences. I have been on horseback since I was a babe, and I ride better than most men. If the bay is not available, tell them any horse of 15 hands or smaller will do well."

"Whose hands, ma'am?"

Cat stared at her a moment before she remembered that Agnes had spent her life in a town. The maid had probably never dealt much with horses.

"My husband's hands will do. In fact, tell them to let Lord Rhys choose a horse for me. He will know what I need and how to saddle it."

"You Welsh truly are a strange lot." But the maid moved through the door, calling, "I will try to tell them, ma'am, but I cannot say what will come of it."

Cat thanked her, imagining what whispers and gossip her request would stir in the kitchen later. As soon as the maid left, Cat picked up the overtunic. The light scent of lilies flashed a scene into her mind: the thud of horses' hooves, a brisk wind against her face,

Princess Elinor laughing back at her with delight as they rode across a field. Elinor! The princess must have left the dress here last year, fully expecting to return this summer with her first child.

A pang of sadness filled Cat as she held the green linen to her nose and breathed deeply. Then she straightened and drew on the overtunic, welcoming the scent and willing her former princess' spirit to her as she arranged the fabric. A matching cloak and crisp white cap—a barbette, Elinor had called it—lay on the bed. Elinor had never worn a veil, but the maid must have found it in the chest with the dress. Cat picked up the barbette and tied the band under her chin. Then she spotted her pack peeking out from under the pillow.

Should she hide the pack or take it with her?

First she set the bed to rights and placed the pack back under the pillow. But how ambitious was Agnes? Would she pull the bed apart to remake it after they had gone? Unsure, Cat picked up the pack again. What if she and Rhys had a chance to escape? If she hid the pack, they would have to return for it. No, she had to take it with her.

Cat tied the pack around her like a child's sling, and tried arranging the cloak over it. She craned her neck to view the result: the pack appeared to be hidden fairly well under the folds of her outfit. She was adjusting her barbette again when Agnes returned.

"Very well, ma'am," Agnes told her, holding the door open. "They are saddling the palfrey for you."

"And how did Sir Stephen receive the news?"

"He—he laughed, ma'am," Agnes said, her voice holding a mix of surprise and a little awe.

14

Hyw marvelled at the flex of his new muscles and how easily he carried the weight of a person on his back, across country toward Criccieth. He could feel Margred's hands in his mane and he let himself follow the pressure of her thighs and knees. His mind translated the commands effortlessly as he became one with the nature of the horse.

As they began to climb one rocky, narrow path, Hyw realized he had lost the sense of the prince's spirit inside him. In a panic he stopped, closed his eyes, and sought Llywelyn's now-familiar presence. The prince stood behind him, as always, but he was pale and the lines around his eyes and mouth had deepened. The constant shifts in form had taken a toll. But Llywelyn merely nodded and waved Hyw on. Margred shifted on his back, and Hyw opened his eyes again.

He could give them one advantage, whether through his gift or the horse's heightened instincts for herding: he could sense the horses of the English soldiers whenever they drew near. Several times he stopped and shook his head, communicating to Margred that the way was not safe. At first, she seemed to understand his reluctance and allowed him to turn their course in whatever direction he chose. But as the delays caused them to lose time, Margred began to urge him onward. The next time he tried to stop she kicked his side with her heel.

"We will never get there at this rate," she hissed into his ear. "We must go this way."

He wanted to buck her off then, to rub against a tree and remove her from his back. But he had agreed to the arrangement, and he had to honour it. He fought the instinctive fear of the prey animal and regained control, trying to follow her commands and lead them away from the English at the same time.

As they crested a hillock, a group of English riders came into view. She slid from his back and ran into the bushes near them. He made his way into the thatch as best he could without changing shape, and stood with his head bowed. He was surprised by the strong pull of their pounding hooves and his longing to join them. He fought off the urge, wondering if they sensed him in turn and knew their running called to him.

When the soldiers passed, Margred returned and they continued on their way. Finally, they could see the spires and flags of a castle flapping in the distance.

"Criccieth," he heard Margred whisper. She urged him on, but he could smell smoke and something darker. Burned flesh? He heard her intake of breath, and knew she smelled it too. He tried to stop, but she pressed harder and tugged on his mane. Then he saw the birds. Wheeling and diving, blackbirds and crows circled overhead and then dipped toward the ground. He thought of Dolbadarn, and his stomach churned. When she kicked him with her heels, he heard the sobbing in her throat, and he galloped.

At the edge of the town, he shied away. He could see the charred remains of thatched roofing, and what looked like a twisting, shaking black pool on the ground. She slid off his back again, and as she ran toward the mass, it dissolved into shrieking and cawing birds.

"No," she cried. She picked up a discarded broom and batted at the birds as she ran.

His bones gave a grinding crackle as the change took him, shifting him from horse to man again. Never had the return to human form hurt him more, even as he tried to rally. She had tied his clothing to him in case they were separated, and he struggled into it and stumbled after her.

She was screaming now, screaming at the birds as she twirled, using the broom like a sword. Birds hit the ground, stunned by the force of her blows.

Then he had her, he held her, he stroked her hair as he would a child. She hit at him at first, but soon she shuddered and finally sobbed against him. The birds continued to swoop at them until Hyw used his gift to send the bravest of them away. Inside his mind, Llywelyn began to sing, and Hyw joined him, loud enough for Margred to hear. Gradually, she quieted. The song ended, and she pushed away without looking at him.

"We will kill them," she said. He knew she meant the English. "We will find the ones that did this, and we will kill them all."

From deep inside him, he heard Llywelyn's rumbling voice. *Yes.*

When she had recovered enough to continue, they checked the town for survivors. "There were more people than this living here," she said.

Hyw looked up at the high walls of Criccieth Castle. Anyone watching might see him or Margred if they stayed in the street. He led her to the remains of a smoldering wattle-and-daub hovel, where he bade her crouch beside him, low enough to be out of sight.

"Stay here," he said, turning to face her. "I'll go check the castle yard. Our people may yet be alive." A flicker passed through his mind of the ways he had seen the English force people to talk, during his time with them. He glanced away from her, clamping down on the thought quickly.

She shook her head. "I know how to get in without being seen."

"So do I."

She tossed her head. "When were you last here? Your magic might get you in, but how will you get the others out again?"

"I have ways."

"Tell me."

Her challenge startled him into answering. "Prince Llywelyn."

No! You must not tell her.

Hyw closed his eyes and answered without speaking the words aloud. "You trust no one."

Nor should you. Even your sister cannot know what man—or woman—will break under pressure.

"Yet I am not like you. I must trust someone." Hyw opened his eyes and spoke to Margred, over Llywelyn's continued protests. "My magic, as you call it, extends beyond even what you know. When the prince was murdered, his spirit remained and—and somehow bonded with me."

For a moment she stared at him without speaking. "You mean, he lives in you? In your mind, even now?"

He nodded. "And right now he is not pleased."

"But he will help us?" She stared past him for a moment, in the direction of Criccieth. "Even so, you must let me show you what I know."

Best hear her, Llywelyn said in his inner ear. *This was her home for many years. If it has secrets, we may need to know of them before the day is out.*

As the afternoon shadows grew longer, they moved carefully through the streets. She pointed out the road to him, explaining the layout as they went. In truth, Hyw was glad to learn there was no tunnel this time. When they finished, he scanned the sky. He could simply use the eyes of a passing bird to scout again, but a restlessness took hold of him. He left her and crouched behind a long trough to prepare for the change. He closed his eyes to check Llywelyn as he settled, and left his clothing in a neat pile for later.

The transformation was swift and almost comfortable, as if Hyw were assuming a more natural shape. Stark contrast to the change back from animal to man, he huffed, and he shook out his wings in the waning sun. He chose the small, fierce goshawk to cast the least shadow. The castle spread out below him, and he dipped toward it.

Margred had done a good job of explaining the various buildings and quarters, and he took stock of all he could, in case it was needed in Dafydd's bid to retake the country. He counted seven men tied together in the yard. Landing soundlessly on one of the poles the English had set up to practice sword-fighting in the yard, he watched the line of bound men with the sharp hunter's eyes. He could not tell if they were warriors or villagers. Most were still, or lying prone, and he heard soft groans. Ropes tied their wrists behind them. They had been badly beaten and then left in the courtyard. Their guard stood staring at the castle, his body slouched with boredom. Others would surely come to collect the prisoners for questioning, or perhaps to drag them to the dungeon Margred had mentioned.

Hyw looked back at the line of bound men. One man moved his shoulders from time to time, and Hyw realized he was working the ropes, trying to get free. He looked familiar, and Hyw wondered if he had been one of Llywelyn's guards at Garth Celyn. In bird form, Hyw could not use words himself to ask the prince, although he could understand when the prince whispered.

This one numbered among my teulu, a new recruit only last year. Glad I am to see him, but not like this. You must help him, Hyw.

Hyw bobbed his head and settled in to watch the guard with the patience of a hunter. The guard fidgeted, chewing on a slender wheat stalk. At one point he picked up a stone and threw it, without much force, in the direction of the Welsh prisoner who was moving his shoulders.

"Settle down," the guard growled, and the warrior tensed. The guard stared at him for a time, but the prisoner remained still, keeping his eyes on the ground. After a few long moments, the guard slouched against the pole, taking out another stock to chew. The warrior began to move his shoulders again.

Hyw wanted to scratch his talons across the guard's bald head, but he held the hawk's instinct at bay. He remained still, the breeze ruffling his feathers slightly. His bones felt light, as if he could perch there for hours, the sun warming him as it inched across the sky. The pole swayed as the guard sank heavily into a sitting position, but Hyw moved only his neck, to stare down at his prey.

Before long, the guard's head nodded. When he heard the heavy breathing of sleep, Hyw flew to the ground nearby. He landed near the Welsh prisoner, who eyed him warily.

"What do you want, eh?" the man crooned softly in Welsh. "Do not harm me." Hyw moved his head up and down, hoping to gain some measure of trust. The man was seated half-facing the others, with his arms twisted away from the guard as he worked at his tether. Hyw hopped a little, using his wings to bring him closer to the man's bound hands. It was a marvel the man didn't flinch. Hyw bent his sharp beak and pulled at the knot, loosening it, and then hopped away before the man could react.

"I know not what you are, but I thank ye and the gods who sent ye to us," the man whispered, his eyebrows raised in shock or surprise.

Hyw repeated the action twice more. The man quickly wriggled out of his tether and untied the others, keeping his eyes on the English guard and shushing any who made a sound. Hyw flew toward the secret entryway Margred had told him about, perching on it. He had to repeat the movement again until he was sure the men would follow him.

Swiftly he flew back to Margred and landed, making the difficult transformation where he had left his clothes. As he shrugged on his tunic and breeches to join her in hiding, he gestured for her to remain quiet. He could feel Llywelyn moving restlessly inside him.

Now we wait, Llywelyn said grimly.

Soon they saw six halting figures making their way toward them. Margred stood and waved, but Hyw pulled her down. The men had seen them and moved in their direction, crouching behind bushes and scuttling from cover to cover. When they finally arrived, Margred gave a little cry and bent to one of the injured men.

"Drem!" she said. Hyw could see the man was a little older than himself, and wondered how she knew him. But she said nothing more as she looked at Drem's wounds, and used some cloth from her pack to bind them. Hyw turned his attention to the rest. Four still seemed able to walk, and they had braced the other between them as they ran.

"You were seven, but I count only six here," Hyw murmured to the one he had helped to freedom.

"Dewi was already gone," he replied. "We could not save him. *Saeson* bastards." He spit on the ground, and then his eyes roamed over Hyw. "How did you see us?"

Hyw realized his error, and struggled for an explanation. He pointed to the mountain behind the castle walls. "I have been trained to scout."

"You seem familiar to me."

Panic flooded Hyw. The man couldn't have guessed his secret? Llywelyn's voice murmured almost soothingly in his inner ear. *Greet him for me, as I cannot.*

"I am Hyw ap Bran, late of Garth Celyn," Hyw told him, reaching out his arm.

"I thought I was all that remained of my home. Glad I am to see another. I am Odgar ap Math, also of Garth Celyn. Well met!" He clasped Hyw's arm with his own. "I knew your da. I was a farmer's son until he took my measure and bid me serve the prince. And how is Lord Bran?" After they had exchanged news, Odgar went on, "We came to bring the people to safety, but instead we met up with the traitor priest." He spat on the ground.

"There are yet more of us," Hyw assured him. "Da and Aeneus hold Dolbadarn for *Tywysog* Dafydd."

Odgar looked back at Criccieth as if checking their way. "Strange and stranger are the times we live in, and stranger yet they may become," he said softly. "We must move from hence, Hyw ap Bran. The ropes that held us did for our guard, and we hid his body where it might not easily be found. For a time they may believe we have been taken back to the dungeons, but they will seek us before long."

Hyw nodded. "We must hasten back to Dolbadarn. The *Tywysog* will welcome more warriors to his cause."

"I am the only warrior among us. These others are villagers, good men all, but not yet seasoned."

Hyw nodded, realizing that Odgar had been the one to kill the English soldier, and saw the cost of it in the man's haunted eyes. Llywelyn spoke softly in Hyw's head. *No man should be glad to kill another. Keep account of this man, Hyw. He will be as worthy in peace as in war.*

Then Odgar gestured and the others picked up their wounded. Hyw found himself searching for Margred. He could hardly believe there had been a time when the loss of a horse concerned him more than the danger she had put herself in. Then he saw her, smiling up at Drem and supporting him as he walked. Hyw wondered again how she knew the other boy, but she did not look his way. Had that been the real reason why she came? Had she used him to rescue a former love? A strange tightness gripped his heart, but where he had expected jealousy, it quickly turned to something else. Relief? He shook his head slightly as he moved to the front of the line to act as their scout.

15

Cat couldn't help but smile as the pretty bay palfrey with black points neighed in greeting. The company of more than twenty armed knights fanned out around the horse, to fill the courtyard of Bere castle. Cat glanced around, hoping to catch a glimpse of Rhys. He leaned forward, as much to catch her attention as to pat his mount's broad shoulder, and sent her a reassuring glance. She saw his horse's reins were held by a mounted knight beside him. Without control of his horse, it was unlikely that her dream of escape would become a reality—at least, not today. She looked around farther and spotted Cynfrig standing near a group of soldiers.

De Francton manoeuvred his horse between them, as if to prevent their silent communication. "So good of you to join us, Lady Catrin," he said.

She held her head up as she walked past him. "I enjoy riding."

"I hope you do. And I see you've brought your pack with you."

Cat automatically covered it with her left arm. He smiled to let her know she was too late.

"It seems your husband had little luck in finding Prince Dafydd yesterday," he went on. "It must be hoped that you can use your skills"—he nodded to the pack—"to help guide our company to greater success today."

So he had decided she was indeed a witch and carried her spellcraft in the pack. Even better. If he had communicated as much to his men, this might be easier than she had hoped. She allowed herself some relief at having made the decision to bring it along, but it was short-lived.

"To ensure your cooperation and that of your husband, your steward will remain here with my men. Pray tell me if there is any way we might assist you to make the journey shorter."

"I am glad to follow your advice," she told him, "and keep my time in your company as short as I possibly can."

Cat walked to the left of her horse, glancing at Cynfrig, who nodded without smiling. One of the soldiers cuffed him for it, but Cynfrig barely moved as his body absorbed the blow. The older man's drooping moustache gave him a forbidding look. Cat moved her skirts to cover her as she mounted deftly, ignoring the knight who held up his cupped hands to assist her. The bay took a few steps back as Cat adjusted herself on the saddle, and she saw a lead connecting her horse to de Francton's.

"Very well, Lady Catrin," de Francton said, giving her the same courtly smile as before. "What direction do you suggest?"

A horse gurgled, and she turned to look for Rhys, but his face was a mask of stoicism. She wished they had had a chance to confer, but she was equally sure that de Francton would prevent them from doing so. A heavy sorrow thrummed through her as she glanced around the castle yard. The English had settled in so well, it was hard to believe it would ever have been her castle. She felt their eyes on her. Spreading her fingers to rub the smooth fabric of Elinor's green overtunic, she tried to straighten her shoulders. What should she do?

"Your husband and his steward would be grateful to you for suggesting the direction today," de Francton said. He rode closer and spoke to her in Welsh. "No doubt you missed your husband last night. My apologies, but he was needed elsewhere. Nevertheless, if you divine the right direction for us today, you will be reunited at dusk. Would that please you?"

"I could think of nothing that would please me more," she responded. "And our steward?"

"He will yet live to see another dawn." That smile returned as de Francton caught her eyes and held them while he continued. "But take good care, lady. If we do not find the prince soon, both

Lord Rhys and his steward will spend the night in chains so we may inquire with other means."

The colour drained from the morning as she was sure it drained from her face. "I must—" she began, and gulped down the bile that threatened to rise in her throat. De Francton tilted his head as he waited for her to continue.

Cat knew where the prince was hiding. If she pointed de Francton and his company toward them, she would become the instrument that made her vision come true. Yet if she did not, Rhys and Cynfrig would be at de Francton's mercy. Visions of their torture rose in her imagination and she had to close her eyes. She had no doubt that Rhys would die before he told them anything. She struggled to control her breath and force her eyes open again.

"I must consult the Fates," she finally said. De Francton stared at her a moment longer. "As I said, a stream or a lake will do nicely."

The Englishman bared his teeth in what might have been a smile as he raised his other hand. When he gestured toward the gate, the company fell into place behind them. Cynfrig and the little group of soldiers receded behind them as they rode out.

Several times Cat tried to swivel in her seat to see Rhys or find some way to tell him what she had planned. Rhys managed to give her a reassuring nod, but as she expected, de Francton's men watched them closely. She was thankful when de Francton finally pulled them to a halt on the road.

"Dismount," boomed a voice behind them. The knight holding the reins of Rhys' horse must be de Francton's second-in-command.

She smoothed her skirts with one hand as she disengaged a foot from its stirrup and lightly stepped off the other to the ground. The little palfrey took a step to the side. She patted its neck to steady herself, and the horse turned its head to look at her, its brown eyes calm. As a knight stepped up to take the palfrey's reins, Cat drew a breath and turned to de Francton.

"I must have privacy," she said.

"That won't be possible. I can assure you that I will not tell anyone what I see."

His face was smug: he meant to stay with her while she,

supposedly, performed some ritual. She would need to do something to protect the contents of her pack. Panic returned in force and she blurted the first words that came into her head. "I need Lord Rhys to assist me."

"Lord Rhys?"

She blinked. "If you understand the craft as well as you say you do, you should understand that." She was inventing as she went, but she had to hope de Francton was no more knowledgeable about witchcraft than she was. Apparently it was a good guess, because he nodded gravely and turned to wave at his second-in-command to bring Rhys to them. Would that mean more English eyes on them?

"We must have privacy for the ritual," she amended lamely.

De Francton snorted. "I've already told you that won't be possible. I can promise you that I will be the only one with eyes on you, but my troops will be a whistle away."

So, no chance that they might run or light a fire and escape in the smoke. She searched for options. She could hear the murmur of a river or stream, somewhere nearby. She might as well use the opportunity to find out everything she could to help them. "I must have water."

De Francton took off his water skin and held it out to her.

"No," she said. She pointed in the direction of the sound without taking her eyes off him, hoping it would look like the gesture of a true witch. "We will find a stream a short way down the trail in that direction."

De Francton drew back, as if shocked by her knowledge, and her panic began to subside. This English captain had a good measure of belief but no clue about the craft. Perhaps this would not be as impossible as it seemed.

By the time they could see the brook, Cat had worked out part of a plan. "I must have my husband near me," she told de Francton. "He knows the words."

"As I said," de Francton began, but she interrupted him, pointing to an area behind them.

"You may watch from there." She moved slightly so her back was to de Francton.

Rhys moved closer to her now, as if he knew this might be their only opportunity. "The words?" he asked quietly.

"Never mind," she said, pitching her voice to Rhys and trusting the brook's fast and noisy current to prevent de Francton from overhearing. "Did Gawain find you?" She slanted her eyes so she could see Rhys without raising her head.

"We must lead him in another direction."

She nodded. "For as long as we can."

"Cat, you must not let him know."

"Is there not some way we can get word to them?"

He cast a glance back at de Francton. "Unless you can control the ravens?"

She shook her head slightly. "We must try to escape."

"If opportunity presents itself. And Cat, if you have the opportunity, you must take it. Go back to the holding near Abbey Cymer, where we left the others. Emrys will see you safe there."

She could feel her vision blur with tears. "De Francton threatens to torture you."

"Then he will," Rhys whispered back. "Do not fear for us. We will not break."

No, you will die, she wanted to say, but her voice was lost in her throat. She turned her head away from him and caught sight of the river. A sudden longing for her mam nearly overwhelmed her, and she wished she was a little girl again who could ask for guidance. She saw her mam's face clearly in her mind's eye—

—and she felt herself falling. Around her someone was playing a crwth, the music inviting her to dance, although she couldn't see the player. She saw something like a curtain in front of her, and then realized it was smoke. She felt a strange heat, and heard a crackling near her, and then she was right above it. She was on Ynys Môn, the sacred lands, but flames devoured the fields. Through the smoke and flames she could hear the voice, still calling to her. Calling her but not only her. Around her she had many Sisters, all the same as her. There was something she must

do, she and her Sisters. But the smoke made her strangely calm, almost against her will.

She listened for it again, the voice. The voice so melodic and lilting that she wanted to go to it. Like her Sisters around her, she struggled and danced and stretched toward the voice. It was calling for all the creatures of the air to come and save the land. But it was so faint. She looked for the tall tower of orange that called them home, for the Fire That Did Not Burn. The Fire of Blackthorn, Birch, and Willow. Earth must be born again. She must go to the voice. Where was it? She and all of her Sisters should be flying toward it right now. Instead they lay still, all around her in the grass. The smoke from another fire held them still, a man-made fire that seared and burned. Confusion and pain choked her. She was small, very small, and she couldn't move.

Help us, she wanted to call, but she could not. Help us. We cannot hear you. We cannot come. The creatures around her stopped struggling. Grew still. The land crackled. She wanted to call to the voice, but the smoke and flames choked her. A tree crashed in front of her as the flames seared—

—and she found herself on the bank of the brook again. Rhys had come closer to her to hold her up, as if she had almost fallen into the rushing waters. No spirit or sword rose from its surface to help them.

Calan Mai. The day the land should awaken to its promise of summer. But instead there was fire, and smoke, and bees lying dead in the fields. Although she could barely understand what had happened or why, she had lived and died with her tiny brethren. She felt them deep within her still. And like the bees, she ached for her mam—not only as her human daughter now, but also as a creature of air and earth. But her mam was too far away, and like the bees, she could not reach her.

"What did you see?" Rhys asked her, an urgency in his voice.

"What ho!" de Francton called out, coming closer. "What news, Lady Catrin?"

"Bees," she whispered to Rhys. "Dying in the field."

He looked at her, uncomprehending. "You—you did not see Dafydd?"

Cat shook her head.

"What tidings do you bring for us?" At de Francton's voice, Rhys gripped her shoulders more tightly.

"Do not fret." Rhys bent as if to kiss her and whispered, "Use what you have already seen. Send them east." Then he captured her mouth with his, and she closed her eyes and leaned into him. De Francton and his captain pulled Rhys away and she almost stumbled. Rhys reached out to her but the soldiers had him, dragging him away from her.

"So, what did your—" de Francton gestured to the stream "— little adventure tell you? Do you know what foxhole Prince Dafydd has found to hide in?"

Cat used the moment Rhys had given her to compose herself to meet de Francton's sallies. If she did not tell de Francton what he wanted to hear, he would torture Rhys and probably her as well. If she told him, he would most likely kill her family along with the prince. *Calan Mai* was yet to come. Surely she could keep de Francton from Dolbadarn for two more days. Then the first of May would be over and her visions avoided. Drawing herself up, she composed her face in a careful mask, as she had seen her mam do more than once. She drew a long breath to calm her heart, which was surely beating fast enough for everyone to hear.

"Not foxhole, but castle," she said.

De Francton huffed. "We have taken all of his castles."

"And he has taken one back."

She could see the uncertainty pass through Rhys' eyes as he shrugged off the guards. He moved as if to stop her, but the soldiers grabbed him again. She turned to them and raised a hand as if to stop them, but de Francton grabbed her arm and yanked her around to face him. Behind her, she could hear a struggle.

"Is this the extent of your cooperation, Lord Rhys?" de Francton said, looking over her head at the scene behind her. "You would do better asking her to tell us all she knows, if you expect to see morning." She itched to turn around and help in some way, but de Francton held her by the arms as he switched his eyes to her. "Don't worry, my dear. If you tell us what the spirits have shared with you, you will save his life. I am sure he will forgive you. And we can finally leave this god-forsaken rain behind us."

A flash of her knife hitting the English soldier passed through her mind. If she had truly sent a man to hell, even by accident, then how could a lie—especially to an enemy—blacken her soul anymore?

"You need not fear our loyalty," she said, speaking in English so that hopefully the guards would also hear her.

De Francton's jaw clenched. "Then share what you have learned." He waited and she knew some response was necessary.

"As long as my husband is safe, I will, of course," she began, keeping her eyes trained on de Francton's chin so she wouldn't give herself away. He nodded behind them and the sounds of struggle abruptly stopped.

She breathed out, not realizing she had been holding her breath. Rhys was out of danger, at least for the moment. Her mind swept through what she knew of witches and witchcraft, hoping de Francton hadn't heard as many stories around the cooking fires as she had. "What I can see through my craft is not plain but must be interpreted. I can see a castle surrounding Prince Dafydd. A castle to the east of us."

"How can you know that?"

She glanced up and realized he was serious. "The position of the sun and the moss on the trees, of course."

He nodded at that and she moved her eyes to his chin again to hide her expression. She could have told him anything. He knew little of tracking and nothing of the mountainous Welsh forests.

"What castle?" he asked.

"There are many Welsh castles in the area, my lord." She pursed her lips, searching her memory for names of the castles to the east of Dolbadarn, as far away as she could lead them from Dafydd and her family.

He tightened his grip on her arm. "Which one?"

In the end, he would probably kill them all anyway, but she would lead him on a merry chase first. "Would not a prince in hiding think you too lazy to search a ruined castle? I know of one that would be his best choice."

De Francton searched her face. She held firm, keeping her face as composed as she could. The Englishman let her go and turned to his men, as she almost stumbled back in her haste to move away from him.

De Francton shook the rain from his cloak and turned to the knight on his right with renewed energy. "Bellamy, have the men mount up. We ride east."

Cat glanced toward Rhys and saw his knees bend in readiness. Now was their chance. While the English went off chasing shadows, they could slip away and finally get the relics to Prince Dafydd. But de Francton turned back and, almost as an afterthought, gestured to the knights behind them to bring them both along. A knight's hand touched her elbow. Her knees almost buckled but she tried to shrug away.

"Now that she has told you what you want to know, will you not let me take my lady wife to safety?" Rhys said.

"Is that what you thought," de Francton again asked, turning the question into a statement. He studied Rhys. "What happened to your pledge of service?"

Rhys kept his face impassive. "I will bring more of my men to join you."

De Francton's eyes crinkled as if he was going to smile. "Ah, the twenty men with horses."

"At least let her return to the castle." The crack in his voice gave Rhys away, and the anguish in his eyes told her they both knew it.

"We may well have further need of her—skills." De Francton gestured again. "Come along, now. Both of you."

Cat tried to send Rhys a reassuring look as the knights fell in behind her, herding her onward.

16

Hyw was forced to rely on stealth and scouting skills on the trek back to Dolbadarn. His human skills had grown rusty, so he reached out with his mind to the animals around him. As the sun began to set, he used the keen eyesight of a long-eared owl to help them find a thicket where they could spend the night. Hyw tried to thank the owl, but as he made deeper contact he had to yank himself away from the pull to assume its shape and gain its knowledge first hand. While he was recovering, Margred appeared beside him.

"While I waited for you, I found dried meat in the village, and packed as much as I could." She held out some of the meat and a small, slightly withered apple to him, but Hyw took her hand.

"Who is Drem?" he asked. She freed her hand from his, and he let her.

"He is the son of the butcher in my village," she told him.

"I mean, who is he to you?" Hyw's voice sounded odd in his ears. Was he jealous?

"We have known each other since childhood. We—we promised ourselves to each other as children, long before my father brought me into his world. My mother was a servant in the castle, and after—when she came with child—my father found her a suitable match with a local mason. We were happy."

Hyw thought about his own childhood at Garth Celyn, when he and Emrys and Bronwen cared only about who could run fastest or swim farthest in the pool below the waterfall. If he could find those days again, wouldn't he? Shouldn't she? He looked away from her.

"Then one day my father saw me, and the next I was taken to live at the castle. He sent Mam and her mason away." Margred laughed harshly. "Mam told me beauty is a curse. But I won't be bartered to an old man to help my father make alliances."

Her light touch feathered his shoulder, but he did not trust himself to look at her. Should he be angry? Shouldn't he be angry?

"You brought me here," she went on. "Know that you have helped me more than I can ever repay. Your secret will remain safe with me. We must return to the castle for protection, I see that now. But when we arrive at Dolbadarn, I will renounce my father's name and marry Drem." She leaned forward a little and removed her hand, whispering. "I will not ever again command you, Hyw ap Bran. I know my own mind now. And you helped me find that."

She is her father's daughter, Llywelyn said. *And we must trust them to sort it out on our return to Dolbadarn.*

Margred had moved on to distribute food to the others. She deserved to be happy, Hyw told himself. He tried not to look at the spot where Margred had left Drem, wondering if the butcher's son understood his fortune. Margred had proven herself loyal to those she loved, but Hyw found himself thinking of his former foster brother James. Would they ever find each other again? Hyw raised the dried meat to take a bite, but he had no appetite for it. A jumble of emotions warred within him, and he was surprised to realize that the strongest one was loneliness. He tucked the meat and apple into his pouch.

The next morning Hyw tried not to look Margred's way, but he couldn't help seeing her as she assisted Drem to his feet. The young man had a walking stick now, but he seemed to have improved overnight. Hyw was glad when Odgar approached to confer about the path they should take.

Hyw relied on the jays and jackdaws to help him steer the small group away from searching English troops. They made Dolbadarn by mid-afternoon. He gave the password and heard a voice call out. A man looked down over the tower wall. Aeneus! Hyw waved and gestured for the little group to follow him inside the gates.

As they entered the courtyard, he saw his mam, smiling and helping several groups of women gather their children together. She looked young again, almost as young as Margred and Cat, and he knew suddenly what day it was. *Calan Mai.* A breeze lifted the hair from his brow. He searched for his sister, wondering where she might be. He was prevented from transforming into a hawk to seek her out by his father's warm handclasp on his arm. Bran drew Hyw into a hug.

"Glad I am to see you whole, boy," Bran said. "And who are these with you?"

Hyw turned to call Odgar, who was almost overcome at finding them again. Bran clasped Odgar's arm in a warm greeting.

"I recall well the strength of your right arm, Odgar," said Aeneus. "Most I remember the day you helped the Lady Adara secret Baby Gwen through the tunnels under Garth Celyn. Never did you hesitate to hide our exit when you turned back to fight off our enemies. And never did I think to cast eyes upon you again."

"Aye, this was the young knight," cried Adara, rushing forward and kissing Odgar on both cheeks in turn. "We owe you a great debt, Sir Odgar. And glad I am to see you here, on this blessed May Day. Truly God has favoured us."

"I have heard the tale many times," said Bran, clapping Odgar on the back. "I thank you for that service. And I thank my son for the service he has done us today, in bringing us such men, willing to fight for their country."

Drem's leg suddenly jerked and almost buckled under him, and Margred helped him sit down on a stone ledge nearby. His head was down, and Hyw almost went to help them in spite of his feelings. Then Drem's head came up. The look in his eyes was not full of pain, as Hyw expected, but full of venom.

Hyw recoiled, but before he could react, he heard his mam calling for volunteers to accompany the women on their trip to gather blackthorn, birch, and willow for the festivities. Adara insisted that only the women could choose the proper boughs. In the end Bran and a handful of warriors went along, and Hyw took his place among them. His mam had the bearing and lithe steps of a young woman, and his da could not take his eyes from her as she led the others in singing.

Adara is truly beautiful, whispered Llywelyn. Looking around, Hyw could see the same thought mirrored in the faces of the warriors around him. As the song finished, she took Hyw's arm and stepped lightly beside him.

"Careful lest we make you dance the part of Old Man Winter this e'en, Hyw," she laughed, but her laughter stopped when she saw his face. "Or is it a straw man you will be hanging under someone's window?"

Nothing could get past his mother's sharpened sense when she was bringing in the May. She was thinking of those jilted suitors who fashioned a straw likeness of their enemy, cursed it, and hung the *gŵr gwellt* where it might harm the couple. How could he explain to her the complicated nature of his feelings?

"Surely we live in more civilized times than that," he told her, avoiding her eyes.

"So it is true," she responded. "Margred has found her Drem, and you have helped her do it. I know Margred to be loyal and headstrong, but is she truly going to be matched by this butcher's son? I wonder. You must consider, Hyw. It is a woman's right to choose, but it is a man's responsibility to make his case."

Then she was dancing off to join his father again, leaving Hyw more confused than before. His concern over Drem was something he could scarcely understand himself. He was glad when they finally returned to Dolbadarn castle with the wood.

"We must put more logs on the fire," Adara began singing. "It must rise to the sky—"

"It simply cannot be, Lady Adara," interrupted a priest behind her.

"The risk is too great." The second voice belonged to Dafydd. Hyw was surprised to see the Prince of Wales staring down at his tiny Mam. She looked more like one of Dafydd's spirited daughters than the mother of two grown children.

"The land has been fired and smoked and hunted to exhaustion," she told him. "We must call the spirits to help us save it, or we are more than lost."

"With the English so close, we cannot light the bonfire," Dafydd responded, just as stridently. "The English are on our tails, and we cannot take the risk of attracting them hither, or alerting them that any but their own occupy this castle."

Llywelyn rumbled in Hyw's ear. *For once my brother is right. Last year the bonfire rose to the skies, and what good did the spirits do us? Within scarce two months, my lady Elinor was dead in her birthing chamber.*

Hyw moved toward his mam, torn between the sense of their words and her need for the ritual to bring in the May.

"This is not any bonfire. It is already a travesty that we cannot make the ritual at Garth Celyn," she stormed. "If the spirits of *Ynys Môn* cannot see our fires, the bees will not come, and the stirring of plants within the ground will wither. There will be no harvest."

"How dare you!" Dafydd's voice roared out. "I was the one who wanted to march on Garth Celyn. 'Twas your husband, madam, who bade us wait and gather strength."

Bran pushed forward, coming to Adara's side before Hyw could get through the crowd of people that were gathered around them. He saw his father speak to her in a low voice. As Hyw finally drew nearer to them, she threw up her arms and turned away.

"Aye, I know the sense of it," she said, in a quieter voice still thick with emotion. "Only the land cries out to me. I feel the English wildfires upon the grass as if upon my own skin. I hear the new shoots calling out from beneath the smoking mess like children drowning in their mother's blood. Only our ritual fire can quench theirs. The smoke of the blackthorn, birch, and willow are the tonic to this madness."

Around them the people began to murmur, and dread settled on Hyw's shoulders. He was sure only he and Bran had heard her words, but they were far from Garth Celyn and those who knew and loved his mam. Bran tried to gather Adara in his arms, but she pushed him away and turned back to the prince, tears streaking her face.

"Our family has always served and protected you and yours, at all costs. It is that duty that forces me to plead with you now. We must tend the land, or we are all lost."

"Do not speak of this again. There will be no bonfire and none of your pagan games. The English must not catch wind of us, or you and yours will find yourself in the same confinement as did my eldest brother, many years ago—for treason."

As his mam turned away, Hyw took her arm to guide her back into the castle. He murmured words to comfort her, but she did not react. It was as if she could not hear him.

17

Cat swallowed her fear and urged the English east, away from Dolbadarn. They returned to Bere to gather supplies, and Rhys convinced de Francton to let Cynfrig ride along as their guide, since he had been steward of the land for almost forty years. De Francton kept the reins of Cat's little palfrey firmly in hand, while Bellamy and his company of knights surrounded Rhys and Cynfrig. Gradually through the day, as the two warriors made no effort to fight or escape, the English began to relax and the three came to be treated less as prisoners and more as allies.

With Cynfrig's dour assistance, Cat managed to direct the English along the most circuitous route possible. When they stopped for the night, Rhys and Cat were allowed some time together, although Bellamy watched them closely. She tried to act as a wife would, aware that if any of the men knew she and Rhys were not truly married it might go worse for her. Her shoulders ached from carrying the pack, but she could not imagine tying it to the saddle or trusting it to someone else to carry. As she straightened, she winced at the pain in her arm and shoulder. Rhys was instantly at her side, removing the pack with a reassuring look in his steady gaze. He slung it over his own shoulder and rubbed her back and neck for a moment. But Bellamy interrupted their reunion and kept watch over them as they bunked down for the night. He made a place for Cat nearer the fire, keeping the men—including Rhys—at a respectful distance.

The following day, they made their way to the former

stronghold of a castle that had been abandoned long before Cat was born. As they reined in to survey the area, she leaned down to pat the palfrey's sturdy shoulder. She looked over the haphazard pile of charred wood and jagged slate lying around and on top of the earthwork mound. Only the wind stirred in the long grasses. She had heard this castle had fallen into disuse after the larger stone structure at Carndochan took over trade and defences in this area. It would have made a good hideout. Then she frowned. If someone was hiding here, she would be responsible for leading the soldiers right to them.

She caught Cynfrig's eye as he looked around them with concern. Somewhere near here was Cymer Abbey. Her breath quickened as she realized they were also near the holding where they had left Cynfrig's family and the remnants of Rhys' people. What had she done? She started to dismount.

"Please do not," de Francton said, with quiet menace. "I would hate to have to tie you to the horse." Cat recoiled and caught at her necklace again to steady her breathing. De Francton gestured with one hand, and Bellamy dismounted, calling several of the soldiers to him as he started toward the ruin. She looked at Rhys, unable to hide the fear in her eyes, and gestured with her chin toward the group of soldiers. He was still mounted, but holding the reins of his own horse now. At least their efforts at good behaviour had gained him some acceptance among the knights. Rhys nodded slightly as he moved his horse closer.

"I may be of some use in this matter," he began. When de Francton cocked his head, Rhys continued. "I played here often as a boy. There are some choice hiding spots, and some where the structure is not likely to hold the weight of a grown man."

"I suppose you can be trusted not to run, while your wife keeps me company." De Francton gestured, and Rhys slid off his horse to follow the English. De Francton turned back to Cat. "This day must be difficult for you," he said, not unkindly.

Cat arched her eyebrows, not wanting to take her eyes from Rhys as he disappeared into the rubble. "I am out of practice," she said, shifting her weight on the saddle. De Francton looked puzzled, so she continued. "We could not ride much once the armies settled in the valley."

"I was not referring to the ride," he said. She could not think of anything else, and he sighed in some exasperation. "It is May Day, is it not? That means something to your—kind?"

Cat caught her breath and turned her face away to hide her elation. It did indeed mean something! Her family was safe, at least for now. She reached up to touch her locket again, silently uttering a prayer of thanksgiving as she composed herself.

"Thank you for your concern," she told him. "Would it not be possible to dismount for a short break? While the men search the ruin?"

"I suppose a stretch is in order," he said, dismounting to hold her horse for her. He waved his hand and the other soldiers waiting with them also dismounted. While they waited she gathered a few herbs, trying to look the part. The pack she carried had a small pocket where she could place the herbs without opening it fully. As she bent to her task, she watched the fields for any sign of their people. Before long Rhys led the soldiers back, and Bellamy conferred with de Francton.

Rhys came over to escort her back to her palfrey. He leaned closer to her and murmured, "You were right to be afraid. There was a family in the subfloor, but I was able to lead the English away from them."

She gave him a grateful look but their short reunion was interrupted by de Francton's impatience.

"So, no sign of the prince or any other prize in this rubble."

"No, my lord," she said. "But it is so near the abbey, I thought it was worth a look. As I said, sometimes what I see is subject to interpretation. It would be a fine place for him to hide, as I'm sure your men would agree."

"However you came to suggest it, see that you trust your craft more and interpret less."

Bellamy was near enough to them to overhear these words, and crossed himself. Cat pursed her lips and found them dry. De Francton was speaking more freely now, and she would have to come up with a more likely prospect or this could be the final stop for her and Rhys. Or perhaps the Englishman would take out his ire on Cynfrig first. She shivered but masked her fear by shifting her position. She gulped as she went to speak and drew in a breath to steady herself.

"This castle was replaced by a greater prize," Cynfrig broke in, stepping nearer to them, "where no doubt the prince and those with him would be more comfortable."

"Nothing you Welsh call a castle could also be called comfortable," de Francton responded. Bellamy guffawed at that. "Very well. Where do you propose to take us?"

"Castle Carndochan."

"Warwich took Carndochan some two months ago," put in Bellamy. "It is unlikely—"

"That would indeed fit, my lord," Cat managed, keeping her voice steady. "As I said, the prince has taken back a castle that was lost."

"How many men did Warwich leave there?" de Francton asked.

"A small number, as I heard," Bellamy said. "Not even a score of knights."

"Yes, I also heard Warwich was less than pleased with his prize and couldn't wait to get himself and his men away." De Francton mused for a moment.

"If the prince has taken back a refuge for himself and his followers," Cynfrig agreed, "he would be well-advised to try an isolated post like Carndochan."

"It certainly would suit the Welsh more than it did Warwich." De Francton nodded almost to himself. He mounted and turned his horse to lead the way, while hers had no choice but to follow. Rhys angled his horse in beside Cat, and the palfrey accepted being flanked with good grace.

The timber palisades, formidable from a distance, formed an oval around Carndochan castle. It was not as large or foreboding as Bere, but Cat could feel a shiver up her spine as they approached. Two of its three imposing towers were shaped in the traditional Welsh

D, protecting the south and west approach, while a rounder tower faced them. She could see smoke rising from somewhere inside its fortifications. For a moment her heart stopped. Had Dafydd moved his camp here after all, or was some other Welsh family hiding within its ruins? Before she could turn to Rhys, who was riding a little behind her as they made their way up the craggy path of Bala mountain, de Francton gestured for them to quicken the pace.

Fortunately the horses couldn't gallop easily over the craggy slate, but they managed to gain enough speed that their group surged up and around the oval of timbers. As they drew near, she could see also see that the castle had fallen into disrepair, the timber of the palisades broken or rotting with age. The flags flapping in the breeze bore crosses on a red background. She had learned the colours and patterns of Welsh and English sigils long ago, by spying on her brother and his friends in training, and she breathed a little easier when she recognized this one as the English Earl of Warwich. No Welsh in hiding here, but it could not bode well for her, Rhys, or their friends if de Francton found a second castle empty of prey.

The company followed the rocky ditch to the arched entrance, where sentries and armed men with drawn bows stopped them. A sentry came forward to parlay. He wore his battered armour haphazardly, as if he had buckled it on quickly, but his sword was sharp enough as he held it up to bar their way. De Francton ignored the archers and leaned on his pommel to stare down at the sentry, as the riders came to a halt behind them.

"Put it away, man," Bellamy said, stepping his horse closer to join them. "Where is the Earl?"

"Not here," the sentry replied.

"Then who is in charge?"

"The captain, of course."

"And where is he?"

"In the castle."

De Francton huffed in exasperation, but Bellamy continued doggedly.

"We need to speak to him."

The soldier looked at them, turned to look at the castle, and then back to them. "I don't see how you can, without going in, like."

"So let us in!" de Francton growled.

The soldier's sword wavered and he held it in both hands. "I don't see as I can do that, exactly."

"Then call him out," suggested Bellamy.

"Well, I can't do that without leaving my post, like."

Bellamy saw de Francton reach for his sword. Stirring his horse to attract the man's attention, Bellamy pointed to de Francton's cloak. "This is Stephen de Francton, in service to King Edward of England. You can see our colours. We are friends."

Luckily for the soldier, a small group of men had finally left the castle and was making their way toward the gates.

"Let them pass, George," called out the larger knight among them. The sentry turned but de Francton moved his warhorse ahead and all but knocked him over. Cat's palfrey followed, sidestepping more nimbly. Cat took the motion as an opportunity to turn and glance back at Rhys. He caught her eye and shook his head slightly as if to caution her.

The men and horses proceeded toward the square building in the centre of the three imposing towers. The buildings were lighter in colour than she expected, and she realized most were made of wood rather than stone. De Francton dismounted and she followed suit, as Warwich's captain introduced himself as Sir Thomas Grey.

Bellamy had already begun getting the company settled and horses arranged. Rhys came forward to take the palfrey, and paused beside Cat for a moment.

"We have no choice now but to play this out," Rhys murmured. She nodded, and followed him inside. The inside looked worse than the outside. Clods of thatch fell from the hastily-repaired roof. As the men's boots echoed across the floor, they had to step over some of the larger knotholes.

"This is where you saw Prince Dafydd hiding?" de Francton said.

"I saw a castle, my lord," she said. "It does not appear likely it was this one, after all."

He narrowed his eyes at her and moved ahead to confer with Grey. De Francton gestured to Bellamy, who came over with what seemed like reluctance to take charge of them.

"Don't give me trouble and you'll get none," Bellamy said brusquely. Rhys caught her eye and Cat half-shook her head to show she understood. When the knight suddenly stopped and breathed in, Cat nearly stumbled into him.

"It may not be much to look at, but there's a cook on the premises," Bellamy said.

The smell of meat juices and baking bread caught Cat, and her stomach growled in spite of her best efforts. Bellamy looked at her and guffawed, his earlier wariness forgotten.

"Count your fortune," he said. "I've a mind to have a bit of proper castle fare for once. And there is time before we're needed again. So, you two can be tied here to wait for me, or you can mark your best behaviour and join me at table."

Rhys said nothing, but held out his hands to be tied. Bellamy eyed him, and then laughed at his own joke.

"Come on, man," the big knight said, as he herded Cat and Rhys into the great hall. "You're on the winning side now."

Cat wanted to be angry but hunger won, and she made no protest. If they ate, surely they would have the strength to fight later. As usual, Rhys held his face immobile, but he took her arm to help her as she stumbled in the direction they were moving. The room was cavernous and noisy, echoing with voices and laughter, dogs barking, and other sounds she couldn't identify. If she could contrive to sit beside Rhys, they might have a chance to talk about their situation. Even guarded whispers would be better than what they had endured so far.

She couldn't help looking around as they made their way to an empty spot at one of the long tables. From the banners and positions of those seating themselves at the high table, she spotted several lords including Lestrange and de Francton again, who seemed to have the same idea as Bellamy. She could recognize Shrewsbury's sigil among the others. She looked for James, their distant cousin and Hyw's best friend, but she didn't see any younger men seated with the older. If James was here, would he be sitting with the commoners and knights at the long tables that lined the hall?

"Here," announced Bellamy, and they sat beside him. "Eat fast if you want to eat at all." He paid them little mind as he grabbed bread and meat from the platters that were being passed up and down the row. She sat beside Rhys and Cynfrig took the chair on her other side. Rhys grabbed a wooden plate from a spot near him, scraped the leftovers onto the straw at their feet, and began grabbing the food as it passed. He set the plate down in front of her, and she moved it between them before her hunger overcame her manners.

"Cat?" said a voice near her ear, and she saw James crouching between them. Rhys tensed as if ready for a fight and James moved back, but Cat placed her hand on Rhys' arm and leaned forward so they could both hear her.

"Cousin, well met," she said.

"You may not say so when you hear we are hunting Prince Dafydd," he said in a low voice.

"We have heard."

Rhys started and looked around for anyone listening in. "Watch what you say."

"This is my brother's friend," she whispered. "And mine, I hope."

James nodded and leaned closer. "How is Hyw?"

"I have not seen him for days, and much has changed," she told him. She sketched the last days at Castell-y-Bere as quick as she could, without mentioning Hyw's transformation. James looked as if he wanted to ask more, but a page ran up behind them, calling Sir Bellamy's name. Bellamy bent low to listen to the boy.

"You must tell Hyw that I saw him on the field," James whispered urgently. "And that he is released from his bond to me. I would rather have him defend his own life than protect mine."

Cat tried to ask him what he meant, but Rhys touched her arm. Before she could say anything more, James had moved away from them. When she turned, she had to look hard to spot him walking away.

"We bunk here for the night," Bellamy said, turning from the page to his three charges. "Come along, you."

They slept under the crumbling roof in the great hall, under guard by Bellamy or another of de Francton's men, and Cat didn't catch sight of James again. After tossing and turning on the stone floor, surrounded by snoring English forces, she was glad to dust herself off the following morning and mount her palfrey again. She hadn't ridden this hard since their escape to Bere, and she was almost sorry she had opted for the saddle instead of the thicker cushioning of a pillion.

It was nearly evening when they rode into Prysor, another of Llywelyn's primary strategic castles that had controlled the trade routes through Snowdonia. It had fallen to the English months before. Cat saw several thousand troops camped in and around the castle, and Rhys pointed out their standards to her. One was Shrewsbury, so James must be already here. A young messenger flagged de Francton before he could dismount.

"This way, milady." Bellamy took her arm and moved his chin in the direction he wanted her to walk. She ended up across the soldier's camp from Rhys. Bellamy sat her down with some women at the edge of the camp. One of them thrust some mending into her lap, and she was too tired to object. She caught Rhys staring at her more than once, but he had no chance to speak or sign a message to her.

Before long, Bellamy came to gather Rhys and Cat, putting up one hand to stop Cynfrig as he tried to join them. Cat found herself in the centre of a company of knights, marching through the yard and into Prysor castle. She reached out instinctively for Rhys' hand, and Bellamy did not stop her.

As a group, they turned left into Prysor's great hall, where they stood with several other men she didn't know. When her eyes had grown used to the darkness, Cat noticed de Francton across the room. He stood near a well-dressed nobleman, who gestured toward Rhys, and de Francton nodded. Cat gripped Rhys' hand more tightly and he inclined his head without looking at her.

"Is that Roger Lestrange, de Francton's liege lord?"

Rhys glanced over and managed a short nod to let her know she was right.

"Quiet," Bellamy told them. "Speak when you're spoken to, which will be shortly, I warrant."

The long room had been turned into a war room, she realized, with maps and parchments set up on the tables. Around her, men were speaking in English and much of it was too fast for her to follow. One man standing before Lestrange seemed to be giving a catalogue of where his company had searched for Dafydd, but she could scarcely recognize the locations because of his accent. Cat was staring at an elaborately carved wooden chess set to escape the drone when a wizened knight burst into the room.

"We have him," he announced. "Our spies tell us that we have the Welsh devil in our grasp at last."

Cat started. Rhys did not move, but Cat saw his jaw muscle clench. De Francton saluted her from across the room. Her blood froze in sudden terror for her family and friends, as well as the prince.

"We have chased Dafydd from every castle in North Wales," Bellamy remarked. "How do you know we have found him, well and truly, this time?"

"I dunno how, only where," the old man snapped. "We have a man inside the walls who signals us at night."

Rhys caught Cat's eye but she frowned and shook her head. She hadn't seen that in her vision.

"Have you tested him?" someone asked.

"This man speaks aright," Bellamy put in. "How do you know you can you trust this inside man of yours?"

"He came to us in Criccieth when we took that castle," the other answered. "And he agreed to help us in exchange, to get his father out. Butcher in the village, I think."

Cat shivered with a sudden chill. It had been the butcher's son that Margred had fancied, had it not? Rhys went still. He must have remembered at the same time.

"And did he help you?"

"We gave him some minor bruises and set him with the prisoners, but they escaped somehow. We tracked them and one night the boy stole away from the others and found us. It's the way with these Welsh curs. They're only too eager to bite the hands of their masters and steal the food for themselves."

De Francton laughed with the others. Cat saw the muscle in Rhys jaw clench again, but he said nothing.

"When this lad told us what was afoot, we bade him stay with the Welsh and keep us apprised. Now my scout says he has signalled us from the wall walk of Dolby — that is, Dolbay—oh, the devil take these Welsh names. In a castle to the west."

"And Dafydd is there?"

"So he says."

"How many times have we thought him caught in our trap," de Francton murmured, "only to discover he has slipped away again?"

"Precisely, sir. That is the value of our Welsh lad to our efforts. If we wait for his signal, we will have the rat this time."

De Francton stood. "What think you, Lord Rhys?" He turned slightly to encompass the group. "May I have the pleasure to introduce our newest ally, Lord Rhys ap Cadwgan. Former lord of Meirionnydd, and soon to be again, now that he has chosen to follow a king and not a princeling."

De Francton let the angry murmurs circling the room die down. "Come now," he went on. "Would Lord Rhys have brought his lady wife along if he had treachery in his heart?"

"She is Welsh, isn't she? Perhaps she is a better fighter than he," someone remarked. Rhys jerked beside her, but de Francton ignored the speaker.

"He is indeed a renowned fighter and a formidable enemy, especially for the would-be prince. Lord Rhys, what say you?" At that, de Francton looked pointedly at Cat. "Could the rat be holed up in Dolbadarn Castle?"

Cat instinctively took hold of Rhys' arm. Rhys shifted as if to shield her from the room with his body.

"I cannot think it, my lord," he began, but de Francton cut him off impatiently.

"Yet it tallies with our information well enough, does it not." He said it as a statement rather than a question, and turned back to the other man. "At least enough to muster there and wait for the signal from your spy."

The room erupted in noise and babble. De Francton signaled to Bellamy, who pushed Rhys and Cat ahead of him toward the door.

"It'll be every soldier for himself, now," Bellamy told them. "Lucky we have you lot to lead the way."

18

Hyw was exercising with his father and several other warriors in Dolbadarn's courtyard when the boy rushed up with Dafydd's summons. As they entered the conference chamber, the prince's ice-blue eyes were cold. Lord Hywel, standing by the fire grate with his hands clasped behind his back, gave them a faint smile of sympathy. His sons looked away. Aeneus stood up and walked over to them, standing at Bran's right hand.

"What news?" Dafydd said.

"The men on the walk report no movement overnight," Bran began, but Dafydd interrupted him.

"What news of your daughter, Catrin, and her traitorous husband."

Hyw started, but if Bran reacted to the news, no one could read it in his face. "My daughter has no husband, my liege," he said. "She and Lord Rhys were to meet your messenger."

"Were they?" Dafydd gestured and John looked up from his seat near the fire. "Tell them, cousin."

John wearily stood. "I waited in the trees and watched for a night and a day past the appointed hour. Then I travelled back along the route to the abbey in hopes of meeting them. The abbey, my lord..." John's voice trailed off for a moment before he resumed. "It was destroyed by the English. A handful of the brothers were still there, but they said the abbot had been taken, and with him no doubt the treasure."

"But, surely, Lord Rhys?" Bran's question hung on the air.

"The brothers said Rhys and a handful of his men mounted what defence he could, but the English forces were too strong."

Bran stepped forward then. "And my daughter? She was with him."

John shook his head. "One of the brothers said the Lady Catrin brought the English to the abbey, and afterwards, she returned with them to Bere, along with Lord Rhys and others."

Bran looked stricken. "What do you mean?"

John hung back, but Dafydd gestured impatiently. "Lady Catrin was for a time a guest in the castle, but now she and Lord Rhys ride with the English under de Francton's banner," John said.

"She would not." Hyw was indignant. "My sister is no traitor."

Ask who gives them this information, Llywelyn whispered in Hyw's inner ear, and he relayed the question.

"I have seen it, myself." John's voice held no emotion, but he avoided Hyw's eyes.

"If this is true, she is a prisoner." Bran's face was white, but his voice remained even. "Or there is some other reason for it."

Dafydd leaned forward. "Aye, the reason is that she has given the relics to the English."

"No!" Hyw was ready to explode, but Aeneus laid a hand on his shoulder.

Lord Hywel came forward. "We should not jump to conclusions, my liege."

"I have known the girl since she was a babe, and her mother, and her mother's mother," Aeneus said. "They are loyal to House Aberffraw. I would swear it on my life."

"When she parted with us, she was loyal to her betrothed," Dafydd argued. "And Lord Rhys has no reason to love us."

Lord Hywel moved his head in acknowledgement of the fact. "The boy's father was killed at Hawarden, at the start of the war, and his brother a few weeks later. But he has been loyal to your house since then."

"Unless, all along, he was merely awaiting the chance to turn on us."

Hywel moved uncomfortably. "I cannot believe that is the case."

"I must have the relics." Dafydd moved around the room as if weighing the options. "You say he is not yet married to Lady Catrin. Would he take my daughter, the Lady Margred, as his wife in return for the relics? That would solidify his love for me, would it not? What think you, Bran?"

Hyw gasped and looked for Margred in time to see her blanch and become still, like a cornered deer. Hyw heard his father shift uncomfortably beside him.

"Lady Catrin and Lord Rhys have been betrothed since they were children, my liege," Bran said, slowly.

"Engagements can be broken." Dafydd began to look around the room, and Margred quickly made her escape before he could spot her.

"What is it, then?" Dafydd asked, eyeing the elder statesman.

"Castel-y-Bere was his family's ancestral home," Lord Hywel said, "and his father had made a petition last year to *Tywysog* Llywelyn to cede the deed and title. Edward had taken the land in the last settlement, but Llywelyn agreed to intervene. I do not believe it had yet been finalized when he was taken from us last December. It may be that the boy feels he has more chance to gain the land back from the English—more directly."

"I thought as much." Dafydd's hand suddenly boomed down on the table. "Bring me the deed. I will grant the title of this land to Lord Rhys," he said. "After all, it will be mine to do with as I please when we retake Wales from these invaders."

We cannot offer what we do not own. Lord Hywel speaks the truth of it. Edward took the land in return for allowing Elinor to marry me. Hyw was about to speak when Dafydd stood.

"Cousin, you have one more journey ahead of you."

"I am willing," John said.

"Take this offer to Lord Rhys, and see if he will trade land for treasure. If this does not interest him, sound him out on his feelings for the Lady Catrin. It might be timely to remind that lady that we have her family with us. Perhaps she can find a way to persuade him."

Cold prickled the back of Hyw's neck.

You must stop my brother from this madness. Bran has ever been loyal to our house. Dafydd cannot lose faith with your family in this way, not now of all times.

Hyw realized Dafydd had still not accepted Llywelyn's former men completely. His da's stoic expression revealed nothing, but Hyw couldn't help but wonder if he and Aeneus had completely accepted Dafydd.

"My lord and cousin." John had gone to one knee, his face white. "I would always strive to do your bidding, but how—how can I get this deed to one who rides with the enemies' troops?"

"I can do it." Hyw stepped forward. He heard his father begin to object so he turned, raising one hand slightly in appeasement, and looked at his father as he spoke. "As you know, I am known to the English. I can more easily get into the camp to find him." He turned to Dafydd then. "My—particular skills make me the best suited to get the message through the English to my sister and Lord Rhys."

Dafydd narrowed his eyes and gestured for Hyw to come closer. The prince marked the parchment with a flourish as Hyw waited awkwardly. Then Dafydd dripped wax onto it and imprinted it with his ring. He gestured to Lord Hywel, who came to the table. The elder lord gave Hyw a reassuring glance as he looked over the document and signed it as a witness. As soon as the wax had dried, Dafydd cut the copies apart with his knife, setting one on the table and folding the other for easier travel.

"Would that I had my brother's seal for the House of Aberffraw, but this ring must serve for both." As he handed the parchment to Hyw, he held onto one end, staring into Hyw's eyes as if searching for his brother there.

"This must go directly into the hands of Lord Rhys," Dafydd said, his voice low and urgent. "It is of the utmost importance. Can I trust you in this," and his voice dropped to a whisper, "brother?"

Llywelyn stood behind him again, and he shifted in his mind to allow the prince to see through his eyes for a moment.

I will not fail you, Llywelyn said, his voice joining with Hyw's as they answered together.

Hyw found a satchel with looped ties to hold the deed, and packed it into a larger pack with his clothing. He longed to change almost before he was out of sight of the castle. Llywelyn spoke the play for both of them.

First you must find them, and then contrive a way to carry the deed to Rhys.

When they had left Bere weeks earlier, Cat and Rhys had made for Abbey Cymer, but John told them the abbey had fallen and Cat rode with the English troops. Hyw knew of only one way to get his bearings quickly. Hiding his pack behind two slabs of grey slate, he chose the form of a jackdaw and took wing, not pausing to check Llywelyn again. The former prince would only urge him on.

Hyw let the currents guide his wings over the treetops. Welsh castles were strategically placed, but as a bird, Hyw could cover the ground quickly. He could also spot signs of the English: smoke from cooking fires, movement in the forests, and the more dire signs of smouldering villages and pillage as King Edward's massive army cut a swath across the land like the Reaper's scythe.

Soon he caught sight of a larger group and swooped down to circle Prysor, unable to stop himself from scanning for a squire with thick brown hair and gentle eyes. Several companies of men were organizing, and Hyw could recognize the signs of the English army mustering to travel. Then he saw Rhys and Cynfrig saddling horses in the courtyard. Cat would not be far away. His heart leapt into his mouth but his cry was swallowed in the jackdaw's hoarse squawk.

Before he found her, Hyw's attention was caught by the sight of another familiar figure in the castle yard. James was standing beside a large black horse that pranced sideways, its thick neck arched and proud. Hyw landed on a nearby quintain.

It reminded him of the barns at Shrewsbury, when his gift had first come to him and only James knew of it. In those days, James could barely reach the horse's back to saddle it, and Hyw had been glad to manage the horses for him. Now James was as tall as the horse, and his broad shoulders showed his strength. More than that,

James seemed confident and at ease. It was the warhorse of a knight, and it answered to James.

"Your turn, James," a voice called out. James turned and leapt up onto the horse's back. He dug in his heels and rode the rings easily, lancing everything in his path. Around him the other squires cheered.

Hyw was struck by the changes in his friend, even more than he had been when he had discovered James by accident weeks earlier in a practice field. James had allies of his own now. He had no further need of a scrawny Welsh boy in his entourage. James would be able to protect himself in battle and in life. Hyw wanted to be happy for his friend, but his heart was heavy.

Don't give up, Hyw. Llywelyn's voice almost whispered in his inner ear. *Friendship doesn't end because distance or time separates you.*

The thunder of hooves interrupted them before Hyw could respond. A company of mounted men raced toward the castle gate. James and the other squires pointed and waved excitedly. Something was afoot.

We must find your sister.

Hyw pushed himself off the perch and flew above the group. Circling back, he spotted Cat and Rhys mounting their horses. Hyw's heart clenched again. They set off purposefully. He followed them until there was no doubt of their direction. Dafydd had been right to worry. Cat and Rhys were indeed riding toward Dolbadarn, with a full company of armed English soldiers. Hyw's hawk senses refused to count them, but he spotted mounted knights in armour as well as a line of men on foot that must be archers.

Hyw quickly winged his way back to his stash of goods. He switched into fox form and snuffled into the ties that held the pack containing the deed and his clothing. Then he chose the form of a horse so he could make better time, and shifted so the pack pulled firmly around him. It held in place as he moved off and he quickly shifted to a gallop. The animal's herd instincts proved useful, this time in locating the English troop again. He found them at dusk, barely a day's journey from Dolbadarn. Too far to mount an attack, but close enough to make Hyw's heart pound.

How could his sister have led the English against them?

Dafydd's decision to draw up the deed made sense now. There may still be time to avoid this fight, if Rhys and Cat could be convinced to draw the English off again. He had to at least try. Bypassing his human form again, Hyw transformed into a large red hawk. He shrugged out from under the pack and used his sharp beak to open it. He shook it with beak and talons until the satchel fell out of it. With a shriek of triumph, he scooped the satchel up in his talons. Then he flew.

19

With the English always around them, Cat and Rhys had barely a moment to exchange looks let alone confer on their situation as they raced toward Dolbadarn Castle. Worries for her mam and da plagued her. She had to try getting word to them somehow. Hyw! She reached up to touch her necklace, but she could not conjure up a vision of him.

At mid-afternoon they drew up, within sight of the castle walls. Bellamy dragged Rhys and Cynfrig off to regroup for the coming battle. Bellamy gestured to his squire and then to her. She glanced around at the squires carrying buckets for the horses, and noticed they were coming back from the east. There must be a stream in that direction. Bellamy's boy glanced at her and then turned his attention again to the two knights talking near him. As she started toward the squire, she could not help but overhear them, too.

"… So we set fire to the crops on Anglesey and along the coast, as the king commanded," one was saying, with satisfaction. Cat went pale. Anglesey was the English name for *Ynys Môn*. She could see the grass and the smoke in front of her again, as the knight continued. "The crops had barely sprung from the ground, but we fired it so nothing will grow. Winter stores are already spent. Without food they cannot last the season, sunshine or no. We will soon be home again, mark my words."

Cat saw the bees from her vision again, felt smoke burning her lungs until she nearly choked on it. She stumbled past without a word and found herself at the stream. She walked downstream until she spotted a narrow ledge. Looking around, she realized she was alone. The boy must have forgotten her, and she could see no one else about.

The stream was narrow enough to step across in places, but she knelt beside the water and splashed her face and neck. She tried to see into its depths, past her own reflection, and willed her vision to respond. Nothing. Despair crept over her. Someone in Dolbadarn castle had been working against them all this time, but she had no way of getting the information to Hyw or her mam. And she had no clue as to what might be happening to them. What was the point of having a gift if it would not respond to her need?

She turned to the sky and cried out, her voice choked with sobs. "Why? Why did you show me what cannot be prevented?"

She shrugged the abbot's pack off her back and almost tore it open, searching for the Crown of Arthur. As she touched it, the shock of its power thrilled her. She was unable to move, and she became aware of her surroundings. She could see a water beetle skim across the surface on its hunt for food. She could hear the rustle of leaves in the trees around her, and her breathing picked up the rhythm. She tried to recall her uncle's voice, and the words he sang during the time when the three of them had been together. She silently added the song she had heard her ancestors singing in her vision.

Across the stream she heard a rustle and whine, and turned to see a red fox sitting on the opposite bank. She spotted its reflection in the water and found herself looking into its violet eyes—

—and an echo of music and laughter twirled around her. The forest and stream became a meadow filled with fragrant grasses, wild celandine, and clover. The fox transformed into a woman with violet eyes. A woman Cat had seen before, in what must have been a dream. Aylwen verch Arianrhod, woman of Troy, first Briton to learn the ways of the derwyddon or druids. Around them she could hear others, women and men, singing a song she hadn't heard before.

"First mother," Cat said. "Why did you show me the fire, if it was not possible to change it?"

"Last daughter, you have done well to change what you can. You weep for the bees. Yet if only one queen escapes the smoke, it may carry a legacy of generations within it."

"And what of Dafydd? Will we be able to prevent the English from finding him?"

"Some men have a destiny that will find them, no matter how they hide or how they fight. The house of Aberffraw was destined for greatness, and often in greatness, tragedy strikes."

"That's not an answer," Cat said.

"No." Aylwen smiled sadly. "The answer lies not in our fates, Cat, but in the choices we make. Our decisions forge our destiny."

"Yet what good is this gift, if not to influence our destiny? I must get word to Hyw, but I cannot control this gift that you have given me."

"It is not a gift that can be controlled. It must be nurtured, like a growing thing."

"But how?"

Instead of answering, Aylwen began to hum, placing her hands gently over Cat's eyelids. As her ancestor sang, Cat realized she knew the words and began to sing too. Her mind opened and she saw Hyw and her da practicing in the exercise yard. The scene seemed to melt into the great stone hall of Dolbadarn, and Dafydd's angry face confronted them. Then she saw the castle from above, as if from the eyes of a hawk, and knew she looked through the eyes of her brother's gift. Aylwen pulled her hands away.

"We have many gifts within us that can be touched upon, and sometimes unlocked. Your gift must be nurtured, like the bees and the crops, to grow into what you wish for."

"What I wish for is an answer. What I wish for is a sword, that we might fight our way to freedom. Can you not rise, like the Lady of the Lake, and place Excalibur in our hands?"

"You have been given so much, little Cat, without knowing the price. And yet you ask for more."

"Price? What price?"

Aylwen's sad violet eyes grew larger, lighter, turning to liquid that cascaded around her. The scene shifted and Cat saw a man lying in front of her and a woman holding him, singing the same song Cat was singing now. He looked strangely familiar, and he wore a simple gold crown. Then the scene shifted again, and she saw Rhys holding the simple gold crown high in the air. People stood around them, yelling, "Cymru! Cymru!" And then the crown became a cup, like the kind she had seen the priests use in *church. And then even the cup began to disappear and she realized Rhys was holding—nothing. Only his own hand, in the shape of a fist.*

Aylwen began to shimmer. "Wait," *Cat said.* "What does this mean?"

"You have the answer you seek within you. Find the path, that we might find you."

"Wait," Cat tried to reach out as the vision began to fade—

—and she found herself staring into the stream again, as rain dripped and puddled around her. She felt very, very tired. What did it mean? She placed the crown gently back inside the pack and shifted it to her back again.

The nearby shriek of a hawk caused Cat to look up. Its size and copper-coloured feathers marked it as a red kite. Such creatures were usually silent. Her da had taught both her and her brother the variations of its call as a signal. She looked around, but no one else was in sight. No one had noticed her missing yet.

The fluttering of wings caused her to look up again as the large bird swooped down to a closer branch. She frowned. It had flown close enough for her to see it more clearly. Something about it seemed familiar. It blinked at her: blue-grey eyes instead of yellow. Hyw. It had to be. His stare drew her closer.

Hyw dropped something onto the ground and flew a short way off to land. It was a kind of satchel, and she realized he must have been carrying it. Gingerly, not sure how much of her brother remained in the wild creature, she reached down and picked it up. When she had it, Hyw shifted as if to fly off.

"Hyw, wait," she whispered urgently, taking off her pack and setting it down on the ground. "I must speak with you. Can you change?" The bird brandished its wings. In the distance, she heard shouting. Cat looked around. A slight rise hid them from the view of anyone upriver, but she feared Bellamy had discovered her gone and would be coming to investigate.

"I have news," she said urgently.

The bird did not fly off. Could she communicate with a bird? Was Hyw able to understand her in this form? She had to try.

"You have a spy in your camp," she hissed.

The bird shook its feathers again and turned its head toward her. Hyw must be able to understand her words. She let out a breath and focused on her brother's eyes.

"I am not certain, but I believe it is Drem, the butcher's son. Is he—could he be with you?"

Hyw opened his beak and made a shrill sound in his throat.

The shouts were closer now. She heard her name. Time was running out. She put a hand on the pack. "The relics are in here. You must take this pack to Dafydd."

She expected him to change to human form at last, but instead Hyw spread his wings and leapt onto the pack. Cat drew back, startled. He latched on with his talons and tried to fly off. His wings struggled and beat at the air until she could see feathers dislodging, but he only managed to fly a few feet. He began to shimmer. Even as she saw the form of a large eagle taking shape in place of the hawk, she heard the sharp, unmistakable sound of metal scraping metal behind her.

"Your pack!" Bellamy shouted.

Cat whirled around to see Bellamy rushing at them, brandishing his sword.

"No!" she screamed, pushing at Bellamy.

"What are you doing?" The knight pushed Cat and she fell to the ground. Without breaking stride, Bellamy lunged at the bird. His sword sliced down and Cat screamed again as it ripped through the leather of the pack. Hyw lurched into the air with only the strap of the pack in his talons. The heavy pack ripped apart and its contents hit the ground as the bird flew for the safety of the treetops.

"No!" Cat cried out again, but it was too late. Several armed guards came over the rise toward them. Rhys struggled through them until he stood beside Cat.

"Are you hurt?" Rhys reached out his hand to help her back to her feet.

"The pack—" she started and then added, "Hyw."

Rhys stared at her, uncomprehending, but the other soldiers crowded around Bellamy.

"What the devil?" The knight stood, panting with the unexpected exertion, and stared at the ground. The two crowns had rolled out of the pack, and lay exposed on the grass. The reliquary lay half-in and half-out of the pack, as if still trying to shelter the shard of the True Cross.

A bark of laughter sounded as de Francton pushed his way through the men. Bellamy gathered the crowns and reliquary into what remained of the pack, and handed it over.

Cat clung to Rhys' hand, so warm, covering her smaller one protectively. She ventured a look up at his face, wanting to lose herself in the deep blue of his eyes. But he was frowning at de Francton.

"Necessary items, indeed." De Francton peered at the crowns before he opened the reliquary and stared inside for a moment. Then he threw back his head and laughed again. "All this, for a little piece of wood and a couple of rusty rings. Not what I expected." He turned to her with a smile that did not quite reach his eyes. "Do not fear. I will petition the king on your behalf. In return for bringing him these treasures, I'm sure he will grant you a boon."

Bellamy, meanwhile, had opened the smaller leather satchel and pulled out the parchment.

"Sir Stephen," Bellamy said, handing it to de Francton. "You had best take a look at this."

20

Hyw opened his beak but clicked it shut again without making a sound. From the shelter of the tree, he watched the English knight manhandle the pack. The eagle in him longed to swoop down and claw the eyes from the knight's face. Llywelyn cursed over Hyw's shoulder as de Francton appeared with more men, and the knight handed the relics over to him.

We must get them back.

Hyw clenched his talons on the branch but could only watch as Dafydd's parchment was discovered. At de Francton's gesture, Rhys and Cat were led away, prisoners of the English. Hyw sought desperately for a solution but could only think of one thing: get help. Get the news to Dafydd and his father. Without going back for his clothing, Hyw leapt straight into the darkening skies. He changed again, this time into peregrine form for swifter flying.

They were so close to Dolbadarn and his flight so desperate that he was there before he realized it. As he flew over the castle walk, the sound of voices made him pause. Margred and Drem stood together as if sheltering from the wind. Hyw, still a falcon, perched near enough to overhear them.

"It is only that I wish to help," Margred was saying. "I know that something worries you." She stood facing Drem, whose back was to Hyw. The falcon kept still against the wall so she wouldn't see him, but he needn't have worried. She was intent on Drem.

"Fret not," Drem told her. "Go back and finish your supper. I wish only to take some air, and then I will return to you." When she hesitated, he spoke again, more harshly. "You must not crowd me, woman. I am used to being more alone."

"Of course," she said, too quickly. How could the oaf not want to be with her, in the moonlight? She might be only a friend to Hyw, but he knew the measure of her worth by her actions at Criccieth, and the look on her face wrenched his heart.

Sliding farther into the shadows, Hyw held his breath as she came within a foot of him, but her head was bowed. One strangled breath told him she was crying, and rage bubbled inside him. When he looked back he saw that Drem had taken up a stance near the walls, looking out. He had not even the courtesy to watch her leave.

Hyw sought to control his anger, spread his great wings, and flew with the stealth of the predator to the top of a nearby merlon. He could see Drem draw his cloak aside and pull something from under it. The butcher's son cupped his hands in front of a lantern, and moved his fingers in a deliberate motion.

He signals the English! Llywelyn shared the thought even as Hyw realized it himself. Drem had betrayed them. Hyw flew at him in rage, and Drem startled. He dropped the lantern, which blew out as it fell and crashed on the stones far below.

Drem reached for him but Hyw teased back, out of harm's way, talons bared. Rage churned in Hyw's gut, and he heard Llywelyn's voice. *You must warn my brother!*

Harnessing the predator's stealth, Hyw let himself drop from the wall walk until the wind caught his open wings, drifting silently down toward the castle windows. He knew which room Dafydd liked to use to meet with the Welsh lords, and he could see shadows flicker from the lamps burning inside. But the windows were covered with heavy shutters. He could try to push them aside, but when he changed he would have to reveal himself to all of them. He flew across to the next window, and the next, before he found one that opened into a room. He forced himself to begin the change before he hit the floor.

As before, his bones crackled and ground together as they changed from the strong, lithe bird to his heavy, frail human shape. The cold stone floor battered his aching flesh as his skin stretched to cover his human body. Panting with the effort of coming back to himself, he pushed himself to his feet.

The door burst open. Margred stopped half-way into the room, her cheeks still wet from tears. She saw him and quickly shut the door behind her.

"What are you doing?" she hissed, her face flushed. He realized it was her bedroom. And he was naked, standing beside her bed. No feathers, no fur, but skin. He grabbed at a shawl draped across her bed to cover himself.

"It's not—" he began, but Llywelyn cut him short. *There's no time, Hyw. Straighten things out with the lady later, but now we must make haste to Dafydd.* With news that Drem is a traitor. Hyw knew what that would mean to Margred.

"We are betrayed," he managed. "I must get word to Dafydd."

She looked at him strangely. "You are in my room," she pointed out.

"Your window was open." He shrugged helplessly toward it and saw understanding on her face. She leaned forward and grabbed a tunic from a nearby chair, tossing it at him.

"Come then," she said, and he struggled to put it on. The tunic was too big in the shoulders for him, and he did not like to speculate whose it was. She handed him a belt as she opened the door. She led him down the long corridor to Dafydd's room. He heard the voices inside as she pushed him toward Aeneus, who was stationed outside it. No doubt Bran had asked him to make sure he and Dafydd weren't interrupted.

"Hyw has a message for my father," Margred said.

"I have discovered the traitor," Hyw blurted, and then stopped, glancing sideways at Margred. But Aeneus needed no further invitation. He knocked loudly and then opened the door, and Hyw burst inside, repeating his message. Bran and Lord Hywel were both there, in conference with Dafydd.

"Who is it that betrays us?"

"One of our own," Hyw replied, itching to look behind him to see if Margred had returned to her rooms. "I saw him clearly from the wall walk, signalling those in the forest below."

"Who was it?" This time his father grasped him by the shoulder. "Is he still there?"

"Aye, Da," Hyw said, trying to keep his voice low. "I interrupted him as he signalled, only moments ago." Hyw struggled with the need to protect his prince and his family, and his need to protect Margred.

You must tell them. Llywelyn's voice rang clearly in his ears, even as Hyw knew what it would cost him.

"It was Drem, the butcher's son from the village."

"Bring Drem to us," Bran said to Aeneus, who had already turned to leave the room.

Hyw heard the intake of breath behind him and turned to see Margred's pale face. He wanted to say something, anything, but nothing came. She raised her hand and pointed at him, her eyes full of fury.

"You say this out of jealousy. I was with Drem tonight. He did no such thing."

Dafydd stared at her. "I will speak with you anon about your choices." Then he rounded on Hyw. "Is that true, boy? Do you seek to divert our attention from your own treachery by accusing another?"

"No, I—" Hyw was momentarily at a loss. He had to tell Prince Dafydd about Cat and Rhys, and the loss of the relics to the English. How would that look now?

"Hyw is not the traitor." Bran said. "He brought word to us as soon as he knew. Why would he signal them and then tell us of it?"

"To protect your allies from harm at our hands?" Dafydd's eyes were cold.

You must tell them everything, Llywelyn said again.

"My liege," Hyw began, facing Dafydd but keeping his eyes lowered in deference. He trembled and sank to his knees, to keep his fear under control and give himself time to think. "You are right to have noticed my admiration for your daughter. And I believe she is worth so much more than her choice will afford her, but I also respect her right to make a choice. Still, I try to keep her well-being in mind. Tonight, I followed her and saw her conversing with someone. It is true, she was with Drem. I watched her leave him, and I saw what came after."

Hyw bowed his head a little, knowing that if Margred was

listening she would know he had also seen her tears, but he said nothing of them. Instead, he continued, "I should have made myself known to her, to see her safely back, but her companion moved in a curious way. Concealing myself, I watched him. Drem signalled with his lantern into the night. And," Hyw glanced up to Dafydd's face then, "as if with the eyes of a falcon, I could see another lantern signal back to him."

"From the wall walk," Margred said, woodenly. He realized it was not the first time she had left Drem there to have "time alone." The enormity of it hit him, and he knew what it meant for her. The man she risked everything for—her honour, her father's name, and even her life—had betrayed them. He stole a look at her face and saw the tears coursing down her pale cheeks. "It cannot be."

"I am sorry to be the bearer of this news, Lady Margred," Hyw said.

Dafydd suddenly strode over to his daughter and slapped her across the face. She cried out as she fell, covering her cheek with her hand. Hyw jumped forward to try and catch her.

"Take her from my sight." Dafydd recovered himself and turned from her. The elder Hywel ap Rhys Gryg went to her also, and Bran took a step forward.

"Stay here, Hyw. With your leave—" Bran bowed to Dafydd "—I will escort the Lady Margred back to her rooms and then return to question Drem."

Aeneus had already gone, but Hyw raised his hands to stop his father from leaving. "Wait. There is more to tell, and this time it is me who is at fault." He knelt again in front of the prince, hoping to take his attention from Margred. Hyw conveyed the scene without revealing his gift, explaining how he had made contact with Cat under the noses of the English. "She had been protecting the relics while Lord Rhys led the English away from you, my liege. She bade me bring the relics to you, but before we could complete the exchange, the English were upon us. She helped me to get away but lost her liberty in the process."

Dafydd looked grave. "And the relics?"

"They were seized by the English, with my sister and Lord Rhys. The deed was discovered, and Lord Rhys branded as a traitor to the English king. I could do nothing to stop it."

"How is it you came to get away?" Dafydd's ice blue eyes were full of suspicion.

"My sister—placed herself in the path of a knight's sword so I could get away." Hyw's breath caught in the depth of his misery. Would it have been any different if he had been a man, rather than a hawk or an eagle? Would he at least have been able to draw his own sword to fight for his sister and the relics? Or would they all have been taken? He looked up to find his da looking at him, and when Bran nodded, Hyw added, "Not knowing what else to do, I returned here as swiftly as I could, to warn you."

"My son and my daughter have made me proud in service to the House of Aberffraw," Bran said, his voice husky with emotion.

"Indeed, you have good reason to be proud," agreed Lord Hywel. "Hyw and Lady Catrin have kept faith with you and your house, Prince Dafydd."

"Where are the English?"

"Very near," Hyw answered. "Perhaps a day's ride. Perhaps less."

The prince's eyes widened, but he nodded with his chin at the door. "Send scouts," Dafydd told the others in the room. "I will speak with the traitor."

"Lady Margred, come with me." As he helped Margred to her feet, Bran caught Hyw's eye. "Aeneus has not yet returned. He may need your assistance."

Hyw and Aeneus searched the wall walk and then the castle itself, but Drem was nowhere to be found. By morning, Aeneus sent Hyw to his bed, but after a fitful hour Hyw rose, unable to sleep. He could feel the tension in his gut and knew it would not be long before the English were upon them.

Prince Dafydd had warned them to prepare for a siege, and several warriors manned the wall walk, making preparations. The prince held a meeting with Bran, Hywel ap Rhys Gryg, and others of his council. As they emerged, Hyw could tell from the lines on his father's face that the situation was grim.

In the mid-afternoon, word came from the warriors on the walk that the English had been spotted. But instead of circling the castle for a prolonged siege, the English rode up to the gates. Warriors manned the wall walk to rain arrows and rocks down on them, and to pour the oil that had been heating since the morning.

The onslaught turned the tide of English riders back, but Hyw turned in horror at a grating noise as the portcullis began to rise. Aeneus had his sword out and was heading up the stairwell two at a time. Hyw followed, along with his father. A warrior lay with his throat slit at the top of the stairs, and the doorway was barricaded. Drem! He must have hidden from them through the night, and then snuck up into the entryway to lift the heavy portcullis for their enemy.

"Traitor!" roared Aeneus, but there was no response.

"Find your mam," Bran told Hyw. "Tell her to meet us at the tunnel entrance."

And see to my daughter's safety, Llywelyn agreed.

"Take as many of our people as you can gather and get them out," Aeneus said grimly. Two of the men remained on the wall walk. Their eyes told Hyw they knew the cost. "Very well," Aeneus said to them. "We will hold them off as long as we can. At least the traitor knows nothing of the tunnel."

Unless Margred told him. But she had not travelled through it. And there was no more time to consider it. Aeneus roared at the others to get Dafydd out. Bran took the prince's arm and they ran.

"Go now," Aeneus yelled again as he began firing arrows, two at a time.

Hyw was already running to find his mam. As he ran for the castle keep, Adara and Elizabeth streamed out the door, already herding the other families toward the tunnel. Some instinct must have warned her. Elizabeth carried Baby Gwladys in her sling and Enid carried Baby Gwen.

Margred appeared surrounded by her sisters. Without speaking, Hyw knelt so one could ride on his back and scooped one of the smaller ones up in one arm. He held Enid's arm with his other hand, as they carried Margred's sisters toward the tunnel entrance. Adara had sprung the latch as soon as she arrived. Prince Dafydd went ahead, carrying a torch, to lead the women and children through.

"Shh!" Elizabeth whispered to a tearful child as they filed into the darkness of the tunnel behind him. "Come, let us go together on an adventure."

"Go," Hyw told his mam and Margred, as he helped Enid down the ladder. "I will close the latch before the English can see it."

"Where is Lord Aeneus?" his mam asked.

"I will fetch him," Hyw told her. "Go you now."

Finally Adara and the others made their way through. Several of the other lords herded the people as quietly as possible into the tunnel and under the castle. Bran touched Hyw's shoulder as he moved after them, carrying a torch to help light the way.

Hyw ran back up the ladder in time to see Aeneus running toward him. Only one of the other two warriors followed. Aeneus twisted and fired arrows back at the portcullis as English soldiers began pouring through it.

"Close it!" Aeneus roared, and Hyw leapt back down the ladder and closed the tunnel gate. The two men raced into the tunnel as the stone scraped shut. Yells of the English soldiers echoed against the stone. Hyw barely had time to pull down the ladder and transform into a sparrow. He darted up and out of the keep as the first English soldier ran into the guardhouse. Hyw circled once to see the confusion of the guards, who stood around the open trap door, staring down at the tunic and leggings crumpled on the stone floor, where Hyw had left them. Then he flew for the mountain entrance of the tunnel.

The light sparrow tired quickly, so Hyw switched to eagle in midflight, keeping watch for English patrols. Even with Llywelyn to guide him, darkness was falling by the time they found the spot. Without his clothing, Hyw opted to switch to owl and waited in a tree branch. He had time then to think about the brave warrior who had given his life on the wall walk to aid their escape, and to wonder if Drem had help from others in the castle who had come through the tunnel with them.

Finally the stone began to move, and the people filed out behind Prince Dafydd and Elizabeth. He could see them easily from his perch, even in the dark. The prince spoke in a low voice, calling them to him, and began to lead them into the mountains, this time by moonlight.

Hyw remained still until the people had all gone. His mam and da were the last to leave, waiting near the mouth of the tunnel to close it again. He could see her looking around for him, and he hooted a signal to her. Without calling attention to it, she took a set of clothing from the pack she carried and casually set it on the rock. Then she closed the tunnel entrance, and moved off with Bran to join the others.

Hyw flew down to make the most difficult change back to his human shape. Once again, he paid the price of waiting. His bones ground and cracked as his spine ripped from the bird's back, and his feathers scratched and tore as they became flesh. The pain burst and split him apart as he was forced back to humanity.

It took longer to recover than he anticipated. Even Llywelyn had little to say. When Hyw was finally dressed, he made his way along the path. He jumped at a cough in the darkness, and Lord Hywel ap Rhys Gryg loomed at his side.

Steady, lad, Llywelyn murmured, as the elder nobleman moved into step with Hyw. For a moment, neither spoke.

"I was concerned that you might have difficulty finding us again," Lord Hywel said in a low voice. "Through your actions this day, you have cleared your name and that of your sister. I believe I know something of your family history. I can guess how you managed it, and that is enough for me. I follow a different path, but I am not sorry to walk this one with you, or any member of your family, wherever your—gifts may take you."

They caught up with the people as they stopped to rest. Lord Hywel smiled warmly at Hyw and moved off to rejoin his sons. Adara hugged Hyw and Bran clapped him on the shoulder.

Prince Dafydd called them to the path again, and the group travelled on. Near morning, they came to a defensible area nearby, where once a hillfort had stood. It was still dotted with a series of caves, in which Dafydd bid the men and their families take shelter. He sent two warriors back to erase their trail, in case the English discovered it and tried to follow.

"Some of you may choose to remain here, and I believe you will be safe," Dafydd told the people. "As for the warriors, we move on Garth Celyn. To be here, the English cannot also be there, so there we must go. Fear not, for we will win back our ancient sanctuary before long."

Dafydd's words echoed Llywelyn's: the living prince and the one in Hyw's mind agreed, for once. Dafydd selected Bran, Aeneus, and two of the others who knew the area to accompany him on a scouting mission. Bran turned to Hyw, his forehead furrowed with too much worry.

"Will you remain to protect your mother and the children?"

I must go with my brother, Hyw. Llywelyn's voice was raw with insistence. *I must learn all I can to help Dafydd win against them. Tell your da that you must go with him.*

Hyw closed his eyes and found Llywelyn staring at him intently. He looked as regal as he had the day he had given Hyw the choice to accompany him on the fateful trip to Builth, where Llywelyn was murdered and their journey together began. Then he had left the decision to Hyw. After all they had been through, what led him to believe that Hyw would not or could not make such a decision on his own?

"I know where my Gift and yours will be of most use," he replied, inside his mind.

Then he opened his eyes, met his father's with determination and spoke aloud. "I go to Garth Celyn. With you."

You are as headstrong as my brother, but at least you make the right choices.

They left the women and children in the caves. He went to say goodbye to Margred, but she seemed so distressed that in the end, he didn't tell her he was leaving. They slipped from the camp quietly and trekked farther into the mountain passes, avoiding the trail of the English army. Llywelyn fretted as the sun trod its path across the sky, and Hyw had to calm him more than once.

21

Dolbadarn was strangely quiet when the English forced their way inside. Cat was allowed to ride, her hands bound in front of her, de Francton controlling the reins. Rhys and Cynfrig ran behind Bellamy's horse, their hands tied to his saddle by crude ropes.

"What game are these Welsh devils playing at now?" Bellamy grumbled.

Rhys and Cynfrig shrugged, keeping their faces expressionless. Cat couldn't help her relief, although she, too, worked to control her composure. The English soldiers frowned and grouched around the courtyard and wall walks, searching for Dafydd or at least something that would explain what had happened. Some crossed themselves and looked around as if they could see Welsh ghosts. A few dead Welsh warriors lay on the wall walk. No one remained in the keep, although some of the tables were set with food on plates, still steaming.

They found Drem barricaded in the area above the entranceway, alone. Before the English even asked a question, the butcher's son began blurting out his tale. He first turned on Cat and Rhys.

"They betrayed you, my lords," he said, pointing his fingers at them as soon as his hands were free. "Her brother was to take them a deed for some land in return for them leading you off. I heard them talking about it. Oh, they thought they were so clever, didn't they? But I heard them. I've always been faithful to you, my lords. Always."

"That we discovered for ourselves," Bellamy said, unimpressed.

Cat's heart pounded at the mention of Hyw, but she soon

realized Drem knew nothing of Hyw's gift or how the Welsh had escaped. After the butcher's son had told them all he knew a second time, de Francton turned to Cat, his mouth curving in a smile but pure menace in his eyes.

"So your gift was a sham meant to mislead us. But your ruse made it possible for me to gain the relics and your husband—along with the deed proving that you were all working for Dafydd. And I have this fool as witness, if he should be needed."

"And my reward?" Drem looked expectantly at de Francton.

"Your reward?" De Francton turned his smile on Drem. "Oh, you will have your reward." He gestured to Bellamy. "Clap them in chains."

"Him too?" Bellamy gestured at Drem, who had gone pale.

"All of them. No, wait," de Francton said, tapping his chin with a finger. Drem looked relieved, but only for a moment before de Francton continued. "Lady Catrin's father serves the prince, does he not? Perhaps she will be of further value to me. Have two of your men—"

As Bellamy turned, Rhys lunged for the other man's scabbard, but several knights surrounded him at sword point. Four knights grabbed him, taking turns striking at his face. Cat cried out and tried to run toward them, but guards reached her first. Then she heard the scrape of steel on steel and turned to see Cynfrig standing over a downed knight, holding a sword.

"Leave off," Rhys called out, but it was too late. Cynfrig engaged the two knights closest to him, dancing around them with sure and practiced steps. He sliced the neck of one as he passed and knocked against another, who fell heavily backwards.

Then Cynfrig turned to take on a third. Cat cried out, but a fourth had already stepped up behind him. For the first time she could recall, Cynfrig stood completely still. His eyes filled with shock, and then pain. A sword stuck out of his stomach, before the knight pulled it backward. Cynfrig's hands covered the hole, already spurting blood. He choked as he saluted Rhys with his fist across his chest, but he held Cat's eyes as he slumped to his knees. Then he pitched forward to lie still in a pool of his own blood.

Rhys was yelling but his captors dragged him off. Another

knight pushed Drem out the door after him. In the confusion, Cat lunged for Cynfrig, grabbing his hand through the blood and holding it tightly. Why had she not foreseen this? She must be the morrigan for him at last. Someone pulled at her arm roughly but she stood firm, breathing steadily.

De Francton said, "Give her a moment. What can it hurt now?"

Slowing her breathing as she had at the stream, Cat closed her eyes and listened. Time stood still, swirling around them like mist. She heard singing in the distance and a light voice whispering, "The path." She drew the mist toward her until she could see Cynfrig's face. His body, whole again. No, his spirit, whole, as always.

The singing grew louder. Behind them rose the towers of Garth Celyn, and Cat gestured toward them. Cynfrig turned toward the towers and then he began drifting, swirling, dancing toward their birthplace. The singing continued, joined by the beating of dark wings all around them, pushing Cynfrig forward, toward Garth Celyn. Away from her.

His hand dropped from hers. She could still see him as she was pulled away by two armed men, until finally she saw no more as they half-carried her after de Francton.

Cat was escorted to a small room. A barred window allowed some sunshine and air in, and she wasn't chained. The room was spartan, with only a straw mattress and table. They left her a pitcher of water and a basin. No Agnes to tend her, although a guard brought her a tray of food. And this time no Rhys to watch for in the courtyard below. She sat at the table to wait for de Francton, and as she had hoped, he finally arrived.

"I need to see Rhys," she said, keeping her nerves under tight control.

"Don't fret so, Lady Catrin," de Francton said smoothly. "Lord Rhys is being held at our expense, until we have word from King Edward. In fact, if I recall correctly, he is being held in the very room where the former prince kept his elder brother prisoner for so many years."

"Prisoner?" Cat's heart thumped at the word. "He is a nobleman. How could you—?"

"He is a traitor. As are you, Lady Catrin. Don't tempt me to betray my gentler emotions and chain you beside him."

"I would see for myself." She tried not to plead but couldn't keep her voice steady. "Surely you can understand. I know you have a wife. Imagine how she would feel if you were captured."

De Francton shook his head. "I cannot imagine she would be asking to see me, under similar circumstances." He was silent for a moment, and then turned to Cat. "You may not know this about me, Lady Catrin, but I came here often in years past, as a simple knight in Lestrange's command, negotiating treaties with the Welsh in Prince Llywelyn's time." Something dark passed over de Francton's eyes then, but he hid it quickly. "And now I use what I have learned to help my king."

With that, he turned on his heel and walked out of the room, gesturing for a guard to close the door behind him. After he left, panic overcame her. She scrabbled at the bars on her window, frantic to get to Rhys somehow, until her fingers blistered and bled. She could not budge them. She paced the little room, thinking of new arguments to convince de Francton to let her speak to Rhys, or even just to see him again, to reassure herself that he was all right. But de Francton did not return.

Guards brought her a tray of food, and she must have eaten but she could not remember what. No one spoke to her, and if she tried to speak to the guards, they crossed themselves and closed the door quickly. She tossed and turned in the hard bed, but she must have slept because she woke in darkness.

"Rhys!"

But he was not there. She had no idea how much time had

gone by. Hours? Days? Finally, she heard the guard's voice at the door.

"You have a visitor."

But it wasn't de Francton this time. A man in a brown robe came in. Her Uncle Gawain. He held a hand up before she could speak. "Child, I have come to offer you succour. Will you pray with me?"

Gawain turned expectantly to the guard, who quickly crossed himself and backed up.

Her uncle held up his hand as if to bless her. She wanted to fall onto his shoulder and pour out her troubles to him, but she struggled to keep her composure. She noted that he still wore the brown robe he had been forced to wear at Bere, instead of his Cistercian white, but he shook his head slightly, bidding her to quiet. She knelt and bowed her head. Gawain cleared his throat and turned to the guard.

"The road was uncommonly dusty and hot, my son. Blessings upon you if you could fill my flask in the kitchens." Her uncle paused, but Cat remained with her head bowed. Finally her uncle continued. "I will watch her in your absence, never fear."

After a long moment, she heard the heavy door of the room close. She looked up to see Gawain put a finger to his lips again, but he didn't need to remind her to speak quietly this time.

"Have you seen Rhys? Where is he? Is he hurt? Is there news of Mam or Hyw?" she whispered urgently.

Gawain shook his head and leaned closer to her. "I know only rumours and speculation. In truth, I am lucky my Franciscan brothers have allowed me to remain with them. It is only through them that I knew de Francton's company was here at Dolbadarn. But it was not until our delegation arrived to give spiritual guidance to this company that I learned you had become prisoners in truth."

She sobered. "Glad I am that you have survived, and that you are here. Tell me what you know."

"It is not good, Cat," he said.

"I would rather know than sit here in ignorance."

"Prince Dafydd remains at liberty, but King Edward vows to wipe house Aberffraw from the world. The English have already started to build two larger castles farther north to announce his presence in Wales."

She considered that. "Garth Celyn?"

"I have not heard, but I will try to get word to you of what has befallen your former home. They have called for more monks to come to Abbey Conwy, and de Francton sent for me. He knows of my background there." Gawain shifted and looked at his hands. "There is a rumour that the king will tear down the old abbey and needs more hands to build a new one, but I cannot believe it."

"Did you learn the fate of the good abbot of Cymer Abbey?" she asked, thinking of the "questioning" de Francton had mentioned.

"Of him, we have heard nothing."

"I must speak to Rhys," she said, jumping up. "He will know what to do."

Gawain gestured to quieten her and whispered. "Where is he? Is he not here with you?"

"No, he was taken. They have him in the tower."

"But surely they want ransom or at least to strike a bargain for him?"

Cat quickly filled her uncle in with their disgrace and the loss of the relics. She could not stop the tears when she recounted the fate of Cynfrig and of Rhys' capture. "And I have not seen him, not since we were taken prisoner."

Gawain patted her hands. "Do not fret. I am to have an audience with de Francton this afternoon. I will see what can be done."

The following morning, Cat clung to the stone wall as she made her way up the stairs into the castle tower, conscious of the guard behind her. She did not know what Gawain had said, but she did not ask when the guard came to fetch her.

Rhys stood near the wall in a damp cell with only straw on the floor. As he came near, she could see the bruises on his face and arms. Bars crossed the heavy door to the room. She ran to it, trying to reach him. Rhys was at the door in two steps, clasping her hand through the metal bars. She laced her fingers into his, lost in the deep blue of his eyes. His face was so close. His lips.

"Here now," said a guard, roughly pushing her away from him. When their fingers parted, a chill ran through her body. "Keep your distance or we'll have to use those." The guard pointed at the chains hanging from the far walls.

At least they had not chained him to the wall. Yet.

Rhys glared at the guard, but Cat voluntarily took a step back. Two armed guards watched her as she stood awkwardly in front of the bars. One guard continued to speak and finally Rhys took a step back as well, looking her direction again but not into her eyes. She leaned forward, and she could feel the heat smouldering in him.

"I trust de Francton treats you well," he said in Welsh. "He will want you unharmed so he can make a deal with your father. You must do all you can to keep it that way."

She struggled to keep her hands from reaching out to him, her voice calm. "I will bargain for your release, my lord." Her voice cracked with the strain.

"I fear there is only one thing that will satisfy them. And they must not succeed." He stared at her for a long moment. "So long ago, it seems, when first they told me the princess wanted to postpone our wedding, I will confess I was relieved."

"Were you?" Cat's voice was barely a whisper.

"What a fool I was. I cannot believe it has only been two months since we two were reunited at Criccieth."

Hope surged within her. He placed his hands behind his back, but the intensity in his eyes told her that he wanted to hold her.

"So much has happened," he continued, shaking his head slightly. "And now you must leave me here and get away if you can."

"Never."

"You must. I have had much time to think here. Your gift and your brother's may be our only hope now."

She started to shake her head, but he cut her off and continued, "Hear me, Cat. The story of the morrigan is old. In the oldest texts, she is King Arthur's healer and leads him to Avalon. And often, she takes the form of a raven."

"Your symbol," Cat breathed, thinking of the ravens she saw after Ifan's death, and the three ravens on Rhys' banner.

"Think on it, Cat. These ravens you have seen, at least once. And who is it that can transform himself into one?"

"My brother."

Rhys relaxed his arms but stopped himself from taking a step toward her, glancing sideways at the guard before he continued. "It is said that King Arthur will return when Wales needs him most. When could that be, if not now? Your connection to the spirit world could be the way to find Arthur."

"How?"

"That I do not know," he said, "but I believe the first step is for you to find your brother. With the two of you together, who knows how your gifts may combine."

"Not without you." Cat could see her vision of Rhys with his fist in the air. She was certain now. "We cannot succeed without you."

His mouth pursed in a sad smile as he shook his head. "There is no chance that they will free me again, lest I fight against them."

"But I have de Francton's word—"

"He is not his own master," Rhys told her. "Whatever his intentions, he cannot guarantee what you ask. I am held at the king's pleasure, and no one but the king can release me."

"Then we must make another opportunity," she whispered. She took a step closer to him, lowering her voice and flicking her head slightly toward the guard, trying to signal Rhys to attack. "We must find a way to turn the tide."

"Cat, I am a prisoner here, under lock and key." Rhys whispered. "Your faith in my prowess is misplaced, and I fear you have sorely misjudged de Francton. You stand on the edge of the abyss with him behind you, poised to push you over it. And I cannot protect you. Now, and for all time, my name will be connected with the fall of Wales." He spun away from her. "You must convince de Francton that you gave up the relics on purpose, as he first suggested." She started to shake her head but he took a step toward her this time. "You must do whatever you can to regain your freedom and find your brother."

"I cannot leave—"

"Cat, listen to me." He took another step. He was dangerously close now, the heat from him almost scalding her, his voice low and intense in the language they shared. "They can scar me and even maim me, but the only way they can break me is if they hurt you in front of me. Do you understand? If you are free, then I can stand this for as long as I have to. You must find a way to free yourself."

"Only to come back for you—"

"Stand back." The guard's armour clanked as he moved toward them. "Enough talk." The guard was there now, pulling her away from him. "And no fraternizing."

"No," she said. "I cannot leave you here—"

"You must." Rhys held her eyes with his, even as the guards pulled her farther away from him, even as they dragged her to the stairs, until she could see him no more.

22

The silence of what had once been Garth Celyn deafened Hyw. Instead of the fragrant wild grasses of his childhood, there was charred ground. The long stone building that had once housed Llywelyn's court was in rubble. One lone tower rose up against the sky, its slate roof crumbled on one side. The little church and other buildings were nothing but charred, burned wood.

He lay prone on the ground, staring down the long mountain at what had been their home. No people stirred, and even the smallest animals had fled. The yard was silent and still. As the roar of wind rushed past his ears, Hyw felt the giant's fist clutching his heart. Garth Celyn was no more.

We can rebuild, Llywelyn began. *If we can but last through this summer, we will rise again.*

Hyw heard the cry of a hawk, high above, and connected briefly with it. He spotted a group of soldiers camped in the area near the ruined *llys*. There were perhaps a score of men, but no more, and Hyw wondered if they had guessed that they would need no more to bring down the remainder of Dafydd's army. They were lounging and gambling with sticks. He stayed with the bird, circling lower.

"Agghhh!" one soldier said disgustedly, watching as another gathered up his winnings. "I have about as much chance of winning as of catching that beggar prince."

A soldier standing on the sidelines of the game grunted, staring out at the rubble around them. "He'll come."

"What makes you so sure, eh? We've been here weeks already, and there's been no sign of him."

"No sign anywhere else, either," the other said. "And this was his brother's favourite court."

"All the more reason to stay away. Everyone knew they hated each other."

The standing man shook his head. "If this prince wants to rally the Welsh to him, he needs to capitalize on the brother's sway with them."

"Doesn't matter either way," said the soldier who pocketed the coin. "We was told to stay here, and that's what we'll do. Either this beggar comes and we take his head to the king, or he doesn't."

"And you take me for everything in my pockets," grumbled the first soldier.

Hyw heard Llywelyn hiss and released the mind of the bird. Closing his eyes, he saw the former prince with his arms crossed.

You must protect my brother. The English have the llys, but they must not get the last living Welsh prince or our children.

Hyw headed back to his da and relayed what he'd heard, including Llywelyn's warning. Bran nodded at Hyw, and drew Dafydd aside with a murmured, "We are outnumbered, and we cannot tarry here. We must make plans."

Hunters had little success that day or the next in the charred areas around the former *llys*, and most of the travel caches they relied on for supplies had been taken in the fire or plundered by English troops. At first, Bran tried to convince Dafydd to move on, and take the children north into Scotland. Llywelyn urged Hyw to speak as well, but the look in Dafydd's eyes stopped them all. Dafydd seemed to take the loss of the *llys* as a deliberate affront, as if it had been his favourite home and not Llywelyn's.

It is pride, Llywelyn commented grimly. *The pride of a child whose friend has taken a toy and broken it. He cannot let it go to find another.*

Bran saw it differently. "Prince Dafydd took up the cause of gaining back the *llys* in his brother's memory. This redemption would have won him the heart of Wales. Without it, he must find his cause again."

Hyw could see signs of strain in Dafydd. Where he had been indulgent with his children, one day he snapped at his son Owain for no reason. Then he hugged the boy to him. Elizabeth came near and massaged her husband's shoulders as he apologized to them all.

Aeneus found a small deserted farmhouse at Nanhysglain, sheltered by the mountains. He and Bran convinced Dafydd to set up his family there. Adara moved in with Elizabeth, along with the wet nurse Enid, who still helped care for Gwenllian as well as Elizabeth's younger children. Bran and Hyw stood guard outside, while several others bedded down their families in nearby caves. They said little, but the handful who remained seemed to trust the caves more than a castle. After what they had been through, Hyw could not blame them.

One day, Odgar ap Math, who had marched with them since Hyw and Margred freed him at Criccieth, took a handful of earth in his hand and seemed to weigh it. "We should soon be planting," he said. The next morning, he was gone.

Dafydd was not the only one to show a brittle temper as dark moods overtook many. Gradually other men who travelled with them began to disappear, one by one, and then in groups. Only Lord Hywel ap Rhys Gryg and his sons remained steadfast, shaking the hands of the men who came to say they were leaving.

Hyw tried not to think about the empty space where Garth Celyn had been. In the daytime he helped the others, moving gear from one hiding place to another, helping them hunt for what scarce game they could find, or scouting the whereabouts of the English. At night, without even a fire in the darkness, he couldn't avoid his memories of the rubble and ruined buildings. He was glad his mother and sister had not seen it.

When Margred went to gather water for Elizabeth, Hyw fell into step beside her. She said nothing, but he was sure she thought of Drem. Hyw finally broke the silence. "You must not blame yourself."

"Who else can I blame?" She kept her eyes down, but her tone was strained. "I knew he was not himself, but I thought the English had harmed him in some way. Tortured him. Something." She shook her head. "And as it turns out, they had no need."

"We cannot know what made him act the way he did," Hyw

began, but she interrupted him.

"Do not try to comfort me, Hyw," she said. "I cannot speak of this. Not with you."

"Then do not. We will speak of other things."

"What else could there be?" She placed the waterskins into the stream to fill, and turned toward him. Tears were coursing down her cheeks, and he wanted to help her in some way. But there was something of the wild animal about her. If he touched her, she might bolt. Instead, he remained still, watching her.

"You helped me find him," she was saying, "and I will never be able to repay you for that. What he managed to do, he did because I let him."

"You believed in him."

"I did," she nodded and looked away from him. "I did."

He stopped himself from reaching out to her. "You loved him."

"I do," she said, turning back to the stream to gather up the water skins. But he understood the word. He found himself again thinking of James—but before he finished the thought, he banished it.

The road to love is not always an easy one.

He had forgotten to hide his thoughts from Llywelyn, but the former prince's gruff voice caused him to close his eyes. Llywelyn's eyes held only compassion. *I betrothed myself to Elinor when she was only five years old, on the strength of her portrait and her father's word. Later, when her father was killed and her family exiled, my good counsellors tried to convince me to choose another. I was the Prince of Wales, after all, and I could have had any woman or man I wanted. And in truth, there were many, more than willing. But I believe in the value of honour, and actions prove the worth of our words. So for me, there was no one else, in all the years before and between. For a time it seemed as if I would never have the chance to show Elinor her value to me, but our years together made it all worth it.*

Hyw considered Llywelyn. Even as spirit, the former prince chose to clothe himself only in black, still in mourning for his wife. They had only been married for four years before she died, birthing Gwenllian, less than a year ago.

After her death, many tried to convince me to find another woman quickly, in order to have a son to secure my position. But Gwenllian was the child of our love, and I would rather change the law to make her princess. A look of great sadness filled his eyes. *Or I would have done, had I been given the chance.*

Hyw wasn't sure how to respond, but Llywelyn went on. *I know you have risked much for my niece's friendship. But I also know that you love another. Do not stop yourself from love, Hyw, in whatever form you find it. In the end, it matters not who you love, but that you love honestly and well.*

Hyw's throat tightened, and he knew again why he had chosen this path, pledging himself to serve a dead prince whose spirit could not rest in one world or the next.

As May became June, Hyw and the others—including Margred—ranged farther afield in small hunting parties that too often returned empty-handed. Each day, Dafydd would send Hyw out to scout the surrounding areas, but still the English hunted the prince and those few who remained loyal. And each time he helped the prince elude them, Hyw felt oddly lucky to be alive and close to Garth Celyn. He had no heart to look on the devastation again, but it was comforting to know they were near his home. Perhaps the English wouldn't look here again for a long while. He even began to hope for the day when they might rebuild.

Then one afternoon, the earth trembled underfoot. Hyw bent down to put his hand flat on the ground. Horses, at full gallop.

Fast horses in wartime never bring good news.

When had he thought that before? The day the messenger came to Garth Celyn, inviting his father and Llywelyn to a meeting they thought would end a war. Only seven months ago, but it seemed like years. He sent his mind out to connect with the horses, and managed to get control of one. The metal armour around the beast's face made it difficult to see, but Hyw made out at least twenty armed knights, riding with a purpose. It almost seemed that they knew where the prince was hiding. But how?

When he warned his father, Bran tensed and turned to look upward. Hyw followed his gaze: smoke wisped from the hole in the farmhouse roof, betraying the cooking fire inside. No one would think it deserted. Hyw was glad that Margred and some of the others were out hunting. At least they would survive.

"We must hide the women and children. Take them into the brush, Hyw."

And Dafydd, Llywelyn warned. *They come for my brother.*

They turned to enter the hut, but Dafydd came out and closed the door behind him. "The children need food and shelter," he said. "Let them remain, and we will lead the English away." He had donned his torque, a simple ring of gold, and carried his sword unsheathed. Gaunt with hunger and hardship, he still looked every ounce the warrior.

Finally, he shows the strength that convinced me to name this brother as my heir, Llywelyn whispered.

Hywel ap Rhys Gryg and his sons stood and unsheathed their swords, as did Bran and Aeneus. Hyw followed their example.

"You are still the prince of this land, and we are sworn to protect you," said Hywel. "I sicken of hiding. Like the brave men of Gododdin, it is time for us to stand against the foe. If it must be, then let it be today."

Hywel ap Rhys Gryg had again found the right words to stir their blood: the poem in memory of the warriors of Gododdin, where a force of only three hundred held off a vast army. Dafydd's force numbered less than a dozen seasoned warriors, against a score of armoured English knights. They moved away from the hut, toward the approaching threat. On Dafydd's signal, as the English were about to burst upon them, they ran from the clearing toward the enemy, yelling war cries.

Hywel's youngest son was the first to fall, and with a cry his father flung himself at a group of knights. He parried fore and aft, and Hyw saw two men fall to his sword. Then he was engaged in his own battle. Hyw swept one man from his horse with his javelin. Three more rode at him. Two men who had been with Dafydd only days ago now rode with the English. Llywelyn's hand moved with his, and together they warded off their attacker. Then his da was at his side.

"Change now, and find Rhys and the others. It goes against us here. If they take Dafydd or the children, find you those who can aid us in freeing them again. I will hold them off here, but go! Now!"

Bran raised his sword at two approaching knights, and Hyw ducked backward, not caring who might see. He was glad this part of the transformation was quicker and easier for him each time. The hawk's beak and talons armed him as he spread his great red wings to take the sky.

As he flew upward, Bran cried out. Hyw turned in mid-air. His father and Aeneus fought back to back, but twice their number flanked them on all sides. The clash of swords increased as they disappeared in the melee.

You must fly for help, Llywelyn hissed urgently in Hyw's ear. But Hyw wheeled around, beating the air with his strong wings. His heart thumped and his beak ached for flesh.

Then the English soldiers moved away to attack another. One soldier snatched Da's sword from where it lay on the grass, but Da made no move to take it back. Hyw started after the soldier and then circled back, staring down at the man who had been his rock, now silent and still. Da's eyes were open, as if he stared at the sky, a fierce grimace still stretching his lips across his teeth.

Hyw heard the hawk's scream from his own throat as he dove downward. He landed and plucked at his da's tunic, but there was no movement. Hyw tried to pull his da off the field to safety, but the air failed him again and again. Finally he hopped onto the broad chest and spread his wings protectively around his da's still form. Near him on the ground lay Aeneus. Hywel ap Rhys Gryg and both his sons lay still and bleeding.

The only man still standing was Dafydd ap Gruffydd, the last living Prince of Wales. The hawk remained still, guarding and watching. Disarmed and bleeding, Dafydd stood tall against the mounted captain.

"Stay your swords, Henry," Dafydd began, smiling calmly and hailing the captain of Edward's troops. "You and I practiced together in the yard, during my time at Edward's court. I assure you, my strength and ability have grown in the past year."

"As have my own," the captain replied, "and the skills of these men with me."

Dafydd nodded. "I'm glad to see my cousin the king assessed our skill aright, to send so many to subdue so few."

"It was your own men who brought us here," the captain said. "You are betrayed, Lord Prince, as was your brother before you. And now you are injured. I must confess, I had expected to find you better guarded."

"My army musters elsewhere," Dafydd replied smoothly. "My sword arm is still sound. Yet I will not fight, but go with you peacefully to Edward, if you will agree to one simple term."

The captain hesitated. One of his guardsmen moved his horse closer. "Do not trust him. The king—"

"The king has changed his mind on this man many times, Sedrig." The captain spoke aside to his guard, although the hawk could hear him. "There is little to gain from killing, where ransom may be more worth." He spoke louder then. "There is no harm in hearing the terms."

"Give safe passage to my princess and her retinue. The Lady Elizabeth you know well, and she has been under Edward's protection e'er this. Swear that no harm will come to her or hers, and I will go with you quietly."

"She is also here, with you?" The captain seemed surprised. Dafydd gestured to the side, where the edge of a farmhouse was visible. "Then you ease our duty. I will agree to your terms. They will come with us to Shrewsbury, but I swear it, as you say. No harm shall befall the Lady Elizabeth or her children."

"Or any with her," Dafydd said. "Swear it."

"I swear. I will see to it myself."

Dafydd nodded. The captain gestured to two of his riders and they rode off toward the farmhouse. The others grabbed Dafydd, trussing him up like a thief. Yet he did not call out, even as they threw him up onto a horse, and rode off.

Safe inside the bird, Hyw watched and waited. Long after the men on horses had ridden off, the hawk remained. A scavenger with two spindly legs stayed behind, and the bird watched it move from body to body. It fumbled at the clothing, ripping anything of value from the still forms on the field. When it came to one better dressed than the others, the scavenger pulled something off and sat on the ground beside the body. Bits of leather. Boots. The bird remembered. For feet. Foolish things, feet. Talons were sharper. But the scavenger pulled the boots on its own feet.

When the scavenger walked in the stolen boots toward the two forms lying together, the bird responded. Talons first, Hyw screamed and flew at the man, who ducked and cowered.

"You're a big'un." The scavenger made a motion across his chest that the hawk recognized as crossing himself. "Hungry, are ye? Well, have them. Precious little meat or booty here anyway."

Hyw knew that he had won. He landed beside the two bodies and watched, fluffing his wings menacingly as the scavenger mounted his horse and rode away. Then Hyw hopped onto the chest of one and settled. He looked down at the still form, the kind face, the eyes open and staring at the sky above them. This was the one who had sired him. Da. He remembered.

He fluffed his wings again, circling the face and cooing to it. All the times he had seen this face, looking back at him. There was a beauty in it once. This had been someone to look up to, someone to make proud, someone to be. Hyw cooed and fluffed and pecked once at the face, but all was still.

He shrieked then, a terrible keening shriek that would carry on the wind to others of his kind. A warning. When the crows and jackdaws came, the hawk would be ready. Already he saw one in a nearby tree. Soon it would bring others. Hyw raised his wings.

Have at us.

Somewhere inside his mind, he heard a voice. *Hyw. We must bring help. Hyw!*

The bird shook and screamed. No. He turned from the voice. He would not listen to the words.

Long after the departing hoof beats of the first scavenger had passed across the mountain, a woman came from the bushes. The hawk watched her. She was beautiful, in her way, although she had no wings. Her lithe body was hunched and bent, her short black hair curling around her face, tears streaming down her cheeks. A word came to the hawk: Margred.

"Hyw," she said.

No. The hawk moved his head down, shook himself, and ruffled his neck feathers. No. She could not have his da. He spread his wings around his perch to protect it. The woman took a step back, and he bobbed his head to track her movements.

"You must transform and help me. We cannot leave them here."

One of the bodies beside him stirred a little. He watched as the woman gave a small cry and dropped to her knees beside it. She took her flask and poured water into the man's mouth.

"Aeneus, you are alive! Hyw, help us!"

Did she not see the menacing blackbirds gathering in the nearby trees? Hyw clacked his beak and flapped a warning to her, before settling his wings around his prize. He would not leave his perch. He watched her fumble in her pack and draw out cloth, which she wrapped around the man's head and arm.

"Aeneus, I must speak plainly," she said to the man. "You knew Hyw's da well?

"Aye, and his mam also. And I have seen this bird before."

"Something is wrong," she said. "Why does he not change back to himself?"

"I have seen men do strange things after a battle," he told her. "Fear not, I will help you with him. I would lay down my life to protect Hyw and his sister."

Margred sat back on her heels and looked at the man. Hyw bobbed and turned so he could watch them more closely.

"I know his mam through her elder brother Twm," he said. "Twm also had abilities that aided him in battle. This brother gave his life for me in the last war with Edward." Then the man looked right at Hyw, startling the bird enough that he looked away. "And I have other reasons for my allegiance. If Hyw is sore afflicted by grief, then I will do my best to see him return to his former self."

Margred helped the man stand and they started toward Hyw.

Hyw spread his wings to defend his perch, but Margred barely glanced at him as she helped the injured warrior hobble away into the bushes.

He turned his attention to the others of his own kind again. Two crows now, hopping near the bodies farthest from him. They tore at the eyes, and bits of shredded flesh dangled from their beaks. Hyw should attack them, but he had to protect his prize. He spread his wings again. The man—Aeneus—lurched out of the bushes, and shooed the crows away for him. Hyw watched Aeneus moving the other bodies.

"Hyw, you must come," Margred said. She had come up from behind him, and he hopped on his perch to face her. "We can dig a grave for your father together."

No. My prize. Hyw bobbed his head at her, clacking his beak and moving a talon up and down.

"I know it's you. But I don't understand what you're doing."

Surely she could see he was defending this place. This one. The one who sired him. Hyw turned, raising his wings a little and carefully moving his talons, to watch the other man again. Were they coming to separate him from his prize? Let them try.

"This is enough," the woman said. "You must come."

She moved around him, and he turned again to keep her in sight. He watched her until something heavy struck him, encircled him, flipped him over. A net! He screeched then, but it was too late. Margred and the bandaged man, Aeneus, gathered him in the net. Hyw struggled, and his mouth gaped open and shut on nothing. He was caught.

Hyw was tethered to a tree stump. The woman reached out and he snatched at the bit of flesh in her hand. Squirrel. The meat was cooked, but he swallowed it hungrily.

"What if it is not Hyw?" the man said.

"It is him," She-who-fed-him said. "Do you not see his eyes?"

"We should release him lest we starve him. We were lucky

to find these squirrels, but this meat is not enough to share with him. He will fend for himself in the wild well enough. He may even change and return to us again."

"Nay, he might change in mid-air and be killed. It has happened to him before. He told me about it on our journey." Her voice faltered, and Hyw stared at her. Margred. Her name was Margred. "And I am not certain he can change back on his own."

Aeneus shook his head. "His mam may know what to do, but she is being held with the princess at Shrewsbury. I had word from a man in the village who heard the soldiers boasting."

"What of his sister?"

"At Dolbadarn, also in custody," Aeneus answered. "As is Lord Rhys. The English have the relic and the crowns." The big man's body slumped, and his words hung heavy in the air around them.

"We cannot give up hope, Aeneus," Margred said. "Think of how my father must feel, in some English dungeon. Or the Lady Elizabeth. Or Hyw's own mam."

Hyw blinked and followed the slight shifting movements of the humans around him. Mam. The word meant something to him. Something had happened to her. Hyw hopped and ruffled his feathers, but the ropes held him firmly. He preened his feathers flat with his sharp beak. Then he trained his blue-grey eyes on the dark-haired woman again as she blew her hair away from her face with a sharp breath. Sometimes she reminded him of someone. Perhaps it was Mam.

"We need Hyw and his gifts to help us get him back. Get our prince back."

A voice whispered again in Hyw's mind, but he shook his head violently and ruffled his feathers again. When the voice continued, he snapped his beak.

"You speak truly." The man was looking in Hyw's direction. Hyw bobbed his head, tracking both of them. "You know what is at stake? Who is—inside with him?"

Margred stared at the hawk and nodded. "Hyw told me that as well, although I did not truly believe it. Do you think..." Her voice trailed off.

"He is still there," Aeneus said. "It must be so."

"We must find Cat," Margred said. "She will know how to restore him to us. There must be a way to get her to him, or him to her."

Hyw knew that name also. Cat. He moved again on his stump but the tether tightened around his leg. He snapped his beak at the tether, trying to bite through it as he had the previous one. Each day the man Aeneus devised some new torture to hold him.

Now Aeneus rubbed his bandaged head. "We need proper tethers for him."

"Then we will get them," she said. "We do not lose until we choose to give up. I well understand why Hyw hides in the form of this hawk. And it's also why you choose to hide away on this mountain. We have lost much, and more is stacked against us. But we remain. While many better men and women are dead, you and I remain free. Surely there is some reason. Something calls to us yet. I cannot speak for you, but I must answer."

Aeneus stirred then, and squared his shoulders. "Lady, you speak wisdom. You do not stand alone. We answer together."

Hyw shrieked and spread his wings, shaking them once before he settled on the perch again.

23

Cat developed a routine to pass the time in the small room at Dolbadarn Castle. After Gawain left, she sang the hymns and services she could recall on her own. Her window faced one of the fields at the side of the castle, so she checked outside for signs of life. She twisted the bars on her windows, more gently this time, but they would not budge. A tightness clutched her chest and she forced herself to breath: in, and then out. In, and then out. Then she began her exercises, going through the motions Margred had taught her at Criccieth.

The next hour, she began again.

A guard manned the door, brought her meals, and escorted her to the garderobe as needed. She stared deep into her basin of water when she washed and into the liquids she drank from her goblet, but neither offered her any glimpses of the future. She lost track of the passage of time, but she couldn't still her panic that time was running out for her and for all of them.

The room was smaller and not as high as her previous rooms at Bere castle, so she could see the courtyard more clearly. One day, as she stared down from the small window, a monk in a brown robe crossed the courtyard, with his hands in his sleeves. Her Uncle Gawain had been forced to wear such a robe, but the way this monk moved told her it was not him. Her uncle always had a slow and contemplative grace, but this monk moved swiftly, almost gliding across the ground. He could have been a warrior dressed in monk's clothing. She craned her neck to watch until he disappeared from view. She forced herself to turn away from the window and begin her exercises again.

Shortly afterward, a noise at the door stopped her.

"Cat," someone whispered.

The monk slipped through the door. Cat started as she recognized Aeneus, the former leader of Llywelyn's *teulu* at Garth Celyn. "How—?"

"Quickly," he hissed. He handed her a similar homespun robe. "Put these on."

"Rhys—" Cat began.

"We cannot tarry," Aeneus whispered fiercely. "We must go. Now!"

"I cannot leave without him."

"You can do him no good from here."

Cat stared at Aeneus a moment. She could still hear the last words Rhys had said to her: *They can scar me and even maim me, but they will break me if they hurt you in front of me.*

Aeneus pulled her back to reality by shaking the robe at her impatiently. "Now."

He helped her put the garment over her head to cover her clothes and then grabbed her arm before she had it properly tied. They pushed past a guard, who lay slumped by the door, and she said a quick prayer for him in hopes that he was not dead.

"Brother," someone hailed from lower on the stairwell. Aeneus shifted the sleeve of his garment, and she could imagine a knife concealed in the fabric. She was sick of knives. Turning quickly toward the voice, she made the sign of the cross and pitched her own voice as low as she could.

"Peace be with you."

Then they turned the corner onto the wall walk. She looked for her uncle but no one else came near them. Aeneus pulled a scrap of leather from his sleeve and handed it to her. He began winding it around her hand and then handed her a second piece for her other hand. He suddenly stopped on the wall walk and held his hand out to Cat.

"Steady," he whispered as she stepped onto the ledge. The 50-

foot drop made her dizzy. Then he was placing her hand onto a rope that disappeared into the trees. "Use your legs too." He gave her a push and Cat had no choice but to cling to the rope as she careened across and downward, swinging her legs to propel herself forward. When she reached the earth, she looked up to see the rope hurtling down toward her as Aeneus disappeared from the wall walk.

"Here," came another whisper from the trees, and Margred appeared beside her, gathering up the rope.

"But Rhys—" Cat began, and Margred shushed her.

"If all goes well, he will join us anon." Margred grinned at her. Cat had no time to ask more as Margred pulled her down into a crouch. Then they were running into the trees.

They shimmied up a tree to wait, and Cat was glad to switch her skirts for the tunic and leggings Margred had stashed there. Cat's feet had been bare inside her prison room, and she was glad to see a pair of leather soft-soled boots. Margred gestured for quiet, and they both sat tensely, staring down at the forest below. After what felt like hours but must have been only a few minutes, Margred shifted and began to rub at her knuckles in a way Cat had never seen her do before. Clearly, something was not going as planned, but when Cat tried to ask, the other girl shushed her again.

As the last bell calling the monks to Vespers, the first prayers of the evening, began to fade, Cat heard a rustling below. A robed figure appeared. Margred punched Cat on the shoulder and started down. Cat followed her.

By the time she reached the forest floor, Aeneus had shrugged off the robe. Under it he was already dressed in a travel tunic and leggings with a pack over his shoulder. He pulled a javelin from its hiding place, and Cat saw a smear of blood on his arm.

"What happened? Where is Rhys?"

He shook his head at her and whispered, "I could not get to him."

"I cannot leave without him."

"Your brother needs you," Aeneus said quietly.

"We must move," Margred hissed.

They ran through the forest until Cat's legs were on fire and her feet screamed with blisters inside the unfamiliar boots. Finally Aeneus raised his hand. Cat could see a clearing, and Aeneus proceeded with his javelin raised. When he was sure the area was free of the enemy, he handed Margred the pack and gestured for her to go ahead of them.

"Where are we going?' she whispered. "We must go back. Rhys is in the tower —"

Aeneus shook his head, cutting her off. "We will go back. But first, you must help Hyw."

"Hyw? What has happened?"

"There is much to tell," Aeneus began, and she noticed how haggard and drawn he looked. At a rustle behind them, she turned to see Margred holding a large bird on her gloved hand. Its head was hooded, and a tether tied its legs firmly to the glove. She craned her neck but could see no one else in the clearing.

"Where is Hyw?" Cat asked.

"He is here," Margred told her.

"Why is he hooded?" She turned to her brother. "Hyw, you must fly back into the castle. They are holding Rhys in the tower."

A warm hand on her arm made her turn back to Aeneus. "He cannot." The warrior's eyes were full of sorrow and possibly sympathy. "We are not sure he can even understand you."

"What? Of course he can." Cat whirled on Margred and the hawk. "Hyw, you must change back into yourself, now. We need your help."

"But he needs yours," Margred said softly. "He cannot change."

"That's—" she began, and sputtered to a stop. "That's impossible. Hyw? You must tell me what is going on."

They heard a noise and what sounded like a hunting horn in the distance. Aeneus crouched instinctively and they followed suit.

"We will," Margred said. "But we must get to safety first."

"Aye," Aeneus agreed, "or at least away from here."

"We cannot!" Cat clenched her fists in frustration. "We cannot leave Rhys."

"One thing at a time, Cat," Aeneus said. "We will not leave him, but we must regain our strength first. We have much to tell you. But first, let us move to a safer hiding place."

24

The bird knew darkness and could not move, but at the same time he felt himself moving. It was difficult to settle. He knew the woman was his perch. He tried to get away but the jesses on his feet and the long line of netting tethered him to the rough perch she held. She-who-fed-him. She should let him go. He would hunt for her, and feed her from his beak the way she fed him. He opened his beak to tell her, but he only panted. He spread his wings, but his talons were tied firmly to the perch.

"Quiet," she said.

Perhaps he would not hunt for her after all. He bobbed his head at her to let her know. Finally the movement around him stopped, and he was shifted onto a tree branch. He moved his talons up and down on the branch. Voices in the darkness. Then no voices. The darkness was wrong but he could not escape it. The sun on his feathers called him to hunt but he could not answer it. The churr of a wren teased him, and jackdaws chattered behind him. He tried to shift on the branch but could not. He was lost. They were all lost.

Then again he heard the murmur of voices around him. More voices now. Something—familiar. He stirred, chasing a long-ago memory. Some instinct in him to fight warred with his need to remember, to think, to hear these voices. In the darkness, everything echoed.

Someone pulled at his hood. He shook his head and the darkness became orange light. She-who-fed-him glowed orange in

433

the setting sun. He opened his beak again. She gave him a morsel of meat. Not enough. Hunger. He was always hungry. Why would she not let him go? Let him hunt?

"I cannot believe it," said a voice, and he looked around him, blinking. Another woman stood there, beside a tall man. Her cheeks glistened wetly. Tears, he remembered. Something stirred in him. He knew her, felt some sense of kinship with her, and yet she was not of his kind. But there was something. He looked away. He opened his beak but no sound came out.

"I have nothing more, Hyw," She-who-fed-him said.

Let me go, he thought, shaking his feathers at her. Behind her was the sky, and he only knew wanting. If he could fly, he could hunt. He could think. Then the other woman came closer.

"You are right," she almost whispered. "His eyes. It is Hyw."

The bird stared at her, unblinking. Then the hood came down, bringing the darkness with it.

25

Cat was shocked by Hyw, but the hawk was only the beginning. The next day, Margred finally told her about Prince Dafydd's capture. It was a quiet conversation as they prepared the few roots and edible plants they had gathered to make pottage.

"Da must have been furious," Cat said. "It is a wonder Aeneus is not with him."

Margred turned to her, and her already pale face seemed to drain of all colour. "With him?"

"Trying to rescue the prince. That's where he is, is it not? Where have they taken Prince Dafydd?" At Margred's continued silence, Cat stopped breaking a root apart and frowned at her friend. "And where is Mam? And Baby Gwen?"

"Shrewsbury," Margred whispered. "Your mam and baby Gwen were taken prisoner, along with Dafydd's wife and children."

"How did Da let this happen?" Cat asked.

Margred wouldn't look at her. "Your da was a hero," she finally said.

Cat frowned again. This made no sense. Then she heard a roaring in her ears as if the ground was rising to meet her. Margred stepped forward and held her up.

Afterward Cat could not remember what else had been said, only the feeling of the rough plants in her hand, and the splash as she let one drop into the pot, still unpeeled. She did not know whether she had fainted or started screaming or both. Some time later, she realized they were seated together on a fallen log. She was staring into Margred's eyes, and it was as if she had just woken up.

"I am glad to see you back," Margred said quietly.

"Back?"

"Your grief is great, and well it should be," Margred said. "We need you, Cat." The tears threatened at the back of Cat's throat, but she swallowed them down.

Cat demanded that they take her to the place where they had buried her father and the others. It was a day's journey away, but in the end they couldn't stop her. She stood staring at the mound of stones, thankful that animals had not been able to dislodge it. She put her hand on the stone, but Da's spirit was already gone. She wanted to claw off the stones herself and hold him to her. She wanted to search for him in the mist and make sure he had found the way to Garth Celyn, but Aeneus pulled her off the stones and held her. She buried her face in his chest and sobbed.

Over the next few days, Cat pleaded, cajoled, and berated Hyw, but the hawk only blinked its blue-grey eyes back at her. These were Hyw's eyes, but the expression in them was alien. She found herself torn between helping Hyw, rescuing Prince Dafydd, returning to rescue Rhys from the tower at Dolbadarn, and freeing her Mam and the baby, if they had indeed been taken to Shrewsbury with Dafydd and the others.

Instinctively, Cat began to sing the song her ancestors had sung in her vision. If only Gawain were here to sing the harmonies with her. These were old sounds, and she was not sure if they were words. She began softly, but gradually her voice grew in volume and confidence. She found a curled leaf and used it to hold water from a nearby stream, staring into it as she sang. Her mind whirled with questions, but the water remained still. She longed to hold Arthur's crown again, to direct her visions and show her which path to take. Then she realized she would never hold it again. The English king had it now, and with it he would drain all of their strength.

She reached up to touch the locket she still wore, with the lock of hair that connected her to Hyw, and her mind focused. Whatever they took from her, from her people, they would not keep Hyw. She would find him. Her brother seemed unresponsive in his hawk form. Where was he now? How must she appear in his mind when the hawk stared back at her? She rubbed her locket, remembering the day he had given it to her. He had taken a lock of her hair for a similar necklace of his own. Did he still wear it? She checked his neck feathers and saw a dark band of grey, almost like a chain that had transformed with him. If that was true, could she use it somehow to connect with him?

Prince Llywelyn shared Hyw's mind. How might that be working, with Hyw trapped in hawk form? She held the locket as she stared into the water, focusing her mind on Hyw's blue-grey eyes and on the former prince trapped inside his mind with him. A mist began to form around her, as it had when she had guided Cynfrig's spirit back to Garth Celyn. She drew the mist toward her, gradually parting it until she could make out a form. A human form. Then the hawk shrieked. Cat broke from her trance with a start and looked around her.

Margred was calming the hawk, which was dancing on its perch and snapping at its tethers. Aeneus drew near to help, grabbing the bird from behind with the net as Margred held it firm, wings closed to prevent injury.

"Whatever you did stirred him greatly," Margred told Cat. "Have you strength to try again?"

In answer, Cat turned to the leaf, and began the song again, louder this time. She eased into the mist again in search of her brother. She heard a sound, almost like a moaning, and she followed it. She almost stumbled over a form, and crouched down to find Llywelyn, lying prone on what appeared to be rocky ground. He stirred like one in a fever, and she bent closer. He was hot to the touch, his face gaunt and ill.

"Waken, my liege," she said. "Hyw is lost to us, and you must help me find him."

Garth Celyn, Llywelyn mumbled, his eyes fluttering and then closing again.

Cat frowned, but before she could react Llywelyn lunged at her. *Save yourself!* The prince's voice was a harsh rasp, and as he grabbed for her, Cat backed up—and out of the trance again.

The hawk seemed even more agitated, but Aeneus and Margred held it firm. Margred nodded to her again.

Cat strove to focus before she attempted to contact Llywelyn again. What had happened? They were miles from Garth Celyn, and the others had told her there was nothing left to see there. Unless—

She had found Garth Celyn for Cynfrig. And once before, with Ifan, the young warrior from Garth Celyn who had guarded them so well at Criccieth and given his life to save her from their enemies. When his spirit fled his body, she had helped his spirit find Garth Celyn, to lay his soul to rest there. Could she find it again now? Could she transport them to it? Would she find her da again there? Part of her longed to know, and part of her knew a strange dread.

In her memory, it was the kind of home the bards sang about around the fire, where she imagined the legendary King Arthur to have lived. Closing her eyes, she sank immediately into her trance. She waved her hand across the mist and saw a glow on the horizon. A tower, windows golden in the setting sun, the way it looked in the evenings when she, Hyw, and the other children returned from swimming at the waterfall. There was Ty Hir, the longhouse. There were the stone buildings and the dwellings that housed Llywelyn's *teulu*, his family of warriors, his bodyguard. Her family. She recalled the people and placed them as she remembered them, one by one: the warriors in their red tunics with gold torques, and the women and children who called them "Husband" and "Da." She heard a sweet voice carrying on the tune of their ancestors.

And there he was. Da. He waved and she longed to run to him, but she felt for Llywelyn in the mist, never taking her eyes off the scene in front of her. Finally she heard the prince stir beside her.

"Look," she said to the prince. "Look now, and see what was, and what will ever be."

Loathe to take her own eyes from the vision she was creating, lest it fade into the white mist that surrounded them, she heard Llywelyn move to her side.

She is there, he said in wonder. *Elinor, my love.*

Cat saw her too, the princess, alive and lovely again, carrying flowers in her arms to decorate the halls. She waved, too, and then the vision began to fade.

Nay, cried the prince. *Tarry there for me.*

"I wait for you, my Lion." The voice was faint but distinctly Elinor's, and they both heard it before the vision dissolved in swirling mist. When Cat turned to him, her tears overflowed, and the former prince covered his face with a hand. His voice was husky.

What do you want of me now?

"My liege," Cat told him softly. "I would not hurt you more."

Do not think it, he said, wiping his face and turning to her. *You have restored me, to know she waits there for me. We must go forward, to the end, whatever it holds for us. What is it that you need?*

Oh, so much, she wanted to say. Da alive, Mam's arms around me, Rhys by my side. But the shadow of their former prince could not help her with any of those things. She wiped her eyes and raised her face to his.

"Hyw is lost, my liege, and cannot return to us."

Now that I am found again, he soon will be. I will reach him. But I may need help to bring him back to himself.

"I will help in any way I can."

I know it, but there is another, a young man who fostered with your brother.

"James!" Cat stared at Llywelyn. "What do you know of him?"

Only that he holds a special bond with Hyw. James may provide a tether stronger than either you or I or any here can give your brother. If he is willing.

They heard a caw and looked up to see a tree branch in the mist, and on it a large black raven. Cocking its head, it opened its beak to caw again. But a large red hawk swooped down at it from above. The raven vanished, leaving one black feather drifting down toward them.

The hawk grew in size, and trained its yellow eyes on Catrin. Yellow eyes? It opened its wings and shrieked at them both. It swelled and grew until its shadow covered them, wings outstretched in menace.

Mind yourself, Lady Catrin, the prince said, keeping his eyes on the bird as he stepped forward to face it.

The feather drifted closer and Cat reached for it almost by reflex. As she grasped it, the feather transformed into a large sword, like the one Llywelyn had wielded in life. It was heavy enough to overbalance Cat and she nearly dropped it. But she kept hold of the hilt and let the tip drop to the ground instead.

"My lord," she said. "This must be meant for you."

Llywelyn glanced back, and the hawk took that moment to swoop down at them, talons forward, shrieking and beating the air with its wings. Llywelyn grabbed for the sword and swung it around. The huge bird drew up in mid-air. Its talons raked at the sword as it dodged away and swerved upward into the air. It circled to come at them again. Llywelyn took a step back. Holding the sword in front of them with one hand, he reached back toward her with the other.

You must go. And quickly.

He pushed her and she tumbled out of the mist and away.

26

The hawk screamed with fury as the young woman fell backward, to disappear in the mist.

And who was she, that she could call the black raven and use its feathers?

No matter. She had trespassed on his dreamtime. These two-legged creatures, these humans, kept him from his freedom. And now this man would defy him again. Too many times the man had tried to interfere. Nightly they fought, and nightly the sharpness of beak and talons drove the man back. Yet, each time they fought, something had kept the hawk from delivering the killing blow.

No more.

Rage made him scream again. The human leapt at him. The bird smelled the tang of the sharp metal as it split the air between them. The force of it ruffled his feathers and he reared back. With his wings, he dragged the air forward to protect himself. He pivoted and turned his wings to gain purchase in the sky, circling overhead, preparing to attack again.

This time he would show no mercy.

Llywelyn raised his sword up and to the side, crossing his hands on the hilt for extra strength. He sliced down with as much force as he could

muster, arcing the blade and swinging through to find the next striking position.

If he could frighten the bird, keep it from attacking again, maybe he could get to Hyw. Where was the lad? He lowered the sword, holding the hilt at his left hip with the long edge up, ready to strike.

Hyw! Where are you?

Llywelyn called out with the battlefield voice that had led his army to success more than once. The great bird faltered, circling, its wings holding the air. As it turned toward him in a long, slow arc, a hint of blue-grey peeked through the yellow eyes.

The hawk crowned his neck feathers. Raising his wings, he bent his head down to stare at the man. He knew this creature. There was something between them. Sunshine, glinting off a longhouse roof. Figures on a board. Someone shouting, Have at us! His voice?

Who did he call? Hyw?

As the bird circled, he saw his own shadow cover the man and the land where he stood. All wings and claws, like some grotesque beast from the past. That was what he was. Yet was it? Something churned inside him. He opened his beak suddenly and screamed.

Kee-eeee-aaah!

Then he folded in his wings and plummeted toward the man below, talons thrusting forward.

Llywelyn stood his ground. His could already see the thrust, using the bird's momentum against it, to skewer it on the blade. Then the impossible happened. The bird grew again. One moment it was the size of a man, and the next it was the size of a gryffyn.

Screaming like a soul damned, it kept growing. The sword would be little more than a pinprick to it now. Its talons thrust toward him, sharp and gleaming. Llywelyn did the only thing he could do. He dropped the sword and dove in a forward roll, under the feathered beast as it plummeted past him.

The beast landed and turned to meet him, surprisingly agile. Llywelyn crouched. The sword was behind the beast now, useless. But it did not attack. It stared at him, eyes turning from yellow to blue.

It was Hyw. Trapped inside a nightmare. A place Llywelyn knew well.

Hyw screamed again, not with rage this time but with anguish. Loneliness. Despair. And Llywelyn felt the sound torn from his own throat.

Elinor!

Then the beast turned and ran into the trees. And all that was left was the black feather.

27

Cat found herself on the ground. Margred knelt near her, holding her hand. The shrieking and thrashing she had heard as she left the spirit realm followed her. When she turned to where Hyw was tethered, she saw Aeneus fighting to calm the bird. Even with the hood, Hyw was giving the warrior no quarter.

Then Aeneus began singing to the hawk. Not the wordless song Cat had sung, but a love song. It was a song of lost love and sorrow, and she shivered at the passion in his rich baritone. She had never heard him sing anything but a hymn in church or a warrior's song around the campfire, but now his voice seemed suited to nothing else. Margred joined in, adding the harmonies.

"Sleep well, my love/ And my dreams of you will last/ Until I hold you in my arms again…"

Hyw stopped fighting to listen, as if the words meant something to him through the haze of his enchanted prison. Gradually he calmed and his struggles ceased. As Cat watched the bird, Llywelyn's words came back to her. *If he is willing.* James was deep within the English camp. Even if she could find him, would he believe what had happened to Hyw? And even if he believed her, would he be willing to help her brother?

As the song ended, Cat struggled to her feet, and Margred rushed to help her up. Aeneus stood near Hyw. The bird was calm now, his hooded head slumped onto his chest as if he slept.

"Did it work?" Margred asked.

Cat tried to give her friend a reassuring look. "Come, both of you," she said, gesturing Aeneus closer to them. "I have much to tell you."

She explained some of what Llywelyn had said. Aeneus stood near Hyw, who was still hooded, and Margred sat on the other side of the bird. Cat wanted to avoid telling it all, or at least to spare Margred. Plus she wasn't convinced that Hyw slumbered. But in the end, Cat could only hold her friend's gaze as she spoke.

"Llywelyn believes there is one who holds a special bond with my brother. He believes this person may offer Hyw a different kind of tether." *If he is willing.*

Aeneus frowned and glanced toward Margred. Margred's eyes showed sympathy but little surprise.

"Who is it?" Margred said.

Cat hesitated. "Have you heard him speak of James?"

"The boy from Shrewsbury? He is a kind of foster brother, I think." Margred showed a dawning understanding. "And will this James help Hyw?"

"That I do not know." Cat glanced at Aeneus to catch a look of concern in his eyes.

"He is English," Aeneus said, looking away. "The English do not easily hold with such—feelings."

"No," said Margred, "but the Welsh believe in love. And James is half Welsh, is he not?"

Cat nodded. "His mam was one of Da's cousins." The loss of her da tore like a barb in her heart even as she said it.

"But he was raised English." Aeneus looked grim, and Hyw suddenly flexed and cried out under his hood. The warrior ducked away, but Margred crooned softly to Hyw without moving.

"You seem—unconcerned. I—" Cat was at a loss to explain. "I thought you two were close."

"We are." Margred watched Hyw. "He was the one person who understood my love for Drem, even when it was hopeless. Perhaps his own love is equally so." She looked back at Cat, her eyes glittering with unshed tears. "You are lucky in your brother, Cat. And I am lucky in my friend."

"As am I, lucky in my friends," Cat responded.

Margred stood. "We must find James." Again, the hawk moved restlessly against the tethers, shifting its head in the hood and crying plaintively. "Do not fret, Hyw. You cannot know the heart of another. And we must ask, for your sake. We need you back, my friend. And we must hope that James needs you as much as we do."

Or more, Cat thought fervently.

Cat pushed them hard, but the route from the mountains to Shrewsbury was not an easy one at the best of times, and they carried the big hawk with them. The trio decided they could avoid trouble best by staying off the main roads. Without Hyw's ability to keep watch on the English, Aeneus and Margred had to take turns scouting ahead. What few plants they passed, Cat gathered as they walked, repeating her mam's lessons over to herself as she pocketed each one. Signs of the English army passing had flattened much of the countryside.

All three took turns holding Hyw on the rough leather-and-netting perch that Aeneus had fashioned to hold him. Hyw was too often skittish and uncooperative, even tethered and hooded. Aeneus was comfortable with falconry, but Cat could tell he was not comfortable with Hyw's obvious distress.

"I almost think he doesn't want us to find this James," he told her once, when Margred was scouting ahead and he was carrying Hyw. "Are you sure we must?"

Cat pursed her lips. "Take off the hood."

Aeneus moved quickly to avoid Hyw's sharp beak. Hyw shook his head and crowned his neck feathers. Raising his wings, he bent his neck down to stare at her with those familiar yet alien blue-grey eyes.

"You must calm yourself, Hyw," she said. "You will do yourself harm, or you will harm one of us." Hyw bobbed his head and lowered his wings, but his neck feathers remained ruffled. He opened his beak suddenly and screamed a long kee-eeee-arr. Cat almost stepped back involuntarily, but stopped herself. She stood her ground, careful not to challenge him by looking into his eyes, and waited until he finished before she spoke again.

"I promise you this: if James does not agree, we will not force him to see you. And if he will not see you, then we will let you go."

"You can't mean it," Aeneus said.

"I do."

Hyw blinked at her. She kept her eyes trained on his neck feathers and held still. He moved up and down on the perch, shook his head and body, and finally preened down the errant feathers. Then he turned to look back at her again. He seemed more calm, and Cat began to sing one of the old songs. She turned to walk, and Aeneus kept pace with her. Hyw did not fight them again.

On the second day, they met up with two Welshmen. Aeneus clasped forearms with one and introduced him as Dai, a warrior who had served with Aeneus in the war of 1277. Dai in turn introduced his son Cadoc, a boy of about twelve years.

"We are bound for the borderland," Dai said. "I would take my son to safety with his mother's people. We have little to share but Cadoc is good with a bow."

"We have but the one," Aeneus replied.

Margred carried her arrows in a quiver on her back, along with her yew bow already tied on one end to be ready more quickly. She moved the quiver protectively away from the men. Hyw, perched on her arm, moved his talons up and down and bent his neck to peer at them. Dai eyed the big hawk, but said nothing.

"You are welcome to share whatever I catch," Margred told them. Hyw flapped and shrieked, but she popped the hook back over his head.

A grin spread across Dai's face. "That one must bring in a good fare."

"He is newly caught and not yet trained," Aeneus said. "But we have hopes for him."

They fell into step together, and Aeneus took Dai for a turn at scouting. Cat wished she had her knives, but she trusted Aeneus' experience. She had more pressing matters to occupy her as they walked. She longed for news of Rhys. In all the time since she had left him imprisoned at Dolbadarn castle, her only vision had come through her connection with Llywelyn in Hyw's mind. What did it mean—and what was the meaning of the raven she saw when the vision ended?

As they passed the English border on their way to Shrewsbury, game became more plentiful. Aeneus tied a long training line to Hyw so they wouldn't lose him, and allowed him to hunt. Cat was surprised to see her brother bring his kill back and drop it at Margred's feet. He could not be far gone if he could remember the hawk's role in the hunt without training.

She and Margred pounded some of the meat into thin strips mixed with berries, and dried it in the sun. They cooked some over a small fire, keeping watch nervously for any sign of enemy troops.

With full bellies they made better time, and Hyw was calmer. Still, it took them almost four days to get to Shrewsbury. The countryside offered rowan, sessile oak, and ancient yew trees. When they made camp near the town, Cat was able to join in the watch by climbing into the branches. Aeneus and Dai used fallen and freshly cut branches to make a lean-to shelter in a thicket. Cat and Margred found an area nearby that had been used for campfires previously, and scoured out a clay pot that looked promising for pottage. It seemed safe enough, now they were in England, to make a small cooking fire in the shelter of the trees.

Dai and Cadoc proved their worth when they slipped away into the town of Shrewsbury, to return with a shank of smoked ham and a sack of root vegetables, although they would not say how they came by the goods. To their credit, they hadn't nibbled even a bite on their way back. Soon all of them were eating well for the first time in several weeks. Dai had other news as well.

"Dafydd is held in the dungeons of Shrewsbury castle," he said. "And that is not all. They say the Lord of Shrewsbury disgraced himself by arguing for clemency for the prince."

"Clemency?" Aeneus asked, frowning.

"Aye, it seems Prince Dafydd is injured, and the old lord

believed he should have a doctor's care. Mortimer built up some connection between Shrewsbury and a Welsh rebel, so the story goes, and had him arrested for it."

Hyw moved on his perch and shrieked.

"What of Dafydd's sons?" Aeneus asked.

"Owain and Llew are to be sent to the south of England, they say," Dai responded. "Gwenllian and the other girls are all being sent to a convent."

"Which one?" Margred asked.

"I heard more than one, Lady Margred, but nothing seems certain. I was thankful to hear your sisters will be treated gently, although the king has not said what he will do with your father."

"Did you hear of my mam?" Cat put in. "Lady Adara? Or the Princess Elizabeth?"

"Some believe the Lady Elizabeth, as they call her now, and other Welsh ladies—could be your mam among them—have returned to Wales. Others say they are in house arrest in the castle."

"Worry not, Cat," said Aeneus. "We will find them."

Hyw shrieked again, spreading his wings impatiently, and Margred spoke up.

"What of Lord Shrewsbury's son and heir, James? He would be about sixteen years."

"No Englishman mentioned him," said Dai, shaking his head. "That would have been cause for talk, I warrant. Most likely he is still at liberty, perhaps within the castle itself."

"James may have news of your mam, Cat," Aeneus put in, before Dai could ask any questions of his own. "I will go and see if I can find him."

"No," Margred stood. "I will go. My father—"

"We will both go," said Cat, breaking in before Margred could finish. She trusted Aeneus' judgement but the friendliness that allowed Dai to find out information could work both ways. He did not need to know who Margred's father was. "We both have kin in the town. Besides, it will be safer for two women to go to market together than one alone."

"Safer still for a man," said Aeneus.

"But not so safe for a Welshman," Dai put in. "Your skills

are formidable in the wilds of Wales, my friend, but you would be a sight in a town like Shrewsbury. Well, you might pass, with all the knights and such coming and going these days. But you would have to speak English."

Aeneus made a gruff sound in his throat and crossed his arms. Dai only laughed before he continued. "There is a market this week. If they can get in and out again before the gates close, it may well be safer for the women."

Later that evening, Dai and Cadoc divided up the remaining food with Margred.

"There's enough to last at least two days," Margred said. "For you and for us."

"You should stay with us." Aeneus clapped Dai on the shoulder. "We will need all the good men we can get to rescue the prince."

Dai turned his head to the side a little. "It is well past planting time," he said. "And my lad's mam will be wondering if he be alive or dead."

Aeneus looked into the distance for a moment, but he nodded. "You are lucky to have them both. Go with God."

Cat watched their two new friends take their leave the following day with mixed emotions. She had enjoyed Dai's garrulous nature and Cadoc's gentleness, but she was glad not to have to hide her brother's true state any longer. Aeneus turned to her almost before the two had rounded the bend.

"I promised your mam I would keep you safe. You and your brother."

"Margred and I have a better chance together than you alone," she said. "We cannot all three go, and Hyw with us, and not raise suspicion in the town. We cannot release Hyw, and know he will come back to us, so one of us must stay to protect him."

"You should remain here, with your brother."

"But only I know what James looks like." At her words Aeneus frowned but said nothing. She touched his arm. "We only have to find James and bring him back with us. We will take no risks. If we do not find him, we will return and find another way."

Finally he reached into his leather boot and brought out a knife, handing it to her. "You may need this."

Cat felt more secure with the knife tucked into her sturdy boot. She and Margred were both dressed in tunics and leggings. They carried the sack Dai and his son had brought with them the previous day, now filled with sticks and leaves, as if they had something to trade in the market. When they passed a farmhouse, Margred gestured with her finger along her lips and pulled Cat down into the shelter of bushes near the road. Margred disappeared for a time and returned with a bundle. She drew Cat further down the road before she let her see the skirts she had obviously stolen from a clothesline. They pulled the damp skirts over their trousers, letting them dry as they walked the rest of the way to the walled town of Shrewsbury.

To get into the town, they would need to cross the Severn River, passing through the six stone arches of St. George's Bridge. As they neared the bridge, Margred pulled Cat aside and they hid at the edge of the lane. Margred gestured to the peasants, traders, and servants passing across the bridge and chatting. Cat was amazed as her friend seemed to transform from a well-bred lady to a slouching kitchen maid. She playfully touched Cat's arm, and Cat tried to imitate her movements, swinging her hips and rounding her shoulders. Margred finally whispered, "Stay behind me and don't talk."

"Unless we need to, you mean?"

"Just stay behind me."

"But how would you know better than me—" she started to ask, but Margred interrupted her.

"My da might be a prince, but my mam was a servant," Margred said. "Trust me. These people, this place, I know well enough. Besides, my English is better than yours."

Stepping in with a group of other market-goers, Margred

led Cat through the Mardol gate into the town without incident. Cat was glad to walk arm-in-arm with Margred as they made their way through the crowd in the town market. The last time they had walked so together had been to Criccieth market, where Margred had introduced Drem. Cat stopped herself from mentioning it, rather than bring up what might now be an unpleasant reminder for her friend. Ifan had been with them, too, and Cat allowed herself to smile at the memory. For so many things, all they had left was remembering.

But Shrewsbury's market was a marvel of paving stones and modernity. Men, women, and even families with young children milled through the market as Cat and Margred made their way to Shrewsbury castle. It lay on a hill at the north end of the town, so neither friend nor enemy could continue into England without passing through it. Conversation rose and fell around them, in English, French, Flemish, and other languages she had heard at court in Garth Celyn. Here and there she heard a spattering of Welsh, but she dared not look in case they knew the speaker and were recognized. She and Margred circled the market, pretending to be interested in the stalls as they listened.

"…seem ripe to you…"

"… the younger the pig, the sweeter…"

"…that Welsh devil… dungeons…"

Cat turned as a woman nearby called out, "Kill him and God be praised." The woman turned away and crossed herself, leaving Cat to wonder if she meant the words or was only trying to stay alive in these troubled times.

"…old lord of Shrewsbury himself…"

"I heard it was his son…"

Margred paused at those words. The two girls feigned interest in a merchant extolling the virtues of "fine English finishing to Welsh wool" as they drifted closer to listen. Cat heard snatches of English and French that she recognized. Margred, more fluent in both, pinched her elbow and whispered, "He will be in the exercise yard now."

"How will we get in?" Cat whispered back.

Margred only nodded and pulled Cat toward the castle. Cat

took a quick look around to get her bearings and realized Margred was leading them into the outer bailey. Margred managed to look like she had a job to perform and moved purposefully into the courtyard. Knights were paired up with wooden exercise swords in the centre of the yard, bashing each other almost as viciously as if they'd been on the battlefield. A water bucket had been hung near a set of quintains, and a young woman leaned against the central pole of one of them, staring off in the direction of the marketplace. Margred headed right for her before Cat could ask what she had planned.

"They need you in the kitchens," she said to the girl. Without hesitation, the other girl ran off and left them to it.

"How did—"

"She was bored," Margred said. "That much was obvious. Do you see him?"

Cat squinted at the knights until she recognized James fighting a bigger boy. She pointed him out as James took a blow to the side that knocked him down. Margred took down the bucket and headed in that direction, Cat following close behind. Margred scooped water into a wooden ladle and handed it to Cat, jerking her head toward James. Cat went toward him as the bigger boy moved off in search of another partner. James took the ladle without looking at her, until she crouched beside him.

"Hyw needs you," she whispered.

James started. "What—? Lady Catrin?"

Before he could finish, Cat took his arm. Margred put down the bucket to help Cat bring him to his feet.

"This way." James followed as they made their way off the field toward the town. Luckily no one challenged them as they walked through the crowd and back toward the bridge.

"What are you about?" James hissed. "I will be missed—"

"You must come with us," Cat said.

"Is Hyw injured?"

Cat frowned. "You know of his gift?" As James nodded, she continued. "Something has gone wrong. He is not hurt, but he is not himself, either."

"If you care for him, you must come," Margred put in.

"Of course."

"No, not of course." Cat stopped him, thinking again of Llywelyn's words. "I made a promise to Hyw that I would bring you only if you are truly willing. I believe you are the only one who can help him find himself. But you must know…" She searched for the words to explain what she was asking. "My brother is a complicated man. He loves few, but he loves deeply. If you are truly his friend, you must know him this well."

"Your brother is my dearest friend," James told her, taking her hand. His warm brown eyes looked directly into hers and she saw only frankness and concern in them. "If he needs me, then I will come. But what has happened to him? You must tell me."

"It's best that you come and see."

James showed them a shortcut through the market to St. George's Bridge. After they had safely crossed it, Cat explained as best she could what happened to Hyw after their father died. James in turn answered her questions about the prince.

"When we heard Prince Dafydd was injured, my father tried to get better treatment for him." James sounded proud of his da, and to Cat it seemed justified.

"Dafydd is a nobleman," he went on, "and the Prince of Wales, as all could see. He deserved better than a dungeon cell. Mortimer said we were Welsh sympathizers. He convinced the king that my father should be secured in his rooms lest he dare something more on Dafydd's behalf."

"And your mam?" Margred asked.

"I have not seen my stepmother since my father was first confined," James said, frowning. "She has returned to my grandfather's home in the south of England. I could have gone with her, but I could not leave my father."

"Have you been able to see him?" Cat asked.

James shook his head. "Mortimer kept on it, even…" James' voice trailed off.

"What?" Cat prompted him.

"He used my mother."

Cat knew James' mam had been Welsh, although she died giving birth to him and his dad later remarried. It had been one of the reasons they chose to send Hyw to foster with Lord Shrewsbury.

She reached out and took James' hand.

"Finally the king had my father thrown into the dungeon along with the prince." James' voice was soft. "Yet it seems we still have friends. An old servant managed to get word from him to me. He told me I should escape if I could. Father fears Mortimer plans to take our castle too."

"Do they not fear you, as his heir?" Margred asked.

"I am too young to inherit and too friendless to win it back." James shrugged. "So I am left to my own devices, it seems."

Cat and Margred exchanged glances. In Wales, he could have been a landowner at fourteen. Cat wondered how long he would have to wait in England, unless he could fight for his due. She raised her eyebrows yet again at the strangeness of the English.

"But who will run your castle, if not you?" Margred, ever her father's daughter, could not let it lie.

"My father serves the king," James told her. "It will be up to the king to decide who replaces him."

Margred shook her head. "The English king, again." Then she reached out to him. "But you do have friends, James. You are welcome with us."

James thanked her, but Cat could see little hope in his rounded shoulders and drawn mouth. That became even more pronounced when they saw Hyw in his present form. The hawk was tethered and hooded, but bobbed his head when he heard James' voice. James tried to move closer, but the hawk began to hop on its perch in agitation and spread its wings.

Cat sang the ancient song, and Hyw calmed. James had left the practice field in armour, with his sword at his side, even though they had been using wooden swords in the exercise. He removed his chain mail and undid the sword belt before he approached again.

"I could not believe it when your sister told me of your fate," James said softly to Hyw, moving closer. "Do you remember the first time I saw you in my father's barn, speaking in your mind with our horses? I could see the truth in you then. And it was wondrous."

The bird hopped again, but this time it seemed as if he was listening intently to James. Cat began her song again as Margred and

Aeneus joined her. The three of them kept watch together as James talked with Hyw.

"But it was you that I saw, Hyw, and I see you now. You cannot hide from me, and you cannot hide from your fate. Or from us, here, your sister, your friends, and I. I thought I had lost you when we parted at Dolwyddelan. So many times I thought I saw you in a passing bird, only to find myself alone again. You cannot imagine my joy at hearing that you were alive and well. When I saw you across the battlefield, I could not believe you were not beside me. We are meant to be together, Hyw. If you will stay a hawk, then I will become a falconer. But if you would be a man, then come back to me."

Cat continued to sing until they saw the hawk's body twist. Aeneus dropped the stout stick he was holding and ran to lift off the hawk's hood and tear the line binding him to the perch. Cat's hands shook as she drew the knife from her boot and cut the jesses around his talons.

"Keep singing," Margred hissed.

Hyw gave a shrill shriek and James called out, "Hyw!"

28

Hyw opened his eyes to pain. He curled his talons around his perch as he heard James calling his name. Cat was still singing that dreaded song. His body twisted again and then reformed into the hawk.

Finally the bindings fell from him. He opened his wings and half flew to the ground. He twisted again, his bones cracking like stone grating on stone. He steeled himself as his spine popped and crackled. Pain ripped through him. His limbs trembled, his muscles distended under the returning skin, and his heart thudded in his ears until his head nearly split. With a yell, he burst into human form.

Finally he lay on the ground, naked, curled into his man-shape again. Hyw stared around him, unable to think through the pain. His shoulder was twisted at a horrible angle, and his ankles were cut and bleeding. His eyes sought—something. And found James, staring back at him. His friend's eyes were round in shock, and he had covered his mouth with both hands.

"Bring cloth to bind his wounds," Cat cried, and Margred snapped to her feet, running for her pack. Someone pulled him upright. Aeneus. The warrior turned him slightly away from the others, grabbed Hyw's shoulder, and twisted it back into its socket. Hyw screamed once, and then stopped. He began to shiver and Aeneus covered him with a cloak and held it firmly against him.

"Better?" Aeneus asked, still holding him up, but Hyw did not respond. Cat rushed forward, grabbing the discarded netting to staunch the bleeding. Margred brought ointment and both women began to apply bandages to the cuts on his ankles. Aeneus lifted Hyw in his arms like a child, and held him while they worked.

"Welcome back, Hyw," Aeneus said, "you and the one within you." Then Aeneus sat him down on the ground, bracing his head and shoulders. They gathered around him, waiting for him to regain his strength. Hyw closed his eyes and saw Llywelyn lying propped against a tree trunk, panting and shadowed. Opening his eyes, Hyw sought James again, and the sight of his friend's blanched face and wide eyes brought him back to himself.

"Do not look at me so," Hyw said, his voice grating in his throat. He attempted a weak laugh. "You make me feel a monster or worse."

James shook his head, but still did not speak. Hyw cringed. How had Margred been able to see him change without shrinking away, when James couldn't bear the sight? Then he felt a hand on his shoulder, through the fabric of the cloak. He turned to find James kneeling near him.

"It—it is strange, Hyw." James looked directly into his eyes, without faltering. "But I have known your secret since we were pages together. I am proud to be one who shares it with you, and I am proudest of you for returning to us."

Us. Hyw lay a few moments longer, recovering. It was not all he wanted to hear, but it was enough for now. James had kept Hyw's secret—even through the beatings by Robert and the older boys— and he was here now. Come back to me, he had said. Hyw reached up to place his hand over his friend's.

And I am proud of you also, Hyw. Llywelyn's voice rasped inside his head.

It took almost a week for the wounds to close on Hyw's ankles. His shoulder had not pained him as much as he expected, after Aeneus popped it back into place. James stayed with him as he healed, although they were not as close as Hyw had hoped. On occasion he reached for James' hand, but his friend found a reason to break contact. Hyw could not blame him, and shame burned through him for what he had made James witness.

Do not think it, Hyw. Llywelyn tried to reassure him, but Hyw would not listen.

Yet James remained, and they talked and talked. James shared the story of his father's imprisonment. Often they were joined by the others, and James shared what he knew. King Edward planned to put Prince Dafydd on trial, but no date had been set for it yet. Elizabeth and Adara were both being held in the castle, but James confirmed the rumours they had heard about the girls being sent away.

"They would not say where they were taking them," James said. "But each rode off with a different company of knights."

"He doesn't make it easy for us," rumbled Aeneus. "And what of Dafydd's sons, Owain and Llew?"

"They were taken as well."

"Then there can be only one choice for us." Aeneus folded his arms across his broad chest. "If we know not where or how to rescue the children, then first we must rescue the prince from the dungeons of Shrewsbury castle."

We must not forget Gwenllian and the other children, Llywelyn said.

Hyw closed his eyes and spoke only to the former prince, so the others could not hear him. "We will not forget them, my liege, or my mam if she is yet with them, or James' father. But we must make a start where we can."

Llywelyn nodded. *Once we have Dafydd back with us again, we can plan their rescue.*

Hyw watched James answering Aeneus but he focused inward on Llywelyn, wondering how the prince would react if he chose to remain with James, rather than going on a rescue mission. If Hyw did go to help rescue the children, would James be content to wait for him to return? Hyw shook himself. There would be time to worry about that once they had rescued the prince and James' father.

One evening Cat was sitting nearby. When James got up to get them more food, Hyw turned to her. "Do you think…" His voice trailed off.

"That it would happen again?" Cat said. "That you might be trapped in the form of a—an animal?"

She looked away from him. Had she meant to say hawk? Did she think even the word dangerous to him? She turned back, speaking quietly and earnestly. "I think we understand more how to prevent it now." She cast a quick look toward James.

Without warning, the hawk form flashed into Hyw's mind, and he looked down at his hands to keep her from seeing his expression. Even after all that had happened, he still expected, even wanted, talons.

Rely on your training, Hyw. Llywelyn's voice rasped in his ear. *You are a warrior now, as agile as any and more skilled than most. You must use what your gift has given you in defence of your country.*

Since their return to human shape, the former prince seemed fiercer and harder to please. Hyw had a vague recollection of fighting with Llywelyn and a lingering sense of guilt that made him try harder to do the prince's bidding. Gawain had warned them: it was up to Hyw to be sure their strange bonding didn't drive one or both of them mad. But no matter what Hyw did, he had a sense that often Llywelyn found him wanting.

As on most evenings, the group sat together after their meagre supper and talked through their options for rescuing Dafydd. They all agreed that they would find James' father and bring him with them as well, to bolster their numbers. Hyw sat on a log, aching to see his mother again, as he watched Aeneus draw plans in the dirt with a twig he had been whittling. The warrior grilled James for information about the castle layout and the number of guards on each floor.

"Where are they holding Mam and Lady Elizabeth?" Hyw asked.

James frowned and shook his head. "In one of the upstairs rooms. I am not certain," he said. "If I went back—"

"No," Hyw said automatically. "It is too dangerous."

"My information is days old," James fretted. "More nobles arrive each day from across England for Dafydd's trial."

Aeneus grimaced and threw down the twig. "We must know more before we act."

As the group broke off to bed down for the night, Hyw could not get over the restless churning inside him. He offered to take first watch, and stood looking out at the forest.

There is one among us who can get inside safely. Hyw closed his eyes to face Llywelyn. The prince's face was as hard as the slate mountain, and his eyes glittered a challenge. *You must try it, Hyw. Aeneus is right. We must have more information, and you are the only one who can get it—if you can keep control of your gift.*

"I can do it."

"Do what?

Hyw opened his eyes to see James staring at him with concern. Hyw realized he must have spoken the words aloud. Surely it was not yet time for James to take second watch. Impulsively, Hyw reached out toward his friend, but softened the gesture so he merely placed his hand on James' arm.

"I can get the information we need."

"You are not fully recovered yet." James placed his free hand on top of Hyw's. "We will find a way, but we must plan it carefully."

"No, I mean I can use my gift. No one needs to set foot in the castle until we are ready."

James shifted to take Hyw by the shoulders, concern on his face. "But if you change—"

Hyw frowned. "I am not as fragile as you think. I can use my connection to animals and resist the full change. I have done it many times before."

"I believe you," James said, releasing him. "But after what you have been through, shouldn't you rest until you have recovered more?"

"What good is there in rest?" Hyw shook his head in frustration. He agreed with Llywelyn, even though he knew Cat and Aeneus would never hear of it. But there was a way, if he could convince James to help him. That now seemed more important than anything or anyone else.

"Mam told me my grandfather had this same gift, and held his form with the help of my grandmother. She was his tether, do you see? As Mam was mine. With such a tether, I can use my gift without fear. I can see through the eyes of an animal without becoming one."

"Yes, there is sense in it." James frowned in concentration.

"But without your mam here, who can act as this tether for you? Your sister?"

Hyw shook his head. How could he explain what he felt? Then James grabbed his arm again.

"Me?" James said. Hyw started to shrug away, but James would not let go. "You mean I could do this for you? You must know I would, willingly."

Hyw half-turned back to his friend. James continued in a rush. "I have always known the truth of your gift, Hyw, and I have never turned from it or from you. And now, with my father in prison as well—"

Hyw could see James' mouth moving, but the roaring in his ears blotted out the sound of his friend's voice. Of course. James would do anything to help his father. That was who he loved. And it was right that he should. James was a good son and it was fitting that he loved his father. Hyw knew the depth of his feeling for James at that moment, but he knew he must put aside his own feelings to help his friend. He drew in a ragged breath and forced himself to listen to the words.

"I will do everything I can to help," James was saying. "If I can turn the tide for you, then only say how, and it shall be done."

Hyw nodded, releasing his arm from James' grip but keeping his eyes averted. "I will find your father, James. That I can promise you. But this must stay between the two of us, at least until I can test the idea further."

Hyw tossed and turned until nearly dawn, when he fell into a deep and unsatisfying sleep. James shook him all too soon, and the chilly grey light did little to raise his spirits as they parted company with the others. They took some snares to set as if they were going hunting, but James took the lead along the same shortcut through the woods that he had shown the girls a few days earlier.

He also challenged Hyw to climb a large ancient oak so they could see over Shrewsbury's walls, and Hyw was surprised at how good it felt to climb with his hands and feet again. The thick branches held and concealed them. As Hyw shifted his leg to make room for James, he caught himself thinking about how much lighter the bones of a bird would be. He pushed the image away, even as he heard Llywelyn say, *Steady.*

Hyw was still concerned about transforming outright, but he wanted to see his mam again to be sure she was well. And of course, he had to find Prince Dafydd and James' father. He could get to the castle easily as a bird, but it would not help him once he was inside. He had found it easier to shift from one animal shape to another than to return to human form, but the pull towards the bird was too strong for him to trust it completely. He could not try it again so soon.

Yet you must manage somehow, Hyw. You must try. Hyw did not want to close his eyes and confront the prince, so he kept his eyes on James instead.

"What about connecting with the minds of animals, as you did before?" James said. "A dog or cat, perhaps?"

Hyw shook his head. "I tried them both, remember?" His early experiments connecting with pets at Shrewsbury had not gone well. "The dogs felt too much obedience for their masters, and the cats too much independence."

They settled on the branch of the large oak in a companionable silence. After a moment, the oak seemed to settle around them. A slight breeze sent its long, lobed leaves rustling. The trills and chortles and whistles of the birds began again, as if the boys had disappeared into the oak's furrowed bark. Hyw relaxed and heard the faint rustlings of creatures around him in the grass. He probed gently toward them with his mind.

"What do you see?" James asked.

"Mouse," Hyw said, with a shudder, but James raised his eyebrows.

"Aren't rodents the natural prey of the hawk?"

Hyw nodded and grimaced. "I have no wish to become one of them."

"Perhaps that's what you need to keep from shifting." James smirked. "And it will manage well inside the castle."

Hyw tried to focus on the mouse, but he was restless and could not seem to settle. James rested near him, and for a moment all he heard was their combined breathing. After a few moments, he turned to James.

"It isn't working."

"Perhaps it is too soon," James said. "Do not fret. We have come this far, at least."

Do not give up, Hyw, Llywelyn said. *We need you now.*

Just as his spirits began sinking, Hyw's stomach growled loudly. James guffawed, and then they were both laughing. Hyw was sure that even Llywelyn chuckled a little.

"Let us go back and break our fast first," James said, still laughing.

Hyw nodded. "But we will try again later," he assured them both.

29

Cat was already awake when the sun began to play its fingers across the dawn sky. She fretted with the weight of her gift and how much they needed it now. Surely she could will a vision to her that would help them. As the others went their separate ways to hunt and forage, she slipped away toward the stream that ran near the campsite.

She recalled the way she had so often knelt on the stones of the riverbank, and she tried that again. She hummed the old songs under her breath, to prevent anyone who chanced to pass by from overhearing. Water beetles played along the ripples of current. She sang louder. But this time, there was no mist, no fox with purple eyes, no stirring along the surface or under the depths of the stream. Nothing appeared.

And that led her mind back to Rhys. Perhaps she really did need him beside her, for her visions to work. Where was he now, and what were they doing to him? She felt a catch in her throat and pushed the thought aside, springing up to find roots for her brother and their friends to eat. She was kneeling near the stream again, peeling and washing the roots, when Aeneus returned, carrying a brace of rabbits over his shoulder.

"You are quiet, Lady Catrin," Aeneus said. "Have you had a vision?"

She shook her head. "Not since we left Dolbadarn."

Aeneus set the brace down and looked at her. "We took you from him."

She knew he meant Rhys. "My brother needed me more, then," she said.

"We needed you." He began to skin the first rabbit. "And even now that you have helped return Hyw to us, we keep you here. What will you do now?"

"You know what I must do."

He nodded, and bent to butcher and dress the rabbit, using his knife deftly. "If you will but wait until we rescue the prince, I will go with you, Cat," he said.

"I cannot ask you to. Prince Dafydd—"

"Yes, and we will rescue him," Aeneus said. "But I will see things right for you as well. Having you and Hyw to look after has given me something to fight for."

"To fight for?"

"You two, and your mam." He took up a long narrow branch and began to strip the bark from it with his knife, fashioning a spit for the rabbit.

Cat watched his deft fingers and thought about all the years he had been with them. Ever since she could remember, he had been like a pillar of support for her and her family, but she had never really thought about him or what his life might have been like. The words tumbled out of her mouth before she realized she had spoken them aloud.

"Was it Mam?"

Aeneus looked sideways at her and his expression was difficult to read.

"I'm sorry," she said quickly. "I don't mean to pry."

"It was an honest question. Your mam is special to me, and I will ever be there for her, as long as I draw breath. But for her, it was always your da." He sat up a little and looked away at the mountains. Cat couldn't help her sense of relief, but she sat quietly beside Aeneus, waiting for him to go on. "And I loved another."

"What happened?"

"The English happened. He was taken in the fighting, the last time they invaded. You were a toddler then, lass, so you would not remember him. But your uncle, Twm, gave his life to save mine." An image popped into Cat's mind of a tall man with a big laugh and a shock of red hair, lifting her up into the air. It was followed by another image, her mam's sad face and Aeneus, equally sad, with his arm around Mam's shoulder.

"As he died, he bade me take care of your mam," Aeneus continued. "And I will honour his memory until the English take me as well." He moved his head to the side and studied the ground. "What think you, Lady Catrin? Will I see him again? After, I mean."

"You will, Aeneus." She promised herself that she would remember this uncle, who had meant so much to her mam and to Aeneus. "You will, if I have anything to do with it."

"Then, glad I am to travel with you." And with that he set to work, fleshing the rabbit skin. "We will rescue the prince and young James' father from the *Saeson*. And then we will rescue Rhys."

Cat nodded. Now all they needed was the plan.

30

It was almost noon before Hyw gestured at James, and they headed into the forest away from the others. They scrambled up into the same tree, and Hyw felt more relaxed with food in his belly and the sun shining through its leaves. He took a deep breath and began to cast about for the creatures he knew were foraging in the grass below them. The hard bark dug into his back and leg, and he jumped when a beetle crawled across his arm. He sighed and shifted his weight restlessly. Then a warm hand grasped his. He glanced at his friend, and James nodded.

"You only need to see through its eyes, Hyw, as you did when we were children. If you start to change, I will pull you back."

At that moment, he sensed the mouse again. It stopped to rub its forepaws against its face. Hyw could feel its nails combing through its fur. Then the paws combed Hyw's face and he made contact with the animal's tiny mind. Llywelyn stood with him, as if looking over his shoulder. The advantage—or disadvantage—of not transforming was that he could now speak to the former prince as well.

Hyw came back to himself briefly and turned to James. "There may be a way."

"If this works, then at least we may know what we are facing before we have to go in," James said. "I confess I would rather see you beside me, here and safe, even if your thoughts are elsewhere."

Let us go, Hyw. Llywelyn's impatience pushed at him. *We tarry too long here and there is much we must find out.*

"It may take some time," Hyw said to them both. "I dare not lose the creature's mind before I have learned all I can."

James looked over at the castle, and then back again. "Can you truly hold contact at that distance?"

"My abilities have grown since we last saw each other," Hyw said. "In spite of what you saw a few days ago, I am stronger, if anything. It is always easier for me to take the animal's shape and harder for me to return. But knowing you are with me will help me to use my mind only, and not the full extent of my gift."

"Then know that I am here." James nodded and leaned back more comfortably. "Settle yourself in a sturdy spot, and I will keep watch until you return."

Hyw shifted to lay in the fork between two branches, near James but giving his friend some purchase in case he needed to climb down before it was finished. Then Hyw sought the rodent again and slipped into its mind. It wanted to scrabble into a hole in the dirt but Hyw bade it, as gently as he could, to Shrewsbury castle. Crossing the mouse paths under the walls into the castle yard was handy enough, if achingly slow.

Finally the tiny creature made its way to a crack in the stones of the hall. Hyw almost lost contact with it in the dark, until it came out through a similar hole into a large room. The creature avoided large shapes and heat: people eating at the long tables and the fire pit in the main hall. He heard a scuffling on the rushes and the mouse went very still. A large muzzle snuffled by him, and Hyw almost broke contact when he realized it was a hound. He slowed his breathing and worked to calm the tiny creature. Someone whistled nearby and the dog galloped off. The mouse took the opportunity to scamper back into the walls again.

It clambered back out into the castle's great hall. Hyw caught sight of a tall stately figure in black and purple robes lounging in a chair. The English king. He looked much the same as he had some six months earlier, when Llywelyn had convinced Hyw to spy on the English. He was blond and fair, and his broad chest held a voice that commanded attention. Now, he wore the reliquary that held the True Cross around his neck. Listening to a group of monks singing hymns, Edward looked every inch the king at rest, his long legs stretched in front, bent at one knee.

You can see how he earned the name Longshanks. Hyw could hear the derision in Llywelyn's voice as he pointed out the king's nickname. The mouse's squeak of fear drew Hyw's attention. A dun-coloured staghound lying at the king's feet suddenly raised its head and pricked up its ears. Likely it was the same one that had snuffled around them earlier.

Those dogs were a gift from me, Llywelyn said, a hint of bitterness in his quiet voice. *There are none more loyal or fierce. I hope he treats them well.*

Hyw calmed the mouse and bade it look around them. The room swarmed with English noblemen and ladies. To the mouse, they loomed like large and frightening spectres, their murmurs as loud as hunting horns. Hyw concentrated until gradually he could make out the words.

"What will he announce, d'you think?"

"Those hounds certainly have the run of the castle."

"What will Lord Shrewsbury have to say about that, I wonder?"

"He can say nothing now that he shares a cell in the dungeon with that Welsh coward—"

Shrewsbury and Dafydd together! That would be a stroke of luck for them.

We must be sure, Llywelyn whispered. As Hyw began turning the mouse toward the dungeon to verify that bit of news, he heard a shout.

"Lo! The king."

King Edward stood and turned a grim face toward them. Edward held up two circular objects in his hand, glinting as they caught the sunlight slanting through the windows. Hyw stopped the mouse's scurrying to watch.

"In this hand, I hold two crowns." Edward raised his voice. "One was given to the traitorous Llywelyn by my father. And now we have taken it back."

A murmur of approval rippled through the crowd.

"This other is said to be the legendary crown of King Arthur himself! Returned now to its rightful place, with the king of all England."

This time the crowd erupted in a deafening noise. Everyone

shuffled a step closer, hoping to see Arthur's crown better. Some reached out with their hands as if to touch it. Guards pushed them back as the king continued.

"These symbols were brought to us by the Welsh people, entreating us to take them into our care. This cross and these crowns will forever remain in my keeping."

Treachery! Hyw could barely hear Llywelyn's voice over the din. The mouse huddled in the corner, desperate to get away. The king turned to a group of waiting guards and placed the crowns and reliquary in a small ornate chest. The guards turned and left the room with it.

Follow them, Hyw.

Before Hyw could send the mouse after them, the king turned to the crowd again and called for silence, holding something up in his other hand. Hyw felt Llywelyn's touch on his arm. *Hold a moment. Let us listen.*

"And here, I hold the smallest but greatest weapon the Welsh have wielded against us," boomed King Edward. "This is not the sword of Llywelyn, nor an axe, nor a hammer. No—it is the prince's seal, a symbol of his authority. That authority was granted to him by my father, King Henry, and Llywelyn's own willful misuse of it has seen it taken from him."

A lie. Llywelyn's voice thundered, but only Hyw could hear it. *It was taken by treachery.*

"Yet these seals may still hold the power to call to arms all the men and women of Wales, in defense of his daughter, the infant princess."

"Never!" someone shouted.

The king nodded his approval. "Never, indeed. For I will not allow it."

"Kill the babe!" someone else called out.

No! cried Llywelyn.

King Edward put up his hand to stay the speaker. "I will not kill the child," the king said, "for she is mine own kin, twice over. Her great-grandmother was kin to mine. Elinor de Montfort, her mother, was my cousin. Nay, I will not harm her, but I will keep her away from the soil of her homeland.

"And to quell any mischief her life may suggest in the minds of the Welsh, I will make sure she will never wield her father's power. I will take this princely seal, Llywelyn's symbol of authority, along with those of his wife and his brother, the would-be prince, and melt them into a simple silver chalice."

A chalice can still feed the people, murmured Llywelyn.

"This chalice will help bring peace to the people by serving an English abbey. In such humility, the seals will do no further harm."

The knights and ladies around him cheered as Edward handed the seals and crowns to a priest standing nearby. Father Maelgwyn! The traitor priest who had betrayed his sister and Margred at Criccieth Castle.

We must stay with them, Hyw, Llywelyn urged. *There may be a way to stop this. We must see whatever we can. All may not be lost.*

Hyw kept the mouse's attention trained on the priest. He bade the mouse twist through the feet of the lords and ladies as they drew away, to follow Maelgwyn from the room. It slipped under doorways and along darkened halls as the priest made his way from the castle to the smithy that abutted the castle wall.

A large, muscular man in a blackened leather apron sat waiting near the forge. The smith. He started as if he had been dozing when the priest dropped the seals into his lap. He seemed to be expecting it, though, and took the seals to a crucible already set on the forge.

"See you make it ready, but I will bring the silversmith on the morrow," Maelgwyn said. The smith made a noise as if to protest, but Maelgwyn continued, "You will not mind sharing your forge for this one small duty. See that you touch it not yourself."

The big smith made a wry face and nodded as if he had heard it all before. "And the crowns?"

"They are already on their way to Westminster Abbey, with the king's guard." The priest left without bidding him a good night.

Keep track of this! Llywelyn's voice was ragged. *We are too late, but we will regroup and find a way to take back the crowns and cross. And for now, this chalice could yet be the Holy Grail that unites our people.*

Hyw thanked the mouse again and bade it move closer. The smith pumped the bellows, making the fire leap hotter. He placed the seals into it, where Hyw lost sight of them. Frustrated, he tried to move closer, but the smith stepped backward and nearly trod on the mouse's tail. The frightened creature ran for the shadows, and it was all Hyw could do to keep control.

Finally the smith poured the silver into a stone mold. As the smith stretched his arms and moved off toward the door, Hyw wondered how long it would be before the silver plate could be pounded into shape. He must return to the others with news of the prince and Lord Shrewsbury as well. It was too much. Panic rose in him.

A mouse holds the key to our dilemma. You must return to watch them fashion the chalice, and find some way to mark our treasure. We cannot lose this, too. Hyw listened to Llywelyn's plan as he released the mouse with another thanks for its assistance.

Returning to himself, Hyw found James half asleep, his hand still on Hyw's. It was near dark, and he ached with having kept still so long. As he stretched, he told James what he had learned. Llywelyn urged Hyw to keep their findings from the others until they could return to the room where the priest had left the hardening silver in its molds. When he relayed the message to James, he could see the concern in his friend's eyes.

"Are you sure, Hyw? Do not overtax yourself."

Hyw laughed shortly. "I have sworn fealty to the Prince of Wales. What choice do I have?"

"But surely he would not expect—"

"He does." Hyw heard the rasp in his own voice and shook his head. "I'm sorry, James. I do not mean to sound angry. Not at you. Without your help, I would not be sure of success. Besides, I have not found Mam or your da yet, not to mention Prince Dafydd. I must go back." He wanted to reach out to James, but he stopped himself. "Come, I only need a good night's sleep. You will see."

The following day, Hyw and James ranged closer to the castle as soon as they could get away.

"I know you said the mind of a dog is too obedient to allow you to direct it against its master," said James. "But if the dogs have free reign of the castle as you say, then why not become one of them?"

But Hyw shook his head. "I will not change again unless the situation is dire. Besides, my sister would have my hide." They laughed and climbed an ancient branching yew tree. Since he knew the way by mouse holes, he made contact with a mouse again and urged the creature to its destination more quickly.

His mam and Elizabeth were likely being held in an upstairs room, James had said. Hyw turned the mouse toward the kitchen, thinking of the staircase. The rodent crept inside the walls. It stopped from time to time in mouth-watering anticipation, only to pick up a crumb of food that would have been too small for Hyw to feel under his boot. He could feel the cold of the stone floor through its paws, but its small nails barely made a sound.

In the end, the staircase wasn't necessary. It knew several shortcuts through small cracks and holes in the wall that Hyw would not have been able to take between rooms. Hyw found himself distracted for a moment by thoughts of James, who must be still waiting beside his inert body. Then hushed voices drew him back to the mouse's view. At his bidding, the mouse scampered toward the sound.

It passed by two guards without notice and entered a room through a knothole in the thick wood of the door. Hyw bade it remain still and used its eyes to scan the room. He spotted two figures in shawls, seated at a table near one window. Mam! Hyw's heart leapt and he almost lost the mouse.

Steady, lad. We are nearly there.

Hyw took a deep breath and looked again. The glare of afternoon sunlight accentuated the lines of worry on their faces. His mam placed her hand on the arm of Dafydd's wife, Elizabeth.

Elizabeth spoke in little more than a whisper, but it was loud to the mouse's ear. "He would not let me see my husband, but I prevailed upon him for news of the children at least. The girls go to Lincolnshire and Sempringham, but my boys have been taken to Bristol."

Heed her words, Hyw, Llywelyn whispered. Hyw quelled his annoyance at the unnecessary reminder in sympathy for the former prince's anxiety.

"Why did they separate them so?" Adara's voice was low and sad. "Could they not have allowed the children to stay together, to comfort each other?"

Elizabeth shook her head. "Edward has scattered my children to the wind. And soon they will send us away as well." She stopped for a moment, and Hyw could hear the strain in her voice. "So far away. What will become of us?" Then the former princess collected herself, and wiped her tears away with the heel of her hand. "I cannot let them see me weak, Adara. I must help my husband, and see my children returned to me."

"Let us think together. Surely there is someone you might appeal to? An uncle or a cousin, someone who might take the children?"

"I have written to my eldest sister. And to my youngest, although from her I have little hope of help."

"Her husband is a Mortimer?"

Elizabeth only nodded.

"Do not lose hope," Adara said. "Write again to your elder sister, more urgently this time."

"Her husband is a good man, but I fear he has little influence."

"What of Joan, your other sister? Her husband is a favourite of Edward's, is he not?"

"I have not seen her since we were children."

"What can be lost in trying?"

We must leave them to it, Hyw. Llywelyn's voice broke into his thoughts. *We must find my brother.*

Hyw tried to focus on the mouse again, but some piece of his heart remained with the two women. Surely there was some way to help them. Perhaps Hyw could find out where Edward planned to send his mam and Dafydd's wife. He and James would manage a rescue, even without the others.

Reluctantly, Hyw set the tiny creature off to learn more. The mouse was glad of a chance to search for more food. Hyw bade it check the dungeons to verify that Dafydd was there. The prince slumped by a wall. Hyw wished he was the mouse, so he could change and try to help. Then he heard a familiar voice from a neighbouring cell.

"How does your wound, my lord?"

It was Shrewsbury! The old lord's surcoat was rumpled, but he appeared unharmed. He stood near the bars of a neighbouring cell, but the prince didn't answer. Hyw almost broke contact then to tell James what he saw, but Llywelyn shouted in his ear.

There is no time. Bring this news to Aeneus later. You must find the chalice. Make haste!

Hyw urged the mouse to find the smithy. The molds were untouched, still in the same corner, and the big smith pounded metal at the anvil. As the smith paused in his pounding, the door opened, and a loud voice spoke.

"See you weigh it first." It was the priest, Maelgwyn, as he entered the room.

"Is it not a special order from the king?" Another man spoke as he followed, but he was neither monk nor priest, by his garments and leather apron. *The silversmith,* Llywelyn whispered. The silversmith's arm muscles bulged and he carried his tools carefully. He nodded to the other smith and moved to examine the cooled material.

"It is traitor's silver." Maelgwyn said crisply. "Pound it smooth, but no more embellished than these others. Make it humble for God's work."

In Hyw's mind, Llywelyn snorted. *Make you humble, priest,* Llywelyn whispered, and Hyw silently agreed.

"And do it quickly." Maelgwyn moved back to the door.

"But a man must have pride in his work, especially for the king," the silversmith replied.

"Your payment will give you pride enough," the priest said, closing the door behind him with finality. Left to his work, the silversmith took a look around him.

"Best bite the coin he gives you first," said the other, gesturing to the workspace. The silversmith twisted his mouth in a rueful smile as he moved a stool over to sit down near the silver. He weighed it, using a set of special weights he kept in his apron pocket. Soon the twin hammering of each smith at his work all but deafened the mouse, and Hyw had to concentrate to keep it foraging near enough to keep watch.

The priest returned to check his work twice, but the smiths ignored him. By noon, the silversmith stopped and turned the metal around in his hands. It had taken on the shape of a chalice and he seemed pleased with it. Using long tongs, he began to warm the metal in the forge, pounding and warming it in turn. When the priest returned, he broke in on the man's work.

"I told you it must be plain," Maelgwyn barked. "I have a mind to make you melt it down and start again."

"It is plain," the man replied. "What monk would drink from a chalice without at least this much embellishment? If it is to do the lord's work, it must appear thus at the very least."

"Very well, but no more," the priest said as he left.

The silversmith placed the chalice on a nearby table, and reaching into his bag, put two similar chalices beside it. Hyw pushed the mouse closer, but he could see no difference. How was he to tell which was which? He felt the panic rise again.

It must be the last one, Llywelyn said. *The one he just set down will be our Grail. Keep it in your sight.*

The doors opened, and King Edward himself came in, along with the priest and two of his guards. The big smith knelt on one knee, and the silversmith followed suit. Hyw had the mouse slink back so they wouldn't step on it. Edward picked up the chalice the silversmith had set down.

"So, this is what remains of the mighty prince's seal?"

"Nay, Your Highness. I was polishing that one to pack for Father Maelgwyn's visit to the Lincolnshire abbey," said the silversmith.

Watch closely now and see what we can learn, Llywelyn whispered.

"It is this one." The silversmith picked up the third chalice in the row and showed the bottom rim first. "I added the weight, here, as Your Grace directed. You can see in the ledger that this is the weight of the silver we melted from the seals." The smith held up the ledger but the king barely glanced at it. The smith set it back down as he continued. "Outwardly, it looks no different from these others. It will be up to the abbot whether to embellish the designs on the other end, but without your knowledge of the weight, he will not be able to tell one gift from the other."

"So, it is done." The king fingered the chalice and laughed. "And with it, I have finally put an end to the Welsh, once and for all. Yet this one must not go to Sempringham. Send this one to Lincolnshire. I would have it kept far from the babe who can do the most harm. These others will be a gift as rich for Sempringham."

I warrant a far richer gift has already been sent there, said Llywelyn, and Hyw nodded. That must be where Baby Gwen had been sent.

Edward set the chalice on the table again. As the priest showed the king around the other gifts for the English abbeys, the mouse skittered across the counter so Hyw could read the weight on the ledger: 30p (L/G). Just then, one of Edward's knights spotted him.

"Vermin!" Hyw heard the word as the mouse was batted to the wall. Hyw abruptly came to himself again on the tree branch. He could only hope the mouse was not injured too badly in the fall.

"What happened?" James sat up as Hyw did.

"Let us climb down," Hyw whispered. "I have much to tell."

31

Cat knew how Hyw must have come by the information as soon as she heard him explaining the chalice to Aeneus.

"You used your gift?" she demanded.

All her brother had to do in answer was duck his head.

"How could you put yourself in such danger? We only just got you back—"

"He did it for us all, Lady Catrin," James said, interrupting her. "And whether we like it or no, he learned much of value. They have my father in the dungeons with Prince Dafydd. Their plans escalate and we can wait no longer."

"The lad is right." Aeneus picked up the twig he had used before to map out their plan. "Tell me all that you saw."

As Hyw described what he had seen, Cat could see the value of his action. At least he had learned their mam was all right, and being held with Princess Elizabeth. Lady Elizabeth now. Cat even helped Aeneus draw lines in the dirt as they discussed ways to get into and out of the castle dungeons.

"But Dafydd won't leave without Elizabeth," Hyw said. "And I won't leave without Mam."

"We won't have to," Cat said. "Margred and I will get the women, while you three free the men."

"No." Aeneus stood up. "I won't lose any more of you."

"Of course you won't," Cat told him, giving Margred a meaningful look. "We can get in and out of the castle without anyone giving us a second glance. All we need is Margred's skills and our borrowed skirts."

Margred grinned. "Good thing we kept them, then."

"Have you had a vision?" Aeneus broke in.

The words were on the tip of her tongue. It would be easy. She only had to say it was a vision, and no one would question her. It was the only sure way to convince them she was right. Aeneus believed in her visions as much as Cynfrig had.

Cynfrig.

Cat could still remember the look of betrayal on the old steward's face when she had pretended to curse the Welsh traitors in de Francton's service. When Cynfrig died, he looked for her help to see him on his way to Garth Celyn, before the guards dragged her away. That was the power that went with her gift, and she could not abuse it again. She would not. Slowly, she shook her head.

"I don't need a vision for this. It is simply the best way. We must go in two different directions, so we must split up." She fixed Aeneus and her brother with a defiant stare. "This will work."

Cat took her brother's arm as Aeneus scuffed over their map with his boot and took up his short hunting bow. James already had his armour on, and now buckled on his sword.

"It is not easy to kill a man, especially one you know," Aeneus said, pursing his lips. "But a quick, unexpected strike may give you an opportunity to get away. There is no shame in running if you live to fight another day."

James gulped before he nodded. "I will do what I must do."

"As will we all," Hyw said. He glanced down at Cat as he disengaged himself from her hand and walked over to James. She watched him go, already missing him, and a grey cloud passed over the sun. It was a long-ago feeling and she couldn't place it. Perhaps she would have a vision after all, or perhaps it was only the wind snaking through the grass. She shivered in its wake.

"Come along, then," Cat said, grabbing Margred's hand. "If

there are women to be rescued, who better than we two to do the rescuing."

Their little group moved single file along the river that ran past the castle, wading in it when they could to avoid leaving a trail for dogs or trackers. When they reached the castle, they stashed their gear and waited for the rafts and boats bringing supplies from down the river. Then Aeneus took up a load and fell into step with the men carrying supplies toward the castle. He would meet them later by the kitchen entrance to speed their escape.

Cat remained with the others, hidden in the riverbank bushes so no one would recognize them. She turned to Hyw, who claimed to have sharper eyes and senses since his return to human form. Her brother watched Aeneus' progress, but she could see he was holding his breath. One word and Aeneus' accent would give them away, but the warrior knew better than to speak.

Finally Hyw gestured, and Margred and Cat donned their borrowed skirts again and moved off together, in the opposite direction. Since James had reported several lords arriving for Dafydd's trial, they planned to infiltrate as kitchen maids or servants. If asked, they would claim to be servants from Chester, but if their luck held, they would not be noticed.

They fell into step with others on the road and managed to get through the gate and inside Shrewsbury castle. Margred began crossing the kitchen toward the staircases. Cat followed as deftly as she could but the cook suddenly turned and thrust a large basket of carrots at her. "Peeled and sliced. Set to it, now."

Cat tried to thrust the heavy basket on the table but it nearly overturned. One of the scullery maids rapped her on the side of the head with a wooden ladle and hissed, "Clumsy! Cook'll box your ears for less."

Cat raised her hand to rub her aching head and the maid thrust a knife into it and pushed her roughly at the basket. With them all glaring at her, Cat had no choice but to begin peeling.

"Here, you'll never get done that way," Margred said, winking conspiratorially at them and grabbing a knife of her own. "Let me show you how it's done."

"Good lass." The cook winked back but glared at Cat before she moved away. Cat felt envious of Margred's ability to move in this rougher world of English servants. But as soon as the scullery maid had moved back to stir her pots, Margred's eyes met Cat's over the basket of carrots, and the concern in them overrode all.

The basket seemed never-ending. Cat was ready to give up on her plan and devise another, when a large red staghound bounded into the servant's area, followed closely by a young man. The man's plain tunic hid his muscular soldier's frame, and his shoulder-length brown hair was unkempt enough to partially obscure his face. It was James.

"Where did he find that dog?" Margred whispered, but Cat shook her head. Then the dog's tongue lolled out and it blinked its blue-grey eyes at her. Hyw! He had used his gift.

Hyw broke away and skittered through the kitchens, snapping at a half-carved ham and upsetting the tables as he ran.

"Here — catch him!" yelled Cook.

"I'll get him!" James called as he ducked past and gave chase.

Margred leapt after them, half-dragging Cat along before Cat had time to put down the kitchen knife. She set it on the sideboard as she ran past. Thinking quickly, she grabbed up a tray with a pitcher and goblets.

Cat caught up to Margred as the big hound skittered past the guards and down the stairs to the dungeon. James followed before they could stop him.

"Don't worry, I'll get him."

"Good lad," one of the guards said. "Those mangy hounds will be the death of us all."

Cat had caught up to Margred by then, carrying the tray in front of her.

"Here, lovely," the other guard said, reaching toward Margred. "Where are you off to?"

Doing her best to mimic James' accent, Cat stepped between them. "You'll have to wait your turn. We must take this tray up to the ladies."

The guard frowned but Cat breezed by with Margred close on her heels. She was shaking by the time they reached the stairs and was glad when Margred reached over and took the tray before the pitcher spilled.

"Like you were born to it," Margred whispered. Cat huffed a laugh, dispelling the breath she didn't realize she was holding and regaining some of her composure.

"Come," she said, leading the way up the stairs. From Hyw's memory of going through the castle in mouse form, and James' knowledge of his former home, they had a rough idea of which room they had to find. They slowed as they heard two guards talking around a bend in the hall. Cat touched Margred's arm to get her attention, and then lifted the stopper to sniff at the contents of the pitcher: it was weak ale. She pulled out a small bottle, one of those items Adara had bade her keep in her kit that she had never expected to use. Cat uncorked the bottle and tipped the contents into the pitcher. Margred raised her eyebrows, but Cat only smiled and moved past, gesturing for her to follow.

"Cook sent us," Cat said, and poured them each a goblet from the pitcher.

"Ah, just in time," said one as he took the mug.

"We shouldn't be—" the other began to protest.

"Cook will never tell," Cat assured him, half pressing the mug into his hand. The man shrugged and drank.

"Here, what did you give us?" the first began, but he staggered even as he spoke. Both men crumpled against the wall.

"Did you kill them?" Margred said.

"I don't think so," Cat said. "I found a flower Mam uses to help wounded warriors sleep, but I've never seen it work so quickly."

"Well, who knows how long it will last. We'd best be as quick."

They pushed through the door and found Adara and Lady Elizabeth. Both women stood, and for a moment no one spoke. Then Cat fell into her mam's arms.

"Da—" Cat began, and Mam shushed her.

"I know, Cat. I know," Adara murmured.

Margred curtsied to Elizabeth.

"What are you doing here?" Elizabeth asked, placing her hands on her hips. "I thought you had gotten away." Then she faltered. "I—I hoped you had, Margred."

"We have come to rescue you," Margred said.

"Come, you must come quickly," Cat said, pulling Mam's arm as she turned to the door.

"You go, Adara," said Elizabeth. "Save yourself."

"We've come for all of you," Cat whispered. "Even now, Aeneus and Hyw are rescuing Prince Dafydd. And our cousin James of Shrewsbury is with them, to find and free his father. We must hurry—"

"My husband will not leave," Elizabeth said, her voice thick with sorrow. "We have made a bargain for the lives of our children. Even if he does—especially if he does, I must remain to see it through."

"What do you mean?"

"My cousin the king will not harm me, and he has agreed not to harm my children if we cooperate with his plans."

"Do you know where they are?" Margred took a step closer to her step-mother. "We will find them as well."

"They have been scattered abroad in England," Elizabeth said. "Lincolnshire for the girls, and Bristol Castle for the boys. Rescue Dafydd and you may mount a rescue for us all. Go now, all of you, before someone comes."

One of the guards groaned in the hall, and Cat pulled her mam's arm again.

"Mam, we must hurry," Cat said again. "Come now!"

But Adara turned toward Elizabeth. "How can I go, Lady, and leave you here?"

"You must." The former Princess of Wales drew herself up. "I will face the king's men, and remind them of his bargain."

Adara turned to Cat. "You must save yourself, you and Hyw. I cannot leave her, Cat, any more than you could have left Princess Elinor when she needed you. And I cannot leave Baby Gwen to her fate. Our family has served the House of Aberffraw long and well, and I will not break with that tradition in this final hour. I must stay and see this through."

Cat stared into her mam's determined eyes and her vision

blurred with tears. "But I cannot leave you."

"You must, Cat. I must know that you and Hyw are safe. Get away while you still can. When this is all over, and we have the children with us again, I will find you. Believe it. Now go."

She pushed Cat toward the door, but it was Margred who grabbed her arm and dragged her through it. One of the guards, still dazed, reached out and caught Cat's ankle and she kicked at him. She caught him in the jaw by accident and his head snapped back into the wall. He slumped down, unconscious again.

"Come on!" Margred pulled Cat behind her as they ran.

32

Hyw galloped to dungeon cell and whined a little as he paced in front of it, his hindquarters shivering. He glanced back over his shoulder: the long red tail surprised him, and it was whipping back and forth. He tried to stop it, but when he looked back at Shrewsbury, it started again. He was wagging his tail. How humiliating! And yet he could not seem to stop. Shrewsbury was alone, seated at a small table. He stood when he saw Hyw and came over, scratching Hyw's ear through the door of the cell.

"What is it, then, boy? How came you here?"

Before Hyw could even whine again, James had caught up to him. Shrewsbury called out to his son, but James shushed him with a gesture. Hyw leapt up and snatched the keys from a hook on the wall. James took the keys, opened the cell door, and beckoned to his father, but the old lord hesitated.

Hyw. You must get my brother out of here. Llywelyn's voice blared like a hunting horn inside of Hyw's head, making him whine again. Hyw had forgotten Llywelyn raised hunting hounds and had a natural ability to command. The cells were cold and dark, lit only by a lantern set on a table for the guards, but Hyw could sense the way easily. He snuffled at James' hand and bumped against Shrewsbury, herding them both toward the opposite cell. Shrewsbury reached back to grab something from his bench.

"My servant brought it, and we may have need of it yet." It

was a small leather purse, and Shrewsbury placed it inside his tunic as they rushed across to find Dafydd.

"Ah, the warrior and the young *bleidd-ddyn*." The term meant werewolf, Hyw realized with shock. The voice was low and strained, but easily recognizable. Dafydd laughed softly but it turned into a cough.

He is injured. Help him, Hyw.

"Dafydd," whispered Shrewsbury, pushing inside as soon as James got the cell door open. "Here, James, the keys."

"'Tis but a scratch."

Hyw whined again, and James laid a hand on his head to steady him. Then James and Shrewsbury lifted Dafydd, who had obviously been beaten, and recently. Shrewsbury began struggling with the lock that held Dafydd's chains, trying key after key.

"You were fools to come," Dafydd said harshly. "You all must escape now. Any man who mounts my rescue dooms my children. If I comply, Edward will let them live."

I do not trust Edward's word, Hyw. Dafydd is a fool. He languishes here while his children are separated and dispersed throughout the land. What will happen to them once Dafydd is dead? Hyw tried to tell James but the words came out as a complaining wo-wo-woof.

Dafydd weakly pushed Shrewsbury away. "It is too late for me now. What of the next Prince of Wales? I must not jeopardize my son's chances." He gestured with his chin to a cell across the way. "And take the bard with you."

Hyw whirled around with a whine to see Gwilym ap Einion leaning on the bars of a neighbouring cell. The bard had been with them at Dolbadarn, but Hyw could not recall seeing him when Dafydd was captured.

"My lord, our rescue is at hand," Gwilym said.

"I've been through this with you already," Dafydd said. "Even if the giant Idris himself came to rescue me, I would not go with you now. I have given my word. Take your chance, Gwilym." The prince's voice was almost a growl. "Get Shrewsbury out of here while you still can. If you truly wish to help the House of Aberffraw, find Llew and Owain."

"Come with us," James said.

"Here, let me." Margred pushed past them all. Cat stood behind her, her face awash with tears. Margred rounded on the hound. "No, your mam is not with us. Nor is Elizabeth. We found them upstairs but the Princess of Wales would not come." Margred whirled on her father. "Elizabeth is as stubborn as you are."

"But she is well?" Dafydd asked.

Margred looked closely at him. "She is better off than you are, it would seem."

Hyw whined, and this time James could interpret for him. "Could you not convince your mam, Cat?"

"She is determined to stay with Elizabeth and see this through," Cat whispered.

"We were able to subdue the guards with one of Cat's potions, but they were already stirring when we left. You must come now," Margred told Dafydd.

"Daughter." Dafydd reached toward Margred, clanking his chain against the wall. She gasped as she reached for a piece of linen wrapped over his arm as if to staunch the bleeding. It was filthy and caked with dried blood. Margred started to remove the linen, but Dafydd stopped her.

"Leave it. It is all I have left of Elizabeth, now." He reached up and pushed a curl off her cheek. "You must know I care for you deeply, Margred."

"I know." Her voice was thick with unspoken emotion. "I know you do. And I, you. You must let us get you out of here."

"What will it serve if I escape, only to see my children killed in my place? You are all precious to me. Every one of you. That's why I took you from your mother, Margred. Not to shame you or her, but to keep you safe."

Margaret's lip trembled, and Hyw's heart went out to her as a single tear rolled down her pale cheek. "Please, Da. You must let us get you out of here."

"That is the first time you have ever called me Da."

"Voices," Cat hissed as she moved into the cell. "On the stair."

They heard a gruff voice calling, "Boy, do you need some help with that mutt?"

"I've got him!" James called back and threw Gwilym the keys.

"Here, what's this?" A guard appeared in the hall, but before he could cry an alarm, Hyw leapt at him and knocked him into the bars. The guard's head cracked against the iron bar and he slumped down. Hyw snuffled at him but the man was still breathing. Having the strength of a large hound without the obedience had its advantages.

A second man rounded the corner, and the force of his charge caused him to trip over the big dog. Hyw bounded to the side and whirled back around to see the second guard prone on the floor beside the first. Gwilym stood over them.

"Prince Dafydd said you were a bard," James said.

"*Pencerdd,*" Gwilym said.

"What?"

"A master bard." Gwilym grabbed the guard's helmet and put it on. "And I wouldn't be worth much if I couldn't defend my words, would I?"

Hyw made a sound like a whine again and James said, "Go, Hyw. We're right behind you."

"Wait," Gwilym said. "Hyw?"

"Never mind that now," James said. "We must be off."

"All right, but if we live through this, I will expect the full story."

"Go now, and be safe," Dafydd said, wiping the tear from Margred's cheek. "Gwilym, if you would truly help me, take my daughter from this place. Shrewsbury, I charge you, keep my children as safe from harm as you do your own."

"As you wish, Lord Dafydd," Shrewsbury said.

Prince Dafydd, Llywelyn said, but only Hyw heard him.

"Swear it," Dafydd said. "Swear it on your honour."

"I so swear," Shrewsbury said. Gwilym picked Margred up, carrying her over his shoulder as if she were a sack, and started down the hall.

"No," she cried, struggling, but Gwilym held her firmly. Hyw tried to leap toward Dafydd, but James grabbed him by the ruff and pulled him along as well.

"Go, quickly," Dafydd whispered urgently.

"Come, Hyw," James called softly, and Hyw could not help but respond.

"This way," Cat whispered, catching Shrewsbury by the arm. As they rounded the final hallway before the stairs, they heard footsteps and more gruff voices. James reached for his sword but Hyw bounded in front of him up the stairs. As he reached the top, one of the guards grabbed for him but Aeneus appeared out of the shadows. He boxed the guard's heads together before they could sound an alarm. Gwilym set Margred down but when she turned to go back down the stairs, he grabbed her arm.

"They will kill us all."

She stopped resisting but Hyw could see her eyes bright with tears. Then they were moving swiftly back out of the kitchens and past the courtyard.

They managed to gain the safety of the market before a cry went up from somewhere inside the castle. They heard armour rattling and scattered. James and Gwilym, visors down, marched off toward the city gate with Shrewsbury between them. Aeneus picked up a sack of something he had obviously placed nearby and headed off in the direction of a supply boat, tied at the river's edge.

Hyw bounded behind Margred and Cat into the market. Two soldiers clanked by them at a run, and the girls turned to look at a bolt of cloth as Hyw squirmed under the clothier's table. He saw Cat grab Margred's hand, and scrambled after them, almost upsetting the table. The girls walked swiftly to the corner, and then they all ran down the shortcut James had shown them previously.

Arriving at the pier, they spotted Aeneus in the small supply boat. Gwilym and Shrewsbury were already seated in it, and they grabbed the poles. James sliced the rope with his sword and climbed in after them. Cat and Hyw ran down the bank and leapt into it. Margred pushed them off and Gwilym reached out a hand to pull her to safety. Guards burst onto the riverbank, but their swords were useless as the current picked up the little boat and took them farther from shore.

"Archers," Margred hissed. Aeneus grabbed her bow and quiver from the bottom of the boat and tossed them to her. Shrewsbury made a small sound, and James pushed his father flat to the bottom of the boat.

Hyw scrabbled down beside them. He whined as an arrow

glanced off James' back, where the tunic hid his armour, to land harmlessly in the water. Another thwacked into the side of the boat. Then they were careening down the river and the arrows finally began to fall short.

"We made it, Father," James cried, holding the old man close and raising him to sit in the boat again. Shrewsbury groaned softly as he brought his arms around his son. Then Hyw smelled the blood seeping through his surcoat.

"No!" James cried.

Cat knelt near and gasped as she saw the arrow protruding from the old lord's side.

When they pulled into shore again, Shrewsbury collapsed on the riverbank. He had already lost a great deal of blood. Aeneus moved to help him run, but Shrewsbury shook his head and turned to his son.

"Go you with God," the old man laid the sign of a cross on James' forehead. "And know that whatever happens, you are my legacy. I am proud of you, boy."

"No, father," James cried as he hugged the old man tightly. "Stay with me."

The old lord reached for Hyw with his other hand. "Do not forget your pledge to me."

Hyw whined and licked Shrewsbury's hand so he would know he was in earnest. There was no time for him to change back.

"What is wrong with you all?" Margred's cheeks blazed red with rage. "What are the young without the old? You must not die."

"We must all die someday, child," Shrewsbury said, his voice kind. "I am sorry that your father would not leave with you. But I am proud to make the same sacrifice he makes. You—all of you—are our future. See that you live it for us."

Then Shrewsbury looked beyond them at Aeneus and Gwilym. "There is a purse in my tunic. Use it to help my son. It may give you an edge in what is to come. Do not let them find James. Send me back into the river, that they may find me, and God willing, they may leave the boy be."

Aeneus raised his eyebrows but nodded. "As you will it, my lord."

Then Shrewsbury hugged James to him and kissed the top of his head. "See that you live," he said again. And with one ragged breath, he was gone.

James would not let him go, and Hyw could not bear to tear him away. After a moment, Aeneus reached down and disentangled the boy's arms from around his father's body.

"There is no time, lad. We must do as your father wished."

Aeneus and Gwilym laid the old man's body gently in the boat, and pushed it out into the river. James was leaning against Hyw, still in canine form, for support. Their small company watched without speaking as the current caught it. Then Aeneus turned to James.

"You are welcome with us, for as long as you wish. And you will have my help, whatever you may decide."

Hyw raised his voice and howled into the darkening skies. No one tried to shush him.

33

The failed rescue attempt haunted Cat. Shrewsbury's death shook her deeply. And seeing Dafydd chained to the wall brought nightmares of Rhys in the tower at Dolbadarn. It had been over a month since she left him there to help her brother. What had happened to him in that time?

They moved camp farther into the forest, having no doubt that there would be a hue and cry. Hyw resumed his human form but never left his friend's side. Cat wondered if the qualities of the animals he chose to become had any lasting effects on his mind or behaviour after he returned to human shape again. She shivered, recalling the yellow-eyed hawk that had attacked her when Llywelyn pushed her out of Hyw's nightmare. Touching the locket that connected them, she uttered a silent prayer that the better qualities would stay with him while the rest dropped away.

Cat buried her thoughts in consoling Margred, who had begun to tremble as soon as they returned to their makeshift camp. Margred had rallied to help them escape, but she became overwhelmed with emotion after the danger was over. Cat held her and rubbed her back and shoulders as she fell into a fitful slumber. Gwilym tried to help but Margred pushed him away. Aeneus handed the bard a bow and took him into the woods to hunt.

Margred finally dropped into an exhausted sleep. When she heard James' settled breathing and knew he slept, Cat gestured to Hyw. He walked with her toward the fire, a few paces away from the others. She handed him some stew on a leaf, and they ate quietly. Finally Cat could put it off no longer.

"I must return to Dolbadarn for Rhys. I have already tarried too long here."

"It won't be safe there for you." He moved his head to the side and raised his eyebrows. "Unless you've seen something?"

She shook her head. "But something has changed." She tried to explain the difference in the vision when she helped Cynfrig's spirit back to Garth Celyn, and the strangeness of her meeting with their ancestor Aylwen. She also told him what Rhys had said, about her and Hyw being connected in some way. She mused over the meaning of the ravens that often appeared when she used her gift in that way, as well as the one that had been chased away when she made contact with Llywelyn's spirit inside the hawk.

"If only Gawain or Mam was here," Hyw said, slowly. "They might have some idea what this means. What about Rhys? Wasn't his sigil three ravens?"

She nodded. It seemed like another sign pushing her to go to Rhys, whatever the outcome. Then she took a closer look at her brother. He seemed pale and drawn, but perhaps that was natural given his friend's grief. "What about you and James?"

He reached for her hand and she could see the uncertainty in his eyes. "Llywelyn bids me fetch the chalice, and I am sworn to it."

"You must, of course. But you must stay with James, now that you have found each other again. He needs you now, as you still need him."

"I will go with your sister, Hyw." Aeneus spoke softly from behind them. Cat was always surprised that such a large man could move so quietly.

"I do not hold you to that promise, Aeneus," she whispered. "Prince Dafydd—"

"Made his wishes clear." His face was set. "I pledged my fealty to the princes of Aberffraw. He that now lives in Hyw was the greatest of all, and what he brought us could have changed the world, but that he was cut down by treachery. I served Prince Dafydd because Llywelyn named him heir. But from now on, I will only serve a prince that is worthy of my sword arm. If it be Llew, then so be it. I will find him and set him free, or die trying." He stopped again to look at her. "But before I can do that, I have a debt to you."

"Then I release you from it," she said. "You have saved me and taken care of me and Hyw. And it gained you nothing. I owe you more than you could ever owe me."

"Whither thou goest, Lady Catrin, I will go also. At least until I can return Rhys to you, and see you safely together."

She reached up to touch the locket and then straightened her shoulders. "Then have no fear for me, Hyw. I've always got this with me. Aeneus and I will rejoin you again as soon as we can, with Rhys."

"Join you where?" Margred had slept through the meal earlier, and she was still paler than usual, her mouth set in a determined line. Cat handed her some of the food she had saved. Margred took it without looking at it.

"Cat leaves us to find Rhys again," Hyw told her.

"I will accompany you, of course," Margred said, without hesitation.

"But your da—" Cat began, and Margred interrupted.

"My da has made his choice," she said. "I took you from Rhys to help repay my debt to Hyw." She raised her hand before Hyw could react. "For your assistance at Criccieth, Hyw. The outcome of that was not your fault. By bringing Cat to you, we learned how to save you. For that I am not sorry. But now—"

"You owe no debt to me, Margred," Cat said. "Hyw is my brother, and I was glad to help in whatever way I could. But now I must return."

"Of course you must," Margred said. "We will find a way to rescue Rhys. And he in turn can help us find my sisters."

"As I will, when we are reunited," Hyw put in.

"Do you mean to use your gift yet again?" Margred was startled. "How fared you with it?"

"It was… difficult." Hyw shrugged. "Yet it will most likely be necessary."

"Hyw, you must not," Cat began, but he raised his hands, palm up.

"I must do whatever I need to fulfill my pledge." He hugged her to him. "Now it is I who must tell you not to fear," he said, releasing her and gesturing toward James, who remained asleep. "I am not alone in this. And if the need arises, get word to me and I will find you."

With mixed feelings, Cat touched her locket as she watched him walk away to join James. She was overjoyed to see them together, but she already missed her brother.

34

Later that evening, James awoke and gnawed on a little of the rabbit Hyw had saved for him. When Hyw filled him in on their plans, James immediately said he would remain. Hyw felt torn between his need to hold James and his fear of scaring James away. Before Hyw had a chance to decide, he spotted Gwilym returning from the woods. Instead of a brace of rabbits, the bard carried a woollen sack slung over his shoulder.

"I was not much interested in hunting, after all." The bard grinned as he reached into the sack and brought out a bundle of dark cloth. "Aeneus filled me in on your plan earlier." He unwrapped a plain chalice. "I'm sure they'd have donated it, out of pure Christian charity, if they knew our need." Gwilym shrugged. "It was an English church, after all."

Llywelyn's laugh rumbled. *A switch. We exchange one chalice for another, and the priests will never know they have been duped with their own handiwork. How fitting.*

"Why would Aeneus tell you our plan?" James asked.

Gwilym bristled. "Aeneus has known me for more years than you have been alive." Then he seemed to catch himself, and when he spoke again his voice was calmer. "You are lucky that he did. Your priest was already planning his route for tomorrow."

"What?" Hyw stood up in surprise.

"Maelgwyn, wasn't it? I happened to overhear him discussing the wages he would make for delivering a special chalice to

Lincolnshire and some gifts to the Gilbertines at Sempringham. He will leave at dawn with two other priests and a special saddlebag, apparently, which is even now being packed for him, somewhere in the castle."

"Then we must follow their trail," James said quickly.

Hyw gave him a conspiratorial look. "But we could always use help."

"There's something I still don't understand." James frowned, turning to the bard. "How did you come to be in that cell?"

"Can you believe it?" Gwilym responded. "Someone complained about my music."

"Even I know that can't be all there is to it," said James. Between them, they kept asking questions until they got Gwilym to admit he had been caught trying to break Dafydd out.

"You would try that alone?" Hyw asked.

"I was alone. What else could I do?" Gwilym answered. "Prince Dafydd had sent me to recruit three loyal men from a holding near Caernarfon. We were attacked by a troop of English." Gwilym looked away from them. "I was knocked unconscious, but I awoke before the soldiers could finish their grisly business and managed to get away. I walked back to Nanhysglain to find stone mounds and an empty cabin. A farmer fed me and gave me news of Dafydd's capture, so I came here." He turned to Hyw. "And there's something I don't understand. How is it that you gave your name to a staghound? And where is said hound now?" Gwilym leaned toward him. "Or are the rumours about you true, after all?"

"Rumours?" James asked, moving between Hyw and Gwilym.

"You have nothing to fear from me," Gwilym said. Hyw and James exchanged glances, and the bard laughed. "Very well. However it came about, I thank you for deliverance. And for the meal and lodgings. Tomorrow I will go about my business."

"And what is that?" James asked. "To rescue Prince Dafydd? Or die trying?"

"I have pledged my skill and my sword to the house of Aberffraw, and I will follow that path, wherever it leads me."

He would be a worthy ally, Llywelyn said. *But you will need to let him into your confidence.*

"In that case," Hyw said slowly, "we may have a better use for your sword than in the dungeons of Shrewsbury."

Hyw was swinging his sword in ever increasing circles around him, circles of red mist. Droplets flew into his face. Tangy and vile. Blood. The red mist was blood, flying all around him. Faint groans became screams of anguish and pain. He was screaming. No, the voice was not his.

It was Llywelyn!

The former prince was screaming and thrusting at anything that moved around him.

Hyw's first thought was of James. He leapt up, ready to protect his friend. But everything around him was quiet, and the fire had died down. James stirred sleepily beside him.

"What is it?" James whispered.

"Nothing," Hyw whispered back, feeling himself shaking. "Go back to sleep."

It had been a dream. Llywelyn's dream? Hyw closed his eyes and found the former prince, crouching and covered in blood, sword raised.

"My lord," he started to say, but Llywelyn dropped the sword and ran at him, taking him by the throat with both hands and flinging him down. Hyw gasped and lines of red began to form across his vision.

"My lord." He struggled to speak but could barely get the words out.

Llywelyn uttered a cry and let go, turning in a huddle on the ground, shaking and moaning. Hyw coughed and struggled to sit up. When he tried to touch Llywelyn, the prince jerked away.

Give me space, he rasped.

"What's wrong?" Hyw started to ask, and then looked around him. He was surrounded by a battlefield strewn with bodies, some in long gowns and turbans, some in battle armour, all dead. "Where are you? We? What—?"

Crusading. Llywelyn gave a shaky laugh. *I was younger than you are now, Hyw.* He wiped his hand across his face. *But I have fought so many battles. It could be any one of them. Fighting for a piece of land in Wales or the borderlands. Fighting in desperation to get to Simon de Montfort before he was hacked to pieces by the whelp of a boy they now call king.*

"Has this—does this happen often?"

Not for many years. The White Abbot helped me, and for a time I had control of it. And now he suffers for his loyalty. With Elinor I found a kind of peace. And she died because of it." He drew a breath. *"I have a gift too, Hyw. The gift of war.*

Hyw considered that. "Did you never long for peace?"

All my life, said Llywelyn. *And I had it, for a few short years before it was taken from us. After Elinor and I were finally married, I was content. I could have been bound in the space of an acorn and still have been happy with her, Hyw.* Llywelyn's expression was sombre. *Treachery and deceit plagued me and plague me still, even after death. But your sister has shown me the life to come, and my lady Elinor waits for me there.*

Sorrow thrummed through the prince's words, and Hyw felt the pain in his own chest. "What can I do?"

Llywelyn almost smiled. *You would have made a good addition to my teulu, Hyw. I am sorry that we never had the chance to fight together, side by side.*

"We seem to have done nothing but fight, with each other and side by side."

Llywelyn shook his head and gave a gruff laugh. *Go back to sleep.*

But sleep would not claim either of them for the remainder of the night.

The following morning, Hyw longed to tell Cat or Aeneus what had happened, but they were anxious to get on the road to Dolbadarn. Gwilym bowed low to Margred, and for a moment it seemed the bard might change his mind and go with her. But at the last minute, he turned back to stand with Hyw and James.

Cat waved a final time as she, Aeneus, and Margred fell into stride together. Hyw stood for a moment, watching as they disappeared from view. James bumped up against him.

"Don't worry. She'll be all right."

Hyw considered telling James about Llywelyn's dreams, but he wasn't sure how much of this magic his friend could tolerate. Instead, he opted for, "I'm merely tired."

"The dog was probably too much. Too soon. And…" James' voice trailed off but Hyw understood. Their plan couldn't prevent James' father from dying.

"I wish it had been me instead."

"Don't say that," James said roughly. "I can't lose you again."

Hyw felt a tiny surge of hope as they followed Gwilym to pick up the trail of the priest.

The following day, Hyw enlisted a passing jackdaw to find the right direction. Maelgwyn was riding with another priest, and the two made camp early that afternoon in the rain. Gwilym suggested waiting for darkness. Hyw could make the switch later that night, while the priests slept.

"He'll do this without taking the form of a beast, then." James' tone boded no question.

Gwilym grinned at him. "He'll need both thumbs to open the saddlebags."

"Why Hyw?"

"I can keep the horses calm," Hyw said. "That is our best chance of success."

"And the two of us?" James turned to the older man.

"Keeping watch, in case something goes wrong." Gwilym touched the sword he now wore, stolen from the guard in Shrewsbury's dungeons.

"Nothing will go wrong," Hyw said.

Hyw watched from the branches of an oak as the priests made a fire to boil water. Soon the smell of cooking mutton made his stomach growl. He thought instantly of James, wondering if his friend could smell the meat as well from the shadows near the tree. The priests scraped the pot clean before they knelt for evening prayers. One made a show of crossing himself. Hyw was about to shift position again when the priest changed his movement to a stretch and looked up. Right at him. It was Maelgwyn.

Hyw held his breath and tried to shrug into the tree. A rush of fear blasted through him and he instinctively steadied himself. His fear melted away as his eyes grew sharper, and his bones firmer and lighter. He knew the tree branch now as if he were born in its shelter. He looked down and saw feathers. Talons where his feet should be.

Steady, Hyw!

Llywelyn's voice shocked him. Hyw had a sudden urge to strike with his beak.

Calm down, lad!

Hyw struggled to keep control. He had a nightmare image of looking at himself in a still pond, but the eyes that looked back were bright yellow instead of his own blue-grey. He stared for a long terrifying moment. Then he saw Llywelyn's hand, as if in his peripheral vision, holding out a small black leather hood.

You must hood the hawk, Hyw. You are the only one who can.

A falcon's hood. Hyw shied away but forced himself, focusing his will. He held the yellow eyes and inched his hand closer to the hood.

Patience. Patience.

Finally he slipped the pouch over his own inner vision, hooding the hawk inside him. The yellow eyes winked out, and Hyw was able to focus on the world outside himself. His human side surged into control again.

Below him, the priest Maelgwyn laughed and looked away to make a comment to one of the others.

Good work, Llywelyn said, his voice lower than a whisper.

Hyw looked down at his own body. The feathers had disappeared. He was still dressed, so he couldn't have transformed. But it had felt so real. Then he saw the pearly skin and sharp claws of a bird's talons where his left foot should be. Llywelyn held him up, a solid presence at his side, with no trace of night terror remaining. Were they saving each other? Or was this what his uncle Gawain had meant, their bond slowly driving them both mad in bits and pieces? October and *Nos Galan Gaeaf* was still months away.

Shaking his head, Hyw grasped for focus. He had to return to human form. Why? He had to complete the mission, regain the chalice, and return it to his people. For Cat. For Mam, caught in Shrewsbury castle. For a moment he wanted to fly to her there, but he stopped himself. For Llywelyn. For *Cymry.*

For James. Llywelyn repeated the words inside his head, soothing, like a lullaby. *For James.*

The air stirred around him, more a feeling than a sound. His talon stretched and splintered as his human foot swelled beneath it. He fell against the trunk as a jolt of intense pain radiated out from his foot across his entire body. The world went black.

He came back to consciousness to find himself prone on the tree branch, his arms curled around his legs. He knew he was dangerously perched but he could only lie still, hugging his stomach until the queasiness calmed. Eyes still closed. Llywelyn's face slowly came into view, and he focused on it.

That's it, lad. Steady.

Hyw knew he had to climb down. Finish his mission. How long had it been? He forced himself to open his eyes and flexed his arms and legs until he was able to move again. Branch by branch. At the bottom of the tree, where he had hidden it earlier, he found the sack with Gwilym's chalice and shrugged it over his shoulder.

Exhausted from the strain of maintaining human form, he could feel his limbs shaking. The nearest horse chuffed and shuffled its feet. Hyw heard Maelgwyn snort in mid-snore. Using his gift to quiet the animals, Hyw stayed as still as possible. The priest turned over, and his breathing became steady again. Hyw checked his hand: no feathers. He concentrated on his hand and steadied himself, focusing only on his breath as it moved into his lungs and out again. Slowly his hand quit shaking.

Returning to the task, Hyw drew near the tethered horses and checked the saddlebags lying near them. He pressed on the outside until he found a bulge. Reached in slowly, he felt two lumps wrapped in soft cloth. He opened the next one. This time, he reached in and removed a bundle of cloth, lifted the wrapping long enough to feel the round lip of the chalice and run his fingers over the marks on the bottom rim.

One of the horses moved its foot. He sought its mind, soothing it before it could nicker and give him away. Sleep, he urged it. Sleep. When he felt it still again, he breathed out slowly.

Now for the hardest part. He reached into his own sack and removed the other chalice Gwilym had brought them. He set the two on the ground, took Llyweyn's Grail from the cloth, and replaced it with the other. He set the precious Grail in his sack before he wrapped the fake one up and placed it into the saddle bag. The priests should have no reason to detect the switch, at least not until it was too late.

Finally Hyw turned and slipped away into the night. James and Gwilym joined him in the darkness, and they ran until they could no longer see the glow of the priests' fire. The sun streaked orange across the sky before Gwilym stopped them to examine the chalice. It seemed exactly the same as the other one.

"How can we tell this is the right one?" Gwilym frowned. Hyw pointed to the marks in the silver rim. Then James spotted a folded scrap of parchment in the cup and removed it. Opening it up, he read it for a moment, and then handed it to Hyw.

It was a scrap of parchment penned in Latin by a scholarly hand, unsigned. Perhaps Maelgwyn's own hand. Or the silversmith's. It appeared to be little but an inventory record to pass to the Lincolnshire abbey: Melted silver, 30p (seals L/G). The same words the mouse had helped him read in the ledger. "L" and "G" for Llywelyn and Gwenllian, the seals of the Welsh royal family. Hyw wondered if the English king would ever know he had given them the means to confirm what only Hyw had known for sure.

Gwilym smiled now. "We must return this to the rightful Prince of Wales."

One such prince is already grateful, Llywelyn said. *But you must dissuade him. Dafydd will never break his word, even now.*

"Prince Dafydd?" James asked, before Hyw could speak.

Gwilym shook his head. "I heard Dafydd. This time." He grinned ruefully. "And Bristol is a fortress, if his young sons are truly there. But I have an idea, if you care to listen."

James looked sideways at Hyw, who nodded.

"We must return it, and someday we will. In the meantime, we must keep it safe. And there is one person who could provide safekeeping for the chalice and an immediate solution to the stability of Wales. Lord Rhys." For a moment, no one spoke. Hyw wondered if Gwilym was more interested in Rhys or in the Lady Margred. But James nodded, slowly.

"He is the only one left who has fighting men he can rally to him."

Many have fought beside him, and know his worth. Llywelyn's voice thrummed with hope. *He might have a chance.* Hyw relayed the former prince's words to the others.

"Dolbadarn it is, then," the bard said.

They had travelled another two days the opposite direction, chasing the priests, and his sister had a four-day head start. Hyw raised his eyebrows at his friends and set a brisk pace down the road to close the distance.

35

It took longer than Cat expected to return to Dolbadarn Castle. They travelled over steep craggy mountains and deep ravines. Aeneus and Margred were careful to watch for signs of English troops as they hunted for scarce game in the charred and smoking countryside. Cat tried her hand at fishing. She stared into the waters, trying to call a vision, but her ancestors were silent.

Everywhere they went, she was reminded not only of Rhys but also of Cynfrig, his belief in her and his questions. Why had she not foreseen his death? Or Rhys' imprisonment? Had she been too focused on her own family? Or on the prince and his family?

Through it all, a persistent voice inside her kept asking how she had expected to protect the relics with tricks and dissemination. Why hadn't she hidden them or let Gawain keep them with him? As the miles stretched, the voice became more demanding. Cynfrig had warned her that if the True Cross fell into English hands, it would leach the spirit from the Welsh. Now they—she—had lost it to de Francton. How could they go on without it? And what of the Crown of Arthur? Would she ever have a vision again, now that it was lost? Now that she had lost it?

To still the voice, she concentrated on Rhys. Once she had Rhys back again, they could decide what to do. He could call for Welsh warriors, and they would come. Then they could go back and convince Prince Dafydd to lead them. Or find his son Llew. Or they could drive off the English once and for all and return to the old ways, with Rhys at the head of Meirionnydd, Llew at Gwynedd, and the remaining sons or grandsons of other lords leading other territories. Ideas churning in her head did nothing to help her sleep when they bedded down for the night, and she was happy to take her turn at the watch.

They made it to Llanberis Pass in four days. Cat welcomed the sight of the craggy cliffs and fast-flowing river if only because it meant she was closer to Rhys. Surely it would not be long before she saw him again.

"Slow down," Margred said. "We need to find a place to camp for the night."

"We need to make a plan," Cat said, temper flaring.

"Let me have a look around," Aeneus suggested. They stood on a rocky crag between the two lakes, Llyn Padarn and Llyn Peris. "This place offers shelter and would serve as a good camp for us."

"We need to get Rhys and get out before we lose the element of surprise," Cat said, her voice sharp.

"We just got here," Margred said, sitting against a rock and removing one worn boot to massage her foot. "I've got a blister the size of Idris himself. We need to rest and regroup. Aeneus is right. Let him scout the area to see what we're up against."

If Cat sat down, she would not be able to rise again. One part of her knew Margred was right, but she had been pushing herself for too long.

"We have had no food and little rest," Aeneus said. "You two fish, if you can. I will take a look around."

He disappeared down the path before she could protest. Cat watched him go and then turned to Margred.

"I'm sorry," she said. "I have some herbs that might help."

Margred threw her a grateful look and put her boot back on. "Let us get those fish first. I could eat at least three myself."

Cat made a face. "Only with a fire to cook them on."

Margred laughed. "Don't let Aeneus hear you say that."

They found a shallow cave where they could build a fire, and by the time Aeneus came back they had washed, scaled, and spitted the fish. He gave his report as they ate.

"There's a full company in the castle yard now, rebuilding and fortifying the walls. When I got you out some weeks ago, Cat, I could not get near the tower, and at that time there were fewer guards." He grimaced. "Now there are at least twice as many as before."

"It can't be hopeless," she said.

"No," he replied, quietly. "But it will take some planning, and a good night's sleep."

He left the two women inside the warm cave and took first watch. Cat tossed restlessly, unable to turn her mind off for long, until sleep finally took her.

The following morning, Aeneus was gone when Cat awoke. Margred slept on, so Cat found some wood for the fire and set the remaining fish from their previous night's meal on a flat rock to warm. Margred awoke to the smell, and Cat divided what was left in three. When Aeneus returned, he was grateful for his portion.

"I found the tunnel entrance that Hyw and your mam led us through when we fled Dolbadarn," Aeneus said. "I am sure I found it, but it would not open. I remember Hyw opened it from the inside for us, and later Adara did the same. But even if we could get in that way, there would be no safe way to get to the tower."

"How can that be?" Cat demanded. "We were able to get to Dafydd at Shrewsbury."

"These are hardened soldiers and mercenaries, used to fighting together," Aeneus said. "Not like Shrewsbury, with so many new faces coming and going. The chaos worked for us there."

"But if we could use the tunnel," Cat began, something stirring in her memory. Cat had often hid behind the curtains to listen to family conversations without the adults knowing. Llywelyn had chosen to keep his traitorous brother Owain ap Gryffudd there. Wasn't that why Llywelyn had closed off the tunnel? But Mam had known all the secret entrances and exits her family had made for the Welsh princes, and Mam had sent Hyw to open it from the inside. If her mam couldn't open the tunnel from outside the castle, how could Cat expect to succeed?

Then Cat recalled her vision of the ancestors. *Find the path, that we might find you.*

Could this be what Aylwen meant? The old songs had coaxed Hyw's mind to open up to her. Could she use the same songs to coax the tunnel open?

Driven by her need to find Rhys, Cat jumped up and started down the road. She had heard of the tunnel from Margred during their talks and knew roughly where to look, trusting her instincts to guide her.

"Cat, wait," Aeneus called softly, but she did not stop. Soon he and Margred caught up to her. "We can help, you know."

"Of course," she said, examining the mountains ahead of them. "I want to have a look."

Margred reached out and grabbed her arm, pulling her to a stop. "Wait."

They heard a sound like rock clattering on rock. Hooves. Aeneus grabbed Cat's arm. "Full gallop."

They were exposed on the narrowest part of the path. He gestured to Margred and pulled Cat back with him, running toward the cave. But they had come too far.

Two horses raced toward them. Aeneus pushed past both women to face the oncoming English soldiers. He drew his sword and dagger, but the soldiers were in full armour. One pulled up when he saw Aeneus, but the other horse reared and lost its footing on the narrow ledge. It screamed and struggled, but the path crumbled beneath its hooves and it went careening off the mountain, taking its rider with it.

The fate of the first took the second soldier by surprise, and he lost time in drawing his sword. Aeneus feinted toward the mountain, leaping upward to stab the soldier, who tried to raise his sword to parry. The sheer force of Aeneus' charge threw them both to the ground. The unlucky animal tried to turn but had no way to prevent itself from falling off the narrow ledge. Cat covered her ears against the screams of the dying horses echoing up the cliffside.

The two men lay in an unmoving heap on the path. Cat ran to Aeneus, who gasped with pain.

"It's nothing," he tried to say, but his shoulder hung at an odd angle. Margred rolled the English soldier over, but his head lolled. Aeneus had buried his blade into the soldier's neck, between his mail shirt and his helmet. Aeneus struggled to rise, holding his side. Cat stooped to help him.

"We have to get you back to the cave."

"Wait," he said. "He is dead. Unbuckle his sword, but I must roll him over the cliff. With luck the English will think the cliff gave way under their horses and not look too closely at him."

"I'll do it," Margred said.

"Lady Margred," Aeneus began, but she shoed him and Cat away.

"I will do it. Take Aeneus back and tend his injury."

Cat struggled to hold Aeneus up as they made their way back to the shelter of the cave. She helped him lay down where she had slept the previous night. Margred returned with the sword, helmet, and gauntlets. She set them down near the fire without speaking.

"All will be well," Aeneus said, his breath thready and rasping.

"Of course it will," Cat told him fiercely.

All seemed lost when Cat heard a hawk shriek in the underbrush behind them. She jerked around, her heart leaping in her chest. Hyw! Lost in the shape of a hawk again. She watched carefully, but no hawk appeared in the sky or in the branches of the nearby trees.

Then her eyes caught sight of figures moving in the underbrush, almost invisible, but human. She was overjoyed to find Hyw in his human shape, and pleased to see James and Gwilym.

She and Margred had been fishing in the small stream. Cat reminded them of the English soldiers, who still patrolled the area around the castle. They gathered up the buckets of water and fish, and she led the way back to the cave. Gwilym whistled softly at

Margred's description of Aeneus' battle with the armoured English soldiers. Cat noticed she left out the part about rolling the body over the cliff. Margred might speak of hating the English, but it was another matter to treat them as faceless enemies. Especially with James among them.

They had tied Aeneus' arm in a splint, and he was sitting near the entrance to the cave when they came back. He had heard their approach and was seated with the sword in his uninjured hand. He set the sword down and clasped Gwilym's forearm as Llywelyn had taught them. Hyw asked about the castle.

"If you could get us inside again," Cat said to him, "I know we could get to Rhys and bring him out."

Aeneus coughed. "They have garrisoned up in recent weeks. I do not believe we can succeed by that ruse again."

Gwilym gestured to Hyw. "We brought something that might brighten your spirits."

Hyw lifted his sack from his back and opened it, while James drew the items out. "Our former Prince Llywelyn calls this the Holy Grail that will unite our people again," Hyw said.

"This is the chalice?" Margred asked, a puzzled look on her face. "It is so plain."

Cat hugged him to her for the second time that day. "I cannot believe you did it!" She thought of her vision. "And I know whose hands must hold it."

36

Hyw managed to connect with a mouse again and got inside Dolbadarn's tower to find Rhys. Hyw could not bear to tell Cat the state he found Rhys in, but he was grateful to have James to confide in.

"Rhys was chained to the wall and the guards sat in front of the cell and shouted insults at him. Then they unchained him and took him to another chamber, where they beat him until I could no longer watch."

"What did they want? They already have Dafydd."

"They asked him where Cat was and where his men are hiding." Hyw stared at his hands. "But in truth it seemed that they beat him for sport, James, and did not care what he answered except that it gave them an excuse to hit him again."

"Is he..." James began, and then faltered. He reached forward and placed his hand on Hyw's. "How is he managing?"

Hyw's heart sang at the gesture but he did not move, not sure how to react and not wanting to ruin the moment. "He laughed in their faces until they beat him senseless. Then they dragged him back and chained him again. Yet still they did not leave him alone but set up their chairs to wait for him to revive again. I could not help him, and I could not bear to watch."

James put an arm around Hyw's shoulder then, and Hyw let himself be comforted.

After the evening meal, they held a war council to come up with a new plan. After tossing out and rejecting several ideas, Hyw sighed.

"If only I had the strength of our grandfather's gift."

"But you are stronger," Cat said, almost absently.

"I am not."

"You are. Mam often said so. She said you would have the strength of the legends once you were grown."

"He has grown so much already," James put in.

Hyw flushed and huffed out a laugh. "Very well, I am legendary."

"This gift you have is very close to the legends, Hyw," Gwilym put in. "The strongest of the *Tylwyth Teg* could transform into anything, even other people."

"If I could turn into King Edward, we should surely succeed," Hyw quipped.

"But if you could…" Cat suddenly leaned forward. "There is one closer to home that would ensure our success."

"Do you mean…?" Hyw's voice trailed off. As soon as she said it, Hyw knew exactly who she meant. The others stared at each other and shook their heads. Hyw held up one hand to convince them to wait and closed his eyes to find Llywelyn.

"I would need your agreement to succeed," he told the former prince. As Hyw explained his idea, Llywelyn's face first reflected rage. Then a calculating look narrowed his eyes. Finally he bared his teeth in a feral smile. He bent his knees slightly and brought up his sword, two-handed, over his shoulder in readiness.

Have at him!

Hyw opened his eyes to see the faces around the low fire staring at him in the dim twilight. "If we cannot get to the tower through the tunnel, then we must walk in through the front door." He turned to his sister. "Tell me everything you can remember about Stephen de Francton."

Between them, they had gathered three swords, two helmets, and one coat of mail. James wore his own mail, his sword sheathed at his side, and the helmet Gwilym had salvaged in the dungeon covering his head. Gwilym used the sword he had taken. Now he knelt at Margred's feet as she placed the helmet she had salvaged onto his head.

"How could she help but succumb to him?" James asked.

"Gwilym?"

James nodded, staring at the bard. A barb jabbed into Hyw's heart, and he crossed his arms across his chest.

"He is not worthy of her."

"I think they make a good match," James said, turning to Hyw. "What? You look like thunder, Hyw." Hyw remained silent, and James suddenly laughed. "You are jealous!"

"Of Margred? I am not. It is only that we are friends and I don't want to see her hurt."

"I think she will hold her own well," James said. "But I am right. You are jealous. And not of Margred."

Hyw raised an eyebrow and half turned toward James. "Well, he is a bard, after all. He is—eloquent and—well-spoken, and who could resist him?"

"Oh, come now." James took his arm. "Never fear. Your stories are equally as good as his."

"Think you?"

"Riveting. You could have been a bard."

Hyw wished James was not wearing his armour at that moment, but Gwilym stood, and it was time for them to go. Hyw took a deep breath.

Gwilym turned to Hyw. "The tricky part is left to you."

"I disagree," Hyw said, still a little rankled by James' appreciation of the bard's performance. "It will hinge on keeping de Francton from the castle long enough for us to succeed."

"Leave that to us," Cat said. Aeneus took the third sword in his hand and joined her. His swarthy skin was paler than usual, and he leaned against a new javelin he had whittled the previous night, but he stood as straight as always. Margred stood beside him with her bow and quiver of arrows. Hyw smiled.

"Have at him!"

37

Cat walked toward the gates of Dolbadarn castle alone, but she could feel her friends behind her, Margred with her bow trained on the castle walls and Aeneus holding his new javelin.

Cat had used what remained of her linen to tie a while flag of truce to the stake Aeneus presented to her earlier. Even knowing they were at her back, her hands trembled. She waved the flag in front of her to make the movement look more purposeful.

"What! Ho!" someone yelled from the castle walls.

"I have a message for Stephen de Francton," she called up to the soldiers on the wall walk. Imagining Princess Elinor at her side, she pulled herself up straight and raised her voice. "Tell him the Lady Catrin of Bere wishes to convey her greetings and an urgent warning."

"Wait while we open the gates," the soldier called back.

"Nay, I do not trust him or you," she called back. "He must meet me on the mountain, where we have more equal footing. Tell him to come quickly."

With that she turned and ran into the trees. Her legs flew over the ground, and she was sure at any moment arrows would rain down on her head. But either the soldiers understood the flag of truce or they were so shocked to see a woman that they didn't react in time. She made it to the trees and climbed to the spot they had chosen for the meeting.

Her job was to negotiate with de Francton, and make him believe she would keep her end of the bargain if he kept his. They all relied on how much she knew of the man and his actions in the past.

"He has just left the gates," Aeneus said. "He is on horseback and he has too many men with him."

"Wait in the trees," Cat told them, thinking quickly. "I will face him alone. Do not move against him unless he tries to take me."

"That is too dangerous," Margred said.

"I know him," Cat said. "He has always been honourable, although he wouldn't want anyone to know it. Besides, if he can overpower us anyway, what choice do we have?"

Aeneus looked at her for a long moment before he nodded to Margred. "We can at least even the odds and give her a chance to get away. Let us hope that Hyw is able to fulfill his part of the plan. You must—"

"Keep him here as long as I can," she finished. "Yes, I know." She gestured to them and they disappeared.

The minutes dragged on as Cat waited. She stood for a time, and then her legs began to tremble. She sat on a ledge of rock, then stood, then sat again. She picked the piece of white fabric off the stake in case she needed to run, so she wouldn't have to leave it behind. Or perhaps she could wave it at de Francton. She started to crease it in her fingers and then stopped, in case that made her look nervous.

She wanted to ask Margred and Aeneus if they could see de Francton coming. She stood and shielded her eyes to look up into the trees, trying to catch sight of either of her friends. Then she quickly looked away lest anyone spot her and guess the ruse. She wanted to look down at the castle and see if Hyw had arrived at the gate yet. But she knew she couldn't, because that would also give away the ruse. Finally she sat again, took a deep breath, and released it. She could do this.

She heard the horses' hooves against the rock before anyone appeared. Two soldiers rode in front, rounding the corner of the path and stopping when they saw her. One soldier moved his horse around and de Francton rode past them both. Two others rode into the area, and she saw the soldiers scanning the rocks and trees. Watching for a trap, no doubt. She had a moment of fear for her friends, and took a deep breath again to steady herself. She couldn't see how many soldiers he had brought with him in all.

"Should I be flattered?" she said, her voice thinner than she hoped it would be. "I am not truly so frightening, am I?"

De Francton dismounted and walked over to her. "You are alone, Lady Catrin?"

"I would not be, if you would release my husband."

He leaned against a slab of rock, facing her. "Ah, the Lord Rhys. I'm afraid we have little to gain by that, at this point."

"So, you don't want to hear about the rise of the Welsh resistance?"

He stared at her for a moment. "And why would you want to tell me of it?"

"That should be obvious," she said. "I want my husband back."

He settled against the rock. "Perhaps we can come to an arrangement."

And so it began. Seeing Gwilym again had reminded her of one of his battle songs, from the war over 100 years ago when the Welsh mustered to its leader, who was also named Rhys—Rhys ap Gruffydd. Not so much had changed, really, whatever the English might think. The House of Aberffraw would remain as long as its people could remember them. She felt herself calming as she started her story.

Hyw watched as Cat ran towards the woods. The commotion she caused in the castle would have been humorous if he hadn't had his heart in his throat. He breathed more freely as she disappeared, and James clapped a gloved hand on his shoulder.

"Brave woman," James whispered, and Hyw nodded.

"Now we wait," said Gwilym, on his other side. Time dragged but they dared not look away. Finally the gates opened and a troop of English soldiers rode out. Hyw's fear for his sister increased. There was little point in them succeeding with Rhys if it meant losing Catrin. He should go after her.

"Don't worry," James said. "She has Margred and Aeneus with her. And she knows what she's about."

"We must get ready on our end," Gwilym said. They watched de Francton's party enter the woods to follow Cat. She would lead them to the perfect spot, and accomplish the first part of their plan. Now Hyw must lead James and Gwilym, in their borrowed English helmets, back into the castle.

James stood at Hyw's side. "Are you ready?"

Hyw closed his eyes. Llywelyn stood in his armour, as if ready to do battle, his moustache trimmed and bristling.

"You are truly formidable, my liege," Hyw told him, speaking only in his mind. The former prince smiled.

Let us move forward with confidence, Hyw.

Hyw joined hands with Llywelyn. Focusing on de Francton's face in his memory, and joining his mind to Llywelyn's, he began to change. He felt himself grow taller, broader, his nose lengthening as his face changed shape. He heard James gasp but he kept his eyes closed until it was finished. And when he opened them, he saw Gwilym swallow roughly.

"I can scarcely credit it," the bard said.

"You are—him, Hyw," James said. "Or so much like him that I am sure his own mother could not tell the difference."

"Then let us—" he stopped. His own voice caught in his ear, and nearly undid him.

Steady on, lad, he heard Llywelyn say inside his mind, and he closed his eyes to focus on the image again. The moment passed. Hyw breathed out and opened his eyes. He cleared his throat and lowered his voice slightly, trying to add a nasal twang.

"Then let us go and get our prisoner."

"You've got it," Gwilym said. "I couldn't have done it better myself."

They began walking, and soon Hyw's stride lengthened and he gained confidence. And why should it not? After all, he was Stephen de Francton.

"Open the gates," James yelled, as they neared the castle. "Sir Stephen returns."

The portcullis clattered up and they stepped through.

"Where—where is your horse, Sir Stephen?" one of the guards asked.

"Where I left him," Hyw said and kept walking. They were through the gate and across the courtyard, heading for the tower. He passed the guards without comment, went up the stairs, and gestured for the tower guards to move out of the way. James grabbed the keys from the hook as they passed.

The smell hit them first. Sweat, blood, urine, and faeces. More than one man was being kept in this prison.

More than they bargained for.

Hyw kept going. He took the keys from James and entered the cell. Rhys was chained, bleeding, against the wall. Hyw's disguise fluttered as he unchained his future brother-in-law and held him.

Steady.

"Let me go," Rhys rasped.

"Don't fight with us, Lord Rhys," Gwilym said. "Come with us."

Rhys looked at him, then looked back at Hyw. "Who are you?"

Hyw dared not speak. He felt de Francton's face and form flutter again.

"Don't ask any more questions, prisoner," James said. "Or any of the rest of you." James moved like lightening around the room, unchaining men, helping them to their feet, ordering them to the door. Gwilym soon did the same, and they gathered more than twenty prisoners in only a few minutes. Rhys pointed at a piece of brown leather hung on a wall peg, and Gwilym reached out and pocketed it.

Hyw could feel everything slipping away from him. He could feel his face and form begin to dissolve.

Hold on, Hyw. Llywelyn's voice rang in his ears, but it was James who rallied him.

"You must hang on, Hyw." James held his shoulders. Hyw let himself drown in the warmth of his friend's brown eyes. "I will get you through this. But you must hang on a few more minutes. We are lost without you now."

Hyw focused on James, his eyes, his face. His friend. His love. He held on. And the moment passed again.

"Let us go," Hyw said. Then he cleared his throat and tried again. "Let us go."

"Yes." James released him, the look of relief on his face telling Hyw everything he needed to know. They could do this. They could get the prisoners out. All of them.

The guards made a sound and leapt to attention as Hyw strode by them.

"Sir Stephen, what's happening?" one of them asked. "The prisoners—"

Hyw turned around and faced him. "Are you questioning me?"

"Of course not, Sir Stephen. Of course not."

"They are coming with me. That's all you need to know."

The guard backed down, and Hyw turned to lead the procession of men down the tower steps and across the courtyard to the gate. James walked beside the prisoners, prodding them on, and Gwilym brought up the rear, half-carrying Rhys.

They could hear the clop of horses' hooves as they reached the forest. Hyw collapsed against a tree and kept his face averted as the disguise began to dissolve inside him. James pushed the men ahead of him.

"Run," he told them. "You're free as long as you can stay that way. Get back to your farms or climb as high as you can into the mountains and stay out of sight."

Some of them ran, and some turned to look at the English boy. Gwilym had joined James by then, and he added in Welsh. "You heard him. Get moving, and don't ask questions. There's not enough of us to protect you unless you can protect yourselves. Go!"

And with that, the last of them turned and ran. Hyw slumped down and James lifted him back up again. Rhys grabbed Hyw's shoulder.

"Where's Cat?"

"We're out of time," Gwilym said, still holding him up. "We've got to move, and now!"

Cat waited near the hill fort, hiding in a crevasse of rock and watching. Surely Hyw and the others would come soon. Surely Rhys would come soon. She had managed to convince de Francton that she had something to trade in return for Rhys' life. But de Francton had not quite looked in her eyes, and she knew it would never happen. They had one chance to get Rhys back, and that was if Hyw's plan worked. She had faith in her brother, but so much could go wrong.

De Francton had agreed to let her leave with a promise to fetch the Welsh resistance fighters and bring them to him, the following day. Little did he know that the Welsh resistance was an army of ghosts, hiding in the songs of a Welsh bard and the breezes that blew down Cadair Idris. But de Francton had ridden off with his men. She had run without waiting for Aeneus and Margred, trusting that they would watch in case de Francton left a spy or two to follow her.

When Margred and Aeneus joined her, she knew from their silence that there had indeed been a spy. Or two. That no one could be trusted in war, and the only way to win was to stay alive.

And she led her friends back to the caves.

Hyw was so drained he could barely walk. The thing about being human was that it took more out of him, somehow, than being an animal ever could. He wanted to say this to James, but he didn't think he had the breath. He turned to look at James, who was staggering under the weight of keeping them both upright and walking. He should help. He should be walking on his own right now.

"That's right, one foot in front of the other," James said.

Hyw was so lucky to have James. He wanted to cry, but he didn't want James to think worse of him. He would look after James. He would hunt and feed James from his beak. No, that was wrong. He would crawl in between the cracks of the floor and give James a message. No, that wasn't it either. Well. He would sleep, and then when he woke up, he would ask James. James would know what it was he was supposed to do.

Behind them, Hyw could hear someone else, struggling along

the path. He looked back and caught sight of Gwilym, holding Rhys by the shoulder. Rhys was filthy, and bleeding from somewhere. And he stank. He really did. What would Cat say? He should swim in the river. That's what they all should do. Here was the Padarn and the Peris, after all. What better place to swim than the twin lakes?

Aber Falls. That's where. That's the place he and Cat and Emrys and Bron used to swim when they were children, at home. At Garth Celyn. And then he remembered. Garth Celyn was gone. His da was gone. Cynfrig was gone. Likely Emrys and Bron as well. All gone.

All but Cat. And Rhys. Margred. Aeneus. Gwilym. Llywelyn. And James.

"James," Hyw said.

"It's all right. I've got you."

"Let me go."

"We need to keep moving."

"I know. I can walk now. We need to help Rhys."

And then he was walking on his shaky legs beside James. They turned, and Hyw took Rhys' other shoulder, filth and all.

"We've got you, brother," he said. "We'll get you back to Cat."

Rhys made a sound.

"What was that?"

"Not like this," Rhys rasped.

"You're right," Hyw said. "The English be damned. Let us get him cleaned up."

At the stream bed, they laid Rhys down on the bank and used one of the English helmets to pour water on him. His cuts were deep, but with luck Cat's herbs would help cure him. Reeds and leaves were all they had, but they rubbed him as best they could.

"Are these yours?" Gwilym asked Rhys. He had unfolded the brown leather Rhys had asked him to take from the cell and raised his eyebrows at the contents.

"It's for Cat," Rhys managed to say, struggling to get to his feet.

"Some help here," James said. Gwilym pocketed the item, and between the three of them, they got Rhys up and supported him the rest of the way. As they walked, Hyw looked over at James. His eyes really were the warmest brown.

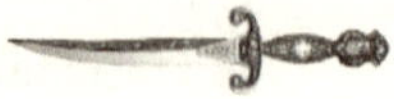

"Rhys!" Cat couldn't help but cry out as she saw him, and she ran to throw her arms around him. Her brother and the others were still holding him up, and she jumped back to check him over. "Bring him in. Quickly!"

They helped him into the cave and laid him beside the fire. Rhys stopped Gwilym before he could turn to go, reaching out a hand. Gwilym handed him the brown leather before Cat shushed him out of the cave.

"Give me space to work."

With trembling hands, she took the herbs from her pouch and sprinkled them into the curve of a stone she had found, adding water from her waterskin. Lucky her mam had never walked without gathering herbs, and never failed to explain to Cat what they were for and how they might be useful. She had to trust that she could remember Mam's teachings and that she had picked the right herbs on their journeys. She knelt to take another look at Rhys' arm, but he stopped her hand with his own. He handed her the leather and she took it with a small exclamation.

"My knives! How did you--?"

"They taunted me with them." His voice was hoarse with emotion. "But it only reminded me of you, and gave me strength."

She threw her arms around him without thinking. He winced but when she tried to move away he held onto her another moment. She finally drew back, but he kept her hand.

"Cat, we must find the relics," he said.

She felt his forehead, but there was no fever. "I—we haven't had much time to discuss it, but you must know…"

"I know," he said. "You did what you thought you had to do. But you must know that I hold my life less dear than my country, Cat."

"But I hold you more dear." She began to clean and dress his wound. "You may see me just as a morrigan to help you win a war, but you are much more than that to me. You are the boy who took me hunting with his friends, when we were still children. And you are the man I am pledged to marry."

He stared at her for a long moment. "You are not 'just a morrigan' to me," he said. "It is true you were pledged to me, but you were young. I told you I would protect you with my name, no matter what befalls us. But my name is dust now, and my claim to my ancestral land is less than dust. I cannot protect you now."

"I think I have proven I can protect myself."

"With me, you can only be a fugitive," he said, turning to stare fixedly at the cave wall as if looking for enemies. "Or worse.

"It may be that we cannot survive what is to come, or that one of us may survive and the other not. But you must know that I love you, Rhys ap Cadwgan."

He recoiled from her as if she had struck him. "It cannot be, Catrin. Do you not see? I will not have your loss of power laid at my feet, too."

"If that is so, then so be it," she said. "I would trade power and crowns and relics of any price for your life."

"And that trade would make my life worthless," he said. "Can you not see those crowns and that relic are the only hope now? Too many have turned to Edward. We must find the relics and save Dafydd. That is the only way to rally the people and save *Cymru.* That is all that matters now."

"Dafydd will not be saved."

Rhys struggled to get up but she pushed him down again.

"Nay, you must hear me," Cat insisted. "I would trade those relics because I know that's not what will rally the people of this country. What we need is you. You, Rhys ap Cadwgan. You will rally Wales, with or without a relic. If it can be done, you will do it."

He stopped then, his head tilted slightly to the side as if surprised. Encouraged, Cat pressed on.

"You are the man we looked to when Criccieth Castle fell," she said. "And you distracted the *Saeson* so Dafydd could escape from Bere. When that castle fell, you led us to safety. Nary a relic helped you then, nor a morrigan whose powers had waned."

"Your powers returned, as I knew they would."

"And whatever they are worth, I pledge them to you—but not because of old ties forged in our parents' day, or crowns or relics. I pledge them to you because I have seen your heart, strong and true. And it is *Cymru*, Rhys. That is the hope of Wales now."

He did not turn away from her. She could still see the anger in his eyes, but something else burned there as well, now.

"If it is relics you need, then have this," she said, opening the pack at her feet and removing the chalice. "This is the relic made from the seals of the house of Aberffraw. This was what King Edward feared the most in all Wales. Not the crowns of dead kings or even a piece of the True Cross, but the seals. The right of a people to govern themselves. The English king feared it so much that he melted it to make this silver chalice. I give it to you. You can decide for all of us what should be done with it."

Then he shook his head as if to clear it. "Can it be true?"

"Ask my brother," she said, standing and walking away from him. "It is for you to decide now."

Hyw brought up the rear of their party, as they snuck into the holding almost a week later. He carried the silver chalice—Llywelyn's grail—in a sack over his shoulder. What little they had, they carried easily among them. They made their way from the caves in stealth, avoiding de Francton's patrols and the English troops removing from Wales, to gain the holding at sunset.

Rhys stopped in the square, his arm around Catrin. He beckoned Hyw over as the people began to gather around them.

"You will have heard by now that Prince Dafydd is taken," Rhys said. "That King Edward has the Cross of Neith, and the crowns of Arthur and Llywelyn. The rumours are true. The English have them."

The people began to murmur and look to their neighbours. Rhys continued speaking.

"You may have also heard that the Welsh are defeated. And perhaps you believe those rumours as well. There may even be those among you who welcome this change."

Now the murmurs swelled, some of the townspeople shaking

their heads, some casting their eyes to the ground. Rhys waited them out. The burnt orange rays of the setting sun lit his face and arms, still purple with bruises. But a few days of rest and Cat's herbal remedies had him standing upright. He drew a breath and straightened to his full height now. Aeneus moved behind them, with Gwilym and Margred flanking them. Hyw reached for James' hand, and James didn't shy away this time, even with the townspeople watching. Finally the people grew quiet, and Rhys began again.

"I am Lord Rhys ap Cadwgan of Meirionnydd. In the past, your rulers and lords have kept truths from you, fearing your idle tongues. And you have no doubt resented them, for taking your bread and your cattle out of the mouths of your children. But those times are gone now. Gone forever. I am here with you, as one of you, and we will stand or fall together against whatever may come."

There was a kind of hush now, as if they could not quite believe him. Even Llywelyn had nothing to say. With Cat's help, Rhys turned to the sack on Hyw's shoulder, and removed the chalice. He unwrapped it slowly as he spoke.

"And so I will trust you with this knowledge, and in it, we will take our power together." He held up the silver chalice for all to see. "King Edward of England made this chalice from the seals of your former princes. He feared the power of those seals more than any ancient magic. Because those were the symbols of Welsh independence and authority. He thought to humble that authority by hiding it away in an English abbey, along with the children of your princes."

There was a cry of "No!" from the crowd, and Rhys turned to it.

"No, indeed." His voice boomed out across the square. "We told him, 'No!'" He gestured to Hyw, James, and Gwilym. "Your countrymen told him, 'No!' Then we took the chalice back! We took it to present it to you, today. So let this be our symbol now. The symbol of a free and independent Wales. A symbol that Edward and his lords must never know the truth of. If we are shackled, let us bear those shackles together, knowing that this is our future."

A cheer rose up among them, and carried from one to the

other until it rang from every throat. And as it died away, a voice shouted from the crowd.

"But how can we hide it from them?"

"The best place to hide the chalice is in plain sight," Rhys answered, as if he had been waiting for the question. "The abbey near our holding was where *Tywysog* Llywelyn hid the relics, and it is the best place again now."

Hyw was surprised Llywelyn had not thought of it. He closed his eyes briefly to see the former prince, his eyes glowing. *This is good.*

"And we will guard it, all of us together," Rhys went on. "We can make a life here, and help each other survive until we can find a way to take back our homeland." Turning to James and Hyw, he added, "There is room for all of us."

And the crowd came towards them then, welcoming Rhys and Cat as if they were conquering heroes. Cat held Cynfrig's wife Haf as she cried. Hyw was overjoyed to find Emrys alive, although he leaned on a walking stick still. When Hyw pulled James over to introduce them, Emrys immediately took his forearm in the old greeting Llywelyn had taught them.

"Well met!" Emrys said, clasping James' arm in turn. "And glad I am to meet you at last."

Bronwen let Hyw feel the baby move inside her. "If he's a boy, we plan to name him Llywelyn," Bron said shyly.

Hyw closed his eyes briefly, in time to see a small and almost sad smile play around the former prince's mouth. *I recall when Elizabeth gave her eldest son my name,* he whispered, and Hyw felt the prince's concern about Gwenllian and Dafydd's children.

"We will find them," Hyw told him. And Margred's sisters, he added to himself. We will convince Mam and Elizabeth to come and join us here.

"With such a silver tongue, you have little need of a bard," Gwilym said, clapping Rhys on the shoulder as he and Margred stepped closer.

"You haven't heard me sing," Rhys responded, wincing a little from his injuries. Then Rhys looked at Aeneus, who stared off into the distance for a moment, and then nodded.

"I have a pledge to fulfill, but first I will see this through."

Emrys took their attention then and began to introduce a few other families that had managed to survive the English and find their way to the holding. Hyw turned to congratulate Rhys, but the former Lord of Meirionnydd and his sister were locked in each other's arms.

Nos Galan Gaeaf

Cat shivered in the full moon that lit *Nos Galan Gaeaf*, the night when the veil between their world and the OtherWorld was thinnest. Rhys put his arm around her shoulders, and she looked around to see Aeneus, Gwilym, Margred, Hyw, and James. Her uncle Gawain had returned to them the day before, bringing the news of Dafydd's death, which had left them all reeling.

She shuddered again at the gruesome details they had dragged from Gawain, in hushed and halting tones around the fire. The former Prince of Wales had not uttered a sound as he was dragged through the streets of Shrewsbury, and then hung, drawn and quartered like a common criminal. The children were thought to be alive still, but knowing Dafydd had made that bargain willingly on their behalf made the act no less barbarous. Aeneus had been speechless at the news, and even now she could see his shoulders hunched with rage and grief.

At least, Elizabeth and Adara had not witnessed it. Gawain assured Cat that her mam and the former princess had been sent away. Rumour had it they had been sent back to north Wales, although Gawain did not know their location.

Still, they had all climbed with her and Hyw to the giant's seat at the top of Cadair Idris, to let the giant's moaning winds blow their hair into their eyes. She looked away from them, into the twinkling night sky. The moon neared the top of its path.

It was time.

Cat stepped forward, away from Rhys. Gawain and Hyw moved to join her. They held hands as Gawain began the song, and Cat joined in harmony with him. She breathed in and drew the mists to her as before. For a moment she lost sight of the world around her. Then she was swirling with and through the mists until she could see her brother again. Behind Hyw, Llywelyn stood tall in his royal armour, topped by a velvet cloak and sash sporting the insignia of the Prince of Wales. An ornate Celtic knot pinned the cloak about the former prince's neck, but it was thrown back over his shoulder. Llywelyn placed a hand on Hyw's arm.

Hyw, you have been my most faithful servant and, at the same time, the master of our fate. Now, our time has come to an end. I will miss you, in spite of and perhaps because of what we have shared. Then the prince turned to her. *I am ready to see my princess and spend eternity with her.*

With a wave of her hand, Cat cleared the mist to reveal Garth Celyn as it had been, and as it could be. An early morning sun slanted off the rooftop of Ty Hir. Sturdy wood and stone buildings fanned out from the longhouse, and the people flooded into the courtyard to greet them. Dafydd knelt before his brother and kissed his hand in fealty before rising again.

All the fallen were among them, even Ifan and Cynfrig. Hywel ap Rhys Gryg and his sons waved at them. Cat scanned the group until she spotted the tall red-haired man who must be her uncle Twm. Then Da moved in front of the others, to stand tall at the head of the line, holding his sword aloft. She almost ran to him, but the mists held her in place, and she heard the songs of her ancestors around her.

And then the people parted, and Elinor walked among them, beautiful in her white spring gown, holding a bouquet of wild daffodils and heather. She held out her hand, and Llywelyn stepped out from behind Hyw. He walked toward her, holding out his hand out to her in turn.

What was, will ever be, Llywelyn said, and the people responded as one, "For *Cymru!*" The sound filled the space around them until Cat was sure it must burst through into the centuries to come.

"For *Cymru!*"

They waited for Hyw to recover before they returned from the mountain. As they walked, a sense of peace filled Cat. James supported Hyw, and the others followed closely behind. She and Rhys could plan their wedding now, she thought, and felt suddenly shy. When they were in sight of the holding, Cat ran ahead, turning to laugh back at Rhys. She entered the hut, hugging Bron once before she took up a kitchen knife to join the women preparing the evening meal.

"We need more water for the pottage," Haf said, turning from the hearth to spot Cat. "Back so soon?" Haf glanced from her to the door.

"He's fine," Cat told her. "It went fine."

The older woman began to untie her apron and head for the door. Cat knew Haf would be going to check on Hyw and James. The older woman had taken them under her wing since their return to the holding. Cat took the bucket from her and went to draw water from the well at the centre of the town. She passed Aeneus on the way, carrying a pack over his shoulder, and stopped him.

"You know what I must do," he said.

"Would it not be better to have companions on the road?"

Aeneus said nothing, and she continued. "You must at least stay for the meal."

He shrugged and turned, heading back toward the hut where the women were working.

Cat drew the water and leaned over the full bucket with deliberation, rippling the water with her fingers and thinking of the violet eyes that led her to Aylwen verch Arianrhod—

—and instead of a vision, her ancestor's skeptical face swam into view as the ripples cleared.

"What have you learned, granddaughter?"

"I have learned the value of pain."

"Then you have learned much. But the lesson is not over."

"No," Cat said slowly. She thought of Cynfrig's final salute, and Rhys' bleeding body. "It may never be over."

"Not until death. So it is for us all." Aylwen's features softened. "And what do you seek?"

"If Rhys and I are married, and I have a child…" Cat's voice trailed off, but Aylwen said nothing. "Will it mean the end of my gift?"

"Your gifts are strong, yours and your brother's," Aylwen said. "We gathered all we could for you, and for your gifts."

"That is not an answer," Cat said. "Will we truly be the last with magic?"

Aylwen laughed. "Magic cannot end. But like all living things, it needs time and nurturing to recover."

"So there is hope, then?"

"There is always hope." Aylwen turned her head to one side. "Is that what you seek?"

Cat took a moment to answer. "We seek freedom. We seek a place where we can be ourselves."

"You have found one," Aylwen said, turning away.

"Wait," Cat called out—

—but the image faded.

Cat returned to the hut. Aeneus was already there, seated with Gwilym. Rhys, James and Hyw came in with Emrys and the others. Hyw was still pale, but James stood close to him and Cat thought how right they looked together. They would eat in groups of three, as was their custom. And she and Rhys would serve them.

"Come, sit with us," Gwilym called to Margred. "And after the meal I will sing."

"Perhaps you will compose a song of our adventures," Hyw said, catching Cat's eye with a grin.

Perhaps no one would believe it, Cat almost said. But she only smiled.

The End

ɧISƆORICAL NOƆE

The year 1282 must have begun with great hope. Llywelyn ap Gruffydd (c. 1223–11 December, 1282), acknowledged Prince of Wales, and his wife Elinor expected their first child. A boy would become the heir to the kingdom Llywelyn had spent his life building—and then trying to keep

By 1282, Llywelyn ap Gruffydd or Llywelyn Ein Llyw Olaf (our last leader), as he came to be known, had gained and lost a kingdom. He reached adulthood in a time of great political upheaval in Wales that included the deaths of his famous grandfather, and shortly afterward, the uncle who had become ruler in Wales. Under Welsh law, a boy came of age at fourteen. Recent scholarship suggests Llywelyn went on the 1240-41 Crusade as a teenager. He was a minor figure in Welsh political life at that time. By 1258, he had defeated his older brother Owain to take control in Gwynedd. Llywelyn began to pull the disparate leaders of Wales into some form of unity. The title Prince of Wales was officially granted to him by Henry III (Edward's father) in 1267, under the Treaty of Montgomery.

Llywelyn was the last prince of an independent Wales under the treaty, lasting some ten years from 1267 until about 1277. We don't know much about that time, because most of the records and artifacts of the last Welsh prince have been destroyed. In his book, Llywelyn Ap Gruffudd: Prince of Wales, J. Beverley Smith suggests that it was a combination of political and military determination. But in my imagination, Wales under Llywelyn's rule was a kind of Camelot.

After a lifetime of fighting, Llywelyn would surely have incorporated peace into his version of a unified Wales. He was known to trace his own lineage back to Troy, so it's possible that, in Llywelyn's Wales, arts and culture flourished and people had a taste of freedoms that were not generally known in medieval times. Llywelyn's letters to defend his dream of a unified Wales have been considered among the most eloquent statesmanship of the time. But it also seems likely that many living in such a Camelot would not have realized their fortune until it was snatched away from them.

Elinor (I have used Welsh spelling for Eleanor to avoid confusion with the numerous other Eleanors of this time period) was the daughter of Simon de Montfort, a nobleman who became a friend and ally of Llywelyn. In 1263, she was betrothed to Llywelyn, although she would have been about five years old. After her father's defeat, the family was exiled to France. Llywelyn apparently kept faith with de Montfort and his daughter: unlike other Welsh leaders, not even rumours suggest other romantic relationships or children in his life. In about 1275-1276, Elinor and Llywelyn were married by proxy. But, as Elinor sailed from France to join her Welsh prince, she was captured by Edward I, King of England, who held her in captivity for three years.

Trying to get her back, Llywelyn lost a major battle to the English king in 1277. The country split into North and South Wales, with parts of the south held by lords who served King Edward. Under the Treaty of Aberconwy, Llywelyn kept his title but had to pay a stiff tribute in money and sign away most of his land. He retained only Gwynedd in North Wales.

Finally, in 1278, Edward allowed the wedding and led Elinor down the aisle to meet Llywelyn, her future husband. Between 1278 and 1282, Llywelyn and Elinor appear to have been happy together. Then in the spring of 1282, Llywelyn's younger brother Dafydd attacked the English, who were, in his opinion, terrorizing his people and castles. Llywelyn tried to avoid committing the country to war by not joining with his brother.

On June 19, 1282, Elinor died giving birth to a baby girl, Gwenllian. Llywelyn went into mourning. The Marcher lords on the border between England and Wales increased their attacks against the Welsh. Llywelyn tried to prevent war by appealing to the pope on behalf of his people, and Edward sent the English Archbishop of Canterbury to visit the Welsh court in the autumn. The Archbishop stayed there in the first week of November, during a truce on all sides. During his visit, the Archbishop offered Llywelyn lands and personal gain if he would relinquish his title and surrender to King Edward. Llywelyn and his nobles refused. On November 6, the English forces broke the truce and attacked by water across the

Menai Straight. Llywelyn's forces defeated the English, and many died. The Archbishop later proclaimed the Welsh heathen and in need of subjugation by English forces.

Llywelyn was killed suddenly and unexpectedly on December 11, 1282. There are many stories about how and why he died, and whether or not he was preparing to go to war with Edward. Some stories suggest he was surprised while meeting allies near Builth, and killed by a Shropshire soldier named Stephen de Francton, who did not recognize him as the Prince of Wales. De Francton profited little from his actions, since others took Llywelyn's head to the king.

Edward hung Llywelyn's head on a pike at the Tower of London, where it remained for close to a decade. The prince's seal and letters that may have contained evidence of treachery against Llywelyn were stolen from his body and taken to the Archbishop. Later Edward melted Llywelyn's seal, along with Elinor's and Dafydd's seals, and made them into a silver chalice, which was sent to an abbey in Lincolnshire for safekeeping.

Llywelyn was the last true prince of an independent Wales before its conquest by Edward I of England. This is where this story begins.

# # #

By May of 1283, independent Wales was in a desperate state. After the murder of Llywelyn ap Gruffydd, the English began hunting down his brother Dafydd, who some say was trying to hold the country together by assuming the title of Prince of Wales.

During the first six months of 1283, the English forces chased Dafydd from castle to castle throughout north Wales, but did not capture him when the castles fell. At various points, Dafydd was accompanied by Llywelyn's daughter Gwenllian, as well as his own wife Elizabeth, at least one son and daughter, and several illegitimate daughters. Although he eluded them at first, Dafydd's forces dwindled until finally he was betrayed and captured in June of 1283. He was tried and executed at Shrewsbury in October 1283, becoming the first nobleman to be hung, drawn, and quartered.

# # #

My personal introduction to Welsh history began during a family trip to Wales in 2006. It encompassed a rather rambling self-guided tour, including a sheep farm in the Snowdon mountains of Gwynedd and a restored 13 th century wattle-and-daub cottage in Ceredigion. As we toured castles and historical sites, we read and heard more about the country's history. We were especially impressed by the restoration of the Welsh language. The highway and street signs were in Welsh first, English second, and school children are taught in Welsh. How could a language outlawed 800 years ago come back to thrive in the 21 st century?

According to family lore, the Powell family was apparently the "keeper of the Holy Grail." After our first trip, I read in J. Beverley Smith's book that the Welsh royal seals were melted into a silver chalice. A "grail" and a "chalice" are both essentially cups. My imagination was sparked, and the story began to unfold.

Over the years, I've relied on many research sources, a selection of which are listed under Further Reading. I found inspiration in the historical traditions of The Brothers of Gwynedd series by Edith Pargeter and the Welsh Princes series by Sharon Kay Penman. As well, I was influenced by modern fantasies such as The Dark is Rising by Susan Cooper, Tomorrow's Magic by Pamela F. Service, and The Farseer by Robin Hobb.

Like all fiction writers, though, I chose to deviate from the historical research as the story required. For example, through the Shropshire archives, I confirmed there was no lord of Shrewsbury castle in this time period, so I invented one. Although little is known about Llywelyn's early life, most Welsh children in this time would have fostered with other families, including the English, so I've used that in the story. A Welsh boy came of age at fourteen; since Llywelyn's bodyguard or teulu were known to wear red tunics, I invented a red sash as a visual way to show this transition to manhood and his status as a warrior.

I have also used artistic license in other areas, such as having Bran and other Welsh warriors wearing torques, which may have been rare by the 13th century, as symbolic of their Welsh heritage. Likely there was no pit of rotting bodies, since medieval people usually burned bodies, but in Wales the constant rain caused me to speculate about other possibilities, considering the sheer numbers killed in this invasion. Although Rhys ap Cadwgan and Gwilym ap Einion are fictional, Cynfrig ap Madog is a historical figure credited with managing the negotiations at Castell- y-Bere, which I have called "Bere" in the story, and a well-known bard was also thought to be present. Hywel ap Rhys Gryg was a historical figure, and I include him as a representative of those who stood with Dafydd, defiant to the end. I also speculated about the characters of Stephen de Francton and Dafydd's illegitimate daughters, Margred and her sisters, and how events may have unfolded.

People in the English marches and Wales would have spoken several languages, including Norman French, but I've limited references to English and Welsh. Since free use of the Welsh language ended with the Welsh defeat in 1283, I have included a few Welsh words and used Welsh spelling whenever possible. Also, I have altered names when it seemed necessary. For example, Llywelyn married Eleanor de Montfort, whose mother was also Eleanor de Montfort; King Edward's wife was another Eleanor (de Castile) and his mother was Eleanor (de Provence). To lessen confusion, I've used the spelling Elinor, which I found in some sources, for the princess. As well, I've referred to the English as "soldiers" or "knights" and the Welsh as "warriors" for easier reading. Although the English term "cavalry" was used for mounted knights on horseback in this period, I avoided it when describing the English invaders because it can carry the connotation of rescue.

The poem mentioned on pages 86-87 of Spirit Sight is "Y Gododdin," which is considered the earliest surviving Welsh poem. I have written words for Llywelyn's poem to avoid conflicts with copyright, but the original can be found in translation by Siân Echard in the Broadview anthology, and by Joseph Clancy, among others (listed below under Further Resources). Similarly, one inspiration for the scene in Chapter Eighteen was the YouTube video Mari Lwyd by Trac: Music Traditions Wales; the link and other resources for the greetings, insults, riddles, and other aspects of that chapter can be found in Further Resources.

Scholars disagree about what castle fell on what date during the 1282-83 invasion, and on the location of the royal llys at Garth

Celyn (or Garthcelyn as it appears in some sources.) My main written source was the Smith biography, as well as the Cilmeri, CADW, and Castles of Wales websites.

The list of sources under Further Reading provides more information about these topics. In changing or leaving out some details, as always, I hope I have left room for readers to find their own stories.

GLOSSARY

Annwn (AN-oon) ~ Welsh for OtherWorld (see OtherWorld); Arawn was its king (Cŵn Annwn are the Hounds of Hell)

anon ~ soon, in a little while

bard ~ singer and/or storyteller: Welsh bards or beirdd also had other duties, such as oral historian, legal advisor, and skilled political negotiator; there were three orders: Pencerdd or master poet, bardd teulu or family poet, and cerddor or minstrel

Bere or Castell-y-Bere (KAS-tethl-uh-BEH-rreh) ~ castle in north Wales built by Llywelyn the Great; it was besieged by English forces and fell in April 1283, but the English failed to capture Dafydd there

Builth (bilth or BEE-ehst) ~ castle in mid-Wales

Cadair Idris (KAH-diyr EE-drrees) ~ mountain in North Wales, known as the "giant's chair" for the legendary giant Idris; also thought to be the legendary hunting ground of the Tylwyth Teg (or Welsh fae)

Caergwrle (kiyr-GOO-lee) ~ castle in northeast Wales built by Dafydd, near a town called Hope, built on a mountain known as Hope Mountain

Carndochan (karrn-DOH-khan) ~ castle in Gwynnedd, North Wales, built by Llywelyn the Great

Carreg Cennen ~ castle in south-west Wales

Cistercians ~ religious order in Western Europe started in the late 11 th century, known as White Monks; they lived in solitude and isolation, had no personal property, kept a rigorous way of life, worked the land by hand

coat of arms ~ distinctive heraldic design representing a particular individual or his retainers, often on a cloak, shield or banner

compline ~ end of day (about 7:00 p.m.) in a monastery, a fixed time for evening prayers

Cornish ~ people from Cornwall, England

crest ~ a heraldic emblem usually on a helmet

Criccieth (KRIK-ehth) ~ castle situated on the northwest coast that fell early in 1283

crwth (krooth) ~ a musical instrument similar to a lyre

Cymraeg (KUM-riyg) ~ Welsh language, related to Gaelic

Cymer (KUH-merr) ~ an abbey near Castell-Y-Bere; also a nearby native Welsh castle overthrown in the early 1100s, still visible as ruins today

Cymru (KUM-ree) ~ the country of Wales

Cymry (KUM-ree) ~ the Welsh people (the Welsh called themselves Cymry, "compatriots," and thought of themselves as people of Britain by virtue of their ancestors, the Brythoniaid or Brythons.)

Dderwyddon (ther-oo-ITH-oyn) ~ Druids (people of the derw or oak), an ancient people said to possess magic

Desenni valley (aka Dysynni) ~ valley in Northwest Wales

Dolbadarn Castle (doll-BAH-darn) ~ castle in North Wales

Dolwyddelan Castle (doll-with-ELen) ~ castle in North Wales that fell after five days' siege, on January 18, 1283, and was a strategic loss for the Welsh

Eryri (eh-RRU-rree) ~ medieval Welsh for the Snowdonia mountains or land of the Eagles fealty ~ special kind of service (especially military), loyalty, and allegiance, usually pledged by a knight to a noble

Feast of the Holy Innocents ~ an early Christmas feast day, dating from the 5th century, celebrated on December 28 to commemorate the children King Herod killed in his search for the infant Jesus

Feast of Saint Stephen ~ On December 26, people gave leftovers to the poor to honour a deacon known for his good works who was stoned to death in 36 AD; referred to in the carol, "Good King Wenceslas"

foster ~ in medieval times, boys were sent to live with another noble family to train to be knights; they began as pages, then advanced to squires, then to knights

garderobe ~ toilet in a castle, often a wooden bench with a hole in it

Garth Celyn ~ dwelling of the royal family of Wales at Aber and Llywelyn's headquarters; may have been a castle or fortress made of a combination of wood and stone, with a traditional longhouse and other buildings, but the area was levelled by Edward I in 1283 and replaced with English castles; the English manor house at Pen-y-Bryn, built in the 1600s, is thought to contain one tower of the original Garth Celyn

gŵr gwellt (goorr GOO-ehstht) ~ Welsh folk custom where jilted suitors fashioned a straw likeness of their enemy, cursed it, and hung it in sight on May Day

Gwyn ap Nudd (gwin ahp neeth) ~ King of the Tylwyth Teg (faeries)

Gwynedd (GWIN-eth) ~ district in North Wales, held longest by the Welsh royal families

Hawarden Castle ~ former Welsh castle near the Welsh-English border; Dafydd's attack here in Easter 1282 is blamed for the start of the final war with the English

keep ~ fortified tower within a walled castle, often with a large hall inside

King Arthur ~ legendary king who united the warring chieftains of Wales in early Medieval times

lauds ~ early morning prayers in a monastery, focused on praising God (in contrast to evening prayers which were focused on thanksgiving)

laverbread ~ tasty mix of seaweed in rolled oats, usually eaten at breakfast

Llyn valley ~ district in North Wales, in the Snowdon mountains

llys (thlees) ~ Welsh term for the royal court

Llywelyn the Great or Llywelyn ap Iorwerth (c. 1172-1240) ~ Llywelyn ap Gryffydd's grandfather, ruler of Gwynedd and most of Wales

Marcher lords ~ fierce knights who were given land in return for policing the English-Welsh border

Marches ~ the lands along the English-Welsh border

Mari Lwyd (MAH-rree loyd) ~ New Year's tradition, still celebrated today, in which a skeletal horse's head (grey mare) is invited into homes to help bring good luck for the year

marriage by proxy ~ a marriage where the bride or groom is not present but is represented by another person

Meirionnydd (may-rree-ON–ith) ~ region in North Wales, once a sub-kingdom of Gwynedd

Menai Straight ~ treacherous body of water between North Wales and the island of Anglesey Ynys Môn)

morrigan ~ a gift of prophecy, based on an Irish mythological figure or goddess who could predict the outcome of major battles, to offer favour to warriors, and to predict a warrior's death in battle; represented by three sisters who appeared as crows or ravens and had the ability to shapeshift.

Nant Peris River ~ river in North Wales nones ~ ninth hour (3:00 p.m.) in a monastery, a fixed time for mid-afternoon prayers

Nos Galan Gaeaf (nohs KAL-an GAY-ehv) ~ Welsh term for Halloween: the eve of winter, or the night before Calan Gaeaf (the first day of winter); also known as Ysbrydnos or Spirit Night

OtherWorld ~ the place, known as Annwn in Welsh, thought by some to be where people went when they died, and by others to be more of a parallel world identical in most ways to our own; in Welsh legends, people sometimes exchanged bodies with people who lived in the OtherWorld

pibgorn ~ Welsh pipe-horn (phibau) with one reed (sounds like a bagpipe)

Prysor Castle ~ castle in west Meirionnydd thought to have been the location of a llys or royal court; King Edward sent a letter from this location in 1284

quintain ~ shield rigged to swivel on a wooden pole; when training, boys would ride horses toward the quintain as hard as they could and try to hit the shield squarely with a lance; after the hit, the wooden apparatus swung around behind the rider to unhorse the unwary with heavy swinging sandbags

rhaeadr ~ waterfall in Welsh (Rhaedr Fawr is Aber Falls)

Rhuddlan ~ castle in Northwest Wales near the Welsh-English border

score ~ unit of measure—twenty (of anything)

sell-sword ~ one who sells his services with a sword; a mercenary

sext ~ sixth hour (noon) in a monastery, a fixed time for midday prayers in praise of God's works

Shrewsbury ~ town in northern England, near the English-Welsh border

Simon de Montfort ~ English lord who fought for an early form of democracy and was brutally hunted down and killed for it by King Henry and his son Edward, who later became Edward I; Llywelyn may have fought beside de Montfort, and in 1263 Llywelyn was betrothed to his daughter Elinor

Sir Gawain ~ knight in the legends of King Arthur, and Arthur's nephew

solar ~ private sitting room for a lord or lady in a castle

telyn (TEL-in) ~ Welsh harp

terce ~ fixed time for mid-morning (9:00 a.m.) prayers in a monastery

teulu (TAY-lee) ~ "family" in Welsh, a Welsh prince's personal bodyguard (Llywelyn reportedly had 160 in his teulu, more than any other Welsh prince had before)

torque (tork) ~ ring of gold thought to have been worn by Celtic warriors around the neck, often crafted with intricate designs

trencher ~ English tradition: flat loaves of bread, cut in half and used as plates for food

Twelfth Night ~ English tradition: last day of the 12 days of Christmas, on January 5, celebrated today as Epiphany; often the day when gifts were given, ending the Christmas season

Tŷ Hir ~ the longhouse, possibly the royal dwelling at Garth Celyn

Tylwyth Teg (tuhl-with taig) ~ faeries in Welsh

Tywysog (tuh-WUH-sog) ~ leader in Welsh, translated as Prince

unshriven ~ without the process of confession, penance and absolution by a priest

vespers ~ evening prayers of thanksgiving

vigils ~ prayer service at night; in some traditions, specifically at midnight

Watchers ~ legendary characters that sleep within the Welsh mountains, in some Welsh legends thought to be the Old Ones (faeries) and in others King Arthur and his knights; it was said that the Old Ones would return to the people of Cymru in the time of their greatest need

weft ~ filling yarn in weaving

Y Calan ~ traditional Welsh song for the New Year

Ynys Môn ~ Anglesey, the island off the northwest coast of Wales

FURTHER READING

Nonfiction Books

A Collection of Welsh Riddles by Vernam Hall and Archer Taylor
A History of Wales by John Davies
Broadview Anthology of British Literature: The Medieval Period, edited by Joseph Black
Cadw Guidebooks on various castles
Castles of the Welsh Princes by Paul R. Davis
Castles of Wales by Alan Reid
Celtic Gods and Heroes by Marie-Louise Sjoestedt
From Medieval to Modern Wales by R.R. Davies and Geraint H. Jenkins
Life in Medieval Europe by Danièle Cybulskie
Llywelyn ap Gruffudd: Prince of Wales by J. Beverley Smith
Medieval Wales: c. 1050-1332: Centuries of Ambiguity by David Stephenson
Medieval Welsh Poems translated by Joseph P. Clancy
Stories and Ballads of the Far Past by Nora Kershaw Chadwick
The Age of Conquest: Wales 1063-1415 by R.R. Davies
The Journey Through Wales: The Description of Wales by Gerald of Wales
Wales and the Welsh in the Middle Ages edited by R.A. Griffiths and P.R. Schofield
Trioedd Ynys Prydain (Welsh Triads) by Rachel Bromwich
Welsh Wars of Independence by David Moore

Online Resources on Welsh History

Archeology of Northwest Wales: http://www.archaeoleg.org.uk/areanorthwest.html
Anna Belfrage: "Historical People ~ Elizabeth who? A reflection on the life of a medieval woman." https://www.annabelfrage.com/2018/05/27/elizabeth-who
Castles of Wales: http://www.castlewales.com (articles and essays)
Cadw Dolwyddelan: http://cadw.wales.gov.uk/daysout/

dolwyddelancastle/?lang=en
Cadw Dolbadarn: https://cadw.gov.wales/visit/places-to-visit/
dolbadarn-castle
Llys Rhosyr: http://www.heneb.co.uk/palaceoftheprinces/rhosyr.html
Gathering the Jewels: Castles of the Welsh princes: http://education.gtj.
org.uk/en/item10/28986
International Heralds and Heraldry: http://www.
internationalheraldry.com
Medievel Insults: http://www.funnyjunk.com/funny_
pictures/4254438/Medieval+insults
Medieval riddles: http://www.increasebrainpower.com/easy-riddles.
html http://www.justriddlesandmore.com/riddlearchive.html
Sarah Woodbury: "Making Sense of Medieval Wales" video series,
https://www.youtube.com/watch?v=IQfG6WlyxEU
Midlands: "Shrewsbury Castle and Town Walls," in Castles,
Forts and Battles http://www.castlesfortsbattles.co.uk/midlands/
shrewsbury_castle_town_walls.html

Online Maps of Wales:

http://commons.wikimedia.org/wiki/File:Wales_after_the_Treaty_
of_Montgomery_1267.svg (Alex D.)
Source: Wrex County exhibition:
http://www.wrexham.gov.uk/english/heritage/medieval_exhibition/
struggles.htm
http://commons.wikimedia.org/wiki/File:Gwynedd_after_the_
Treaty_of_Aberconwy_1277.svg
Gwynedd General Map (James Frankcom):
http://en.wikipedia.org/wiki/File:Gwynedd_General_Map.jpg

Fiction

After Cilmeri (series) by Sarah Woodbury
Assassins Apprentice: The Farseer by Robin Hobb
Lord of the Rings (series) by J.R. Tolkien
Ranger's Apprentice (series) by John Flanagan
The Brothers of Gwynedd (series) by Edith Pargeter
The Dark is Rising (series) by Susan Cooper

The Once and Future King (series) by T.H. White
Tomorrow's Magic by Pamela F. Service
Welsh Princes (trilogy) by Sharon Kay Penman
Wheel of Time (series) by Robert Jordan
"Y Gododdin" in *The Broadview Anthology of British Literature: The Medieval Period*

MARIE POWELL

Marie Powell's adventures in castle-hopping across North Wales to explore her family roots resulted in the award-winning YA Fantasy series, *Last of the Gifted*. Marie is the author of more than forty traditionally published children's books, and her award-winning short stories and poetry appear in such literary magazines as *subTerrain* and *Room*. Among other degrees, she holds a Master of Fine Arts (MFA) in Creative Writing from the University of British Columbia. Marie lives on Treaty 4 territory in Regina, Saskatchewan, Canada.

Learn more about the world of *Last of the Gifted* at mariepowell.ca